"From the first
kept me on th
have you shive
New York Times bestselling author

"Gripping, atmospheric, and fabulous! Watterson has created a fascinating and determined detective in Ellie MacIntosh. I'm already looking forward to see what Ellie tackles next."
—Carla Neggers,
New York Times and *USA Today* bestselling author of *Saint's Gate*

"Chilling! Watterson draws you in and keeps you riveted until the last page."
—Laura Griffin,
New York Times and *USA Today* bestselling author of *Twisted*

"Watterson's evocative prose brings a Wisconsin winter to life, where the most dangerous threat isn't the cold but a cunning killer who will leave you chilled to the bone."
—C. J. Lyons, *New York Times* and *USA Today* bestselling author

"A tale of psychological suspense that builds to a chilling ending . . . Will keep you turning the pages late into the evening."
—Jamie Freveletti,
international bestselling author

"Taut, tense, and completely original—I couldn't put it down! Kate Watterson is a terrific storyteller, and this compelling page-turner will wrap you in gripping suspense until the very last page."
—Hank Phillippi Ryan, Anthony, Agatha, and Macavity award–winning author

TOR BOOKS BY KATE WATTERSON

Frozen

Charred (forthcoming)

FROZEN

Kate Watterson

TOR®

A TOM DOHERTY ASSOCIATES BOOK • NEW YORK

FROZEN

A Tor Book
Published by Tom Doherty Associates, LLC
175 Fifth Avenue
New York, NY 10010

www.tor-forge.com

ISBN 978-0-7653-6960-4

First Edition: January 2013

Printed in the United States of America

0 9 8 7 6 5 4 3 2 1

For Bruce Muggenburg and David Nordgren.

You are both intelligent, articulate, and a little bit eccentric in your own way. I happen to admire that very much. I count myself lucky to have you in my life.

ACKNOWLEDGMENTS

Many thanks to my editor, Kristin Sevick, for insightful advice, the necessary guidance I sorely needed, and her delightful sense of humor as we walked this road together. As always, Barbara Poelle is a joy to work with, and she is both a canny agent and not just a colleague, but a true friend.

Several detectives in northern Wisconsin were kind enough to take time from their busy schedules to help answer my questions. I truly appreciate their courtesy, and as I think most of us do, their dedication to such a difficult job. Any mistakes are strictly my own.

FROZEN

Prologue

He was never sure if the cold influenced him. It should be the opposite. That as the ground grew more unyielding and the air frigid he would sleep better. It just didn't work that way.

Odd.

There were fewer of them this time of year. It didn't really matter—it just was. Each month had a certain draw. Perhaps that was why he was so hungry. He had to work for it this time of year.

The summer was too easy. He'd done the summer first, but there really was no challenge in it. June. July, August, September.

Even October had been child's play.

The woods were quiet, sleeping, waiting, full of shadows.

Perfect.

The car sat there, tucked into the side of the road between two white pines on a level spot, nose into the shadows, carefully parked in the turnoff, all windows up. Detective Ellie MacIntosh walked past it twice, a full circle, the empty windows not talking to her. No movement inside, no signs of violence, the patches of frost on the windshield starred with symmetrical snowflake crystals. Autumn leaves tickled her ankles.

It was absurd, but she'd taken her gun out. She didn't even realize it until she lowered the weapon, her breath leaving her lungs in an audible exhale. "There's no one visible in the vehicle. Try not to touch anything that might give us fingerprints, but open the trunk."

"Yes, ma'am." To his credit, the county officer who had called in the abandoned car didn't point out he'd already told her that no one was visible inside. He instead nodded at another officer and between them they took a crowbar and went to work. In the meantime, several other law enforcement vehicles had arrived, the meandering curve on the remote road taking on color and movement, the naked trunks of the trees reflecting the swirling blue lights.

She'd hoped . . . Well, she'd just *hoped* this call hadn't been the one they were waiting for, because if it was . . .

It meant it had happened again.

The wrench of metal screamed, the trunk popped open, and the two officers peered inside. One of them said, "Detective? Want to take a look at this?"

Ellie took two steps and stared into the trunk. Did she want to look? No, she sure as hell didn't. Whatever was in there, she didn't want to see it. Her palms were damp and hot despite the cold; her heart pounding.

The plain interior held a blanket and a flare for emergencies. There was also an atlas with a torn cover.

Nothing else.

She muttered hoarsely, "That bastard."

Chapter 1

He was a stage prop in his own life.

Now *that* was enlightening realization. Bryce Grantham eyed the darkening sky as he turned off the highway and took the small county road. Trees clawed tearing hands at the sky, the wind picking up enough that it moaned in rising protest through the branches. The shriek was audible above the music, even when he flicked up the sound.

He'd forgotten what it was like up here in late October.

The north woods held a special kind of melancholy this time of year. Gray skies, falling leaves, naked branches, and deserted roads. No more tourists, no more summer cabins full of life and light, nothing but a vast engulfing silence and autumn dying into the chill, inexorable grip of winter. Most of the places were shuttered, roof supports put in under the rafters to handle the heavy snow load, the boats hauled out of the water and beached, covered with canvas like gray shrouds, lining the shores of cold lakes that would eventually freeze into thick silent ice packs.

There, I'm all cheered up, Bryce thought in grim amusement as he guided the SUV around a turn, the wheels humming on the wet pavement. It was misting, just enough to get everything wet but not enough for windshield wipers. A soliloquy on the bleak state of his surroundings wasn't going to improve his mood any more than the lackluster meeting he'd just attended in Wausau.

A long, boring-as-hell day with a bunch of similar boring-as-hell colleagues, and a cold, lonely night ahead. What more could a man want?

Food, he realized. A man could—and he did—want food.

All sarcasm aside, he was hungry, and the lunch provided had been little more than catered lasagna, wilted salad, and generic garlic bread. A stop at the grocery store might not have been a bad idea before he headed for the cabin. It was too late now and all he could hope for was some canned food still on the shelves when he got there, and if that didn't pan out, he had a case of beer in the back of the car.

He hadn't drunk his dinner since college—not even during the thing with Suzanne—but this just might be the night.

With his first stroke of luck of the day, he caught sight of the little tavern on the corner of the last intersection before he turned for Loon Lake. He'd assumed it would be closed already for the season, but a beer sign glowed in the window and the lot held six vehicles, most of them pickup trucks or four-wheel drives. Bryce pulled the Land Rover in next to a battered Ford Ranger and got out, turning up his collar against the whip of the wet wind. At least he could get some pizza, if he remembered correctly. The frozen variety, cooked in a little electric oven behind the bar, but he really wasn't too picky at the moment.

For a man who thought he wanted solitude, he was surprised to find he craved the warmth of light and human voices.

This trip wasn't set in stone, he reminded himself sharply as he held the door for another refugee who also hurried to get in out of the weather. The young woman shivered as she slipped past him, giving him a fleeting smile. "Nasty out," she murmured. "And it's just going to get colder, isn't it? I hate winter."

If so, she should probably choose somewhere else to live, but Bryce smiled back, grateful himself to be out of the blustery elements as he followed her into the place, hit at once by the smell of food and the yeasty scent of spilled beer. In the corner, Willie Nelson wailed out a lament from the jukebox, and three men in flannel shirts sat at the bar, idly talking. Several of the other tables were occupied also, and the two of them drew cursory looks, but everyone went back to their drinks and murmured conversation.

He said politely, "Yeah, northern Wisconsin isn't the best place if you don't like the cold."

"You're telling me. And I don't." She shivered again and looked around as if picking out a table. "Like the cold, that is. It seeps into your bones up here. If I didn't have to be here, trust me, I wouldn't be."

Even a little wet and windblown, in a padded coat appropriate for a blustery October evening, she was very pretty, he realized in an offhand sort of way. Dark hair cut in a clean swing at the line of her jaw, blue eyes, very little make up because she really didn't need it, blue jeans hugging nice curves. Young. Early to midtwenties maybe.

Bryce glanced back at the doorway. No one else had arrived with her as far as he could tell, and given how few people were in the place, if she'd been meeting someone, surely the person would have said something or motioned her over.

He was actually a little shy with women most of the time—too damn shy according to Suzanne—but to his own surprise he found himself saying in a perfectly normal voice, "I was going to have a beer. Can I get you one too?"

She hesitated, her gaze assessing enough that he wondered how he measured up. He needed a haircut one of these days but had been putting it off, so his hair was probably a little on the shaggy side, his leather jacket slick with rain, his expensive tailored slacks and Italian loafers out of place in a roadside tavern. Still he must have seemed harmless enough because she gave an almost imperceptible nod. "Actually, that'd be great. Thanks."

There were no waitresses at the Pit Stop. Bryce went to the bar and asked for two drafts of Old Style, paid the bartender—who looked like a lumberjack right down to his bristly beard—and when he turned around, found the young woman had selected the table in the corner farthest away from the door. Good choice; he didn't want the blast of cold, damp air every time someone came and went either. Bryce carried their drinks over and set hers down in front of her, but held on to his for a second. "Mind if I sit here too, or are you expecting someone?"

Bold for him. Maybe all of Suzanne's cutting remarks had had an effect after all.

"No."

That was kind of hard to decipher. No, he shouldn't sit? Or no, not expecting someone?

So much for his attempt at being a little more outgoing. He stood there like an idiot, trying to decide if he needed to make a strategic retreat, until the young woman noticed his dilemma and laughed. "Sorry, I didn't really answer that well, did I? Out of practice, I guess. Please, sit. I'd like the company."

He pulled out one of the rickety chairs, trying to ignore the wobble of legs probably attached to the base in the 1950s. The scratched surface of the table also dated back decades, and over time people had etched their initials in spots. His companion fingered her glass of beer—it was in a plastic cup actually—and looked at him.

Of course. This was when he was supposed to make witty conversation and wow her with his intellect, but chances were he'd just bore her to tears.

Been there, done that.

Gorgeous eyes, he thought, luminous, dark in color, more indigo than anything, framed in wet lashes. Now that she'd taken off the shapeless parka, he could see that she wore underneath it a shirt in a soft pink material that clung to her breasts. "I get the impression you are not a native. You live close by?" he asked, trying to sound conversational.

"I'm a grad student from Madison actually. I'm up here doing a research project."

"Beautiful area." He took a sip of beer and continued. "My family has had property on Loon Lake for years."

"My place is only a couple of miles from there. I rent a cabin, which considering half of them are deserted this time of year was harder than you might think. I had to find one that was winter-proofed enough I wouldn't turn into an icicle by mid-November. I expect to be here until spring."

"What sort of research?"

The jukebox clunked and started as some man in a checkered shirt and Brewers ball cap put in some change. His choice proved to be Patsy Cline proclaiming her state of mental health, but actually, Bryce had always liked the song, aside from the melancholy message.

Everyone was a little crazy in some way in his opinion.

The young woman across the table sighed. "You had to ask, didn't you? It's pretty boring really, unless you are getting a master's degree in biology with a focus on northern aviary species, in which case we in the field find it fascinating, actually."

"Birds?"

"Birds. Ornithology . . . exactly. I'm here to study the winter habits of nonmigratory North American birds for my thesis."

It had been awhile since he'd smiled spontaneously. "I see."

"Told you so. Boring, huh?" She drank more beer and watched him over the rim of her cup. "Why are you up here?"

"I think I have you outranked in the boring department. I came up for a technology conference in Wausau. I thought a few days at my parents' place might be a nice change."

"My family used to have a place here too. They sold it a few years ago."

"Hey, it happens," Bryce commented, with regret

recalling how little his family used the lake cabin now. "My parents go to Florida or the Caribbean in winter. Someplace where it's warm, not forty degrees at night in the middle of July sometimes, and has beaches. I can't say as I blame them. I'm still wondering why I decided to come up at this time of year myself." He paused and then added, "I'm Bryce, by the way."

"Melissa," she offered.

"Nice to meet you." He was easily ten years older. At least. But what did it matter? It was just a drink in a small tap in the middle of nowhere.

"Same here. I hope you're staying for at least a few days."

Bryce stopped in the middle of a swallow of beer, not sure how to interpret that comment. Patsy Cline crooned from the jukebox, two of the patrons—local guys from the way they joked with the bartender—started a game of pool, and Melissa just looked at him with that same engaging direct stare.

Was she flirting? It seemed like it . . . at least maybe a little bit. It wasn't that women didn't flirt with him—they did—but he had a habit of keeping himself out of social situations since the divorce.

He was pretty good at avoidance. It was a honed skill, and it had ruined his marriage if you listened to his ex-wife. So, since he had no idea how to respond, he just didn't. "I was thinking of getting a pizza," he murmured.

"I've had it here before. It's frozen," she warned, still toying with her glass, a small smile on her mouth. "Not too tasty. But there aren't a lot of choices around here. Merrill and Rhinelander have more options, but this is much closer."

"I'm desperate," he admitted with a slight shrug.

"Bachelors often are. For that matter, I'm still technically a starving college student. There have been times when I thought frozen pizza was ambrosia."

He liked her laugh. It was sweet and easy. She *looked* like a college girl in the stylish jeans and simple clingy blouse.

How did she know he was a bachelor?

No ring, you idiot. When would he get used to the missing gold band on his left hand?

"School isn't without its sacrifices," Bryce told her, meaning it. "I remember undergrad and grad school all too clearly. But how much better is that than having no clue as what you'd like to do? Though I do have to admit I design software because I think I'm pretty good at it, but I am still not sure it's how I want to spend my life."

So fucking true. All of it. A degree from MIT, good money, nice house: all just bullshit if a person went to bed alone every single night and felt like the day was . . . wasted. People cared about him, he knew that. But so few of them were involved in his day-to-day existence. It made a difference.

"Life is short," he added, his voice quieter than he intended.

"And for the birds." His companion laughed and raised her glass.

"In your case, that's the truth," he agreed, finishing off his beer. "Want another?" He gestured at her glass. "I'm going to get one and order some food."

"Sure. Thanks. It's a short drive home."

He got up and ordered a sausage pizza and another two drafts. The burly man behind the bar grunted something, took his money, and Bryce went and sat back down. Outside it had begun to rain in earnest, the sound loud on the tin roof. That sound reminded him of childhood.

One of the other patrons left, and just that brief opening and closing of the door let a waft of cold, damp air touch them even in their corner.

"It's getting worse out," Melissa remarked, her lashes lowered as she stared at the small windows, the glass running with moisture, the rattle of the wind audible. "I hate nights like this."

"Introduce me to the person who likes them."

"I suppose that's true. It just gets so *dark* up here." Slender fingers smoothed condensation off her glass. "It sounds corny, but I thought it would be a romantic ideal . . . you know, cabin in the woods, solitude, the works. But the only reason I'm in this tavern right now is because it is a lot more lonely that I imagined. I mean, I love to read. I think I had this idyllic notion of quiet woods and nights with nothing to do but finally read *David Copperfield* from cover to cover. You know, catch up on the classics and actually get in eight hours of sleep, that sort of thing."

The tip—just the pink tip—of her tongue touched her upper lip and wiped away a bit of foam from her drink.

"That's why I went to grad school. I thought I might write a novel one day."

"Really?" She looked interested. "What genre?"

"Literary." He gave a negligent shrug. "It hasn't happened yet."

"I'm intrigued. I'd like to know more about you and the book."

Bryce had a moment of doubt. Was he being propositioned? By this pretty girl such a short time after they met? He eyed her face over the rim of his glass and decided he had no idea. That said a lot about his level of sophistication when it came to the opposite sex. There were signals; he just didn't know how to read them exactly.

It made him feel awkward, but he'd never been good at the game, not even before he was married. He was too serious . . . maybe that was it. The way his brain worked, he liked a straightforward explanation for everything.

Straightforward? Was that even possible with women?

"Pizza." The proprietor walked over, plunked the cardboard circle on the table, and handed Bryce a couple of napkins.

Not exactly four-star service, but the pizza was hot, and for what it was, it looked edible.

"Help yourself." Bryce pushed one of the napkins toward her with a slight grin.

"All right." She smiled back, and she definitely had a pretty smile.

As bleak as the evening had turned outside, Bryce didn't even mind the bland taste of the pizza or the vague stale smell of spilled beer in the air.

As they ate, she told him about attending the University of Wisconsin in lighthearted snippets of small talk, and they both drank their second beer.

It was over way too quickly.

"I'd better go. The weather sucks." She stood and reached for her jacket. She probably was right. The raw night wasn't getting better. After a small pause, she offered her hand. "It's been nice."

"Sure." He no longer felt quite as comfortable just because of the music, lights, and people all around them, and he needed to leave too. It was full dark now. The cabin would be ice cold.

She put on the puffy coat and they walked out together. Her vehicle was a somewhat battered Jeep that had ice crystals on the windshield. Melissa swore softly, the sound whipped away by the wind. "It's getting icy. That's the worst."

"Be careful." What a banal thing to say, but Bryce couldn't think of anything better. "The roads will be slick."

She nodded, her ebony hair brushing her jaw, and gave a small wave as she dashed to her car.

He unlocked the door of the Land Rover, cold rain pelting his head, plastering his hair to his skull, and he slammed the car door closed against the icy deluge.

Car started, defrost on . . . but he found the faint glaze on his windshield wasn't going away without a little help, so he sat a minute or two, startled when he heard a knock on his window. It was Melissa, and when he rolled down his window, she said quickly, "I swear this is not some kind of reverse line, but my car seems to be dead. I can't even get it to turn over. That makes me really nervous."

Well, he supposed it wasn't a night to get stranded. "Let me try."

"That's sexist, but at this point, I'll take you up on it."

She was right, he thought as he eased out of his car, ran around with his collar up against the bleak wind, and got into the front seat of hers. It *had* been sexist. She could turn the key as well as he could apparently because he had no better luck. The lights worked, so it didn't seem to be the battery, and that was about the extent of his skill with cars.

"I'd suggest a tow truck," he said apologetically.

Melissa huddled in the passenger seat. "Great. I guess I'll run back inside and see if someone can tell me who to call."

"I'll wait." It seemed like the right thing to do, and if he wasn't smooth, at least he liked to think he was a nice guy.

"You don't have to." In the dim illumination, he saw her bite her lip and then nod. "But thanks. I'd appreciate it, actually."

"No problem."

She disappeared back into the lights and warmth of the little tavern and he made the pilgrimage back to his own car, happy to see the defroster was taking care of the film of ice on the windshield. By the time Melissa emerged from the bar again, ten minutes had passed. Instead of heading to her vehicle, she opened the passenger side of his car and slipped into the seat. A cell phone was pressed to her ear, but she flipped it shut with an unhappy sigh.

"I had to leave a message," she explained, her eyes luminous in the semigloom. "Can I ask you to possibly give me a ride home? It's only about ten minutes from here."

"Sure." Though he had absolutely no objection, he was a little startled. He was, after all, a stranger.

It must have been obvious because she said, "The tow truck will take awhile. It might not even happen until tomorrow. I have experienced the vagaries of the local service before. I need a new car. Since I can't buy one tonight, you seem nice enough and we pulled in at the same time. There's no way you could have done anything to my car because you haven't been out of my sight. I have mace in my purse, by the way."

He sensed she was only half joking, so he chose to be amused, not insulted. "Noted. Where to?"

She gave him directions and, luckily, it was on his way. He pulled out of the lot, driving slowly because the road held a treacherous gleam he'd seen before. Around them the woods gathered like a secret army, closed in ranks, the few remaining leaves clinging to the otherwise naked branches, the sound of crisp rain drumming on the car. It was dark in only the way it can be in the northern woods; hushed, secretive, shrouded, and distant. They passed a few turns, the road glistening, the beating rain a steady presence. Then abruptly, Melissa said, "Here."

Bryce braked. "Here?"

"Yes. Second drive."

He wouldn't have even known it was there but he caught it, a gleam of gravel, and he turned in at the last second, the car sliding just a little. "Whoa."

"I wish I'd left the lights on now." She gathered her coat a little closer.

He came to a stop and there was only a glimpse of a dripping roof and blank windows, but she was right, it was damned dark "Want me to walk up with you?"

"No need. Remember my mace?"

"I'll stay and make sure you get in safely. And if you ever want to share another cardboard pizza, let me know."

There. That was an understated come-on in his opinion.

Melissa paused, one hand on the door. "I just might. You have a cell phone?"

He did, in his pocket, and he fished it out. By the dashboard light she slid up the cover and expertly started pushing in buttons. Then she handed it back. "My number, programmed right in."

Then she slipped out of the car. He waited patiently until lights flickered on in the windows of the square structure.

Maybe, he thought as he backed up the Rover, this trip was a good idea after all.

Chapter 2

He . . . hummed.

There was nothing like it. Nothing like the insidious chill of autumn creeping in, signaling winter; a promise of what nature could dish out. He thought about it all the time. Hunting season soon. That helped. He did it all. Deer, squirrel, grouse—he'd even hunted bear with a bow. Sopped stale bread in grease as bait, his breath puffing in soft clouds the air was so cold, the forest quiet as death, his compound bow propped next to him as he waited ten feet up in the air. Now that was a good challenge. A tree stand didn't mean much with a deer. All it was there for was insurance against detection. Taking a full-grown bear with a bow took some guts, and using a tree stand might mean the difference between being the hunter or the prey. Besides, there was always the chance you wouldn't get it right the first time. Bears could climb and then there was nowhere to go . . .

But he usually did get it right, no matter his target. Hunting was a mind game as much as a physical one.

You had to be smarter than your quarry, more cunning. More ruthless. Stack the deck in your favor if you wanted to win.

It was almost November.

Fuck, he loved this time of year. Especially on nights like this one when it was black and inhospitable . . .

Ellie pointed with her fork. "The report is in and inconclusive. She sold real estate so she takes different people around all the time in the vehicle we found. Lots of forensic evidence to process, but who knows how much of it is worth anything. There was no blood in, on, or near her car." She speared a piece of lettuce and ate it.

Across from her, Jody raised her brows. "Seriously, could you not do this?"

The lights flickered. It was only raining out but the wind was high, so Ellie glanced at the window before she responded. "Do what?"

Blond, petite, and annoyingly happy with three small children and a husband who worked at an insurance company, Jody sighed. "I love you, but didn't we go out to dinner for a nice sister-to-sister chat? I realize you live and breathe the job, and I doubt it is easy to be around that much testosterone every single day and hold your own, but I don't want to talk about Margaret Wilson's disappearance. I'm just as spooked as every other woman in northern Wisconsin, but honey, I like my chicken salad without gloom and doom hovering over it."

It took a moment, but Ellie shook her head with a small rueful laugh. "Oh, yeah. Sorry. It's this case."

Damn. Can't help myself. That was always part of it. She had an undeniable tendency to focus. How could she explain the juxtaposition of the horror and the hunt? She hated one and loved the other. And as far as she could tell, no one else in her sphere understood it.

Jody took another biscuit and broke it in half, but she set both pieces on her plate. "You work too hard."

If so, why was it some days she thought she didn't work hard enough? The hours didn't count—well, they did—but results were all that mattered.

"True enough." Ellie took a bite of walnuts and cranberries and changed the subject. "So tell me about the kids. Is Della still in dance?"

A half an hour later they were both standing in the foyer of the little restaurant, putting on their coats. Icy rain sluiced across the glass door, and Ellie braced herself to step outside into the cutting wind.

Winter was coming.

And that wasn't the only cold cruel thing out there.

The cabin was cold, the musty smell of disuse already heavy in the air, and his footsteps echoed loudly as Bryce fumbled for the flashlight kept on a shelf by the front door. He found it, flicked the switch, and muttered, "Shit."

Nothing. The damn battery was dead. He never had understood why his parents were adamant about the flashlight always being put back in the same place when in his memory it didn't have fresh batteries when they needed the thing. Disgusted, he shook out his wet hair, groped around so he could set down the leftover pizza—no box, Paul Bunyan back at the bar had wrapped it in some foil—and stumbled off blind to the fuse box in the back bedroom to switch the electricity on. It wasn't the easiest thing to do in the pitch dark and he whacked his ankle on the corner of the bed frame hard enough to make his eyes water, but he finally found the metal box, fumbled it open, and flipped the main.

It helped to have light, he thought, as the glow of the little lamp on the side table banished the impenetrable darkness of a small room with the draperies drawn against a rainy late fall night. The bed was stripped, of course—his mother always did that when they closed up for the season—clean sheets were in a small cedar chest in the hallway, a patterned blanket neatly folded at the foot of the bed on top of the mattress pad. This was the room he'd had as a kid and still used as a grown man when he had the time to come up for a few days.

The blanket has little cowboys on it . . .

Suzanne could do derisive like no one he'd ever met. If a man had an urge to be emasculated with a few words, she was a pro.

He'd shrugged and told the truth. It was a perfectly good blanket and his mother was of pragmatic Scandinavian stock. Nothing wrong with it except it was bought years ago for an eight-year-old boy. She wasn't going to throw it out and it was a *cabin,* for God's sake.

He could still see the look on his wife's face the first time he'd brought her up to Loon Lake for a vacation. The *only* time. She'd hated the whole week. She didn't like to fish, to swim in the cold water, there was no television, no Internet, no upscale restaurants, no shopping—you name it, she'd complained about it.

He hadn't understood her aversion then, and he still didn't understand to this day. Trees, sparkling clear water, the smell of a woodstove with a crackling fire. What wasn't to like?

No, it wasn't elegant. That wasn't in dispute. None

of the furnishings matched. To this day his mother said the place was furnished *à la dump,* but it was comfortable and homey not in spite of it, Bryce thought as he moved to the kitchen, but maybe *because* of it. The tin cupboard for the dishes by the sink, the open shelves holding battered iron skillets, chipped casserole dishes, a vintage coffee pot that still made coffee so good it put Starbucks to shame. The floor was linoleum, worn through here and there but immaculately clean, and the counters held various styles and colors of jars to store pasta, flour, rice, sugar, all with good seals because mice could chew through anything but glass or metal.

Bryce went back out to his car for the beer, his suitcase and laptop. He put his suitcase in the bedroom, flicked on the baseboard heat in the living room, removed his wet jacket, and flopped down onto the couch facing the long windows overlooking the lake, toeing off his damp loafers. He couldn't see anything outside because of the darkness and rain, but the comfortable sound of the rhythm on the roof was soothing. He drank his third beer of the evening in solitude and thought about Melissa.

Pretty girl. Interesting too. It had been awhile since he'd met someone like her.

His cell phone rang just as he was dozing off, the half-empty beer in his hand. He hadn't even bothered to turn on the radio, just sat listening to the soporific sound of the rain slapping against the shingles. It took him a minute or so to blink awake and realize the phone was ringing, sitting on the table by the woodstove he hadn't bother to light. Bryce surged to his feet and fumbled to retrieve it, finally managing to open it by the seventh ring. "Hello?"

"You made it okay?"

His mother. The sound of her voice was as familiar in the surroundings as if she stood there. "Yeah." Bryce ran his fingers through his hair. "Everything is fine. Weather could be better, but I think you can say that ninety percent of the time up here. Stop worrying."

"It's on the lonely side on the lake this time of year." There was concern and reproof in her voice. "I'm not sure what you're going to do there all day."

Neither of his parents had believed he wanted to spend his vacation in late October at a lake that didn't have a single inhabitant except himself. All the other places were summer cottages and the road wouldn't even get plowed if it wasn't for the fact one lake over there was a couple of people who lived there all year.

"I'm going to work on my book." Though she couldn't see it, he gestured at his laptop, now sitting on the table by the windows. He felt foolish and laughed quietly at himself. "I brought my computer and a backup battery and I can check my e-mail on my phone, so I'm set. I'm fine."

"When we saw you last month you looked tired."

"Hence the peace and quiet. I always sleep like a rock here, Mom. Besides, you can reach me at any time. I can't believe I get a good signal here, but I usually do." Bryce squinted at his watch. "Is it really only eight-thirty? It must just feel later because of the rain."

"Have you eaten?"

Once a mother, always a mother. Since the divorce became final every phone call between them had included that question. He hated to disillusion her, but Suzanne hadn't been much of a cook. They'd usually eaten out or he grilled something. He could do that all on his own.

He had to, actually. Suzanne was gone.

"Some pizza." He really just felt strange, as if he should go to bed and sleep off the seminar. Sleep off the past twelve months of trying to find himself again as he struggled to accept the failure of his marriage.

"Make sure you have something more healthy than pizza tomorrow."

"I will." Probably a lie, but it was a nonmalicious one, designed to ease her mind. "Thanks for calling."

"Keep in touch with us."

"Okay. Have a good night."

It was funny he thought as he ended the call, but he didn't miss his ex-wife. That wasn't the problem.

What the hell *was* the problem?

She couldn't sleep.

Again.

Fuck it.

Ellie sat up and shoved aside the covers. Barefoot, she padded out to the living room and picked up the remote. The rain was supposed to stop by midnight but it gave no sign of letting up yet if the steady drum against the skylight was any indication.

A lamp burned on the end table by the sofa, casting the comfortable room in a low haze of light. She never used to leave the lights on, but now . . . well, let's say she always left a light burning. It would be helpful if she hadn't inherited her father's colorful imagination. There was a monster in the woods, and if this was one of the picture book stories he'd read to her as a child, someone magical would come along and find it so it wouldn't ever scare anyone again . . .

She sat down on the couch and stared at the façade of the fireplace. It stared back, a blank canvas of river rock and the gaping hole of the hearth. Water dripped from the eaves outside.

Unfortunately, she was supposed to be that someone. But she wasn't magical. Far from it. The monster so far had the advantage and she didn't like it one bit.

The ever-present question lingered. *Let's look at this logically again.*

Like she hadn't said *that* to herself before. Notes lay scattered all across the antique walnut table in her dining room. Some were dog-eared, some had coffee rings on them, but she knew each one by heart.

She drew her robe more tightly around her, pressed a button, and ironically saw a cop show flicker over the screen as the television popped on. One of those where they solved the mystery in an hour.

I could use you guys. Tell you what, I'll give you two hours on this one. It isn't all that easy, there's no evidence, and we haven't got a single body . . .

A year and a half for her and she was no closer to knowing what might be going on in this corner of Wisconsin than she had been when the first missing person report landed on her desk. It might be more accurate to say she was more in the dark than ever. Two leads had petered into nothing and it kept her awake at night.

Like now. The investigation had stalled.

Resigned to the fact she wasn't going to go to sleep anytime soon, Ellie got up and went into the kitchen. It was neat and shining, but she absently wiped off the countertop anyway as she waited for the electric kettle to heat up. When the light flashed on, she brewed a cup of tea and went back into the dining room. She sat down, took a sip from her cup, and began to go over the cases in her mind, or case, as she thought of it, because she was sure they were all connected.

Or pretty sure. She was methodical about investigations and that was part of the problem with this case. Forcing the round peg into the square hole instead of going with her gut like she wanted to, which had told her from the beginning that they had a very, very serious problem and the enemy was . . . canny.

Margaret Wilson made the third missing woman in seventeen months. Tomorrow would mark day ten of her disappearance. Her car had been found, unlocked and abandoned by the gate of what used to be the county dump before it was shut down. The vehicle had been in plain sight but off the road. She'd been reported missing by her husband when she didn't show up at home after work one evening and he couldn't get ahold of her. The car had been spotted the next day by a sheriff's deputy. A special crime scene unit had been called from the Division of Criminal Investigation, because while they had a county scene investigator, there was no way they were taking any chances on missing something and processing the scene themselves, not with another possible serial homicide. Without any bodies and with no evidence, no matter how many departments were cooperating, there had been no progress.

From the first disappearance it had been serious, but it was starting to get *really* serious.

There had been no blood in Margaret Wilson's car, no tire tracks nearby that could be cast because the ground had been hard as a rock then. They lifted prints, but as she'd told Jody, Mrs. Wilson had been a Realtor and plenty of different people got in and out of her car, so it would only be helpful if they had a suspect later. None of them showed a match when ran through the federal database, so if whoever kidnapped her was careless enough to leave a print, he was a new bad guy, not an old one.

And Ellie had a feeling he was a very, *very* bad one. They hadn't found a single trace of the bodies or even a struggle. The second missing woman had been just like this one: car driven off the road a discreet distance and left there, nothing stolen, and no sign of a struggle. The first had disappeared in a different way. Julia Becraft had been camping in a recreation area near Birch Spring Lake and opted to stay in the tent and sleep in when her two friends went off for an early morning canoe paddle. They came back to find no sign of her but hadn't panicked until later in the day, thinking maybe she'd decided to go for a hike on one of the trails.

If so, that was one hell of a hike, because she'd been last seen seventeen long months ago.

Ellie sipped her tea and gazed morosely at the flow charts she'd painstakingly made. The victims didn't have much in common except they were female and fairly young. The oldest was twenty-nine, the youngest nineteen. None of them knew each other.

"Nineteen," she muttered out loud. "Christ. Nineteen." She was thirty-one and wouldn't have given up one single day.

It was two-thirty. She'd have nice circles under her eyes in the morning. Oh wait, it *was* the morning. Correction, she'd have circles under her eyes in a few hours when she got up to go on duty.

The furnace clicked on with a small swoosh of

sound, the rain more of a gentle patter now. Maybe it would let up before daybreak anyway.

Ellie rose and stretched, flicked off the television, which she hadn't watched, and went down the hall to her bedroom. Sometimes lying there and closing her eyes worked if she waited long enough.

And sometimes it didn't.

At four she was still half awake, restless, her mind working, strange dreams drifting in and out as she dozed off. Dark woods, wet leaves, and the metallic smell of blood; she could feel the slippery and hot glide on her skin . . .

She jerked back into full consciousness.

With a clammy sheen of sweat making her pajamas cling to her body, she decided that maybe having insomnia wasn't so bad after all. At least there were no nightmares when you were awake.

Then she thought about those three missing women and knew she was wrong.

The nightmares were there all the time.

Chapter 3

When he was five years old his father had given him a small pocket knife. He still had it. Carried it in his pocket at all times. It was strange how such an insignificant gesture could turn a person's life in an unexpected direction. Though he tried to not equate that event with anything except what it appeared to be on the surface—a gift from father to son—he sometimes wondered about it.

Knife. Blood. Death . . .

Symbolism was not to be discounted when it came to the human psyche.

Maybe that was why he'd taken the knife out and used it the first time.

Though by then, he had to admit, it was all over.

Bryce sat at the table by the long windows and watched the sun come up.

He'd woken early, made coffee—it was a little stale from the grounds being months old in the can on the counter, but better than nothing. The rain had moved on toward the Canadian border and the morning was pretty, the lake shining steel gray, a light wind rippling the surface of the water. The cabin sat up high on a hill, surrounded by birch in their ghostly splendor, stately elms, hemlock, and a scattering of white pine. Winding mossy steps led down the steep hillside to the dock, the latter now raised on a hinge with a winch to keep it out of the mangling grip of the ice for the winter. The solitude was complete, nothing moving anywhere except for the gentle lap of the water on the rocky shore.

In the Land Rover he had about a dozen books he'd been waiting to read, and he'd made a vow to himself when he'd decided to come north that he would write, read, and relax for the next couple of weeks. This last project had been a tough one. He deserved some time to sit with his feet propped up.

But he was not interested in starving to death. It was seventeen miles or so back to town, but he knew there was a little café there, and Hathaway's—a true old-fashioned general store where you could buy everything from minnows to roofing nails to ice cream. He could pick up some essentials until he decided to drive into Tomahawk and do some real grocery shopping.

So he changed into jeans and a clean shirt, brushed his teeth with bottled water he'd brought along in the car, and drove off toward Carney.

The sound of Beethoven's Fifth Symphony about sent him off the road, the sudden break in the silence unexpected enough he swore and jerked the wheel.

What the hell?

It took a moment before he realized the music was coming from somewhere in the region of the floor of the SUV on the passenger side.

A phone, he realized. Not his phone either, for not only was the ring different from what he had programmed but he patted his jacket pocket just to be sure and the weight of his cell was there, small and square.

He found a small turnoff and pulled his car into a patch of dying goldenrod, the ground still sodden from the rain as he got out. It made him glad he'd worn boots instead of his expensive shoes. He went around the vehicle, opened the passenger door, and bent to try and locate the source of the noise, which had stopped. He spied the cell phone on the edge of the floor mat, almost under the seat.

It had to belong to Melissa. He remembered she'd been leaving the message for the tow company as she'd gotten into his car, so maybe that was when she'd dropped it, or maybe it had just fallen out of her pocket.

He weighed it in his hand. It wasn't a bad excuse to see her again, which he wouldn't mind. Almost as if it was meant to be. Besides, she was probably half frantic without it, especially since she didn't even have her car. In his experience most people couldn't function without their cell phones—he sure couldn't—and obviously someone had just tried to get in touch with her, maybe even the towing company. He got back into the Rover and pulled out onto the pavement again as he headed toward the road that snaked off the county highway to her rental cabin.

Fifteen minutes later, as he tried to judge just where exactly she lived, Bryce slowed the car to a crawl, searching for the driveway. It had been pitch dark, wet, and nothing looked particularly familiar, but finally he spotted the dip of a drive, and through the leafless branches the roof outline of a small cabin, almost invisible from the road.

Yes, this was it, or so he thought, but in the light it was all different, though he was reassured by the gouge of fresh tire tracks going up the muddy drive. His tires splashed through standing puddles of water as he turned in.

The place was small, neat, with weathered siding and a stone chimney. There were brilliant scarlet and yellow wet leaves plastered to the shingles on the roof and the drapes were still drawn. Bryce glanced at his watch. It was only about eight-thirty and a Saturday morning. Did bird-watching grad students sleep in on weekends or was her research project a seven-day-a-week job? He hesitated to wake her, but on the other hand, she no doubt wanted her phone back. Without it she was literally stranded.

He got out, slammed the door, and walked around to where a small set of wooden steps led to a miniscule porch that had a pot of long-since-withered ferns sitting by a wooden screen door. It opened with a protest of rusted hinges and he knocked.

No answer. The morning was chilly and his breath blew puffs of steam. Bryce shoved his hands into his pockets and waited.

Nothing stirred inside that he could hear. He tried again, resisting the urge to lean over and look through the slight part in the curtains in the window next to the door.

He knocked again a little bit louder.

It was possible, of course, she was out working on her project. He could just leave the phone on the stoop, he supposed, but he hated to do that because it wasn't cheap and electronics didn't always do so well when left outside in the damp of late Wisconsin October.

She couldn't have gone far without the Jeep. He

glanced around, wondering where she'd go on foot. Birds, he realized, were everywhere.

He went down the steps, looking around at the slender stands of trees crowding the narrow drive, and wasn't sure quite what to do. He could go ahead and go to town, do his shopping, and then come back and try and catch her . . .

It was at that moment he saw the shoe.

And the blood.

The swirl of blue and red lights on a quiet Saturday morning was all wrong, Ellie thought as she pulled up, seeing the wash of revolving color against the white scarred bark of the slender birches. The first police officer to step forward was a square-shouldered, square-jawed blond man, a silver deputy's badge pinned to his jacket, his familiar face set. "Could be we've got another one," he said by way of greeting as she got of her car.

Not quite what she wanted to hear. The lack of sleep made her eyes gritty. "Fill me in."

Rick Jones nodded once. "Got an emergency services call from a man who says he gave a woman a ride home from a bar last night. She left her cell in his car and he came here to return it. No sign of her, but we do have blood, a pair of shoes, and it looks like she might have been dragged off into the woods. He says she was a grad student from UWM studying birds or something."

"How'd he know that?"

"They had a couple of beers at the local tavern. She told him."

"Did he know her before?"

"According to him, no."

"Show me."

Rick motioned to where an officer stood and she walked over, saw the discarded shoe and dark splotches on the leaves. She wanted to cry, right then and there, but it wouldn't do this possible victim any good. Instead she swallowed hard and straightened. "I think I see why he called it in. However the blood got here we know it must have happened after the rain stopped, which was about midnight. That's a start."

"He found her other shoe too, in a small stream about a couple of hundred or so yards from here. That's when he says he really started to get the feeling something might be wrong."

The investigator in her went on full alert. Usually the blood alone would send a normal citizen straight to his phone. "Why did he go out that far? Did he say?"

"Thought she might be out doing whatever people who study birds do. He walked around a little in the woods, saw more blood, and then found the other shoe."

"Where is he?"

"Over there. Name is Grantham. I took his statement, but I figured you would want to interview him."

"Good call." It was cold and Ellie tugged her gloves from her pocket. "Do we know anything about this guy?"

"No outstanding warrants. No record. I ran his plates. He's some kind of freelance computer software designer."

"All right. I'll talk to our Good Samaritan and you keep me informed on how soon we can get more officers here to start searching the woods. I don't want another Margaret Wilson."

Rick looked at her. His nose was red from the cold and his eyes were somber. "No one does."

"What about tire tracks?"

"If there were any, he probably ran over them when he pulled in. According to our witness, her vehicle is still probably sitting in front of the tavern. No sign of a break-in either, but the door was unlocked, which seems unlikely considering all the current media focus."

That didn't sound good. A heavy weight had already settled in her chest anyway. Having instincts wasn't always an advantage. "Okay."

The man who had called in stood by the side of an expensive SUV, hands in his pockets. Tall, athletic looking, maybe midthirties or so, she noted, and visibly tense, his head bowed a fraction. He wore a denim shirt under his jacket, jeans, and his boots were new. When she approached he turned to watch her, his gaze steady.

Would I let him drive me home from a bar? she asked herself. She could see where a young woman might be tempted, but as a police officer, no way in hell would she let anyone get her alone with what had been happening in this county lately.

"You are Mr. Grantham?" She didn't offer her hand but just looked at him.

"Yes."

"I'm Detective MacIntosh. It's cold out here and I have a few questions. Shall we sit?" She motioned at his vehicle.

"That's fine."

The man came over and opened the passenger door for her. Ellie glanced at him sharply but he wasn't being obsequious that she could see; he didn't even seem to register the polite gesture. It was automatic, not calculated. She nodded and climbed in, taking in a quick survey. Not a smoker, at least not in his car, the only odor one faintly of coffee, probably from a cup still sitting in the holder on the driver's side, and maybe a hint of spicy cologne. Bryce Grantham went around and got in also, his features set.

Dark hair curled around his face and the shadow of a one-day beard emphasized the line of his jaw and the height of his cheekbones. If it wasn't for his dead pallor, he would be a good-looking guy, but right now he was pasty and looked like he might just pass out. The grazing of whiskers stood out against his skin in stark contrast.

"I could see if anyone has some water," she said quietly.

He shook his head. "No, not necessary. I'm just a little rattled."

"I can understand that," Ellie murmured. "Not a great way to start out the day. Care to tell me exactly what happened?"

"I've already—"

"I know, sir, but let's go over it again."

The curtness of her voice clearly stopped him. But he cooperated. He outlined in a measured voice that he'd stopped in at the Pit Stop the night before and about collided with a young woman in the doorway, ended up inviting her to have a beer with him, they'd talked, eaten some pizza, and when her car wouldn't start, he'd taken her home.

Here. Where the other participant in his impromptu date didn't appear to be, but a bloody shoe lay in the driveway and another one in the woods where even now officers were preparing to start a search. He claimed he didn't even know her last name.

After he finished, she sat there, thinking it all over.

"When did you realize she'd left her phone in your car?"

Dark eyes regarded her blankly. She had the feeling he was thinking of something besides her question. It took a moment. "Someone tried to call her. I about drove off the road when it started ringing out of the blue."

Not for the first time, she wondered if she was too sensitive for the job because she could imagine all too clearly the moment the young woman realized she was not just without transportation in this remote place, but without any form of communication either. Ellie knew it would leave a sick knot in the pit of her stomach.

She had one there now, wondering if they had another victim.

Jones had noted the man said he wrote computer software programs. She'd pursue that later. "I'm going to need your address here besides the one in Milwaukee."

"Loon Lake." He attempted a smile. "The only inhabited cabin right now. Third drive off Pine Lane."

Ellie took in the sensitive line of his mouth. "You up here for long?"

"I'm not sure."

"Hunting season?"

He shook his head. "Not up here for that. I just wanted to get away from Milwaukee for a while."

Okay, so he didn't hunt. She wasn't surprised. It stretched the imagination to picture him in camouflage gear with a scoped deer rifle in hand. On the cover of *GQ* maybe; he had that lean build and angular bone structure. He just wasn't the hunting type. And there *were* types. She lived here all her life and knew the signs. Her father and uncles had all been avid sportsmen, though she never could understand why freezing your ass off in the dark in a tree stand in the middle of the night held any appeal. "Any reason why?"

"I just finished a big project and there was a technology seminar in Wausau. I attended and came up here to use my parents' cabin afterward."

"Mind telling me when you were here last?"

For the first time, Ellie suddenly felt she had his full attention. He turned, those dark eyes narrowed as if he struggled to focus on her. "What? Where?"

"Just want to make a note of your last visit to the area."

Bryce Grantham stared at her. After a moment he said in a careful voice, "Am I missing something here? Do you mind telling me how that could be pertinent?"

The Land Rover had comfortable seats. It should. After all, she'd thought about buying one but they were way out of her price range. Ellie responded coolly, "Anything could be important to the investigation."

Important to me, she wanted to add. At this point she was living and breathing this case. Yes, she had other investigations, but this one *haunted* her. Margaret Wilson's disappearance had brought it back to life, and this new possible disappearance might hold the clue to catching the bastard.

If she had a purpose on this earth, this was *it.*

The man in the driver's seat took a minute to think it over. A lean hand came up and rubbed his jaw. His eyes looked bloodshot. "Around the Fourth of July. The week before. My whole family came up."

Ellie sat very still. The timing was close to the second disappearance. Really close.

Did he realize it?

"I'll stick it in my notes." Hopefully her voice sounded casual.

He nodded, his gaze straying to the woods again.

"Thanks." Ellie went to slide out and paused. "Does Deputy Jones have your number?"

In any case, the emergency services would have it, but she wanted his reaction. He simply shook his head. "I have no idea what else I can tell you, but I have no objection if you want it."

He rattled it off, obviously still distracted.

Ellie wrote it down and got out of the car. "Thank you, Mr. Grantham, for being so cooperative and also for reporting your find. You can go."

He just nodded and started the engine as she shut the door.

She walked over to where Rick Jones stood by the muddy edge of the road, watching the SUV pull away. After nearly a year and a half of working together on the task force and getting nowhere on this case, she expected he felt the same as she did; apprehensive it was all just escalating and they still had no solid evidence of anything. She said, "Interesting."

"I thought so too." He jerked his head sideways to where the Land Rover had been parked. "So? Did he say anything else helpful?"

"Not really." She brooded at the line of trees, most of them bare-branched, and the leaf-strewn hillside, the different colors giving it a pretty patchwork effect. Two officers stood by talking on their phones but largely they all just waited.

Too much of police work was that way. Waiting. Waiting for test results, for paperwork, waiting for bones to turn up in a remote place . . .

"I don't mean to sound callous, but I was kind of

hoping when you called me this morning you had a break in the Margaret Wilson case," she murmured. "That maybe you'd found her so we'd have *something* solid."

Rick hunched his shoulders. He was built thick, like a football player, maybe five-ten but at least two-twenty and not an ounce of fat on him. The good news was all that muscle was balanced with an agile mind. Though he didn't have any homicide investigation experience, he was learning fast. He nodded. "Ten days she's been gone, Ellie. The likelihood she's still alive is pretty low. You don't sound callous. I'd bet she'd want us to find her first too, if she had a choice. We need a body."

They did. *God help us, we need a body.*

She thought about that second shoe in the stream. "What the hell is going on here?"

"Whatever it is, it's not good." Jones looked back at where the Land Rover had disappeared now around a curve. "Grantham sure seems shook up, and he called it in, but you and I both know—"

She interrupted. "Killers can be impatient to let others see their handiwork and we haven't done too well finding it out on our own, have we? He also admits to being here around late June this past summer. It goes without saying, let's check Grantham out."

"You don't believe his story?" Rick lifted sandy brows. His eyes were pale blue and at the moment held the kind of jaded amusement that only comes with law enforcement. The mind was always working, always distrustful in some ways.

"I do," she said thoughtfully. "And then again, I sure as hell don't."

Chapter 4

He'd slept.

It happened afterward. A rebirth in some ways, but he wasn't really that poetic, he just felt better, more relaxed, able to breathe again.

Like when spring crept in and he first noticed with surprise that there were buds on the lilac bushes. A pleasant revelation. A sign life had changed once again; the process eternal and inevitable.

Even Mother Earth had secrets. Birth and death. No one could predict when either would come.

He didn't know much about the first, but the latter . . .

The Hunter rolled over, realized how late it was, and rubbed a hand over his face. From the sun streaking against the curtains, it was going to be a nice day.

Pity.

He liked the challenge. The cold. The wet. The flesh-biting wind.

The chase.

* * *

He had no idea what else to do so Bryce drove into Carney as planned, pulling into the parking lot, the rutted holes there full of water from the overnight rain. His enthusiasm for having breakfast at the diner was completely gone, his stomach churning from both tension and hunger at a guess. Mostly he was still stuck in this numbed place.

It had seemed logical to call the police given the shoes, those blood-splattered leaves, and Melissa's absence when she didn't have a vehicle, but he didn't know where she did her bird-watching either. How he'd been treated by the officers had been disturbing, he had to admit. Not that anyone had been anything but polite, but he couldn't shake the image of Detective MacIntosh with her blond hair back in a no-nonsense ponytail and a dark pea coat over a pair of jeans, looking straight through him.

All he'd done was give a pretty girl a ride home and try to return the property she'd left in his car.

It didn't matter, he assured himself as he went up the wooden steps to Hathaway's Store. What he hoped was that he'd made a fool of himself and Melissa was okay.

Inside the place was warm, smelling of everything from coffee beans to shoe polish. So much was crammed into the space that it was hard to navigate, but he stuck with the grocery section and picked up bread, mustard, a couple of apples, and a bag of potato chips. There was no fresh meat counter but a glass case containing cold cuts and cheeses gleamed at the back of the store and he rang the little bell for service.

Bryce knew it was warm in the place, but he still felt unaccountably cold. He attempted a smile when a young man hurried up to help him. "A pound of ham," he said. "Some cheese too. Swiss, I guess."

"The brick is local." The name embroidered on his apron said Neil, and the clerk had short blond hair, hulking shoulders, and a friendly smile. "Trust me, it's really good."

The conversation was absurdly normal on what had been *not* one of the most normal mornings of his life. Bryce nodded, cheese not really a subject he wanted to debate. "Fine."

"The coleslaw is fresh. Just made it."

A vague voice in his brain told him vegetables in some form would be a good idea. "Sure. Sounds great."

Actually, he wasn't sure he could choke down anything, but maybe later he would feel differently.

The same young man came to the front of the store to check him out, his gaze inquisitive enough Bryce wondered just how upset he might look. He paid, went outside, and then climbed back into his car. To get back to the cabin the usual way, he would have to go right back past the place where the police still no doubt swarmed over the woods, looking for the owner of the bloodstained shoes.

Mind telling me when you were up here last?

The pretty detective had meant it too. Maybe it was just usual procedure. It was unsettling just the same to have anyone actually ask that question.

He took the long way around, driving past the turn for Three Mile Road and circling around the recreation area until he could double back in the opposite direction. It took him thirty-five minutes instead of around twenty, but he didn't think he could stand to drive past all those police cars.

Once he was back at the cabin he stowed the groceries in the refrigerator and poured another cup of coffee. It was lukewarm but passable, and he wandered back over to the window where he'd been sitting before he made his ill-fated trip.

He hadn't talked much to the police, but he did feel like talking to *someone*.

Or maybe he didn't. What was he going to do? Call up and go, *Hey, how's your day been? Mine? Well, not the best ever. It started out with a beautiful sunrise but then I realized I had a stranger's cell phone and when I went to return it there was blood and her shoe lying there . . .*

Best to forget the whole damn thing as much as possible much less call . . . whom? His mother? Father? One of his friends? Or, God forbid, his ex-wife?

There wasn't a very long list.

He didn't know whom to call.

That was an enlightening statement about his life.

It took hours for the crime scene unit to show up. Had it just been the one disappearance, the county probably would have processed it with its own tech, but another possible serial killing was something else altogether. One could have been an angry boyfriend, two even possibly a coincidence, but *four* missing women? So they'd called DCI, the Division of Criminal Investigation, for assistance again, just like in the Wilson case.

It made Rick Jones feel sick.

More than that, it scared him. He wasn't scared frequently and the emotion was unwelcome.

Right after he'd called Ellie MacIntosh to tell her about Grantham's discovery, Rick called home. Jane had answered the phone, sleepy because she worked second shift. He loved the husky sound of her voice in the morning, but mostly he loved it at that moment because it meant she was okay. Alive.

"Just checking in," he'd told her, omitting the reason why. "I'll be home late today. Something has come up."

She knew him. "Something good or something bad?"

He could imagine her sitting up in bed, the comforter to her waist, her breasts bare, and her red hair tousled around her shoulders. She slept nude, even in the dead of winter. He didn't mind it at all, even if his propane bill was higher than it needed to be because they kept the house a little warmer.

Rick hesitated, thinking of the bloody shoe on its side, and then the other, abandoned in the stream, water streaming over the leather. They hadn't found traces of blood in the cabin, but there had been two telltale spots on the steps and those soaked leaves. He said, "We don't know yet. I'll tell you about it later."

"All right." She'd sounded tired.

"Just be careful."

A muffled mirthless laugh. "You have me so paranoid, Rick, do you honestly think I'm not careful? I mean this is happening *here*."

His very point. And she didn't even know yet it had happened again.

Though as usual, they didn't have a body. He and Ellie stayed out with the search teams as they combed the woods around the cabin until Sheriff Pearson ordered them to go get something to eat. If Melissa Simmons didn't show up soon, they would bring in teams with dogs.

He was sitting with Ellie in the little diner in Carney when his phone beeped. He took it out, flipped it open, saw the number, and smiled in relief. He answered briefly and tucked the phone back into his pocket.

"Everything okay?" Ellie picked at her meat loaf, eyeing him across the checked plastic tablecloth.

"I told Jane to call me when she got to work." He found his appetite was renewed and he scooped up some mashed potatoes. "Let's get back to the case."

She tipped her head in a quick nod. Ellen MacIntosh was all business. He'd learned that pretty quickly. Underneath there was a woman too, but she didn't show it on the job. Once he and Jane had run into her and a date having dinner at a resort up in Minocqua. The restaurant was set on the lake, the food good, and every once in a while Rick suggested they drive up there. Ellie had been wearing a red dress with thin little straps, high heels, and her hair was curled and loose over her slender shoulders. No tough detective in sight, she'd looked gorgeous. Rick had been amused, especially since Jane had been at least a little jealous. She'd jabbed in him in the ribs on the way to their table and hissed, "*That's* who you're working with on the task force?"

He'd just laughed.

At the moment the knockout blonde wasn't anywhere in sight. Ellie had on no makeup, her hair was caught carelessly back, and her hazel eyes held that singular glint he'd come to know. An oversized gray sweatshirt concealed the curvy form underneath, and she currently pointed a fork with two peas speared on it in his direction. "Pearson's not going public with this right away. Part of me agrees, but another part is screaming that we need to keep every woman in northern Wisconsin informed about what is happening."

She had a point. But they'd also not do the community a service if they pressed another panic button when they weren't even sure anything had happened to Melissa Simmons. When the sheriff called her parents from the number they'd gotten from her cell phone, they'd told him she frequently spent all day in the woods working on her research project, monitoring her study group of birds.

"We don't know for sure she's missing," he reminded her. "It's early afternoon. She might just have gone off on foot."

"Let's hope she did," she said grimly. "But if she did, she left a bloody shoe behind and then dropped another in that stream down the ravine and it's kind of cold to be running around barefoot. I have a bad feeling, and for the record, I hate having a bad feeling."

The mashed potatoes were good as always, a little lumpy because they were the real deal, and he knew creamery butter when he tasted it. It was early afternoon and the café was empty except for one table where an elderly man and woman sat together in complete silence. A middle-aged waitress wiped off one of the red-checked oilskin tablecloths, glancing at them now and again in ill-disguised curiosity. His uniform was probably a giveaway that he was involved in what was going on just a few miles down the road. Rick had no illusions. It was small here. Small towns, small populations, but the network was pretty good. Radios that monitored police communications weren't illegal. The community already knew something big was happening. He'd stake his life on it.

The only thing that wasn't small was the area where someone who knew what he was doing could easily conceal a body. The sheer range of the forested region was one of the problems. He went on. "If we don't locate her by tonight the shit will hit the fan."

Ellie sighed, finally ate the peas, and then nodded. "This is getting bigger. We *do* know the area. DCI will help us out if we need it, and it seems like we do, but in our defense, so far there's been nothing to go on."

Rick agreed. They both had spent a lot of time on this already. He wasn't ready to hand it over completely to someone else; not now. "We can't do anything until we get the report from forensics on the blood we found this morning. We don't even know it's human at this point. We're still swimming in the dark."

"True." She arched a brow and pushed her half-finished lunch to the side. Slim fingers ran down the side of her plastic iced tea glass in a deceptively idle gesture. "What about Grantham? What do you think?"

Rick took a last bite of meat loaf, chewed and swallowed, and then rubbed his temple. "If he was faking his reaction this morning, he did a good job. Seemed shook up."

"He was obviously seen in the bar with Melissa Simmons. Could be an offensive move to pretend to have to return her phone and 'find' the evidence."

It was possible, but there was certainly nothing conclusive enough to point them that direction. "Let's face it, we'd be hard-pressed to find him if he hadn't called from just a physical description, and that's if any of the patrons of the Pit Stop could clearly describe him in the first place. He could have just driven right back to Milwaukee. He didn't have to call it in."

"Killers like to play games. Hunting is considered a sport, isn't it?"

Jesus, what a chilling observation. But Ellie was like

that, he'd learned. On point, riveted on the job, always trying to get into the head of the perpetrator. He'd wondered more than once about her personal life. If she had one, she didn't talk about it.

Rick mused out loud, "He didn't strike me like that, but God knows we lose the ability to judge without suspicion doing what we do."

She studied her napkin, a faint frown between her fine brows. "You don't think he's a possibility?"

He picked up his glass. There wasn't much except ice but he swirled what was left of it around. "Oh, yeah, he is. But . . . I usually know a scumbag when I meet one. This guy was sort of hard to read. People liked Ted Bundy, so my official position is that I'm not sure. To my knowledge, I've never met a serial killer before. From everything I know, the successful ones are a different breed. He could qualify."

She didn't like the ambiguity. Ellie preferred straightforward answers. It could be a personal flaw, but while her imagination was her nemesis, she also had a direct kind of mind—one that took facts and drew logical conclusions. She had to agree that there was a level of implausibility to what Grantham had told them, because what intelligent young woman would get into the car of a strange man when it was well known in the area women were missing? But it was at least equally as possible it was the plain truth. If her car wouldn't start and a tow wasn't readily available, maybe she'd just decided to take the chance. It wasn't as if she could easily call a cab, and walking by herself through the woods was hardly a good idea.

Rick said, "It won't hurt to look into him, like you said before."

"I think we need to." She added slowly, "You know what my one big fear has been all along once this started? Once we started to get a glimmer it might a serial case?"

Her partner cocked a brow.

"That this guy might be smart." She spread her hands on the table as if laying it out. "I don't mean just psychotic and canny, that goes without saying, for most of them are or they wouldn't go undetected long enough to kill a string of people. I meant *really* smart. Grantham can design software programs and the background check we just got says he also has a Ph.D. It sounds to me like he qualifies."

He does. I saw it just from those few minutes in the car during our interview.

She'd found him interesting, and that was interesting of itself. Rick was right. Dr. Grantham had been hard to read.

"You can't suspect the guy just because he has a couple of letters after his name."

"No," she agreed, turning to pick her purse up off the floor. She laid several bills on top of the little green ticket by her plate. "But I can see if he happens to have an alibi for when our first three victims disappeared, can't I?"

She could and probably should, so Rick didn't disagree, but Grantham wasn't the only candidate. "What about Walters? Should we talk to him again?" Reginald Walters was a convicted felon and had done time down in Illinois for manslaughter. A string of smaller crimes had preceded the fatal brawl with a neighbor that landed him in the penitentiary, but he must have gotten a lenient judge or maybe one who didn't like his own neighbor much either, because he only served six years. Rick had told her he'd stopped him once for speeding and looking into the man's eyes did something interesting to your soul. All he'd seen was a flat landscape of inhumanity mixed in with a good dose of rage. The traffic stop had been routine because Walters wasn't interested in getting in trouble again probably and there was no faster way than hassling a police officer, but Rick had no problem admitting he'd been relieved when the man pulled away in his pickup truck.

Ellie tucked a loose lock of hair that had freed itself from her ponytail behind her ear. "He's not exactly an upstanding citizen but we don't have anything to connect him to the victims. There's no probable cause to keep bothering him except his record."

"His ex-girlfriend filed charges against him," Rick argued, reaching for his wallet. "That at least proves a disposition of violence toward women."

"She dropped them. And battery doesn't necessarily nominate you for sainthood but it isn't murder. Besides, he's got an unbreakable alibi for the first disappearance. He was still in Joliet, remember?"

Rick dropped his money on the table and stood as Ellie shrugged back into her coat. "I've never been one hundred percent convinced the first disappearance is connected to the other two. The others were clear abductions. It's the only one that's different. She went missing from a state recreation area while camping. It's possible she got up after her friends left and went for a swim and drowned in the lake. There are undercurrents there. I know divers looked, but we don't always find the bodies."

Ellie gazed at him, thinking about it. "It's possible.

But neither of us believe that's what happened, do we? It was the same person responsible, and I *so* want to catch this son of a bitch."

At the end of the day she was always tired, especially after a day like this one. Ellie pulled up the winding lane to the circle drive and parked by the shed. She really needed to clean the garage one of these days—it was still full of boxes of things she'd inherited when her father had passed away. It got dark early and she'd worked late, and the motion light went on, illuminating the neat log exterior of her house, the steps leading down a small hill, terraced in with flagstone. In the winter they could be on the treacherous side if it got icy, but in the summer she put pots of petunias and coleus on each step for color, and the effect was very pretty. It was also the closest thing to gardening she ever did. However, set as it was in the woods, her yard was mostly delicate wild ferns anyway, and they took care of themselves.

She fumbled for keys and let herself in. The small foyer was dark and warm compared to the bite of the outside October temperature. She hung up her coat and went into the kitchen, deftly uncorked a bottle of a German Riesling she took from the refrigerator, and foraged for a wineglass in the cupboard above the sink.

It wasn't that she considered the discovery of those splatters of blood and discarded shoes a cause for a celebration, but she wanted to sleep tonight. A couple of glasses might help her relax. She sipped as she put together an impromptu meal for one, broiling some tilapia with a sprinkling of herbs, and was grabbing greens for a salad from one of those convenient bags she kept in the refrigerator when she caught a call from Pearson, the sheriff.

"Just wanted to let you know I'm going to do a press interview after all."

"Sir." She stopped in the act of taking out the blue cheese dressing. "We have nothing. And I don't mean like nothing we can prove, I'm talking literally *nothing*."

He was quiet and she almost thought the call had dropped until he said, "I have to do *something*. I think, you think, and everyone else who knows about it pretty much thinks we have another missing young woman."

It was true, but as they had nothing else in particular to say, it was going to be a short speech.

"Whatever you decide is best, sir."

"What I think would be best would be to be sitting on my couch drinking a beer." His laugh was a short expulsion of breath. "But the media is going to get a hold of this anyway and it's my job to make sure they don't interfere with the case. An ounce of prevention is the way to go."

He was right to a certain extent, but they had no idea still if Melissa Simmons was another victim and an announcement felt premature. After she hung up, she sat there for a moment until she caught a hint of burned fish, swore in colorful language her mother would not approve of, and rescued her dinner just before it crossed the threshold to inedible. She ate, listening to Albinoni's Adagio in G Minor for strings and organ.

The whole time she deliberately kept herself from thinking about the case.

After she was done she washed the dishes, poured a

second glass of wine, settled into the overstuffed chair she loved, put her feet on the ottoman, and flicked on the television.

Sure enough, it was on the ten o'clock news.

Pearson was true to his word. Maybe it was pressure from the girl's parents, but there he was in front of a microphone. It wasn't often this quiet part of the state made the news.

Suitably serious and composed, he gave a brief press announcement on the local station about how an as-yet-unnamed woman had been reported missing that morning. He couldn't speculate if it was connected to any of the other three open cases or not, but he assured the public that state forces and his local officers were doing all they could to find her.

Short and sweet and thoroughly unsatisfactory.

That was accurate. All they could do to find her. Ellie thought she was observant and had shown a knack for investigation from the beginning, making detective at twenty-seven. She'd given everything to the initial disappearance of Julia Becraft, the entire department had, but the investigation had stretched on without any success.

A mere fifteen-mile range between the abductions, so you'd think we could catch this asshole. If he isn't local, he's someone like Grantham. There is a link, if we can just find it.

She just knew infuriatingly nothing about their quarry. No motive, no eyewitness glimpses, no physical evidence left behind . . . just nothing. He was a ghost, a phantom, an evil presence in a beautiful place. As ephemeral as a delicate spider's web dusted with dew in the morning. Touch it and the whole thing disappeared.

The victims so far had no ties either, except they were female and pretty.

How did he hunt them? How did he make the selection? Like any other predatory animal? No. In the wild, it was usually because an animal was young or weakened by injury or age. Not so in these cases. They were healthy, intelligent women with no connection that she could see.

The activity was escalating. The first disappearance had been seventeen months ago. And then another about year later. And Margaret Wilson only eleven days before this one . . .

If this *was* another one. Introspective, she cupped her chin in one hand and let her thoughts flow. She did her best work that way, when she really wasn't on the job, everyone watching, conflicting personalities at work even if they had the same goal. It had been the same in college. She'd been the quintessential sorority girl that first year, social, rudderless in some ways, until Brenda, one of her classmates, had been killed in a hit-and-run accident right on campus.

It had been rather like this investigation. No witnesses, no evidence, and whoever had killed Brenda had never been caught. The sheer unfairness of it had caused Ellie to rethink her major in English and switch to criminal justice.

So *think*. Eleven days. It was too short. The pattern had altered. What had changed? Was it simply opportunity?

What drove this particular killer? She needed to know, to understand so she could stop him cold . . .

"Damn it," she muttered out loud. She was doing it again, every muscle tense though she sat in the most relaxing chair she'd ever owned, her gaze going to the notes still on her dining room table.

Tomorrow she could obsess over this case. Tonight she needed to sleep.

Chapter 5

He liked it when he could visit. Dangerous, he supposed, but some risks were worth it. Predators took chances. That was how it worked. The split-second decision was part of the thrill.

He was a hunter, not a killer.

That was how he'd always looked at it.

At them. At what had happened between them, more intimate than sex.

It was pitch dark, icy cold, dead quiet as he approached the structure, his flashlight skirting dead brush and black water.

Later, he'd take her home, but for now, he'd just drop by . . .

Four of them were missing.

Shock held him momentarily immobile. Bryce stared at the front page of the paper as he stood in the checkout line.

Another disappearance in Lincoln County? It was in bold, undeniable headlines.

What the hell was that? *Another?* It went on. If Melissa was included, four women. Gone. No traces.

Bryce hoped to God the article didn't mention his name on another page. Why it mattered, he wasn't sure, but he'd rather be disassociated as much as possible from a murder investigation, even if he was just identified as the person who last saw the most recent victim alive.

When he thought of it that way, it made him sick inside.

He hadn't realized the situation. He'd been so wrapped up in his latest project for the past six months he hadn't watched the news much. Milwaukee had its share of troubles anyway, so a problem up north usually got stuck away on a back page somewhere. Now that it slammed home in the form of the headline on the front page of the newspaper sitting in the rack in the supermarket, he did recall hearing something about this going on in the usual quiet of Lincoln and Oneida counties. His mother might have mentioned the two missing girls last summer, but he hadn't been listening well enough apparently.

No wonder Detective MacIntosh had been so intense and serious. Bryce reached over, took one of the papers, placed it with his groceries, and his fingers were clumsy as he extracted his credit card and paid.

A hundred and fifteen dollars later he wasn't going to starve in the next week anyway. He loaded the bags into the Land Rover, stopped at the liquor store, added a couple of bottles of full-bodied red wine to his provisions, and headed out of town.

The day had dawned as nice as the one before, but the skies had grown to the color of molten lead and it was colder. He'd need more than baseboard heat this evening if the forecasters were right, though no significant rain or snow was predicted and it was supposed to clear off again and even warm up into the fifties in a few days before the next front rolled through.

Four missing women.

He drove slowly through the thickening afternoon, watching out for deer on the move, dusky forms through the breaks in the trees. A couple of flakes of snow drifted down, but it wasn't supposed to drop below thirty. He took his turn off County B, went past Beaver Lake, and caught the curvy Pine Lane road.

Bryce had spent the day reading. It should have been restful. It was, actually, revisiting old friends. *Paradise Lost.* Milton.

Death . . . on his pale horse.

Perhaps he'd read something else tomorrow.

He'd considered doing his dissertation on Milton but it was overdone. Instead he'd chosen Henry James, though he still wasn't sure even after spending the better part of two years analyzing his work he understood most of the symbolism in the man's writing. The theme, however, turned him off. Death, the possibility of torment trapping human beings in a perpetual cycle of guilt and betrayal . . .

Not that James was very cheerful either. Maybe if Bryce had read one of those romance novels his mother had lying around the cabin instead, he thought with wry amusement, it would have been better. He wanted to relax, not dwell on the intricate dark side of mankind's foibles. A little sex, a love story, and a happy ending. It would be nice for a change.

He pulled into the wooded lane that led to the

cabin and immediately caught sight of the car parked in front of the cottage. Police cruiser.

Why the hell are they here?

Both Detective MacIntosh and Deputy Jones were out of the car, leaning against it, talking. They turned as he drove up and parked by a stand of birches in his usual spot, their conversation arrested. Bryce opened the door and slid out, his stomach oddly tight. Not very brilliantly, he said, "Hello."

"Hello, Dr. Grantham." MacIntosh smiled. It was very slight, and really didn't reflect the emotion in her eyes. She had interesting eyes, he'd noticed that before. Greenish gold in color, and she had an assessing way of looking at you, which he supposed made most people feel as uncomfortable as it did him under the circumstances.

Actually, what *were* the circumstances?

"Sorry to bother you again, but can we have a few minutes?" Her voice was cool, low, just like the day before. A single flake of snow floated down and landed in her dark gold hair.

It was incongruous to the situation, but he found her attractive. *What an idiot*. "Have you . . . found her?"

"This won't take long at all."

The knot in his stomach tightened just a little at her refusal to answer, like someone using a wrench on the nut on a bolt. Next to the female detective, square in his dark jacket, Jones' face was unreadable.

"Sure," Bryce said slowly. "I am not sure what else there is I can tell you, but that's fine. I have groceries to carry in if you don't mind waiting a minute or two."

"No problem."

"I'll unlock the door." To his chagrin he fumbled to find the right key on the ring, but finally managed it, and pushed open the door. "Please, feel free to wait inside. It's getting cold out here."

"Thank you."

MacIntosh went in, but Jones came over to the Land Rover when Bryce popped the back hatch door and hefted out three bags with ease and carried them inside. Bryce managed to juggle all the rest except for the milk and the bag containing frozen meat, which he figured with the temperature outside would be fine for a little while at least. He went in to find MacIntosh standing at the long windows facing the lake. She said, "Pretty view."

"I agree." He could feel them both watching as he dumped the bags on the kitchen counter. For some perverse reason he didn't want to put away his purchases in front of them, as if it revealed something innately personal in whether he preferred Yukon gold potatoes or russet, or what brand of jarred spaghetti sauce.

Like folding your laundry in public, he thought. Boxers or briefs? *Here's the answer for all to see.*

He turned, lifted his brows a fraction. "Please sit down if you'd like."

They both did. He wished they hadn't. It indicated a longer conversation than he wanted. He really didn't want a conversation at all. Both officers chose the comfortable plaid couch, so to face them, he really had little choice but to take the green wing chair by the woodstove.

"We'd like for you to just go over your story from yesterday morning one more time." Jones had a deep voice, a little throaty. Maybe a smoker at one time? He unbuttoned his jacket and took out a notebook.

"I believe I told you and Detective MacIntosh each the same thing at different times. Did something not match? I find that hard to believe since there was only one set of events."

"Just go over it again, Dr. Grantham, if you don't mind."

She'd obviously checked up on him. Found out he had a Ph.D. in literature, though that wasn't how he made his living. Yet. He'd really love to write that damned book he swore was a wellspring inside him, but first his career, then the divorce, and now this, made it really pretty difficult to concentrate.

The detective unbuttoned her coat. Today she was dressed differently. Not quite as casual in gray slacks, a red sweater visible under her dark wool coat, and her hair was loose and shining around her shoulders. She added, "I am sure you understand this is an investigation that could involve multiple cases. We don't want to overlook anything, and what might not seem important to you could be significant."

"I had no idea there were other women missing until today." He pointed at the newspaper sticking out of the top of one of the bags on the counter. "At the supermarket they had the newspaper with the headline there. I haven't had a chance to read it yet, obviously. If the media has been covering the case down in Milwaukee, I haven't seen it or paid attention, I guess. I don't watch a lot of television."

Jones wrote something down. Why the hell he did that, Bryce wasn't sure, but it annoyed him.

MacIntosh said smoothly, "Since you now do know, maybe you won't mind going over your story once again? You are our only witness, or at least the closest we have to one."

The word "story" was one he didn't care for much, but he obligingly went through the events again. The impulsive urge to stop at the tavern because he was hungry, his chance meeting with the dark-haired girl named Melissa, their brief conversation, the issue with her car . . .

"You said she asked you for a ride," Jones interrupted at one point.

"Yes," Bryce said evenly. "*She* asked *me*. The most I did was offer to wait once she realized her car wouldn't start."

"Did she say she was having trouble with her car previous to that night?"

"Actually, she did mention she'd had to call for a tow truck before. Surely you can check that out."

MacIntosh merely nodded. Jones asked, "Who do you work for, Dr. Grantham?"

What does that have to do with anything? He answered, "No one."

Good God, had he really just said that? Talk about a Freudian slip of psychotherapy proportions. When a man referred to himself as no one, he *might* want to take a look at his self-image. He clarified, "I meant I am self-employed and do work for various companies on an independent project-by-project basis."

"Must be lucrative." Jones jerked his head toward the front door. "Nice ride."

"It can be." Bryce furrowed his brow. "I don't think I understand why anything about me matters."

It was MacIntosh who answered. "As you said, we do have other women who have disappeared from this area in the past seventeen months." She pulled a list from her pocket. "Julia Becraft, aged twenty-one, on

June 10 of last year. Then it was quiet, until Patricia Wells, aged nineteen, vanished on July 8 of this year. Just eleven days ago a twenty-nine-year-old Realtor named Margaret Wilson's abandoned car was found about ten miles from here. She hasn't been seen since. Now it seems we have Melissa Simmons."

He'd liked Melissa. Liked that spontaneous sweet smile . . . he really couldn't believe something had happened to her.

Bryce swallowed and glanced between them both. "It's a terrible thing."

"Very." Detective MacIntosh's gaze seemed more searching than ever. "You do understand we can't let any lead go?" Without waiting for an answer, she went on. "I wonder if you could perhaps give us a list of your whereabouts on the day of each disappearance."

Stunned at the implication, he couldn't say anything at all for a moment. He stared at her, trying to process the request. When he did find his voice, it sounded unnaturally hoarse. "You can't think *I* had anything to do with any of this?"

"So far there's no evidence to indicate you do, but we'd like to make sure." Jones sounded matter-of-fact. "It's our job. Nothing personal, sir."

Nothing personal in telling someone he was of interest in a serial murder case? Bryce felt as if his stomach was now a figure eight. With effort he steadied himself. *Relax. Just give them what they want.*

That was the best plan, right?

"Fine," he said, managing to keep his tone civil. "I keep a day planner and use it religiously. I should be able to go back and give you specifics on where I was and what I was doing. It's at home on my main computer though, not on my laptop. I'll have to go someplace and access wireless Internet, retrieve the file, and print it."

"There's a coffee shop in Rhinelander that offers wireless," MacIntosh said helpfully. "Get the file and you can print it at the station, if you like."

He didn't like. He wanted to go nowhere near the county police station. At thirty-six, he'd never been in a police station and very much wanted to keep it that way. He'd find a printer somewhere else. "Is tomorrow okay?" He gestured at the groceries. "I came up here for a vacation. So far it hasn't been all that relaxing and it's getting dark."

"We appreciate your cooperation, Dr. Grantham." MacIntosh stood, slipped a card from an inner pocket in her coat and held it out along with the list of dates. "I hope you have a nice evening."

He took the card and said hollowly, "Thank you."

It took Rick about two seconds after starting the car to say, "What do you think?"

Tough one. What *did* she think, Ellie wondered. Well, for starters, she thought Grantham hadn't reacted in the way a guilty man would, but he had seemed nervous. On the other hand, cops did make people nervous, so that was hardly solid evidence of anything.

So much for getting a real handle on their current only—and only tenuously anyway—suspect. Ellie turned and looked out the window. It was now well past dusk and the cold wind whispered past the windows of the car, the pines with their branches like feathered arms amid starker deciduous trees, stripped to ghostlike bareness as they passed, watchful and close. The headlights picked up flecks of snow in falling crystals. The road looked slick, and probably was.

Another full day of searching and there was no sign of Melissa Simmons. They had found another few traces of blood near the ravine where the second shoe had been left in the water. In Ellie's mind she could picture a woman in desperate flight and a vicious killer right behind her . . .

She needed to quit doing that. It muddled her thinking and made her more victim than hunter. Personalizing the cases too much was a flaw as an investigator.

"I'm going to postulate," she said carefully, "it never occurred to Bryce Grantham we might seriously investigate him. What does that mean? I'm not sure. Is it conceit or innocence? In my opinion, he was shocked."

"Could be one hell of an actor." Jones guided the patrol car onto the narrow road.

"Could be a lot of things," Ellie agreed slowly, sitting back in her seat, the cold around her like a chill blanket. She'd forgotten her gloves. "But he doesn't *feel* that way. Did you get the same vibe? He doesn't really control his reactions well enough. There are things you can fake. Expressions, body language, etcetera, but he went pale when I listed off the names of the missing women. If he didn't expect to be looked at, he either overestimated his ability to hide the crimes, underestimated our ability to solve them, or he honestly didn't realize four women were missing and hearing their names was too much for him."

It was for her. She knew their pictures. Their faces. After the investigations, their lives. She'd always been guilty of putting too much into a case, but she could swear that was what made her a good cop.

Her mother would say it was why she was still

single, and she might even be right. It was fine to be driven, but probably never okay to be *too* driven.

Though at this moment she would swear those four missing women would not agree.

"Maybe he knew more than one of them?" Rick turned, his breath making a wisp of fog despite the heater beginning to kick in. "Maybe he knew *all* of them. I am still not sure how the last abductions took place. If they aren't plastering it on the news down in Milwaukee, that doesn't mean every woman from Mosinee to Hayward doesn't know what's going on. They aren't going to let a stranger into their house or car."

"Melissa Simmons did."

"All we have is his word that was the first time they'd met. The owner of the bar said they were pretty cozy, and since they arrived together, he assumed they had a date. Grantham paid for her drinks and the food. Sounds like a date to me."

"The owner of the tavern isn't exactly a barometer of how to measure the generosity of the human spirit. He has a record."

"True. Just misdemeanors, but I agree, he isn't an angel." Rick stared at the road. "She'd been in there before by his admission. He could have watched them, maybe even slipped out back to take out the trash and disabled her car."

"It's possible."

"But we have nothing but conjecture and he swears they were at a table in the corner, talking like old friends."

"Maybe," Ellie muttered, watching the landscape flit past. That bothered her too. But then again, men she didn't know had bought drinks for her before, and since Grantham said he stopped because he was hungry, it was logical he'd paid for the pizza. "I don't want to harass the guy. It's a fine line. What if he *is* involved? I don't want to point out how little evidence we have. In some ways, he's just what we've been looking for. Someone with access to the area . . . someone women seem to trust."

Rick said nothing, just driving, his expression indecipherable. "I've been going over it too. He has no priors, but that doesn't mean much. Most serial killers don't look like monsters. They can be good-looking guys with money, intelligent, seem nice enough, but there's a blip on the screen, you know? Something out of whack, a piston not firing like it should. That's the kind of guy who kills a girl, and then when we can't—don't, whatever—make any progress in finding him, amps up the tension by leading us to her murder scene like a farmer with a pole taking his bull out to the field by the ring in his nose. Maybe our stupidity frustrated him. Like you said, he's smart."

"Jesus, Rick, spare me the bovine comparisons," Ellie muttered. "And I argue the point we're stupid, if you don't mind. The state police detectives we've used for assistance are just as empty-handed as we are. We don't have a fiber, a hair, a witness, or any other bit of tangible evidence. We don't even have a single suspect unless you count Grantham."

"I'm surprised you didn't ask him about the restraining order his now ex-wife placed against him during their separation."

Why *hadn't* she asked? Ellie wasn't sure.

"One restraining order means very little at this point. If he can't provide proof he wasn't in this area on the dates we gave him, then we'll look into that.

Restraining orders are too often a case of he said/she said. Divorce can get pretty ugly."

"You're telling me," Rick agreed grimly. "My ex gave every stitch of clothes I owned to Goodwill the day we hashed out the fact we both wanted to split. I agreed to go stay in a motel so we could both cool off before we discussed the kids and settlements. When I came back a few days later, I pretty much had no personal possessions. She'd even burned my high school yearbook out of spite."

Having never been married, Ellie couldn't relate exactly, but she'd had a couple of relationships that had bordered on serious and breaking up hadn't been fun, so she could only imagine. "That's petty."

"I think petty is pretty accurate way to describe Vivian." He drove with competence, as he did most things. He was a good law enforcement officer, trustworthy and efficient, and his size didn't hurt either. If she were one of the bad guys, she wouldn't consider a tangle with Rick Jones. He added, "Let's not pull punches. Vindictive fucking bitch works too."

Ellie laughed.

He glanced at her and grinned "Feels good to say it now and again, you know?"

"Thank God, I don't know," she said truthfully.

"Ever come close?"

"To getting married?"

He nodded.

She was surprised. They had worked together on and off for seventeen months now, trying to pick up on anything that might lead them to a break in the disappearances. Ellie had handled other cases as usual, and Rick had his duties with the county, but they met weekly at least to discuss the investigations and rarely did they touch on anything personal. She hesitated and then admitted, “I thought about it once. Right after I graduated from UWM. He was a veterinary student there. Nice guy, but I realized after a while that his commitment was a lot more toward his career than it was to me. Funny thing is, when we talked about it, he said the same thing about me. I think we were both right, actually.”

They had been. She had known it the minute she was relieved it was over, as if the impending question was an anvil over her head, waiting to fall and crush her. Then Brian had come along, and it had been good for a while. He’d even moved in, but they had been playing at it, not serious, and when he’d left she hadn’t grieved.

She wasn’t sure what she wanted, but she was sure he hadn’t been it. They’d been treading water together, that’s all. Where that left her . . . who knew? She certainly didn’t.

“Good thing you were smart then. Viv and I were kids really when we decided to get married. Eighteen. She got pregnant, and you know, even in this day and age, it does seem like the right thing to do to marry the girl you knocked up.”

“If you’re a nice guy.” Ellie thought about that discarded shoe, brilliant fall leaves sifting over the ground next to it, and the congealing pool of blood. She added with somber conviction, “I’m afraid there are some out there who aren’t nice at all.”

Chapter 6

The article in the paper actually bored him. Front page, with a picture of the dark-haired young woman. The Hunter eyed it with calculated assessment, decided it didn't do her justice, and went on reading.

They had the shoes. Some blood. No body, just like the others. They couldn't release more details.

Because they didn't have them, of course.

Tsk tsk tsk. Sounded like a difficult case to solve.

There was a cigarette smoldering in the ashtray and he picked it up and took a blissful inhale. Damn bad habit, but it was a guilty pleasure. Might kill him one day, but that was the way it went.

Unfortunately, life was full of dangerous habits . . .

His more than most.

Sheriff Pearson was wiry, athletic, a long-distance runner in his fifties with salt-and-pepper hair and a Vandyke beard. He'd been to Indianapolis just two weeks before to try to qualify for the Boston Marathon and missed only by minutes, finishing in the top group of the male contestants. His sharp, dark eyes rarely stayed focused on one object for long and he had a slew of restless habits, one of which was flipping a pen around in his fingers. He was twirling one now in short bursts, his face furrowed in thought.

"We've been searching the woods for two full days. I'm going to call it off."

Rick wasn't surprised. He nodded in resigned agreement. Their killer didn't leave the bodies behind. The question was, what did he do with them?

"I understand Dr. Grantham dropped by a little while ago and gave us a printout of his response to your request."

"Yes, sir." Rick took a copy of the spreadsheet and handed it over. "His complete agenda—on paper at least—of where he was when all four women disappeared."

Pearson glanced at it. "What else do you know?"

"He went to MIT. Engineer in computer tech. Then to Marquette for the Ph.D. in literature. Clean credit, not even a traffic ticket since he was in high school, and other than what appears to have been a nasty divorce if the restraining order is an indication, not much else is out there without interviewing family and friends. We haven't gone that far because it seems premature."

The sheriff set the report on his desk. Even in late autumn a fan whirred by his desk, mounted on a small block of wood on one of the filing cabinets. His desk was cluttered, the blinds dusty, and a dying water cooler gurgled in the corner of the room. "Forensics says the blood found by the shoe is human. The Simmons family is frantic. So are all the other families for that matter."

Rick could imagine. He had two kids, one little girl who was twelve and one who was six. They lived with their mother except for every other weekend, when they were his alone. In a purely selfish way, he was glad if this sort of crime had tainted Lincoln County—at least it wasn't some wacko kidnapping little kids. He'd even go to Vivian's to see them if that was the case rather than bring them here, and that was really saying something, because every time he set foot in her house, the visit ended in some sort of argument.

"We're checking out what he gave us," Rick explained.

The sheriff turned to gaze at several framed news clippings on the wall and the pen whirled with even greater speed. "This is getting bigger and bigger. I think you are very competent and Detective MacIntosh is bright and good at her job, but let's face it, there just aren't many murder investigations up here. I hope you'll cooperate with state law enforcement in every way if it becomes necessary. "

"We will, but don't discount MacIntosh. She's done some homicide and she's good at this, sir."

"That's what I keep telling the relatives of these missing women. Margaret Wilson's husband is especially persistent. I can't blame him."

Point taken. Rick got to his feet. "I'll get back to it."

Pearson leaned forward and for once his gaze was riveted. "Four is four too many. I don't want any more victims, Jones."

"No, sir. Neither do I."

"Good. Catch this guy so we can go back to being a sleepy little county with only the occasional hunters shooting each other and a boating accident or two, okay?"

Rick nodded and left, striding out of the office with a purpose, only to crash into Colleen just outside the doorway. The sheriff's secretary, holding a sheaf of papers, staggered. He caught her by the upper arms, and smiled an apology. "Sorry. In a hurry."

"I guess so." She had frizzy, unnaturally dark hair and large breasts, which she concealed under loose baggy tops. Today it was black with orange and white stripes, maybe in honor of Halloween, but it made her look like an overstuffed piece of candy corn. She peered up at him from under the fluffy fringe of her bangs. "You might want this."

"'This' being?" He took the file.

"Updated information on any registered sex offenders in a hundred-mile radius."

"Should be pleasant reading." He took the file and grimaced. "It always is."

She patted him on the shoulder. "You have fun now."

Rick went to his desk and sat down, glanced at his skimmed-over cup of coffee in distaste, and opened the file. Not too much had changed. A few had moved away—they didn't seem to stay in one place long—and a few new ones had moved to the area.

One of them caught his eye. A convicted pedophile had moved to just outside Antigo named Michael Sandoval. It wouldn't mean anything more than any of the other names on the page, except he'd moved up from Stevens Point and that meant he'd had access to the area for a while. Stevens Point was maybe only an hour and a half away.

Rick made a small check next to his name. He'd call the guy's parole officer, get a feel for Sandoval. The missing women weren't children by any means, but they had been young—under thirty, and one had been nineteen.

One other name on the list made him sit back and

take a deep breath. Keith Walters. The last name was familiar, but it wasn't all that uncommon . . . He booted up his computer and sure enough, the address matched. *Fantastic,* he thought with an inner wince. Reginald Walters had a brother. A little brother from the birth date. This was like a fucking birthday present he didn't want. Both of them were bad, bad news. And apparently both of them now lived in Lincoln County.

He punched up a number on the phone on his desk and waited. Ellie was not on duty but she picked up on the third ring, brisk and businesslike. "MacIntosh."

"It's me. Say, want some good news?"

"From your tone I'm going take this with a grain of salt. What's up?"

"Remember how we just talked about Walters?"

"Charming felon from Joliet, filthy beard, monosyllables and unattractive body odor? How could I forget him?" she said dryly.

"Yeah, well, good things come in pairs." Rick leaned back in his chair, the springs squeaking. "He has a brother. A sex offender. You'll be touched to find out they happen to be a close family. Keith Walters just moved in with big bro about two weeks ago. Before this he was in Appleton."

"Are you serious?" There was unmistakable interest in her voice. "That was right before Margaret Wilson disappeared."

"He was convicted on statutory rape about five years ago. I have another lead also, but not as good as this one. While our friend Reginald may have been vacationing in Joliet when Julia Becraft disappeared from that campsite, Keith had done his time and was free and about a two-hour drive away."

Ellie said something under her breath that he couldn't catch. Then she instructed, "E-mail me the information. I want to look it over."

"We should go interview them, Ellie."

"Yes, I'm starting to agree."

"Any progress on Grantham?"

"For Julia Becraft's disappearance, he was at home working, or so his notes say. His office is there. He made a couple of calls we can follow up on, but with a cell, you can be anywhere. He did meet a friend for dinner that evening, but this area isn't that far from Milwaukee. It's a four-hour drive. That's doable. We can confirm the dinner, but I don't know if it'll mean much."

Rick contemplated the fake rose in a vase on the desk of a colleague across the room. It was dusty and hadn't looked real even when new. He blew out a breath. "In other words, it's possible he's still the one. She disappeared before noon. When her friends got back to the campsite for lunch, she wasn't there. He could have been back well in time for dinner."

"Right, but let's see about the others. I haven't been able to spend as much time on it as I'd like so far today. We had two meetings this morning with the lieutenant."

"Let me know how it goes. Tomorrow afternoon let's go over and have a chat with the Walters brothers. Word of warning: Reginald alone makes me nervous. The idea of two of them makes me feel downright uneasy."

Ellie said something he almost didn't catch.

"Did you just call me a pussy? A lady like you?" Rick grinned.

"Nope. I don't use that word." She laughed. "I'll see you tomorrow."

"Right." Rick hung up and thought about Reginald Walters and those flat black eyes. Was he a coward? Nope. He just wasn't stupid.

The clouds scuttled toward the east, and here and there a patch of blue showed in the sky. Bryce had woken to a light dusting of snow but it would be gone by mid-afternoon if the weather forecast was correct. He parked a few spaces away in the dirt lot in front of the Pit Stop and got out. The place looked ordinary and dumpy in the light of day, made of cinder block painted a pale sickly green, a corner of the sign broken out, the roof in need of replacing. It sat in a clearing of woods right off the county highway, one of hundreds, perhaps thousands, of such small Wisconsin bars. There was only one other car in the lot at this early hour. The Jeep owned by Melissa Simmons was gone, probably towed by the police.

Bryce pushed open the door, thinking about the last time he'd been there. A part of him wasn't sure why he'd come.

The burly bartender must be the owner, which is what he'd hoped. He was there behind the long, scratched bar, restocking cups, a half-smoked cigarette hanging from his lips. A huge jar of pickled eggs sat next to the cash register and the relic of a jukebox was silent in the corner. The only other patron was sitting at one of the tables, reading a newspaper and drinking Carlsberg from a bottle.

Bryce approached the bar, chose a stool, and sat down. "Draft, please."

The bartender looked derisively at his leather jacket and tailored denim shirt and asked, "Light or regular?"

No, he supposed he didn't dress like the normal logger type, so Bryce smiled thinly in response. "Regular would be fine."

Proving your manhood by your beer selection, now that is mature. He accepted the plastic cup and pushed a couple of bills across the wooden bar. It was actually a beauty, even scarred and scratched. Solid oak and antique, if he was a judge. Must have come from an old hotel or someplace similar. Bryce rested his elbows on the surface and took a sip. He said tentatively, "I was in here the other night. Do you happen to remember?"

The bartender glanced back, studied his face, and nodded. There was a hint of hostility in his gaze. "Sure do. Police have been here, asking about you."

It shocked him to hear it put that way.

The man went on gruffly. "If it was the summer, I might not have noticed. Once we've got good snow on the ground I might not have either. Lots of people in and out, most of them strangers, up to enjoy the lakes when it's warm, or cross-country ski and snowmobile in the winter. But it's quiet this time of year and hardly anyone comes in but the regulars. You bought two drafts, and then another round, and ordered a pizza."

Bryce took another drink and set down the beer with deliberation. "Then you recall I was with a young woman. Dark haired, pretty, wearing a pink shirt and jeans. She had car trouble and came in to ask about what towing company to call."

Unruly brows lifted. "Yep."

"Was everyone else in here that night local?" Bryce asked him, not even sure why he was bothering with this when surely the police knew their jobs. He wasn't an investigator—not even close.

"Think so."

Yeah, this is a good idea, Grantham. Why don't you draw even more attention to yourself. What is this accomplishing anyway?

"Thanks."

Bryce finished his beer and left, driving on the few miles to Carney. The parking lot at Hathaway's was pretty crowded and he found a spot and went in, this time getting a ten-day fishing license and a box of sinkers, a foam bucket with minnows, and some new hooks. The same young man who waited on him before was back at the deli, but Russell Hathaway, the proprietor who Bryce remembered had always owned the place, was at the cash register. He was iron haired and tall, with stooped shoulders and a good-natured, lined face. His parents knew Russell on a first-name basis, but Bryce doubted the older man remembered him, even though he'd been shopping at the store off and on for most of his life. The once-a-summer visit didn't inspire much of a memory.

He was wrong.

As Hathaway filled out the fishing license, he said genially, "Grantham, right? Son?"

"Yes." Bryce was impressed, leaning over to sign the form. "I'm surprised you recognize me."

"Your parents have been coming up here for thirty, forty years. You look like your dad." Hathaway held up the license. "Want this laminated?"

"I'd appreciate it." He didn't plan on falling into the now-more-than frigid northern Wisconsin waters, but a person just never knew.

"I'll be right back. If anyone comes up to check out, tell them just to give me a minute."

In Milwaukee, no one would walk away from an

antique register that required only a click of one key to open the cash drawer, but things were different up here. Amused, Bryce waited until the older man came back. He accepted the license and tucked it away in his pocket. "Thanks."

"Here's your minnows." Hathaway handed over the foam bucket. "Your place is on Loon Lake, right?"

"The boat is out for the winter," Bryce responded, picking up his purchases. "I might just do a little bank fishing on the Prairie or take out the canoe."

"My parents used to own a little place on the river. Big fish in there." A man who had wandered up behind him with a bag of chips and a loaf of bread spoke up. "Don't go too far up upstream if you get off on 17. The pools get too shallow."

Bryce turned and nodded. "Thanks for the tip."

"My son knows every good fishing spot in these parts. Ask him if you'd like to know where you should go this time of year, depending on what you want to catch." Russell nodded back toward the deli. "From the size of those minnows, I assume you're going for pike. Hey, Neil."

Obligingly, the young man left the glassed back case and came down the aisle, wiping his hands on a cloth. "Yeah?"

"Best spot for northern with minnows right now?"

The man behind Bryce said in good-humored objection, "Russ, I've been fishing the waters around here since before he was born."

Neil grinned. "That's true, Jack, but I actually catch fish."

Jack made a derisive sound but laughed, and Russell ambled off to answer a ringing phone somewhere.

"Don't worry about it, I'm not all that serious about the fishing," Bryce admitted. "It's more the scenery and solitude for me."

Clearly not the correct answer for a true outdoorsman. Both Neil and the other man ignored that statement.

"Wouldn't you say the Prairie, Jack?" Neil pursed his mouth, obviously considering.

"I already did."

"You want lots of fish, try the little turnoff on Goose Road about six miles from here." As he spoke, Neil rang up the chips and bread for Jack and without being asked reached behind him to select a pack of cigarettes from a shelf, which he also rang up and added to the bag. "There's a curve with a bank, and a rocky outcrop, and a big pool between two boulders. You don't even have to bother with your license. Just climb over the gate."

Considering the state of his interaction recently with local law enforcement, Bryce said, "Um, no thanks, I'm not interested in trespassing."

Jack laughed. "No worries. I own it. There's a cabin there, but it's falling apart. It's just used for fishing. Help yourself."

Actually, now that the subject had come up, Bryce knew just where he wanted to go. "Thanks."

"No problem." Jack nodded, his smile good humored. "Hey, if you come up empty-handed, I'll be happy to take you out. I fish about every day this time of year anyway. You can bring the beer."

It was easy to forget, living in a big city, how friendly small-town people were. Bryce said, "I might take you up on that one afternoon."

"Just let me know. Russell knows where to find me. Thanks, Neil." Jack took his bag and departed.

Bryce left too, climbing into his vehicle and backing out slowly, the minnow bucket on the floor on the passenger side. Tonight he planned on grilling a steak, cracking open one of those bottles of wine, and having a pleasant, *relaxing* evening. It was what he came up here for. None of what was going on had really anything to do with him.

None of it.

He'd given the police what they wanted. That was enough.

Enough.

Except he kept seeing Melissa's dark blue eyes in his mind and he was discovering he wasn't good at detaching himself. His tires tossed gravel backward as he gave the Land Rover gas and pulled out of the parking lot.

Chapter 7

Infatuation was a mistake. The Hunter had learned that the hard way a few years ago when he almost tripped himself up and landed on his ass in a mess of trouble that might have ended in a severe lifestyle change.

But he could sense it coming on. It had started the other night and was why he'd been so impulsive and done the girl so soon after the last one. Sexual interest affected his clear thinking and no predator could afford to be careless, but he really couldn't stop the fantasy from lingering . . . teasing him on the edge of his consciousness. He'd even caught himself whistling while working.

Happy-go-lucky, that was him.

The thought made him laugh quietly as he poured himself a beer.

The Walterses lived just north of Merrill close to the Wisconsin River. Ellie saw the drive was nothing but beaten-down dying grass and ruts, and the battered mail box had no number or name on it, rust holes the size of half-dollars spotting it like some loathsome disease. She hadn't been there before because they'd interviewed Reggie at work, and she hadn't been missing much. Still, it was the best—if very slim—lead they had if they discounted Grantham.

Which she didn't. Not by a long shot, but her instincts, which she normally trusted, were sending mixed signals. In retrospect, when she was in college, maybe she should have taken more classes in psychology. Would someone that intelligent deliberately draw attention to himself?

She sure as hell wouldn't, but then again, she wouldn't abduct young women either. It meant she didn't understand their quarry, and it frightened her, not just as a cop, but as a woman. She disliked feeling vulnerable, and whoever was out there had accomplished just that.

So catch him and hang him out to dry . . .

The house was about a quarter of a mile back from the road, in a stand of white pine and hemlocks. It was an old fishing cabin, dingy gray clapboard with a small sagging front porch, and its lackluster appearance made the expensive pickup truck sitting next to it look even shinier and newer. Even if the truck hadn't been there, a thin coil of smoke from a tin pipe sticking out of the roof would have told them someone was home.

Rick parked the patrol car next to the truck. Ellie got out, her shoes crunching the dead weeds. The air was crisp and laden with chimney smoke, but even though it was cool, the sun was shining and the cerulean sky shown only a few wisps of horsetail clouds. Beyond the clearing there was a gleam of silver water.

"The place is a dump, but this is sweet, with the

river right out back," Rick observed. "Biggest muskie I ever caught was in the Wisconsin. Sucker about tipped my canoe. I should have kept him and had him mounted. I was only nineteen and had some idealistic views on live and let live then."

"Which you've since lost?" Ellie noted a flick of the curtains in the front window. Their arrival had been noticed.

Rick let out a snort, and whether it was conscious or not, hiked his gun belt a fraction. His face, usually wearing his easygoing smile, was grim. "Let's just say if I caught a forty-four incher today, I'd be on my way to the taxidermist in a heartbeat. Kind of been on a dry spell in the fishing department. You see we're being watched?"

"I saw it."

"You'd think they'd go ahead and come out to see what we want. I would if a police car pulled into my driveway, but then again, I'm a law-abiding citizen. Guess we'll have to go bang on the door and look all official."

"So let's go," Ellie said. She had unbuttoned her jacket to make sure she could access her weapon easily. After she read the rap sheet on Keith Walters, it seemed prudent. He might be eight years younger than his brother, but he was packing a lot of experience into a short amount of time on this earth. He'd been arrested for possession of a handgun without a license, breaking and entering, battery, public intoxication, and the rape charge that sent him to prison had involved a fourteen-year-old girl. His juvenile record was sealed, but from her brief conversation with Keith's parole officer she'd gotten the impression he'd been getting into serious trouble practically since he could walk.

"Normally I'd say ladies first," Rick told her as he gestured at the rickety steps, "but let me. I'm bigger and he can see my gun."

She had no problem with it. His sheer bulk was intimidating, though she wasn't sure of the effect on two hardened men who had served time in prison. In her experience, the ones who walked out tended to leave their humanity behind, if they'd ever had it in the first place. Ellie said dryly, "So you are. Be my guest. Did you think you'd get an argument?"

Rick did an impressive job of pounding on the door when the first knock wasn't answered. "Keith Walters? Come on, we know someone is at home. We just want to talk to you."

Whomever it was made them wait, though the shack couldn't have more than three rooms. The door finally creaked open a suspicious inch. "Yeah?" said a voice with the rasp of a cigarette smoker. "What do you want?"

"You Keith Walters?"

"And you're asking . . . why?" The door stayed almost shut. "What the fuck is this about?"

Ellie fished out her identification and hung it right in front of the one eye she could see. "I'm Detective MacIntosh. We'd like to ask you a few questions. If you don't want us to come in, just step outside. We can talk right here."

"I haven't done anything, so no thanks. I know my rights. I don't have to talk to you."

"Actually," Rick said conversationally, "if you want us to go away and you haven't done anything, then just answer a couple of simple questions and we'll leave. It's the easiest way. With your experience, Keith, you must know if the police really want to talk to you, we'll find a way. You got a plate on that truck yet? I didn't see one."

It was a good point. Walters said something vicious under his breath and yanked the door open. He stepped out onto the porch and pulled the screen shut behind him. He was unshaven and reeked of tobacco smoke, wearing a dirty pink Grateful Dead T-shirt, stained jeans, and combat boots. His face was angular and gaunt, just like his body, and his hair long, dark, and slicked back. Cracked lips formed a parody of a smile. He had eyes so dark they were almost black, the whites surrounding the irises bloodshot. "I'm out here," he said with sullen intonation. "So talk."

He was high, no doubt about it, but that wasn't why they were there.

"We're investigating the disappearances of Margaret Wilson and Melissa Simmons," Ellie said, taking a picture of Margaret from her pocket and holding it up. "Recognize her?"

"Hell no. Came over here to live with my brother only a couple of weeks ago. I don't know anyone else."

"What about her?" She showed him the photo Melissa's parents had given them.

"You deaf? I just said I don't know anyone here except Reggie."

"That first woman went missing about two days after your arrival, Keith." Rick stood there, solid and serious, his face shaded by his hat. "And now another one is missing. The coincidence has us interested."

"I've never seen either one of them." Walters scratched at his beard and just stared them down.

"Where were you on October 15 anyway?" Ellie put the pictures away. Margaret's husband said specifically he wanted her photo back and she was careful with it.

Melissa's hysterical parents just wanted their daughter at this point.

And unfortunately, she was starting to think she wouldn't be able to give them anything but a body. If that.

His boots scraped the grimy boards of the porch. "How would I know? Hanging out, probably. I'd just moved in, like you said."

Rick glanced at the run-down façade of the house. "Probably a lot of decorating to do, stuff like that, right? Putting up lights for Halloween and getting the candy dish out?"

Walters just looked at him. If the sarcasm had any effect, it didn't show. Maybe he didn't even catch it.

"Her husband last talked to her about five o'clock. She said was going to stop by the store for a few things and then she'd be home. That's the last anyone heard from her. If you could provide us with an accounting of your whereabouts during that time, it would be helpful." Ellie stared back at the man slouching against the door, wondering if she was talking to a murderer. He sure as hell looked the part more than Bryce Grantham. Walters had a nasty smile and it might be his most endearing quality.

"You want to know how I spend my evenings?" he said insolently, running his gaze up and down whatever he could see of her body despite a coat and blue jeans. "Stop by anytime, Detective. I'll give you a hands-on demonstration."

"Forgive me if I pass." It wasn't first time she'd been looked at that way, but it still made her skin crawl. "Besides, I'm legal, so from what I hear, too old for you, Walters."

"Hey, if you're talkin' about my conviction, despite

what the judge decided about the little bitch I screwed being too young, I was sure as hell not her first."

Her knee-jerk reaction to that callous statement was almost overwhelming. Ellie actually took a step forward and Rick caught her arm.

She said through her teeth, "Just tell us where you were on October 15 and 25. If we can confirm it, we'll step out of your life."

"Until you fuck up again, Walters," Rick added. "Just an educated guess."

A bevy of Canada geese flew overhead, honking, low enough the swoosh of their wings was audible. Walters shook his head, greasy black hair moving against his shoulders. "I was here. Watching the tube, hanging out. Reggie has a job in Merrill at a bar. He leaves about three o'clock usually. Today he went in early. I'm sure he'll be sorry he missed you all."

They weren't going to get anything out of him, but Ellie hadn't expected much either. She gave a disgusted sigh and turned, going down the sagging steps with care, hearing the warped boards creak. Rick followed and they got into the patrol car. She settled against the seat, automatically clicked her seat belt into place, and said, "I wish we had *some* kind of damn evidence."

"He's a sleaze and an asshole," Rick agreed, starting the car. "But then again, I expected him to be one."

"A smartass, but not smart." Ellie looked out the passenger window as they backed up, studying the shabby exterior of the house. "Probably not smart enough to be our guy. Margaret Wilson was abducted from her car. Melissa Simmons had to have opened her door for whoever dragged her off. No woman in her right mind would stop her car or open her door for someone who looks like him either. We didn't find evidence of forced entry in the car or the cabin. It makes him a lot less likely as a suspect."

"Probably so." Rick pulled out of the driveway and onto the small county road. "On the other hand, Grantham *is* intelligent, as you said before. More than that, he's a good-looking guy, dresses nice, and is well spoken."

All true. Not to mention those dark eyes. She'd never been a big believer in the phrase "bedroom eyes," but his might just qualify. So far she'd only seen him shaken and defensive, but if he was out to charm, he could probably pull it off. No one expected a monster to look like Bryce Grantham. It was startling to realize she didn't really either when she should know better. Keith Walters, yes. Grantham, no.

She said slowly, "He has a decent alibi for Margaret's disappearance. Not rock solid, but he did have lunch with a client around noon according to his day planner and a receipt. If he jumped in his car and drove straight north, he could have conceivably been here around the time her husband last talked to her, but I don't know how in hell he could have *planned* the abduction. Too many variables like traffic and so on."

"I've never thought it was planned. But I could be wrong. So far I think who we're looking for just stumbles on the right situation and takes advantage of it. Like Melissa Simmons. If he tampered with her car, he had to have the tools to do it with him.

"And he sure couldn't count on her deciding to stop for a drink. Their paths just crossed and it was not her lucky day. What about the rest of the dates? How does he check out there?" Rick shot her a sidelong questioning glance.

"Those aren't quite as solid, but then again, we haven't pushed it yet. Grantham vacationed up here right before Patricia Wells vanished. Claims he left two days before and went back to Milwaukee. I'm sure his family will confirm he did leave, but there's nothing to say he didn't get a motel room for a couple of days and stick around to abduct Wells. As for Becraft, he has the disadvantage of working at home against him, so no one sees him punching a clock, but we don't have a single shred to actually point a finger at him. Once again, no evidence at all. I'm inclined to look for someone else."

Rick frowned at the road. "Jesus, we need a break."

Bryce looped the strap of the lightweight cooler over one shoulder, picked up the minnow bucket in one hand, his fishing pole in the other, and started across the small meadow. In the summer it was fragrant with wildflowers, all shapes and heights, everything from delicate white tiny blossoms that had bell shapes like lily of the valley, to brilliant scarlet stalks with stiff leaves and bristles so sharp if you brushed it accidentally, you could draw blood. It was a beautiful symphony of color, and all of it punctuated by the low hum of bees at work. They'd come to pick blueberries here when he was a kid, and occasionally black bears ambled out of the nearby woods and he'd find himself bundled back to the car by his mother until the unwanted visitor ate his fill and left.

In late October it was quiet, falling asleep for the winter, plant by plant, brilliance fading to the drab shade of death. Pretty still, with the gentle roll of the little field along the edge of the forest and the sky a deep, perfect blue above, but different. He felt alone as he walked, but in a pleasant way. Autonomous, free, no other human beings in sight, maybe none for miles even, and he had nothing to do for the rest of the afternoon but fish, drink a beer or two, and forget the word "stress" even existed.

It was exactly what he came for in the first place.

His boots crunched crisp vegetation as he walked, the only sound other than the birds. The wind was still, and though it was cool and he'd changed his leather jacket for a more practical windbreaker, he was warm with the sun on his back.

The lake was small, maybe twenty acres, but deep and clear. It was surrounded by thick woods and he picked his way over mossy fallen logs and waded through thick piles of fallen leaves. The owner of the property had been a friend of his grandfather, a local businessman who also owned a cabin near theirs on Loon Lake in addition to this property. His family always had free use of it in his memory, though Luke Paris was now in a nursing home in Green Bay, and Bryce had heard his heirs would probably sell both the cabin and this little gem of land. He hadn't needed the friendly Jack's help in finding a place to fish.

Maybe he'd offer to buy the property. The idea was appealing. He'd always liked the spot and he'd considered moving north before. Since he worked from home most of the time, it didn't really matter where he lived, though a convenient airport would be nice and the closest one was a good fifty miles away, maybe even farther than that.

On a day like this, he decided as he eased down the slope to the water, it wasn't a bad thing to be that far away from the nearest airport.

He found a favorite spot in a small cove, settled on

a flat rock, and cast out a minnow on a bobber. The squirrels were busy scampering through the trees and rustling the few leaves left, and the gleam of the water made little sparkles where the sun hit it as a stray breeze ruffled the water. It was idyllic and he needed a good dose of that, Bryce decided after a few hours. He wasn't catching anything though, so he decided to change spots, picking up his gear. He'd had one strike the whole time.

A few hundred feet down was a sandy little beach, and the remnants of what had once been a boathouse was there, the little building listing just slightly to the side. The pitched roof was partially caved in, the walls so weathered it was hard to tell it had once been painted a light blue. Luke had long ago ceased to bring out a boat and leave it during the summer. Bryce half slid, half walked down the wooded slope toward the new spot. There was still a decrepit dock of sorts, framed in the late afternoon sun, the gaps in the boards like broken teeth.

He was about thirty feet away when he noticed the smell.

Faint. A whisper at first. The vaguest hint of decay: noxious but not overwhelming. It blended with the odor of decomposing leaves and water, but was something else, something different and unpleasant. Dead deer, he wondered, glancing around. It happened. One got hurt; hit by a car but not killed on the spot and it wandered off to die somewhere else. His goal was the small sandy beach by the boathouse. Once upon a time it was used for swimming, cleared and smooth for about six feet, and Bryce could put his camp stool there and sit in the remnants of the afternoon sun. It was growing cool under the trees.

The smell got stronger. Enough to make him stop walking, fishing pole in hand. It came from his right, which was puzzling because the lake was that way and he could see nothing washed up on the shore . . .

The odor came from the boathouse.

He realized it in one of those crystalline moments where the world feels suspended, distant and dreamlike. Bryce stood there, unmoving, and even as his brain rejected the possibility of the source, he *felt* it. Nothing earth-shattering, nothing even poignant or frightening, just a horrible sense of inevitability.

With robotlike stiffness, Bryce set down the bait bucket, dumped the cooler on the ground, and carefully propped his fishing pole against a tree. The location of the door on the rotting structure required he step onto the rickety dock, but the boards under his feet were surprisingly solid and he noticed the door hung open an inch or so, listing on rusty hinges.

This close, the odor was indescribable.

Dead raccoon, he told himself. Or a beaver maybe, swimming in under the bay for the boat and getting trapped inside. Only, how did it get trapped? If it could swim in, it could swim out, couldn't it? Besides that, the door was ajar enough to be pushed open, even by a fairly small animal.

God, it had to be something bigger. The stench was so strong, nauseating . . .

Had it been mid-July and hot and humid, he could only imagine it, for even now with the temperature hovering in the midforties and a cool breeze whispering by it was horrific.

There was nothing to *make* him look inside. Even as he reached for the door to ease it open, the insidious thought filtered through. He'd smelled something decaying while out fishing. So what? That wasn't a crime, was it? A person wasn't required to investigate a noxious odor.

But he *couldn't* ignore it. He wasn't perfect, but he didn't think he was a coward, and walking away would be morally wrong as well as an act of cowardice.

Go ahead. Just do it. Maybe you're being ridiculous. Maybe it's harmless, a dead carp, or . . .

Bryce opened the door.

The body lay in a drunken sprawl in the corner, right next to the boat slip. She'd been dumped in facedown, and what Bryce saw was the outstretched arm, hanging over the edge of the wooden platform, and her disheveled hair and rumpled clothing. There was a run in her nylon stocking, running obscenely up the swollen, discolored flesh of her leg and he could see the pink edge of her underwear because her skirt was hiked up on one side.

The putrid odor as much as the horrifying sight drove him back, and he almost fell into the lake he moved so quickly, letting the door go. He caught his balance barely before toppling into the freezing water, the scene of woods and peaceful lake giving a surreal feel to the smell and grisly vision imprinted now on his brain, probably forever.

Dear God.

He managed to stumble off the dock and moved back along the edge of the water until he could take a deep breath of clean air. He was shaking, hot, and then cold, and he sat down on a fallen log for a moment, just to try and collect himself. In the annals of bad vacations, this one just garnered first place.

He'd looked in the boathouse. If he was going to

back away from the situation, he should have turned and walked away before he'd opened that door. His fingerprints were going to be there. On the latch at least. Had he touched anything else?

He *had* to call the police.

They weren't going to believe this any more than he did.

No, he was wrong. They were going to believe it even less, he knew it with dismal certainty.

The woman had been blond. It wasn't Melissa.

Chapter 8

The structure looked cold, lonely even, set back from the road by a long lane. He went on foot, past the old wood pile, his feet dislodging piles of leaves, maybe even leaving prints in the damp soil, but it hardly mattered.

Not yet.

It was quiet, still, the silence reverent. The Hunter took his time, his approach stealthy as he reconnoitered the area. It helped to know the lay of the ground, to understand the flow of the landscape. Like an artist, he thought in terms of images, in possibilities, in flights of fancy, in dreams.

He could imagine the kill. It was the best part of it, because the reality was always more rushed than what he wanted, more visceral, more primitive.

It was a shame really, that it couldn't last longer.

There was a small natural meadow to the left and Ellie noted thick woods beyond. The sky had reddish streaks as the sun began to set, and the air had taken on a late

October chill. Rick stopped behind Grantham's expensive SUV, killed the engine, and both of them got out.

Bryce Grantham waited, half sitting on the bumper of his car. In the fading light, his face was drawn, and there was no doubt when he straightened and stood, his eyes looked odd. Hollow almost.

He seemed tired and resigned. The light from the sunset touched his thick dark hair with crimson glints. Without preamble, he said, "I don't care how this sounds. I'm not going to lie to you. I thought about not doing this."

A strange way to start a conversation with the police.

She put her hands into her pockets. It was really getting downright cold. "I'd appreciate if you don't lie to us at all, Dr. Grantham. Do you mind explaining just what you thought about not doing? Your phone call wasn't exactly informative."

That was the truth. Her cell had rung just as she and Rick were pulling into the parking lot of the county courthouse and when she'd answered and heard Grantham's voice, she'd been surprised.

I think I've discovered something pertinent to your case.

Talk, she'd said.

Come see for yourself, Detective, if you don't mind. Here are the directions.

Grantham just shook his head. He wore jeans that hugged his long legs and a navy windbreaker. The evening breeze ruffled his dark hair attractively over his brow. He looked like one of those beautiful men you saw in catalogues modeling outdoor wear; except instead of flashing a killer white-toothed smile he seemed gray around the edges and tense. "Do you have a flashlight? You might need it."

"Yes." Rick said. "But mind telling me just what we're doing here?"

"Get the flashlight and just follow me," Bryce said. "It'll be easier."

"Follow you where?" Rick asked bluntly, refusing to move. His voice held a reflection of Ellie's own mixed feelings. Confusion, suspicion, and an underlying hint of excitement. Tramping off through the woods with a possible suspect in a serial murder case wasn't that great of an idea probably, but he wasn't armed that she could see—they were—and they'd radioed in their location and who they were going to be with when they arrived.

If Bryce Grantham was dangerous, Ellie at least didn't think he was a fool. Besides, she had a feeling, a gut instinct, the case was about to turn. It wasn't just the call, but his demeanor.

Something sure as hell was wrong.

"It's about a half a mile, I'd guess," Grantham said and started walking off in the direction of the woods. A startled bird whirled out of the underbrush as he passed, but he didn't even flinch.

Rick muttered something and went to get the flashlight from his car. He and Ellie glanced at each other, and then followed, tramping through dead weeds and grass in the other man's wake. The sound of them walking seemed loud in the stillness. Her nose was cold, and Ellie hunched her shoulders in her jacket. The air smelled like winter, empty and forsaken.

Once they gained the trees it was shadowed and there wasn't really a path, so they weaved through the trunks of pine and birch, stepping over sticks and other debris. There was a decent-size lake ahead, she saw, the water dark and glassy. No cabins, no lights.

Grantham led them along the edge until they came to a small sandy beach. There was a dock and boathouse, obviously neither of them in use any longer as both were falling apart and so weathered they looked ghostly in the dying light of day. A soft-sided cooler, a minnow bucket, and a fishing pole were scattered around a fallen log.

Grantham turned and said hoarsely, "Look in the boathouse."

Even as he spoke Ellie caught it, the first whiff of something she unfortunately recognized. A strange sensation stirred in her stomach. "We've got a body," she said tersely. "Give me the flashlight, Rick."

He obeyed, handing it over without a word. Ellie ran the rest of the way across the sand, clambering onto the dock. The door to the boathouse hung open, but it was dark inside and she flicked the switch of the flashlight, the powerful beam catching gray, damp warped wood as she swung it toward the floor. That smell was undeniable and when she saw the corpse she fought to not recoil, though she'd probably seen worse. At least this woman's face wasn't visible.

She'd never—ever—get used to it. Ellie thought that said something about her as a person.

But they had, at last, *a body*.

It was time now, though, to assume her detective persona. If she was going to help the victim get justice, she had to be professional. Analytical.

Even if inside she was . . . sad. Just so very sad.

Blond hair, blue skirt . . . it fit the description she had memorized. Margaret Wilson. It was an educated guess. Patricia Wells had disappeared in July. As bad as this body smelled, it wasn't almost four months old. At a glance there were no blood stains, no visible weapon left behind, no obvious trauma, but she wasn't about to go in there and possibly contaminate the scene. They'd waited too long for this.

"Oh, Christ," Rick said in a strangled voice behind her.

"Margaret Wilson. Look at what she's wearing."

"Smells too bad to be her. This is too new."

"Has to be. Call it in," Ellie said in a voice that sounded strangely detached. "We just got our break. Let's get the crime scene unit here to inspect every single inch of the area. We both know if this is Margaret Wilson, she didn't get here on her own. We need the coroner. Maybe we can even get a cause of death on scene."

"I'm not walking back to the car and leaving you here with Grantham." Rick put his sleeve over his nose. In the waning light, his eyes looked watery. "No way. I'll call the sheriff on his cell and let him organize what we need."

Ellie backed away, wiping her hands on her jacket even though she hadn't touched anything. "Sounds like an idea." She glanced over to where Grantham's lean figure sat on the fallen log, his hands clasped between his knees. "I'll go talk to him." She added on a breath, "I admit I didn't see this coming when he called."

"Who could? If this is a coincidence, it's one hell of a long shot. Vegas would have a ball with this one. Same guy takes one of the victims home and then he finds another in a case we can't break to save our lives?"

"I know." Ellie puffed out a breath and added quietly, "I think he knows too."

She left Rick there, scrolling through his phone, and gained the little beach, walking slowly over to where Grantham sat. He watched her approach, his face inscrutable in the thickening dark. She was afraid the killer was cunning. She was sure she was correct. Just how smart was the perp? Hopefully not as intelligent as the man sitting in front of her.

Unless he *was* the killer.

She agreed with Rick. Such a connection with two victims in just a few days was a bit much. Ellie cleared her throat. "I see why you said you almost didn't call it in."

His dark brows lifted a fraction at her dispassionate observation. "I thought you might."

"You've been through this before, so do you mind telling me how you came to be here and find the body, Dr. Grantham?"

His expression was resigned. "I came here fishing. This property belongs to a friend of my family. I fished for a while down the shore there"—he pointed—"and wasn't having much luck. It was also starting to get cold. I walked over here because the spot still had some sun. Then I noticed the smell."

"So you looked in the boathouse?"

"I couldn't see anything else dead around here and it's so strong." He muttered, "Trust me. I didn't really want to look. I told myself to just walk away."

"Why didn't you?"

Bryce glanced at the boathouse. Rick now stood a good way from it on the beach, talking on his phone. His voice sounded heavy. "Those missing women . . . they have families."

"Did you touch anything? Move the body?"

He stared at her and gave a muffled laugh that held

no mirth. "Touch it? You must be joking. I doubt you could pay me to touch a decomposing body, Detective. All I did was open the door. It was more than enough, believe me. I can only imagine what my nightmares will be like now."

She did believe him. Or at least *that* part of his story. They had that in common anyway. Her nightmares would also reflect black water, that lopsided boathouse, and the grisly contents . . .

Rick knelt in the sand and picked up the cooler. He looked at Grantham, who still sat on a fallen birch tree, his profile limed by the dying light. "Do you mind?"

"Mind what?"

"Can I take a look?"

"Go ahead." Grantham gave him an incredulous look and Ellie didn't really blame him. "If what's left of my lunch is interesting, help yourself. What on earth do you think you'll find in there?"

"At the moment, I find everything about you interesting, sir, if you want the truth. The number-one point of my interest is your ability to locate a victim hidden in an isolated place. The sheriff's department's detectives, and even DCI, haven't been able to pull that off in seventeen months."

"A dubious honor at best," Grantham muttered. "This is *not* how I want to attain my fifteen minutes of fame."

Rick unzipped the pack. It probably wouldn't help anything, but they had nothing else to do at the moment, it was there, and Grantham had just elevated his suspect status in a big way. Ellie stood and watched in the descending darkness, wrapped in her dark coat.

Sure enough, it wasn't much as evidence of any kind, incriminating or otherwise. A wadded-up wrapper from a sandwich, an apple core, and two light beer cans, one empty and one full and not opened.

And all the while, Ellie watched him, thinking . . . thinking . . .

It would take a very scary kind of person to sit anywhere close to the body in that boathouse and calmly eat anything. Was Bryce Grantham that ice cold and frightening? Maybe, if he was involved. He looked suitably upset, and had confessed to not wanting to call in his gruesome find, but on the other hand, maybe they were playing some kind of macabre game.

If so, he was good at it. The chill that touched her wasn't just from the lowering dusk.

"How long have you been out here?" Rick asked.

Grantham rubbed his forehead and exhaled. "I drove out early afternoon. I was fishing quite a bit down the shore from here for most of the time. When the sun started to set, I decided to move here because it was getting cold under the trees. Like I told the detective, I couldn't help but notice the smell right away."

"So you looked in the boathouse?"

"I didn't see anything anywhere else and decided it was coming from the boathouse, yes. It struck me as a strange place for an animal to die. Wouldn't *you* look?"

Rick zipped the case back up. "Probably," he conceded. "It isn't hard to tell where it is coming from. But did you know what you'd find?"

Grantham didn't misunderstand the implication. He looked back steadily, his fine-boned face set. "Did I know before I came here fishing? No. Did I get a bad feeling when I realized something was dead nearby? Can you imagine? I hoped it was a deer. It's bow season for whitetails. I thought at first maybe one had gotten away and died close by to here."

"I suppose that seems reasonable," Ellie interjected. Not that Rick wasn't right to ask probing questions. The circumstances weren't just suspicious, which Grantham obviously knew, but it was an outright defiance of every perceived probability curve.

But then again, coincidences happened.

Rick dropped the case and didn't even look her way. "If you think for a minute that you can toy with us, Dr. Grantham, you can't."

"Toy with you? What the hell does that mean?"

That was a shade too confrontational. She asked her partner, "What did Pearson say? How long?"

"The cavalry should be here at any time. Wisconsin DCI is going to get sick of hearing from Lincoln County." Rick looked over the darkened lake and then directed another question—more contained at least—at their companion. "So, who owns this place?"

"Friend of my grandfather. Luke Paris. He's in a nursing home now, but was always a really nice man. I've been coming here fishing for about as long as I can remember. There are some really nice northerns in this lake. I've caught several over twenty-eight inches here before."

"Keep them?"

"No. Catch and return." The reply was steady. "I'm here for the sport, not food."

"Who else comes here? Do you know?"

"I doubt it's used much." Grantham shook his head. It had grown dark enough that his features were too shadowed to really read his expression. "But I suppose he might let other people he knows fish or swim out here. Since, as you saw, you can't drive out to it, unless you know the location, you wouldn't have any idea the lake even exists."

"I can't believe it," Ellie murmured. "After all this time we might actually have a place to start. A nursing home where?"

"I could get you the address tomorrow the same way I got the dates from my planner." Grantham elevated a brow, his tone ironic. "Any luck with that, by the way? As an interested party, I'm pretty curious to know if you've confirmed the information I gave you."

"We'll keep you informed," Ellie said, not answering the question. She turned and forced herself to look at the boathouse again. Dammit if her vivid imagination didn't conjure up a vision of a figure carrying a body through the woods, probably exactly the way they'd just come. "I think things are about to get interesting."

That was an understatement. "Is there some reason I need to stay?" Grantham asked. He stood, obviously restless and uncomfortable, visibly irritated with her evasive response. "You've both heard my account of what happened and I really don't want to be here for the rest of all this. You know where to find me if you need any other kind of statement. In fact, I'm going to guess you know more about me than my own mother at this point."

Ellie glanced over and Rick gave a slight nod of unspoken agreement. They still had no reasonable cause to hold Grantham and he'd been cooperative enough. Rick said with an edge to his voice, "How long are you planning on staying up here, Dr. Grantham?"

"I don't know. I planned on a couple of weeks, but I think you two can understand if I say this hasn't been the most stellar vacation of my life."

"We'd appreciate it if you'd stick around for a few

more days at least," Ellie told him without inflection. "Just in case we have more questions."

"Are you telling me I can't leave this county?" He stiffened.

"Asking," she responded. "At this point, just asking."

"At this point," he repeated sardonically. "Thanks."

"Look, Dr. Grantham, I'm sorry you're part of this, but when you found Melissa Simmons' blood and her shoes, I'm afraid you—"

"I get it." Bryce Grantham seemed to collect himself. "Staying not a part of this is high on my priority list, but could it count to my credit that I couldn't in good conscience not call you about what I found this afternoon? That said, can I go?"

Ellie nodded. She watched him walk away, and then turned back as his tall form disappeared in the now hovering dark under the trees. Tightly, she asked, "What do you think, Rick?"

"I think this takes the definition of chance to the next level. But I also can't see why he'd call us again if he had anything to do with all of this. It's been a year and a half since Julia Becraft turned up missing. If he had an agenda over the bodies being found, why would he wait all this time and then start leading us now? I admit I don't understand where he fits into all of this, but maybe he *is* just a guy having a really bad vacation."

"I don't know." Ellie chewed her lower lip and then shoved at a lock of hair blowing across her cheek. It was hard to tell if she was physically cold, or if the situation was getting to her, but she was shivering. She said again, "I just don't know. I agree, I really don't get the impression he likes any of this—if he does, he's fooling me, that's for sure."

"Yeah," Rick said slowly, "but some son of a bitch has been fooling us for over a year now, so let's keep that in mind."

Chapter 9

He didn't run on a regular cycle. It built and it receded and the ebb was often erratic. There was power, he knew it, but it was harnessed differently sometimes and when it left him, he felt . . . unfinished.

Yes, that was it. Unfinished.

When it returned the urge was like a flesh-eating bacteria, relentless, invasive, possessing him until he had no choice.

No choice at all.

Bryce's cell phone rang just as he pulled into the winding drive after grabbing dinner in town. Forget the nice steak he had planned, he didn't have the heart to cook it. He fumbled the phone out of his pocket, saw it was an unidentified number, tried to decide if he was too dispirited to talk to anyone, but answered it anyway. "Hello."

"This is Ellie MacIntosh."

Jesus, he was pretty sick of the police right now. Even pretty detectives didn't hold much appeal. "Yes?" It came out curt and he didn't even care.

"You left your fishing pole, minnows, and cooler at the scene. I thought I'd drop by and return them. The area will be sealed off for at least two days, I'd guess. Thought you might want to fish somewhere else, so I'd be happy to stop at your cabin."

"It's not necessary." Clipped, short. He just wasn't in the mood to be pleasant. Though to be honest, she'd been more than decent to him, considering. He knew how bad it looked.

"I agree. Still, the offer stands."

Come to think of it, he *had* just walked away, but then again, he wasn't at his finest after becoming involved in a murder investigation, he was discovering. Of course, if the trend continued, maybe he'd get used to it. "That's nice of you," he said, not bothering to hide the tiredness in his voice. "I stopped and got something to eat so I'm just pulling up to the cabin now."

"I'll be there in about ten minutes."

Ingrained politeness set in. He blamed his mother. "All right. Thanks."

Bryce closed the phone and pushed it into his pocket. He parked under the trees, the gloom complete, and went down the steps and unlocked the front door, the hinges creaking in a familiar sound as he opened it. The place was dark and cold and smelled of pine resin. He flicked on the lights and then the baseboard heat. He'd brought in logs earlier and went to the woodstove, opened the door, piled in some kindling from an old coal bucket that sat next to the brick platform, and wadded up some newspaper. He lit the paper, closed the door, and adjusted the flue. All methodical, all done automatically.

The windows overlooking the lake were like black mirrors. He saw himself in the reflection. Hair on the unruly side, shadows under his eyes, his mouth a tight thin line. Gaunt was the word that came to mind. Bryce turned away, went into the galley kitchen, and stripped the paper bag off of one of the bottles of wine he'd bought in Tomahawk. He uncorked it, poured a glass, and without letting it breathe took a mouthful. It was on the sharp side, but since he'd had the official afternoon from hell, it was adequate for someone who really just wanted to ease the tension that had begun to make the muscles in his neck ache.

Lights arced against the kitchen window and the sound of car came clearly. He heard the car door slam, but Bryce stayed there, sipping his wine, one hip braced against the counter, until she knocked on the door.

He walked over and opened it. Detective MacIntosh stood there, holding his fishing pole and cooler, like a peace offering. "Hi."

The front light shone on the highlights in her hair. She wore the same dark coat she had on the first time he'd seen her at Melissa Simmons' cabin. Other than a touch of mascara to darken her lashes he didn't think she used cosmetics. Her complexion was natural and clear, lips unadorned, hair simply worn straight in a good cut so it brushed her shoulders. She seemed that type of woman, straightforward and without artifice. Confident she was attractive in a natural way, but not concerned over it.

He liked it. He didn't want to like her, but he did, which felt a bit strange.

"Thanks," he said, turning to set his wineglass down on a cabinet so he could take the proffered items. "I'm not sure I'll use these anymore this trip, but I appreciate it. My foray into hiking and fishing so far haven't been a resounding success from my point of view."

"I understand." Her gaze was direct as always. "But it has helped us out. While Deputy Jones and I waited for the coroner and sheriff, we talked. Can I come in for a minute?"

Bryce had to admit the request surprised him. Cynically, he said, "Are you sure you feel safe?"

"Let's just say I'm pretty certain you are intelligent enough to realize Rick knows I was going to stop by and return your gear. You'd have to be an idiot to do anything to me and I don't think you qualify."

Point taken, though it didn't necessarily make him feel a lot better about his current position. Bryce opened the door wider and stepped back. "I'm flattered, Detective. Come on in then."

She walked past him and the sarcasm, into the living room, and took off her coat before selecting the couch and settling down. "This is comfortable. It reminds me of the place my grandparents had up near Woodruff. Knotty pine walls and a mélange of all different kinds of furniture that somehow manages to still look good. Maybe it's the lived-in feeling I like."

"I've always enjoyed it." Force of habit—and the fact he held his glass of wine—made him ask, "Would you like a glass of cabernet?"

To his surprise, she nodded. "Yes, thank you. Been a long day."

Agreed, and admittedly, he was damned curious over what she wanted.

He went into the kitchen, looked in the cabinets, and found a wineglass—it didn't match his, but then again, nothing in the cabin matched, so what the hell—and poured the wine. Then he wordlessly went over to hand it to her before settling into the wing chair opposite. *Like sharing a meal with the enemy*, he thought as he watched her take a drink. A standoff; an unspoken challenge.

"I'm not much of a connoisseur, but that's very good." She took another sip and regarded him over the rim of her glass. In the light from a small table lamp her eyes looked more green than gold.

"Tomahawk isn't exactly overflowing with high-end liquor stores, but the place near the supermarket had a few decent vintages."

"There's a couple of bigger places in Wausau with a good selection. I'll give you directions if you like."

How courteous was he required to be? "Look, Detective MacIntosh," he said deliberately, "that's nice of you, but I'm sure you didn't come here to make sure I don't have to swill inferior wine during my stay."

"No," she agreed with a short, rueful laugh. "I want to make sure you understand how any detail, however insignificant it might be to you, could help us."

"You've pointed that out to me before. I have a decent memory. I just don't know anything else." His hand tightened on his wineglass.

"Would you mind explaining to me why your wife took out a restraining order against you during the time your divorce was being settled?"

The quiet question took him off guard. He'd forgotten about that, but of course, they'd dig it out. It was dirt, and that's what they were looking for, after all.

Bryce looked at her, took a drink of wine, and then cleared his throat. "Actually, I do mind. But I'll explain anyway, since if I don't, I imagine the topic is going to be brought up again."

She just lifted her brows. Nice eyebrows, arched, well shaped, a darker shade than her hair. Were the circumstances different, Bryce thought that he'd enjoy a glass of wine with Ellie MacIntosh. He liked confident, intelligent women and she was pretty in a way that appealed to him: good fine bones, a trim figure, striking eyes.

But the circumstances were about as unromantic as it could get, and rehashing his nasty divorce wasn't high on his list of things to talk about. Bryce sighed and rubbed his jaw. "Fine. My ex-wife is an attorney. I am sure it doesn't surprise you to discover she tried to make me look as bad as possible in front of the judge, but she did have a legitimate reason for the restraining order, or at least it was justified in her mind. I'd moved out but I still had keys to the house. One day I went home to get more clothes, and she was there. Not alone, if you get my drift, Detective. Suffice it to say I wasn't exactly surprised, but walking in on your wife and her lover in your bed isn't a whole lot of fun."

The woman across from him murmured, "I'm not going to argue that point. Anger would be a natural reaction."

"I wasn't angry," he said in a level voice. "I was the one who suggested we separate, and I was the one who moved out because I was sure she was having an affair. It was confirmation I was doing the right thing. I didn't even say a word. I just left. Suzanne was the one who was furious, probably because she'd been lying all along about cheating and now I had proof. The next thing I know is I'm being served with a restraining order. I don't even remember the reason she listed, but I'd never threatened her in any way. Quite frankly, no one wanted more than me to not be given a repeat performance, so the order was unnecessary. Our marriage had failed, but call me old-fashioned, at the time, she was still my wife. Through my lawyer I had a moving company come and remove my personal belongings."

"If we asked her, would she confirm this, do you think?"

Bryce settled back more in his chair, lightly swirling the remainder of his wine. He hesitated, thinking about some of Suzanne's more vindictive demands as they tried to sort everything out. "I can't think of a reason why she'd lie about it, but I'm not going to stake anything on her good behavior either. We aren't friends. My lawyer, on the other hand, could confirm I told him just what I told you."

"I doubt it will really be necessary but we'll get his name if we need it." She stared at the glass in her hand for a moment and then lifted her gaze. "I believe you about the restraining order. I believe most of what you've told us so far, in fact. But I'll be truthful, Dr. Grantham, your involvement in this case bothers me."

Why the hell had she asked to come in? Even as she sipped her wine her palms were just slightly damp. This was taking a chance.

It wasn't how she usually handled an investigation. Even she wasn't sure why she'd decided to do this.

Or maybe that wasn't quite accurate. She found him *interesting*.

"It bothers me also," her host said, his voice holding an edge.

She'd fibbed too, not usual for her. Rick had no idea she'd decided to drop by Grantham's cabin to ostensibly return his expensive rod and reel. He would never have agreed it was a good idea. True, her point was valid and if anything happened to her they would crawl all over Grantham with a microscope, but she still might just be gambling on an entity she didn't entirely understand.

The evidence was so circumstantial it was like standing in quicksand, but it was there, nonetheless, shifting under her feet.

He didn't really have a solid alibi for the disappearances. In fact, by his own account of what happened, he'd been the last person to see Simmons. If he was lying about the restraining order, he had a predisposition toward at least making his wife think he was capable of violence.

Pretty flimsy stuff.

Except he'd found evidence in two different homicides in four days, one of them a body.

He sat across from her, long legs extended in a pose that suggested nonchalance, but she wasn't fooled. Dark curls brushed the collar of his shirt and the slightly rumpled look suited him almost too well, the line of jaw and mouth clean and masculine, and his dark eyes were steady. Ellie wondered obliquely why any woman would cheat on a man who looked like he did, especially since he was also obviously successful and seemed to be nice enough otherwise. She could tell he hadn't been thrilled with her arrival on his doorstep, but he'd still invited her in and offered her a glass of wine.

Murderer?

She didn't *think* so. But then again, it wasn't like she was an FBI profiler either. Other than a book or two she'd read on the subject, she wasn't too well versed in the psychological aspect of why killers behaved in the way they did. She dealt with the results of their actions. Bodies, forensic evidence, opportunity, timetables, and witnesses. They didn't have much of any of that so far, but the autopsy on Margaret Wilson would hopefully provide some clues.

"What don't you believe?" The question was said quietly. The stemmed glass dangled in his long fingers. Soft lamplight lent shadows from his lashes on his cheekbones. The cabin smelled comfortably of wood smoke and old coffee.

"What?"

"You said you believe *most* of what I've told you. What is it you don't believe?"

Fair enough. She didn't mind clarifying if it would make him explain a few things, though his question escalated the tension between them a little. "I think it is odd you decided to pick up a girl in a tavern. It seems out of character to me."

"But then, you don't really know me, do you?"

"No."

Was he challenging her? She couldn't tell.

"For the record, I didn't 'pick her up.' I bought her a drink and we shared a pizza. Not at all the same, is it?"

"And took her home. And now she's missing."

His face tightened. "I'm aware of that, and as sorry as anyone at the idea something might have happened to her."

Might have? An understatement. The blood, the shoes left in two different places, the fact they'd combed the woods with no success . . . and no one had heard from her since. Might have was a probably.

Ellie went on, thinking out loud. There was no harm in letting him understand his current position. "This afternoon is different. You went fishing on the property of a friend, a place where you'd been before. That's logical. It's a pleasant spot, you don't really need a boat on a little lake like that one, and you've caught some nice fish there before. If you'd found Margaret Wilson first, I don't think we'd even look at you."

"Good to know. The next time I embark on a spree of discovering dead bodies, I'll try and do it in the right order."

His caustic tone wasn't a surprise. Ellie sipped her wine and watched him. "Come on, Dr. Grantham, you are an intelligent man. I'm sure you see our side of this. We'd hardly be doing our jobs if we didn't ask the question: Is he finding crime scene evidence or leading us to it because he knows where it is already?"

"If you think it is the latter, then what are you doing here alone with me?"

It wasn't how she'd expected him to react. She expected more of a denial, laced with outrage, which if he was innocent, would be natural. But then again, it would be natural too, if he was guilty, because he'd want her to think he was offended. There was speculation in his dark eyes, as if gauging her reaction to the suggestion she might be in danger.

Why am I being drawn into this?

The head game aspect of it was unsettling. "I don't really think you're who we're looking for." She added before he could respond, "But you're part of the equation somehow."

"Lucky me," he murmured and finished his wine.

Hers was gone now too and Ellie set her empty glass on the coffee table. The piece of furniture was made out of what looked like was part of an old door, cut down to size and painted white, the two base crates painted to match, the sides removed so they were open and held stacks of colorful magazines. A model sailboat in a bottle sat as decoration on one end, and a small piece of pottery with an Indian design rested on the other. The place really did remind her of her grandparents' cabin, everything used, weathered, mellowed.

She stood and reached for her coat. "Thank you."

Immediately he got to his feet as well. "Not at all. Thank you for bringing back my gear. It's really dark under the trees. I'll hit the floodlight."

He was right, it was black outside until he flipped a switch and a halogen light at the pitch of the roof illuminated the area the Granthams used to park their vehicles. Hers was cold as she got in, and Ellie pulled a pair of gloves from her pocket and slipped them on before pulling out of the driveway.

Cold night. It was just going to get colder. Usually they'd had more snow by now.

There were still three bodies somewhere. If they didn't find them soon, it would probably be spring before they had another chance.

The woods surrounded her, quiet, waiting, holding their secrets.

She shivered.

Chapter 10

He'd never liked to share. A personal flaw maybe, but it was what it was. If something belonged to him he kept it. The Hunter was not a giver but a taker.

This was different though, and it confused him. He rolled over and stared at the wall, thinking hard. Nature taught you things. Some of the lessons were painful, some beautiful, some were even terrifying.

Which one was this?

So now they had one of his girls. He could replace her, of course, and the police could consider themselves responsible for it.

It was going to be interesting to see what happened next.

The alarm rang and Rick rolled over, hit the button, and did his best to blink awake. Jane gave a low groan and asked, "What time is it?"

"Six-thirty." He sat up on the edge of the bed wearing only a pair of boxers, and tried to clear his head from a hard sleep he'd sorely needed. "I'm going to escort the body to Fond du Lac once the crime scene guys clear it for her to be moved."

"Sounds lovely." The words were muffled into her pillow. "Yuck."

"Yeah." He stood, the floor cold under his feet, and groped for a T-shirt. "I'm going to make coffee and then hit the shower. Those guys should be on the scene as soon as it's light."

"Seems awful just to leave the body there overnight."

"Not going to make any difference to her."

"I suppose you're right, but still."

Patiently, Rick explained. "The coroner came out last night, took a look, and did all the official stuff and paperwork, but it was too dark to really do much of an examination, and the boathouse too rickety to bring in enough lighting. Besides, we were afraid to move her in case the whole thing collapsed into the water from the weight of the guys with the stretcher and destroy evidence. Two deputies stayed out there all night to make sure no one approached, and no animals messed with the evidence. I'd rather escort the body and sit in on the autopsy than spend a cold, dark night with it. Besides we're really hoping this will tell us something, *anything*, that will help us catch the asshole doing this. Being careful was the only option."

Jane sat up, pushing her hair out of her eyes. "Did the same man who last saw the Simmons girl really find Margaret Wilson?"

Rick pulled the shirt over his head, yanking it downward. "How the hell did you hear that?" *He* hadn't told her.

"Someone mentioned it at the hospital. That's really weird. Is it true?"

It was a big county, but a small community, relatively speaking. Everyone who worked for the sheriff's department was supposed to not discuss cases, especially unsolved ones, but it still happened. Cell phones, radios, voice mail, text messaging, other social media . . . he wasn't surprised the word was spreading fast, and the discovery of the body wasn't a secret, but Grantham's identity wasn't common knowledge. "I shouldn't really talk about it," he hedged. "You know that. I think a couple of the stations in Madison and Milwaukee are going to interview Sheriff Pearson again later. We were told he'd give a formal comment now that we have a body."

"In other words, watch the news?" Jane flopped back down and shut her eyes. "What good is it shacking up with a cop if you can't get the inside scoop?"

"Hopefully it's good in other ways." He really couldn't do a good imitation leer before coffee, and she wasn't looking at him anyway, so he just left the bedroom and went into the kitchen. He poured out the old coffee from the day before, rinsed the pot, and got out a new filter. As he measured the grounds into the basket, he wondered how the sheriff had fared with Matthew Wilson. Breaking the news to the husband of the victim couldn't have been easy. The guy had been frantic after his wife turned up missing, and really, who could blame him?

Any day of the week, Rick would rather take the body and sit through the medical examiner's clinical dissection of what happened to her than talk to the distraught family members of someone who may have been murdered.

But at least it was over for Matthew Wilson.

With Melissa Simmons, maybe it was worse. All

the waiting, the hope gradually deteriorating to resigned despair, the days going by in a shimmer of fear that news will come, and that it will be the very last thing you want to hear.

Both of them connected somehow by Grantham.

Couldn't be a coincidence.

While the coffee percolated Rick stood under the hot stream of water in the shower. Thinking about it all. Grantham. The abductions. The bloody shoe. A decaying body stuck in a rotting boathouse. Grantham again.

He'd seen bodies before. Older people reported as not answering their phone or collecting their mail who had lived alone and had died at home. Traffic accidents, hunting accidents, boating accidents; some of them pretty bad. It happened in the course of law enforcement. Not the most pleasant part of the job, but inevitable. The difference was, of course, whatever happened to the missing girls was not accidental. Margaret Wilson hadn't ditched her car and walked miles and miles to die in a dilapidated boathouse.

It was the inhumanity that got to him, Rick mused, lathering his face to shave. The way the body had been just dumped and left there, like refuse, in an untidy sprawl, her skirt hiked up immodestly. The county coroner was an aging doctor who had retired from his general practice in Green Bay and moved permanently to his vacation home near Carney. Since Dr. Phillips had only done a cursory exam without moving the victim, he'd been unable to determine the cause of death from the appearance of the body, but did say the victim was wearing not only her underwear but panty hose, so he'd guess there hadn't been a sexual assault unless her abductor allowed her to dress again afterward.

Since the woman was dead, it wasn't much reassurance, but had it been his wife, Rick would have wanted her to suffer as little horror as possible. He hoped that there was no rape proved to be true, but wasn't sure what solace it would offer the families of the missing women. Since they had found both her shoes, it was likely Melissa Simmons had been dressed also when she'd run, or been dragged, from the cabin.

When he finished up in the bathroom, he put on a clean uniform, and then found Jane in the kitchen in a fuzzy blue robe and slippers, frying eggs. She glanced over her shoulder. "It doesn't sound like you'll be home for supper. I thought I'd make you something to eat now instead. The bacon is in the microwave. Take it out, will you?"

He did, stealing a piece, thinking of how different his life was since he'd met her. The idea of marriage scared him because his first one had been bad—really bad near the end—but Jane was nothing like Vivian and he wasn't eighteen this time.

He should ask her to marry him. She'd never said so, but he was pretty sure she wanted him to propose. They'd talked around it a couple of times since she'd moved in, but he had a feeling she understood his reservations even more than he did.

She wasn't beautiful—on the taller side, able to look him in the eye, a bit heavy in the hips, but he liked the curves, the full softness of her pale blue-veined breasts, and most of all the character in her face. Her heritage was pure Irish, and when they first met he'd half expected her to speak with a brogue, but she talked with the normal Wisconsin inflection, as if living in the north woods gave a special cadence to life, including speech patterns.

That fiery hair too looked hot when it was spilled over the sheets of his bed. Right now it stuck up on top of her head and resembled a frizzy clown wig. She religiously straightened it every day, but at night her hair reasserted its rebellious nature. Jane put the plates on the small little round table in the corner they jokingly called the breakfast nook, sat down opposite, and poked the yoke of one her eggs with her fork. She watched him eat for a few minutes before she said quietly, "I'm thinking of buying a gun. Would you teach me how to shoot it?"

She could have said she'd decided to flap her arms and fly to the moon and it would not have surprised him more. She was a pacifist in every way. The woman had a catch-and-release policy for spiders inside the house for God's sake. Rick stared at her for a moment, then crunched into a piece of bacon, thinking it over. When he swallowed, he shook his head. "You hate guns. People who hate guns and are uncomfortable with them shouldn't carry a weapon. Pepper spray is a good alternative. More accessible and no training necessary. Point and push."

"I knew Margaret Wilson. Her mother was a cancer patient at the hospital. She came in pretty much every day." Jane stared at her coffee cup for a minute. "It makes this all very immediate, you know? Her mother dying was an act of God, or if you don't believe in that, a merciful act of nature then, because she didn't have to add to her misery on this earth and know her daughter was found dead before they met in heaven."

That was one of their hang-ups. She was a devout

Catholic. He wasn't so sure about religion anymore. Maybe it was the job. It wasn't any great secret it could harden a person. "I know," he said.

"This is different," she said fiercely. "Why do people do shit like this? Kill each other? There's no purpose to it. Here's some of us, the doctors, the nurses, the lab techs, researchers; all of us working so hard to make sure other human beings live we devote our life to it. And then there are sick bastards out there who just *kill* them. I think I'm more angry than scared."

"*Be* scared." Rick said with emphasis, looking at her across the table. "I understand what you're saying, but, baby, you should still be scared. Because one of those sick bastards is out there and he's way too close."

"Jody told me. How awful."

Ellie cradled the phone between her shoulder and ear and folded a towel. She hadn't done laundry in almost a week. Not that she minded doing it, she just hated putting it away for some reason. "I won't deny we're pretty busy all of a sudden."

On the other end of the line her mother said, "A woman murdered . . . it's terrible. Who did it?"

Her laugh was short and explosive. "If we knew that, the investigation would be over, wouldn't it? How's Florida?"

"Warm."

"Brag on." An earlier glance at the thermometer outside the kitchen window had tagged the temperature at thirty-four degrees. Not bad, but not great either.

"Come see me. Sit on the beach. I'll make key lime pie."

"Pulling out the big guns as a bribe, I see." She

retrieved a pair of lacy black panties, wondered why the hell she paid so much for lingerie when no one ever saw her wearing those expensive little bras and thongs, and put it neatly in the pile. "When this case is finished, maybe I'll fly down. I have time coming, that's for sure." It sounded nice. A beach, fruity drink in hand, the sun warm on her skin . . . and her mother did whip up a killer key lime pie.

If they ever solved the case. At the moment they were still infuriatingly empty-handed.

"Bring a friend."

"I'm not seeing anyone."

"Since Brian, I know. Rather a long time, isn't it? Jody and I talked about that too."

Ah, what were sisters for? Ellie shut the door on the dryer and carried clean sheets into the bedroom. "I've had a date here and there, and really, Mom, I don't mean to be rude, but not your business."

There was a bit of dry humor in the response. "You work with a lot of men. Surely in a target-rich environment like that, you find someone attractive?"

Actually, the only man she'd found intriguing lately was the main target of their investigation and that was unsettling on many different levels.

Somehow she was sure her mother might be horrified rather than gratified to hear it. "Any romance with a coworker is ill-advised and I've never been sure that male cops like female cops in the first place."

True enough. Though she'd never been precisely harassed in any definitive way, she wasn't convinced that all of her colleagues thought women should be on the job. On the other hand, there were a lot of guys who had no problem with it at all. Like most of life, there was a balance.

After about five more minutes in which she dodged a couple of other interrogations about her personal life, Ellie managed to get off the phone, start another load of laundry, and methodically dress for work.

She hoped the case was moving forward, but Melissa Simmons was still out there. If there was any chance . . .

She slipped her Glock into her shoulder holster, buttoned her coat, and quietly locked the door behind her.

Chapter 11

Fate. He'd looked up the definition in the musty dictionary left in the spare room on the shelf. He'd always thought it funny his parents had put it there, like Webster's was some sort of decoration that would welcome guests and make them feel at home.

It said: Primarily a divine decree or fixed sentence by which the order of things is prescribed . . .

Or better yet the list of synonyms; destiny, doom, fortune, death, destruction.

Yes, the Hunter believed in fate.

The medical examiner's report sat on the desk and Ellie stared at it as if maybe her prolonged scrutiny would summon up something new from the neatly typed words.

"She wasn't raped," Rick said. He took a drink from a Styrofoam cup, his face somber. "I'd already thought there was no sexual assault because of the panty hose. I can't really imagine trying to get a pair of panty hose back on a dead woman. Really, why the hell would he bother?"

"Why the hell would he kill anyone in the first place?" Ellie asked woodenly. "Let's face it, we don't get how these guys think, Rick."

"Good point," he admitted and looked away for a minute.

"What about the cigarette butt?"

"It was pretty unproductive. Not old, but then again not fresh, and forensics was skeptical about getting any DNA."

"Grantham doesn't smoke."

"Not that you know of."

True. She'd been in his car that first morning, when he reported Melissa Simmons missing, but there were some smokers who were careful and only did it outside. She'd give him that point, but she hadn't smelled it at the cabin either. "It could have been another fisherman who stopped by before, or after the crime, and maybe didn't smell the body because it wasn't there yet, or because it hadn't been there long enough yet."

"A long shot, but okay, I'll give it to you."

They sat at her desk on a busy Thursday morning, the bustle of the rest of the department around them. The office always smelled like coffee, the tiled floors the same institutional color as the walls, the ring of the phones punctuated by the conversations of various officers at other desks all around them.

She tapped the document with a forefinger. "She was strangled. Manually. I suppose we have that. At least we know the cause and manner of death. That means it is officially a homicide investigation and switches this whole thing into a different gear. I was hoping for more, for some DNA, but at least we have something."

"It doesn't look like she struggled."

"The ME's report says there is a bruise on her knee. Residue around her neck that indicates latex gloves, and it was cold out the day she disappeared. He probably wore a coat and it protected him."

Rick eyed her from across the desk. "It's something, yes, but not much. Where are we going next?"

"The families have been interviewed, and I doubt there is much point in doing it again because they don't know anything." Ellie sighed and ran a finger down the paper with her notes. "Even if the guy—and yes, I think we can assume now we are dealing with a man because if she was strangled, he was stronger—picks his victims at random, there still has to be a common thread. Our victims didn't know each other, weren't in the same places, and didn't live near each other. He's snatching them at different times of the year, but still, there's got to be a pattern."

"He has a definite connection to this part of Wisconsin, we know that much. Public records show Grantham's grandparents bought that property in the forties." Rick eyed the contents of his cup, apparently found something unappetizing, and set it aside. "Bryce Grantham fits in several ways. He's not a small guy either, taller than me, looks pretty athletic. Physically I'd say he's capable of overpowering and strangling a woman easily. One tiny bit of physical evidence shows up, and I say we arrest him."

"We can't and you know it. We still have a pretty tight timeline on Margaret Wilson, and even if he rushed up here after that lunch that gives him an alibi of sorts, why did she stop for him? She was in her car." Conjecture didn't hold up in court.

"You like him."

The slight tone of accusation took her off guard. She glanced up. "Excuse me?"

"Grantham."

"I think he's telling us the truth."

Unless he was very, very good at acting and she was overestimating her ability to tell the difference.

Shit. She wasn't sure what to think.

So, in other words, trust your gut feelings, but . . . not too much.

That helped.

The phone on the desk rang, making her glance up. Rick answered, said a few clipped words, and then hung up. "Margaret Wilson's husband is here again. He knows we have the results of the autopsy and insists on talking to us."

Ellie rubbed her forehead. "This should be fun."

"Pearson said he's pretty on the edge." Rick looked stoic. He leaned back in his chair and it creaked, the small squeal sounding like a dying animal. "I can understand why. They'd only been married a couple of years."

"What? It would be easier if they had been married longer?" Ellie gave him a sardonic look. "You know, you don't do much for the image of holy matrimony."

"I didn't have a good experience. I had a shitty experience, actually. As a result, I'm not a fan, but it had some good results. I've got two great kids."

Ellie had seen their pictures, both of them in little dance costumes, smiling and waving. Occasionally she thought about children, wondering if the urge to have one was ever going to kick in, but then again, she hadn't met anyone yet she wanted to share that kind of a commitment with, and look at Rick. He was stuck dealing with his ex-wife for the rest of his life.

The Wilsons had no children. Good or bad thing? She wasn't sure. At least some child wasn't left motherless, but then again it might be some consolation to Matthew Wilson because Pearson was dead right about his current emotional state. When he pulled out a chair at their invitation and sat down, he looked both shaky and on the verge of tears. His thin face was tense and he continually ran his hand through short brown hair that was already receding from a high forehead. His sweatshirt had the UW badger on the front of it and looked as if he'd pulled it out of the dirty clothes hamper. "What happened to her? What happened to my wife?"

God, Ellie hated some parts of this job. *She's dead and we don't know why, or who did it. And we can't promise you we ever will.*

Those were not words of comfort.

Rick was the one who said succinctly, "She was strangled. There was no conclusive evidence of sexual assault or defensive wounds, so we think she was taken very much by surprise."

"I'm sorry." Ellie spoke gently. Rick had sat in on the autopsy and she knew what he said was a repetition of the observations of the medical examiner, but they sounded cold and unfeeling, which wasn't surprising, given the vocation of the person who had originally said them. Still . . .

Wilson stared at his hands and blinked rapidly. "No one had any reason to kill her." He was wrong. There was a reason in someone's really screwed up mind. Ellie knew they just didn't understand the incomprehensible nature of it.

Rick got up and went to the coffee pot in the corner, poured some in a white cup, brought it back, and extended it. "Here you go. Might help a little."

The other man looked at the offering as if he didn't know what it was.

Dear God, Ellie thought, sympathy rising, almost choking her. "You're right, sir. No one had any reason to do her harm. We're going to do our best to find out what happened. You have my word."

It sounded old-fashioned and stupid. *You have my word.* Like she was the marshal of a town in the old West or something. Wilson didn't seem to mind. He just nodded. "I keep telling myself there should be something I could tell you. Something I know to help in all this. I keep thinking and thinking. But I can't find it."

The bewilderment in his voice was evident. Ellie was sure he was right; he didn't know anything that could help. They'd looked at him already. Checked out his whereabouts, his financial records, all the usual things. He was an accountant in Merrill, went bowling with the guys on Wednesday night, and he and Margaret had just bought a little house about twelve miles out of town. All pretty bland and unsuspicious for a man about to kill his wife. Not that as the husband of the third woman to disappear he was really under suspicion anyway, but there were no possibilities they were going to ignore.

"She was on her way home from a showing and we needed a few things." His voice was pathetic.

"We know." Ellie nodded. Margaret Wilson had said she was going to stop for milk, a can of green beans, and a jar of spaghetti sauce. The items and the receipt hadn't been in her car, so she hadn't made it there.

"I really don't think she'd have stopped for someone. All the women around here are scared."

He'd told them the same thing before, in varying forms, over the past thirteen days. Ellie had no idea really what to say now that his worst fears—and theirs—were confirmed. Even before, when Margaret didn't turn up in twenty-fours, then forty-eight, and so on, she'd been at a loss. She wasn't a counselor, she was a cop. Catching the bad guys was her job, not helping people cope with their loss.

"We're puzzled by that too, Mr. Wilson," she said, wondering if he was even listening.

"I guess they're going to give me the body for the funeral now."

How on earth did a person reply to that?

He rambled on. "The newspaper said the same man who found Margaret was with the other girl that night before."

That unusual aspect of the case had been leaked out somehow, so Pearson had confirmed it. Too many people knew about Grantham's grisly run of luck in the corpse discovery department for it to stay quiet, but at least his name hadn't been included. Neither she nor Rick responded to the question in Wilson's voice. "We're looking into every possible angle, sir," Ellie said.

"I can't believe this, you know?" His hand lifted for some purpose, then just fell back limply into his lap. "In the streets of New York, yes. Chicago, sure. I read somewhere Philadelphia has one of the highest murder rates of anywhere. But here? It's so quiet. Safe."

Ellie could have pointed out that Ed Gein, one of America's most infamous serial killers, was from Plainfield, just a few hours south. She'd been through

Plainfield. It was quiet too. She decided not to bring up the subject. When she was a little kid, Ed Gein was the real bogyman in her mind.

"We'll catch him," she promised firmly.

"We will." Rick backed her up, but there wasn't nearly as much conviction in his voice.

One of the advantages to being married to a lawyer for five years was you tended to meet a lot of lawyers as a result. After sitting and unsuccessfully trying to read for several hours, giving up to pop a movie into the DVD player and being unable to concentrate on that either, Bryce got out his cell phone and looked up one of the numbers he called infrequently but hoped was programmed in there. To his relief, it was. Predictably, because it was a weekday toward lunchtime, he got voice messaging when he called. He left a brief request for a call back because he might need some professional advice and hung up.

He went back to the movie. The motivation to write didn't exist and there wasn't much else to do.

An hour and half later, Bruce Willis had successfully foiled an entire building of armed terrorists and Bryce was drinking a light beer in the aftermath of testosterone and violence, when his phone rang. Outside the big windows facing the lake, the wind rippled the water and big fat crimson maple leaves floated like spots of blood near the shore.

"Bryce, it's Alan. How are you?"

"Fine." Maybe fine. Maybe not. It was the automatic polite phrase. When he went to the doctor last year because he had strep throat, he'd told the physician the same thing, for God's sake.

"Glad to hear it. What can I do for you?"

Brisk, professional, to the point. Alan was probably sitting in his expensive office, gazing out the window at his expensive view, wearing a designer suit that cost over a thousand dollars, a half smile on his affable face. Alan Silver was one of Milwaukee's best defense attorneys, or so Suzanne had always claimed. To awe Suzanne took some doing, so Bryce believed it. All he knew was that Alan played golf with a handicap and usually humiliated him when they went out for a round, which happened about three times a year, even since the divorce. They were friends, and the humiliation on the course was due to superior skill, not a superior attitude. Bryce liked Alan, and he needed advice.

"I'm up north," he began. "I've run into a situation and I am trying to decide if I need to talk to a lawyer."

"Any lawyer? Or me?"

"You."

"You think you might need a defense attorney?" There was a hint of disbelief in the tone.

"I don't know. You tell me. They've asked me not to leave Lincoln County."

"'They' being the police?"

"Sheriff's department, yes."

A pause.

"Maybe you'd better tell me why." The voice on the other end changed subtly from friendly and curious to professional.

Bryce gave him a brief overview of what had happened.

At the end of his abbreviated recital, there was a small silence. "That's you? I saw a small bit on the news about it last night."

"On the news?" Bryce felt vaguely sick.

"The Milwaukee station. It wasn't CNN, but it

could be on there. One man connected to two missing women in such a short amount of time. It's an unusual story."

"The overuse of that word in reference to me telling the truth is getting irritating," Bryce muttered. "It's a recounting of what happened, that's all, not a story. I feel like the guy who gets repeatedly struck by lightning. Not so lucky."

"I can only imagine." Alan sounded thoughtful. "I see where the investigation includes you right now because of the anomaly of the two victims. But really, unless there is some physical evidence to show a connection to a crime, they don't have a case, even without solid alibis for the disappearances. You are a person of interest, no more, and I'm going to guess that's only because they don't have anyone else."

It was a relief to have his own thoughts echoed by someone who knew what he was talking about. "Good to hear."

Alan laughed. "It should be. Do you have any idea how much I charge an hour?"

Bryce sat down on the couch, aware he had just relaxed muscles he didn't even realize were locked in viselike tension. "I hope I never have to find out, to be honest. There's still a problem though."

"As in?"

"I don't really have an alibi for the other disappearances. You know what I do. I work at home most of the time. No one sees me come or go. I don't want to hire you, but I'm worried enough to consider it."

The brusque response was reassuring. "Don't blame you there. I wouldn't want to have to hire me either. I'll tell you for free you don't have to stay up there, and the lack of an alibi doesn't matter until they can prove you need one. The police just don't want to have to haul themselves down to Milwaukee to talk to you if they think up another question. I feel confident you've told them all you can, so if you want to leave, go ahead. Just let them know you're going. That will make them either move forward with some charges if they really are leaning that direction, or agree you can do whatever you want. "

The word "charges" made his stomach do an interesting sick roll.

Bryce said thickly, "Thanks for the help."

"No problem. I'll call you in the spring and we'll hit the new country club course." Alan paused. "Suzanne know about all this?"

It might be natural for him to ask, since he and Suzanne were colleagues, but it was still an unwelcome question.

"No," Bryce said grimly, "but I suppose she might find out. She took out a restraining order against me when we separated to keep me away from the loft. The police have already asked me why. If they continue to target me as a possible suspect, I suppose they might ask her. I get the impression that because the victims are female, they are looking for someone who has a violent predisposition toward women in general."

"What will she say?" Alan sounded neutral. Perhaps he'd heard everything already and wouldn't be surprised, even by the behavior of his friends.

Bryce sincerely hoped he never became that jaded. "God only knows," he replied. "She wasn't kindness personified during our divorce, but the restraining order was all for show. She felt guilty for screwing around on me so she tried to make me look like someone who deserved it."

"I see." Neutral again, no inflection.

Maybe Alan believed him, maybe not.

When the call ended, Bryce stared out the windows. A steel gray pall had settled over the sky and the clouds resembled bunches of dirty cotton dusted with soot. With the leaves off the trees he could see the other cabins across the water, shuttered and unoccupied. His mother was right, it *was* lonely. October lonely with the trees going to sleep and every creature bracing for the coming deep freeze. Most of the birds were gone, the squirrels industrious, the turtles burrowed into the mud to wait it out.

It was cold and bleak.

In retrospect, maybe he should have gone to Florida.

Chapter 12

He'd drunk two beers, watching the news, quietly laughing to himself, feet up on an old ottoman.

Law enforcement was clueless, but he'd known that all along. They didn't seem to get the single most important rule: You have to know the animal you're hunting.

That was it in a nutshell. They didn't know him, what he could do, what his capabilities were . . . or how dangerous he could become.

If you don't get that, you are just some idiot stumbling around with a gun.

Hell, that described most of them perfectly.

Not Detective MacIntosh though. The thought took the edge off his slight buzz; sobered him up a little.

She might be trouble.

Rick wandered over to the television, decided against turning it on because he couldn't find the remote to switch the channels at will, and glanced at the clock on the wall. When Jane worked second shift, she didn't come home until close to midnight, if not later, and he had the evening to himself.

If only Vivian hadn't called. He usually equated calls from his ex-wife as being as much fun as having his gums scraped, or at least if he'd ever had the dental procedure, he imagined it would be about as enjoyable.

Tonight had been no exception. The antagonism still hung in the air like the smoke from a bad kitchen fire, rancid and palpable. They'd argued over money, but for them, any subject was a good excuse. She'd signed up Amy, their oldest daughter, for some kind of expensive gymnastic lessons and informed him he had to pay for half.

Jesus, it pissed him off.

She did similar things all the time, like agree to hundred-dollar tennis shoes—the same shoes he'd firmly told the girls were ridiculously expensive and refused to buy—and hand him the bill. It ticked him off to the point he'd even skipped out on his visitation rights with the girls twice now, canceling at the last minute and hopefully ruining the plans Vivian had for the weekend. It wasn't the most mature way to strike back, but half the time both Amy and Adrienne complained anyway because they couldn't see their friends when they were with him. When he and Vivian split, she had moved back to Green Bay.

He didn't need her shit right now, not with this case staring him in the face.

Rick walked through the untidy living room, telling himself he should really take the time to haul out the vacuum and do a couple of loads of laundry, but not feeling like it. His coat hung on a peg by the back door and he shrugged it on and went out to the battered Jeep he'd bought for when the snow got really deep. His house was about five miles outside of Merrill and he was in town in minutes, for a moment startled to see the plethora of porch lights and pedestrians everywhere, even though it was now fully dark. Halloween, he realized wryly as a small troupe of witches and ghosts were shepherded across at a light on Main Street by a set of attentive parents. He waited until they were safely across and turned, went down two blocks, and then parked in front of Gil's Bar and Grill.

Inside the place was full as usual and on the noisy side, busy even on a Thursday night. Low, fake stained-glass light fixtures hung over the tables, most of which were occupied. Rick headed for the bar, sliding onto a stool and propping his elbows on the wooden surface. Joe, the bartender, greeted him with familiarity. "Hey, Rick. Leinie?"

"Sounds great."

Joe, going to fat around the middle, his bald head shining in the artificial light, fished out a frosted bottle of Leinenkugel from a big cooler behind the counter and popped the top off with an expert flick of his wrist. He put the beer on a small white napkin and wiped the cold from his hand on his green apron. "Jane working?"

"You got it." Rick took the bottle and took a sip. "Thanks."

"I hear you're working too. One of those missing girls was found. I sure hope you can catch this maniac now."

He thought of Margaret Wilson's decomposing corpse in the weathered boathouse and took a deep swallow of beer. She wasn't precisely a girl, but still . . .

much too young to die. "We're sure as hell trying. I'm not sure how crazy the guy is, by the way. We haven't been able to touch him for nearly eighteen months."

"Got any suspects?"

"We're following some leads," Rick said evasively. It was always difficult to explain how you couldn't discuss the case. So far Grantham's name hadn't appeared in the media, but it was only a matter of time probably, especially if they got wind law enforcement was doing a little sniffing around his background. Ellie finally had agreed that maybe they should go talk to his ex-wife to get a better sense of Grantham's past behavior. His explanation for the restraining order might or might not be true. Right now they were still trying to get a feel for how much they should pursue in his direction. If there was a history of intimidation or violence, it made him much more interesting.

One of the other patrons, sitting on a stool next to him, a young man with tousled sandy hair, wearing a jean jacket, glanced over, obviously listening. "You a cop?"

Rick nodded at the obvious question, fingering his beer bottle. "Sheriff's deputy. Local."

"I'm with the Division of Criminal Investigation crime scene unit." He held out his hand. "Tom Jessup. I thought maybe you looked familiar. Out of uniform sometimes it's hard to tell."

Rick shook cordially with a brief nod. "We keep calling you guys up here."

Jessup shrugged. "We go everywhere around the state. Lincoln County more than most this week, it's true. Somebody isn't playing nice around here, that's for sure."

Joe moved off down the length of the bar to serve

someone else. Rick smoothed the damp label of the beer bottle. “You all didn’t find much.”

“Nope.” The other man agreed. He was drinking draft and finished his beer. His accent was more Chicago than Wisconsin. “There were a few stray fibers on this last victim. Hard to place, or at least not obvious in origin, but I wasn’t the one who analyzed them. She had an interesting scratch on her face though. It didn’t look postmortem to me. What did the medical examiner have to say about it?”

Joe was only a few feet away, listening avidly. Rick said, “You want to grab a table? I’ll buy you a burger and a beer.”

So much for getting away from the murders, even if only for a few hours. His whole body seemed to hum this case.

“Sounds good. Thanks.” Jessup got up and found them a booth. It was close enough to the front door that every time it opened they would both get an eddy of cold, the last of October Halloween chill, but was more private than sitting at the bar. Rick told Joe he wanted two of the house burgers—which meant bacon, barbecue sauce, and loads of brick cheese melted in a gooey cholesterol pile on a charred patty of meat—and asked for two more drinks. Joe nodded but looked disappointed they were going to carry on their discussion out of earshot.

When Rick went to slide into the booth, he said, “Sorry. This is a small town. I don’t see any reason I can’t talk to you, but I don’t want the few tidbits we have discussed at the next meeting of the ladies’ church circle.”

“I get it.” Jessup nodded and grinned. “Big cities don’t have networks in the same way.”

"Gets cold up here. There isn't much to do but talk in the winter."

"Or hunt. At least before it gets so cold you freeze your damn balls off. That's why I'm still here. I'm off for a few days and decided to take advantage of the end of the whitetail bow season. I'm not hardy enough for muzzle loader. Deer hunting in northern Wisconsin in December is for the gung-ho types."

"I do it," Rick admitted. "The cold is part of the experience."

"Not the best part."

That icy morning, the dark, the hunt . . . the silence until you hear the telltale snap of a twig, or rustle of a leaf. The lift of the gun, the cold of the stock, the pull of the trigger . . . There was a surreal feel to the whole thing, even the killing of the animal. "I won't argue, but it's an integral part of it."

"So you said." Jessup glanced up and briefly thanked the waitress as she deposited his beer in front of him. She wore a kitten costume, or her version of it; cotton blouse, undone to a revealing degree so they could see a hint of lacy bra, and a short denim skirt, all punctuated by a pair of dark ears perched on her blond head, and black streaks mimicking feline whiskers on her face. She winked at Jessup, smiled, and sashayed away.

"Friendly girls up north here." Jessup tilted his beer to his mouth.

"Don't get too flattered. They get bored. It's the cold again." Rick sat back.

The music was loud enough to be distracting but it also meant no one could overhear them talking either. Not that he had much to say. "To answer your question, though our killer didn't use a weapon, the ME said the scratch on the victim's face came from something sharp. Metal maybe. She was decomposing by the time he got to examine her. Lucky for us, as you saw, she was in that structure so there wasn't scavenger damage. At least it was sort of lucky. We still didn't get much to go on. We now know she was strangled, but who is to say all the missing women were killed the same way."

Jessup looked at him somberly. "You guys up here are floundering, aren't you?"

Rick nodded and confirmed, "We sure as hell are."

Ellie answered her door wearing sweats, a T-shirt that had a Stevens Point beer logo on the front, and padded neon pink slippers. None of her outfit matched, but she'd been asleep when Rick called and he would just have to deal with it. She stepped back and he came in, his thick shoulders hunched under a down vest, his boots scuffing on the tiled floor of the entryway of her house.

"I'm glad you were still awake." He had the gall to not even look tired. "Sorry to call so late."

"I wasn't awake," she pointed out. "But that's okay. Come on in. What's up?"

He walked past; large, restive, edgy. A faint whiff of beer followed him in along with the night air. "I ran into one of the crime scene techs tonight at Gil's. We had a couple of drinks."

Ellie frowned, shutting the door. "Yeah, I can smell it. Are you sure you should be driving?"

"I didn't have more than two. Well, might have been three. Okay, maybe driving wasn't a brilliant idea. This damn case . . . I tell you, now that we have a body, I can't think about anything else. Ask Jane. I talked about the autopsy report at dinner last night. She's a nurse, and even she eventually asked me to shut the fuck up. Make me some coffee?"

Ellie knew she'd be up all night again if she drank coffee now, but she nodded, curious over what had him so wound up. It was after eleven and she'd gone to bed at ten, early for her, and wouldn't you know, this was one night she'd drifted right off.

Rick went and dropped into the chair every male who came into her house instinctively chose, a recliner she only kept because it had belonged to her father. Her mother hadn't been able to bear the sight of it after he died, but it held fond memories for Ellie. In her heart of hearts, she was sure he wouldn't have wanted some stranger to buy it from a thrift shop. It was worn, and even new the beige color wasn't something she would have chosen, nor did it match any of the rest of her furniture, but she liked having it there. It had only been a year now, and she still missed him with a throat-tightening ache when she allowed herself to remember he was gone.

She went into the kitchen, dumped the old filter, rinsed the pot and poured water into the machine, and spooned out fresh coffee. After she pressed the button, she went back into the living room and sat down, looking at her partner expectantly. "So? What's this all about?"

"I think I might have an idea. I don't know if it means anything, but it occurred to me while talking with Jessup, the crime scene guy, tonight. I sat there and the more I thought about it, the more I wondered if this might be the lead we need in this case."

"Hey, I'm all ears." Since she was already awake and he probably needed to stay awhile to make sure he was under the legal limit to drive home, she might as well hear it. Of course, he could have told her all about it during the four-hour drive to Milwaukee tomorrow. Though she'd been understandably curious, Suzanne Colgan-Grantham had agreed to see them. At first she'd said if they were investigating one of her clients they needed to come during office hours, and on Fridays she worked from home. Ellie hadn't explained in particular what they wanted, but she had said the questions were related to her personal, not professional, life and she preferred a face-to-face interview, rather than a phone conversation. For an articulate lawyer, Grantham's ex-wife seemed nonplussed but had agreed to meet with them anyway.

"We've been looking for a link," Rick said. His blue eyes were just slightly bloodshot, either from the smoke in the bar or from the alcohol he'd consumed, and his boots had trailed mud across her floor but she didn't comment. "Margaret Wilson was abducted from her car and strangled. The medical examiner also said the level of decomposition was inconsistent with the amount of time she'd been missing."

"Actually he said it was slightly inconsistent in his opinion." The one hour of sleep made her feel fuzzy around the edges. "That decomposition rates vary a lot due to external conditions such as temperature." Ellie wasn't sure whether to be exasperated or interested. "Rick, I know we both are living and breathing this case, but we'll have eight hours in the car together tomorrow to talk about it. I, for one, wouldn't mind some sleep."

He leaned forward, putting his hands on his knees. "I think he keeps them somewhere. That's why we don't find the bodies. Because he keeps them until we've exhausted the search around where we can pinpoint their last location.

"The blood pooling in Margaret Wilson's body didn't match the position she was found in at all. That means she was killed somewhere else and dumped in the boathouse later."

"Humor me and get to the point, please. Anyone reading the report would come to that conclusion."

"I think maybe he keeps them alive for a few days."

Ellie stared at him, not sure how to feel about that idea. It gave her an unwelcome chill, because while being attacked by a murderer was bad enough, being terrorized for days was worse.

She argued, "Melissa Simmons was bleeding."

"Yeah, she was, or someone was, but though we found blood, we didn't find a lot of blood." His jaw was set. "The dogs tracked her a mile and a half through the woods to the road. It's obvious at that point she was put into a vehicle."

In the kitchen the coffee pot stopped making percolating noises. Ellie got up and went to one of the birch cupboards, got out two thick ceramic mugs, poured them each a cup, and diluted hers liberally with milk. Then she took the coffee back into the living room, thinking hard the whole way. Rick accepted his with a nod of thanks, and she sat back down, one leg curled under her. "I admit it could be possible."

"This is a fairly unpopulated area. Lots of small deserted buildings, old summer cottages . . . plenty of hiding places."

"Your theory doesn't give me a warm fuzzy feeling, Rick," Ellie muttered.

"What if it means Melissa Simmons is still alive?"

Chapter 13

He never parted with them lightly. It was a matter of progression. The Hunter mused, in the end, it was really like a couple falling out of love, the process insidious and yet inevitable. No more use for each other, the feelings gone like the ending of a season, the waning gradual but noticeable.

In short, the game was over.

He opened the door and descended the stairs, the air dank around him, his flashlight gleaming off the chill walls.

Usually he took them home.

This was the first time he'd given one of them to someone else.

The first day of November dawned cold and clean, with enough frost on the fallen leaves they crackled with each step. Bryce trudged up the hill, ax in hand, his breath blowing puffs in the icy air. He caught a glimpse of something red through the stands of trees and realized it was a fox. The animal stopped, poised, snout in the air and one foot elevated, then seemed to dismiss him as a threat, trotted away, and disappeared down the hill toward the lake.

Nothing like being shrugged off with little more than a cursory glance, Bryce thought in amusement, though as an ax-toting human he thought he should get more deference.

The woodpile was located under a rough lean-to he remembered years ago building with his father, the structure just a few two-by-fours nailed together, open on each side, with a shingled roof above to keep moisture off if it was raining. Lighting wet wood in the stove inside was a challenge, but since the memory of constructing the makeshift cover was twenty-plus years old, the roof leaked and it really no longer was as functional as it had been when they put it up. It was half full of logs covered with lichen and small, interesting growths of fungus, cracked birch with peeling bark, pine, and rough odds and ends from the last summer project, which had been to repair the dock. Bryce picked up a log off the top, set it on a nearby stump, and took a swing with the ax. There was something satisfying about splitting wood. Chips flew, he vanquished the log as it cracked into two pieces, and then he went over for more. Something white caught his eye and the first flicker he felt was nothing but curiosity.

Then everything stopped dead. It was as if the world hung suspended, no longer spinning on its axis. A bird twittered and he registered the sound through the slight roaring in his ears.

The bone sat nestled intimately between a chunk of gnarled hemlock and a peeled length of pine. It was in the second row, so he hadn't seen it when he hauled off the first log, but now it was exposed, vulnerable, naked. He stared, a prickle of sweat glossing his skin under the cover of shirt and jacket. It was long, knobby at the end . . . Tibia? he wondered with a detached clinical resurgence of some college class on anatomy he'd taken for the challenge of it. The ax dangled from his hand and fell on the ground with a dull thud that reverberated in the quiet morning.

It looked human.

He blinked, tried to swallow and failed, then drew in a whistling breath. There was an odd buzzing in his ears, like an angry beehive.

This is not happening.

Right. Not. Happening.

It wasn't human, a voice somewhere inside him insisted. He was no expert. Why would he think it was human? Bryce worked loose his frozen jaw and took a cautious step forward, as if the thing could levitate and attack him.

There were more skeletal fragments. Glimpses of bleached white among the stacked logs, layered in like a terrine in a fancy restaurant. No skull, not that he saw, but his vision was a bit on the blurry side. Arms at his side, he struggled with disbelief and a horrifying sense of incredulity.

No animal would crawl between the logs and die in such a way. At least he didn't think it was possible, but without pulling the logs out and really looking, he couldn't tell. Whatever creature it had been, that was a long bone . . .

On shaky legs, he walked around the small lean-to, the morning sun filtering through the mostly bare branches of the crowded trees warm on his head and shoulders. It felt good, he thought remotely, because he was freezing. The sharp odor of pine resin and rotting leaves filled his nostrils as he tried to get a better look.

Something crunched under his booted foot. It seemed inordinately loud and he stepped back as if he'd been shot. In a nightmare daze, he bent and picked up what looked like a small twig nestled in a pile of damp oak leaves.

It was part of a bone, delicate and small, snapped in half from his weight. A finger fragment, Bryce guessed. He knelt and saw there were more pieces scattered among the leaves, the small array of bones in the fecund debris of the fallen vegetation in no particular order but he knew they were from a human hand.

The area was a mixture of restaurants, office buildings, high-rise banking institutions, and side streets that had been reclaimed into the new urban ideal of fashionable living. Ellie saw the building they sought was warehouse chic with a plain brick façade and no place to park. The anonymity of it all made it hard to determine if they had the right address, but they eventually found a space on the street about a block away, and walked back to find a small, glassed-in foyer and stairs upward. They pressed the appropriate button that corresponded to the Grantham loft, and there was a click as a green light on the security door glowed. Rick opened it for her, and muttered, "No trees, no yard, no thanks."

"It's how professionals live now," Ellie answered as they gained the second story and found themselves in front of a polished door of what looked like alder wood, with gold numbers discreetly embossed that declared it the right place. "Close to work, shops, culture. All the amenities of downtown life at your fingertips.

Just think, it's walking distance to the pricey restaurants that charge fifty dollars for a steak, or you could buy a Coach purse at one of those boutique shops we just passed."

"Yeah, well, I'll pass. I guess I don't need a new purse."

Ellie thought about her modest cozy house tucked into the woods and smiled. "Me either, but it's kind of a moot point. On our salaries, Deputy, we have to pass. She's obviously expecting us to be punctual."

Suzanne Colgan-Grantham *was* waiting. She answered the door on the first press of the doorbell. Bryce Grantham's former wife wore a clingy silk blouse tucked into designer jeans on a Saturday morning, the scarlet color showcasing her dramatic coloring. A perfect fall of glossy dark hair swung at her shoulders and either she had the smoothest skin Ellie had ever seen or else those prohibitively expensive cosmetics really worked. Almond shaped eyes, expertly outlined for maximum effect, and a touch of lipstick completed the picture, and it was easy to imagine that when they had still been a "they," she and Bryce Grantham had been a striking couple.

Those dark eyes studied them as Ellie explained who they were. Rick, in his uniform, negated the producing of badges and the ex–Mrs. Grantham didn't ask for more formal identification. She just stepped back to invite them inside. "I saw you drive by, and there aren't too many county sheriff vehicles in this neighborhood, Detective. Come in."

No wonder she'd seen them, as the wall facing the street was entirely glass. There were also soaring brick walls, exposed beams, and furniture out of *House Beautiful* defined the space. A giant oil painting hung next to a sleek, polished wood staircase that slanted upward to a different level, the style modern in slashes of bold, vibrant colors. Their hostess led them over to a grouping of leather furniture and glass tables perched on an Oriental rug and indicated they should sit down. She chose a chair, sank into it with a graceful, almost feline movement that seemed a bit contrived, and lifted her brows. "I admit you have me curious. On the phone you said this had nothing to do with one of my clients. I've been in the meantime assessing my personal life and can't come with a single reason a sheriff's deputy and a detective from northern Wisconsin would want to interview me. How can I help you?"

"We'd like to ask you a few questions about your ex-husband, ma'am."

The perfectly plucked brows soared higher. "Bryce?"

Ellie nodded, wondering if the surprise was feigned or real. It seemed real, but the woman was a lawyer after all. Since her ex-husband's family owned property in the area of their jurisdiction, surely it had occurred to her it involved him somehow. Trying to up the shock value, Ellie added, "We're investigating a homicide with the possibility other disappearances are linked to it."

Now the surprise was real. Suzanne Colgan-Grantham didn't know what to say, and for an attorney, that usually took some doing. After a moment, the woman blinked and found her voice. "You think Bryce is linked to a *murder*? In what way?"

Rick so far had been silent. He usually was, since she had more experience in these kinds of investigations, but he said, "Ma'am, we get to ask the questions if you don't mind."

She obviously didn't like a sheriff's minion pointing

that out and her mouth tightened, her tone acerbic. "I'm not denying cooperation, Deputy. I am just understandably taken aback."

"Could you please explain why you took out a restraining order against your husband during your pending divorce proceedings?" Ellie asked, intervening.

"What on earth does our divorce . . ." She seemed to catch herself and straightened a little. She had a lithe, trim body to go with the well-maintained, expensive surroundings. One hand restlessly rubbed her knee and she took a moment to formulate the answer. "We had separated. He had come in unexpectedly once or twice and it frightened me as I wasn't used to have someone suddenly in the house. I asked him not to do it any longer, but we weren't really communicating all that well, as you can imagine. The restraining order was insurance he would keep out."

Light from the tall windows lent slanting blocks of illumination on the rug, making the colors glow like jewels. The glass coffee table didn't even sport one speck of dust. "You weren't frightened of him physically?" Ellie asked.

Was the hesitation because this was an opportunity to malign her ex-husband? Or was it because Ms. Colgan-Grantham didn't want to admit she *had* been frightened? After a moment the woman shrugged. "No, I wasn't afraid of him physically. I wanted him to stay out of the damned house. He was the one who moved out, so he could just stay out, in my opinion."

Short and sweet with just a hint of resentment left that maybe Grantham had made the preemptive strike. Ellie was no psychologist, but it sounded that way to her.

"Your ex-husband never threatened you?"

"If you are investigating a homicide and consequently investigating *him,* it appears, you'll have met him, Detective. Bryce really isn't the threatening type. I think I saw him lose his temper about three times in the course of our five-year marriage, and those were because I really pushed his buttons. Usually if we argued, he just shut up."

That meant nothing, of course. Plenty of serial killers had been perceived as nonconfrontational and mild mannered.

"Under what terms did you then couch the need for a restraining order, Ms. Colgan-Grantham?"

"Basically, emotional duress under the heading of harassment." Her beautiful face wore an expression that reflected no remorse. "Perfectly legal. We were done and we didn't need to see each other anymore."

"Did he respect the order?"

"Yes. If I hadn't thought he would, believe me, I wouldn't have bothered. He even waived the hearing and accepted it in writing."

So, in short, she'd counted on her now ex to be law-abiding. Ellie knew what she meant too. Restraining orders were frequently ignored, for until they were violated, there was nothing the police could do. A restraining order was filed in civil court, not criminal court, and until the subject of the order did something criminal to break it, the police really weren't involved. Unfortunately, every once in a while, a tragedy happened when the subject of the order found the one who'd placed it and exacted the revenge that had been the fear all along. In those cases, the police came along after the fact and scraped up the damage, having not protected anyone. Ellie would feel worse about it, but she wasn't the one who made the law. She just tried to enforce it as best as possible.

"Can you tell us anything else about his emotional state or past that might help us?"

Suzanne settled more firmly in her chair. "How do I know what will help you? I don't even have an inkling of why you are here talking about my ex-husband. Let's also keep in mind I haven't seen him in over a year."

The investigation was on the news already and Ellie had a feeling his identity would break soon anyway. Evenly she said, "We have four missing women in around eighteen months. Law enforcement hasn't been able to find a trace in all that time. Dr. Grantham was with one of the victims the night she disappeared and found the body of another just a few days later. The suspicious circumstances could just be bad luck, as he claims. We're just trying to make sure."

"Holy shit," Suzanne said in a less than elegant mutter, a contrast to the setting and her carefully orchestrated attire. "I read about that in the paper. That's *Bryce*?"

"Now do you understand why we're here?" Rick sat stolidly next to Ellie, his formidable size a contrast to the quiet question.

"Yes, I think I do." Suzanne stuck out her lip theatrically and blew out her breath. She rubbed her cheek and frowned. "I'm just taken off balance. Give me a minute."

They waited. Ellie shifted a little on the leather couch, not sure how to interpret the other woman's reaction.

"Is that all you've got?" Suzanne straightened her spine and crossed her long legs. Her tone had turned crisp and professional again. The lawyer phoenix rising from the ashes of disbelief. "It doesn't sound very conclusive to me."

"Counselor, you know we aren't going to reveal to you details of this investigation," Ellie said with what she hoped was patience.

Suzanne regarded her, those almond shaped eyes direct. "All right, you want a statement, and I'll give one. Bryce and I aren't married any longer and things didn't end on a very friendly note, but truthfully most of the animosity was on my side. Even when I treated him like crap, he didn't get nasty back really. In a way, I'd have preferred it. I argue with people every day. It's my job. His tendency to walk away from confrontation made me crazy. It just built up until I couldn't take it anymore. Even when he was in the right, he didn't defend himself. I could never decide if he was just too passive, or if he was so secure he didn't feel the need to put himself through the ordeal. I think it was the latter."

The picture she painted was far from enlightening. "So you're saying what, exactly?"

"I don't think the man I was married to for five years would voluntarily hurt anyone." Suzanne sighed and ran her hand through her shining dark hair. It irritatingly fell right back into place in an immaculate curve. "He wants to write a book, but his mind works in circles not straight lines. To him if a person wants to embark on something like the great American novel, they get a Ph.D. in literature, of course. Never mind the cost, the time, the fact it might not help at all when he was already doing well in consulting . . . we aren't in the least alike. He's a dreamer. An extremely smart dreamer, but nonetheless, a little impractical. He makes a good living at what he does. Do you have any idea how much he could make if he started his own company?"

The fact that Suzanne Grantham liked expensive possessions wasn't exactly a secret from the chic and understated opulence of the home they'd once shared, but the insight was a little valuable anyway. "No," Ellie said dryly, "but we've seen his tax records and he does pretty well already. I'm a civil servant, so don't depress me."

"You think we're barking up the wrong tree." Rick didn't look as if he agreed, his mouth set in a mutinous line.

She gave a typical lawyer nonanswer. "Look, I've had clients that lie, steal, cheat, and still are elders in their church. Bryce was seeing a therapist, but I doubt that information will do you any good. Confidentiality is like a chastity belt on patient privilege."

"Dr. Grantham was seeing someone for psychiatric help?" Ellie's interest sharpened.

"No. He saw a clinical *psychologist* for a while. Right after he moved out. I don't know if he still does. The only reason I know he did it at all is that when he started, he was still on my insurance."

"Do you happen to remember the doctor's name?" Rick plucked a notebook from his pocket and clicked his pen. Until now, there hadn't been much worth writing down.

"No, not off the top of my head, but I might be able to find it for you. But I assure you the effort is hardly worth my time or yours to look into it."

"Just the same, we'd appreciate that."

"Even if the doctor won't tell you anything?" Ms. Colgan-Grantham looked faintly amused. "Ever tried to get information from a mental health professional, Detective?"

From the moment the woman had opened the door—no, from the phone call she'd placed yesterday—Ellie had felt an irrational dislike toward her. Well, maybe it wasn't irrational. Anyone who would take out a restraining order to make sure she could have sex with her boyfriend with impunity in the house she still owned with a man she hadn't quite yet divorced, was not all that admirable. If she had cheated—and since her version fairly well matched Grantham's it seemed likely—that really wasn't great character endorsement either. So the superior remark struck the wrong chord all the way around. As if the highly paid attorney in the big city knew the police officer from rural northern Wisconsin wouldn't understand the workings of various laws covering medical privacy.

Well, she did.

Keeping her voice very level—noticeably so—Ellie said, "We'd still like the name, if you could. We are just gathering whatever information we can at this point."

"Give me your card and I'll call you." Suzanne rose, graceful and dismissive. Her smile was perfunctory. "I'm sorry I can't help you more."

Ellie sat in the passenger side of the cruiser and looked out the window. Two hundred miles south of Lincoln County the trees still held some color and it was in the upper fifties, which felt positively balmy.

"What a bitch. Not an overt bitch, but it's there just the same," Rick said as he took the exit.

"Lots of people aren't at their best when talking to the police," she murmured.

"She a friggin' lawyer, Ellie."

"True. And I agree. She seems a little hard-edged."

The traffic was not heavy on a Friday afternoon in November and they merged easily onto the interstate, going the speed limit. She was always amused at how everyone seemed to find religion about how fast they were going when they spotted a police car, even if it was a county sheriff's cruiser quite a ways from home. She usually did just about what everyone else did and drove five miles over, maybe a little more now and then, but on the interstate she liked to watch everybody be honest.

"I don't think that visit did us much good." Ellie was more resigned than anything. She'd met women like Grantham's ex-wife before. Bitchy was an apt description, but not quite enough.

Rick shrugged. "Oh, I don't know. She pretty much confirmed what Grantham told us about the restraining order, though she left out the part about how he walked in on her screwing her boyfriend. I almost asked about it, just to see what she'd say, but give me a medal, I held back. It was enough to see from her expression that she wondered if he'd told us that part."

"I got that impression too," Ellie said.

"But if she was trying to convince me he isn't our guy, she didn't. The opposite, I think. What did she say . . . he thinks in circles? Well, fuckin' great, because whoever is making these girls disappear has us sitting around scratching our asses."

"Speak for yourself," she said, grateful to at least be able to laugh.

He grinned. "Figure of speech, of course."

"The affair . . . not every man would want to mention that." Ellie shook her head. "For a good reason. Even if they were separated, it still would be tough.

You'd really have to be over your wife to just let it go when you walk in on her with someone in your own house. Then she files a restraining order against *him*, who is actually the injured party. Nice."

It was warm in the car and Ellie unbuttoned her coat. When they'd set off that morning it had been below freezing up north so she'd chosen a long wool jacket to ward off the chilly temperature and blustery wind.

The cold would probably resurface again somewhere around Stevens Point if the weather forecasters demarked the correct line. She said tentatively, still thinking out loud, "This therapy thing . . . I don't know if it has any significance. Since we have no idea what Grantham might be seeing the guy for, I doubt we should even pursue the angle. As much as I hate to say it, his ex-wife is right, it takes a subpoena to access medical records of any kind, and you have to have one hell of a good reason to get one."

"Still, the first disappearance coincides pretty closely with the filing of that restraining order." Rick flipped on his turn signal and changed lanes to pass a semi. "Can I mention how that whole deal would piss me off? If my ex-wife did something like that . . ." He trailed off.

"The trouble is, the coincidences are piling up," Ellie said, because his wife had done exactly those sorts of things and now the two of them hated each other. "I usually don't much believe in coincidence in police work. It happens, but in this case, the timing issues . . . I just don't know."

It was true. The date of Grantham's separation was pretty close to the disappearance of Julia Becraft from the campground.

Rick gazed ahead at the ribbon of asphalt. "If you're theorizing that the episode might have set him off for the first time, I totally agree."

Was she?

"Set him off? I don't know. I'm not a psychologist. I just know we've got four women missing, one of them dead for sure, and he had opportunity in all four of the cases as far as we can tell, and his life was turned upside down right about the time this all started."

That was true. All of it.

Rick stubbornly stuck to it. "I wonder if Grantham started seeing the psychologist right after he walked in on his wife and her boyfriend? Surely we could get that information? No details, just the date of his first appointment. I bet his ex might even be able to find out for us from her insurance company. If so, with the disappearance of Julia Becraft just within a few weeks of the time frame, maybe we could get a judge to look at it."

"It's all circumstantial," Ellie argued. "Even if we do find out the therapy coincided with that incident and the first disappearance took place at that time, so what? For all we know the therapy had something to do with being cut from the basketball team in high school. He'd just split from his wife. It follows he might want to talk to someone about how he was feeling. Work it through. It's weak."

"True enough." Rick agreed with obvious reluctance. "We have no idea. Maybe he wets the bed or something. Or maybe he went to see someone because he's having some pretty interesting aggressive feelings about his wife and the fact she's diddling someone else. Maybe he doesn't like to argue because he internalizes the feelings instead, and because he's a smart guy, he knows he can't touch the about-to-be ex, so instead he starts strangling innocent women."

Ellie looked at him. He was right, but he was also wrong. Grantham was easy, and she wanted a quick arrest too. But even a vindictive ex-wife hadn't quite hung the man out to dry. "I'm sorry but we need more than amateur psychoanalysis to even try to invade Bryce Grantham's therapy records. One piece of physical evidence would help."

Her partner's face tightened. "Then let's find it."

Chapter 14

The anticipation was killing him.

Funny phrase, wasn't it? And even more amusing when you thought of it in this context. The restless day had the Hunter unsettled, not sure if he needed to sit down or pace, and he distracted himself instead with simple tasks, but in the back of his mind was always—always—this evolving relationship.

It was one. A mutual attraction, he thought, because as he moved through the motions of normal life, he knew it to be true.

Grantham.

It was interesting to imagine what could happen next.

The rising sun that had illuminated his unwelcome find had started to set in a spectacular array of spiky red streaks across a fading sky that had gone from brilliant blue to deep indigo. Bryce sat, feet up on the coffee table, and morosely stared out the wall of windows.

Fucked.

It was a crude word to describe his situation but maybe appropriate.

He'd thought about it all day. At one point he'd made himself a bland sandwich of sliced deli turkey and a store-bought tomato on rye bread in an effort to keep the neurons firing. He'd forgotten the mayo, decided to not get up and bother to correct the oversight because it all tasted like dust anyway, and ate it while drinking a beer.

That was hours ago. The same litany was still running through his head.

Which made him more stupid? Calling the police, or trying to get rid of the evidence in his backyard?

Both choices made him want to break out in a clammy sweat. Especially, he'd discovered over the past hours of unwanted introspection, the latter.

To make matters worse, he had a feeling that somewhere out there a killer was smiling at his dilemma, the bastard.

He could try it. He could go out there, pick up all the bones he could find, place them in a garbage bag and put the lot of it in the back of the Land Rover, drive it out somewhere remote, and dump it. At that point, the skeletal remains of whoever resided currently in his parents' woodpile would be moved off the property and he wouldn't have to report discovering another body to the police.

Logic told him there were a few problems with that decision, however.

The first and foremost was his conviction that even if he got past the ethical part of his dilemma over not reporting this, he still couldn't find every scrap of dead humanity sprinkled among those logs. The odds he could were very low. That body had been *hidden*. Three times during the day he'd walked back outside to make sure he wasn't dreaming all of this, and he'd unfortunately determined he wasn't. The bones were dispersed in a way that signaled a lack of symmetry and the guidance of something other than the elements.

The chance the person who had put those pieces there didn't have more that he or she could plant at will—or didn't have an agenda over reporting this anonymously to the authorities if he decided to take other action—seemed small. The skull wasn't there as far as he could tell. The skull would identify the victim; could they find out who it was without it? Maybe he should have gotten a degree in forensic science in retrospect instead of his useless Ph.D., since he certainly wasn't writing a damn thing on this trip. Knowing exactly how the evidence worked would be a nice boon at this moment anyway.

It became more macabre all the time. And he was a hostage in an almost literal sense of the word.

If he didn't report this and the police became interested enough to explore the property, then he was in real trouble. As someone they were already looking at, how would it seem to have human remains about a hundred feet up the hill from the cabin if he'd told no one?

Not good, a voice in his brain echoed monotonously. And the same sardonic voice reminded him he probably wasn't good at hiding bodies, though he did seem to have a talent for finding them. Being caught with a garbage bag dumping bones in a remote spot spoke of a nightmare glare of guilt he didn't even want to contemplate. He'd be crucified. If he wasn't already in trouble, the police could at the least get him for tampering with evidence and obstructing justice.

The alternative, he realized with an inner exhaustion of tension, wasn't a lot better. If he called this in, he was about to go from ankle deep in the mire of these murders to midthigh and sinking fast.

But a good day-long session of contemplating subverting the law told him he wasn't cut out for it. Say he did hide the bones successfully, managed to quell his conscience over how some poor family was denied the knowledge of the whereabouts of their loved one, and went back to Milwaukee. What if then, later down the road, his father or one of his uncles, who also used the cabin, found more of the skeletal remains? Being law-abiding citizens, they would call the police, and Bryce would be right back where he was now. He couldn't live with the suspense of not *knowing*. For that matter, what if the police really got serious about him as a suspect and decided to search his parents' property? Things could get nasty if he was caught circumventing the investigation. For that matter, he didn't *want* to interfere with the police catching the killer.

For a very good reason. If those bits of bone were planted there, someone was trying very hard to incriminate him, or else was playing a very sick joke.

He drank a second beer as he watched the blood-red orb of the sun sink below the tree line on the opposite end of the lake. A gaggle of Canada geese flew overhead, honking loudly, the arrowhead spear of their progress heading south.

It was five-thirty when he picked up his cell phone, fumbled with his wallet to find the detective's card, and with a cynical attempt at some form of humor, programmed her number into his phone. Then he pushed the button.

* * *

It seemed strange that Grantham didn't want to meet at his cabin, but then again, the call itself had been strange, and since he specifically asked to see her alone, she supposed it was neutral ground.

The place was typical of the little bars that scattered the Wisconsin north woods. On a Saturday night it was fairly busy, with the click of connecting billiard balls and a wailing jukebox in the background. A television mounted in one corner played a rerun of the earlier Packers and Colts game.

Ellie saw that Bryce Grantham was already there, sitting at a table in a corner of the place. Two cups of what was presumably beer were on the scratched surface of the table, one in front of him, one in front of the opposite chair. He'd noted her entrance but didn't quite meet her eyes as he waited for her approach. He rose to his feet as she got close.

No one extended that courtesy anymore it seemed. Did that make him weird or just nice?

Ellie took off her coat and sat down in one of the spindly looking chairs, relieved to see the tabletop was clean, if worn, propped her elbows on it, and pointed at the beer. "This for me?"

"Absolutely." Bryce sat down too. "Or would you like something else?"

Would she? There was no delicate way to point out it was stupid to accept a drink if a woman couldn't see the man offering it to her pour it. The only reason she'd taken a glass of wine the other night was because Bryce Grantham hadn't known she was coming by. She took a second, and said, "Thanks, I'll get my own."

It took him a moment, but then he caught on, his smile humorless. "You have no need to worry, but help yourself."

She did, going up to the bar, and her purpose wasn't just to make sure she saw her drink being served from the tap, but she'd already noted Gravelly behind the bar tonight. He recognized her too, his gaze sliding away as if he didn't, but it was obvious enough. "Yeah?"

"Draft, please."

He smoked unfiltered cigarettes, she noted by the ashtray near the cash register, or it was most likely him, though he had the good sense not to during business hours. Always a good source of DNA if they needed it. She paid for her drink and took it back to the table. "Sorry to keep you waiting."

Bryce Grantham's mouth twisted. "No problem. I'd put off this meeting indefinitely if I could."

To say that comment made her curious was an understatement. His tense expression said he was probably serious. This evening he wore a soft flannel shirt open at the throat, blue jeans, and his dark hair fell in the usual attractive unruly waves around his face. A leather jacket hung over the back of his chair. Long fingers moved in a restless mannerism on the condensation on the side of his cup and the set of his lean jaw spoke of an obvious inner conflict.

In the background someone made what must have been an impressive pool shot because there was a series of whoops and shouts from that area of the bar rendering conversation impossible for a moment. After things settled down, Ellie said as evenly as possible, "Put it off why?"

"Because the truth is, I don't want any part of this."

"'This' being the investigation right now under way because women are being abducted and some of them are turning up dead? Please, Dr. Grantham, it's our job and we don't want to be part of it either."

He gave her a humorless smile. "At this point, let's admit your end is better than mine. What I have to tell you is just going to make it worse." For a minute his dark eyes looked unfocused and tired. "I tried to think my way out of this scenario, but just couldn't. I can't really figure out how to deal with this, but have reconciled myself to the fact I do know how I *can't* deal with it."

That cryptic statement didn't do anything except exacerbate her interest. She drank her beer and waited. A country song started on what could be the oldest jukebox in the world. The beer was a little flat and the song depressing, but the atmosphere seemed to suit the mood of the discussion.

The man across from her gave a ragged laugh that held no mirth at all and ran his hand through his ebony hair. The rumpled result made him look younger and more attractive than ever.

Why the hell she had to notice that she wasn't sure, but she *did* notice.

"I don't know how to say this but . . . Oh hell, let me rephrase. I *really* don't how to say this, but I'm going to give it a try. Look, Detective, for whatever reason I believe that another one of your victims has turned up on my parents' property."

It took her a moment to absorb the roundabout confession. Ellie blinked and stared incredulously at Bryce Grantham as it sunk in. *One of your victims . . .*

"Can you clarify?" Her voice sounded hoarse. She cleared her throat and didn't wait for him to respond. "Are you telling me you found another body?"

He shook his head, his eyes haunted. Then he nodded. Just one quick inclination of his head. There were lines incised by his mouth and his lips looked pale.

"Not quite sure, but yes, I think so. Not a body, though. It's just bones, and I'm not positive they are human, but . . . well, I guess certain enough I called you."

She sat back in the chair so abruptly it creaked loudly, the implications whirling through her mind. After a moment she said more sharply than she intended, "Tell me what happened."

With obvious reluctance he complied, outlining an early morning trek to the woodpile to split wood—it *had* been damned cold the night before—and how he hadn't noticed the skeletal remains at first until he took off more logs.

The cop in her was outraged. "It's evening," she said unnecessarily, jabbing a finger toward the darkened narrow windows in the front of the room. "You found it this *morning*? Why did you wait? Now we can't process until tomorrow."

"I debated calling the police the last time," he shot back defensively. "What would you do if you were me? Put yourself in my shoes, Detective." His face was tight.

That stopped her, hung on the threshold of her anger. Ellie took in a breath and splayed her hands on the tabletop. She was disconcerted, off balance, and didn't know precisely what to do. It was one thing to have the discovery of a possible homicide victim called in. *That* she knew how to deal with. To have the tidbit dropped like a bomb over a drink in a nondescript tavern was something else. After a moment of inner debate, she said slowly, "I don't know. This is too . . . weird. If you are innocent of anything to do with these women, the way you stay in the middle of this investigation is beyond coincidence and well into a horror novel."

"I agree." He glanced away, a muscle in his cheek twitching. "I have the advantage of knowing I had nothing to do with any of this. The first two times just happened, Detective. Call it coincidence or good luck, or bad luck depending on your point of view. This morning . . . that was *planned*. I've had all day to think about it. Who all knows my name in connection to the finding of the bodies?"

Ellie digested the insinuation. "You think those bones were planted?'

"*I* didn't do it." Bryce sounded strained but reasonable. "And when you see how they are arranged, I think you'll agree there isn't anything natural about it."

"Shit," she muttered.

Bryce went on. "Let's say you are the killer out there and someone is connected to two of your victims. Maybe the chance aspect of it amuses you, or maybe you realize this is an opportunity to pin everything on someone else. To deflect the police in a different direction."

Sonny and Cher started singing "I Got You, Babe." Ellie rubbed her temple and tried to block the song out. "Probably the entire sheriff's department knows your name. It wouldn't surprise me. It isn't a big secret and there is no reason to keep it out of the reports. I'm surprised the media hasn't picked it up yet, but give them time. For all I know it was on the six o'clock news as I pulled into the parking lot outside. Don't forget the coroner's office either. I can't give you an exact roster of who knows."

"I assume that includes all their spouses, maybe neighbors, friends, grandmothers . . . this thing is pretty high profile up here. I'm screwed." He made a gesture indicating futility with his hand.

And maybe, if he was law-abiding and innocence personified, he had a reason to be unhappy with the system poised to perhaps vilify him, and if not that, at least play with the idea of it.

All right, she felt a glimmer of sympathy for him. Maybe it was the slight wobble in his voice. "It *should* be high profile," she countered, trying to sort out this new development. "There are four missing women, one of which turned up dead. That's a lot for a big city, much less a county with less than thirty thousand year-round residents."

"It isn't that I don't concede that point. It's just I don't want to be a part of it. Now this son of a bitch is doing his best to see I have no choice." The bitterness in his tone cut through the cloying sentiment of the song playing in the background.

"It looks like it," she agreed, thinking about it. Grantham became more of a suspect with each ticking minute and he was sitting right in front of her. She'd set her purse on the floor and she retrieved it, took out a pen and a notebook, and clicked the pen open. "Go over this for me step by step again."

He did. Waking up cold. Frosty crisp leaves. Wood chopped for a stove that needed to be lit. Bones supposedly stacked amid those slumbering logs suddenly noticed.

Ellie looked again at the flat black of the windows of the tavern. Outside it was pure early Wisconsin November. Pitch dark, cold, enigmatic. It was pointless to try and investigate the scene at this time of night.

"You didn't touch anything?" she asked out of habit.

"I'm getting pretty good at this by now," he said with a sardonic smile. "No. I touched nothing on purpose but I stepped on some evidence. I went around the back of the woodpile to make sure I wasn't hallucinating. I'm not an authority on the matter, but I'd guess it was part of a hand. It crunched . . ."

He stopped, his voice cracking. Then he exhaled heavily and turned away so the clean line of his profile was all she could see as he stared at a neon Coors sign in the window. "It crunched. *Jesus.*"

At that moment, she believed his distress. She had, for the most part, all along. The question was did this third discovery exonerate him or implicate him more? "Is it possible the bones have been there for some time?" she asked with less of the interrogator in her voice.

"I suppose they could have been put there anytime during my stay this week but they weren't there before my arrival up here. My father puts a tarp over the wood when they leave each time. It was tied in place and covered with wet leaves when I took it off the other day. I didn't pay close attention, of course, but I'd say it hadn't been moved since their last visit in September. Either it was done while I was out during the day, or done at night. If it was at night, he must have come on foot. I would have heard a car."

Once again, unfortunately for her, Ellie had an excellent imagination. She had no trouble picturing a stealthy figure creeping through the woods, carrying a bag of human remains.

A serial killer who had retrieved one of his grisly prizes and was intent on a personal delivery.

Crap.

She shut the vision off. "Dr. Grantham, maybe you shouldn't stay out there alone tonight. Our guy seems to have taken a personal interest in you, and I don't know how you feel about it, but there is no one I'd like less trespassing on my property while I'm asleep. Besides, I'd like the least amount of traffic possible through there until we can get in and see what we've got. There's a Super 8 motel in Merrill and a Comfort Inn in Tomahawk. In the meantime, when was the last time you had something to eat?" Ellie checked her watch. "For me it was a fast food hamburger almost eight hours ago. I'm going to call this in and talk to the sheriff. Then if you'd care to follow me into town, I'll buy you dinner."

He looked bemused at the offer, his ebony brows lifting a fraction. "Are police officers supposed to take suspects to dinner, Detective?"

Ellie stood and started to put her coat back on. He got up at once and helped her. His mother had done a good job in his youth, apparently, for it seemed reflexive, not something he even thought about. She adjusted her collar and gave him a cynical smile. "Look at it this way, Dr. Grantham. It's an easy way to keep an eye on you."

Chapter 15

He was restive, in another place, nervous in a way he remembered too well, ready for it to be over.

The room was dark and smelled off, like old meat. He pulled the chain and the light came on, the quiet oppressive when it had once been peaceful.

The Hunter walked over to the corner and opened the door.

It was time to say good-bye again.

The red of the taillights on Ellie MacIntosh's small Toyota four-wheel-drive flashed in front of him as she pulled into the busy parking lot of a weathered lodge with a rustic sign that proclaimed it THE ANTLER INN. Bryce parked four spaces away in one of the only other available spots on what was apparently a busy Saturday night.

Eight days. Eight days ago he'd arrived in Wausau for that boring conference and things had taken a steep downward slide since that less than auspicious beginning. He certainly hadn't ever pictured himself having dinner with a police detective because he was the focus of interest in a murder case. He should probably call his parents and warn them before the horrific presence in their woodpile splattered across national headlines.

Had Ellie MacIntosh not been quite so pretty, and his desire to go back to the cabin at such low ebb, he would have declined her invitation. As things stood, he was glad of the company, even if it was an attractive woman not completely convinced he wasn't a serial killer.

Nice way to score a first date, Grantham. Very clever.

She waited for him in the covered entry, the light wind ruffling her honey-colored hair. Her hazel eyes were as always disconcertingly direct. "I'm assuming since you fish, you eat fish. They have great walleye here. The steaks aren't bad if the fishing thing is a façade."

He assured her it wasn't a front, and opened the glass-fronted doors for her. Inside the place smelled wonderful, a mingling of grilled meat and cholesterol-laden fried dishes, and the hostess led them to a booth accented by the log walls, red faux leather seats, and low, fan-shaped lighting. The menu was printed on the place mat and the silverware wrapped in a paper napkin. Ellie ordered a glass of Chablis and he chose a Heineken dark.

"I'm famished," his companion said. As usual she wore almost no makeup as far as he could tell, and in the unreasonably dim light from what might have been a twenty-five-watt bulb in the light fixture above their table, she looked younger than she probably was, more college girl than detective.

"I can't tell," Bryce admitted. "I'd guess I must be hungry if I consider the amount of time that has passed since I last ate. If anyone wants to go on a radical diet, they might try switching places with me this week."

"You look a little blurry around the edges," she agreed, studying his face. "That's part of why we're here."

Blurry around the edges was a nice of way saying he looked like hell. Unfortunately, he could imagine it was true. Bryce turned and smiled gratefully at the middle-aged waitress as she delivered their drinks. The beer was ice cold and delicious.

They both ordered walleye dinners and he wondered why he didn't feel more awkward. Surely this had to be one of the worst possible reasons on earth for two people to have dinner together.

The hum of conversation around them was like a cocoon, the warmth and smells of the restaurant making the bizarre events of the morning distant and unreal. A basket of warm rolls was delivered along with butter and honey and Bryce discovered maybe he was hungry after all.

After Ellie generously slathered a roll with butter and took a bite, she said conversationally, "You went to MIT and then on to graduate school later in a completely different field. Impressive. I understand MIT because of what you do, but why a Ph.D. in literature? Seems a little off the wall."

"I love to read." The roll was soft and delicious. He swallowed another bite before he added, "Just because you're good at something doesn't mean it is your favorite thing to do. When I was younger I decided I'd love nothing more than to write. To that end I decided graduate work in literature would help immensely."

She looked interested. "Your ex-wife mentioned that. Did it?"

"If I ever hit the *New York Times* best-seller list, I'll say yes. Let's just leave it that it was much more enjoyable reading Joyce and Voltaire than it was studying computer engineering. The Ph.D. was an indulgence. Then I got married and . . ." He trailed off and gave a slight shrug.

The woman across from him knew everything about his life if he had to guess, but he knew very little besides her rank-and-file placement in Wisconsin law enforcement. "How about you?" he asked. "Are you a native?"

"Madison," she confirmed with a nod. "I went to UWM and majored in English at first. I thought about law school but something happened to steer me another direction. My degree is in criminal justice. I thought about applying for the FBI, but you know, I like it here. It's beautiful. Not just in an abstract sense, but really beautiful, even when it's cold. I like the aura of northern Wisconsin, if that makes sense. It's familiar, and it's home."

"Perfect sense." Bryce ran his fingers down his beer bottle, wiping away the condensation. "I've been vacationing up here since I can remember. I think my grandfather built that cabin in the fifties."

The cabin. The woodpile with its strange layered of bits of humanity . . .

No, he wasn't going to think about it. Quickly, he asked, "What about you, Detective? Are you married?"

"No." She smiled. "Never. Most of my colleagues are men, but still, women in the police force sometimes have a hard time with romance. Men too, for that matter. The hours alone are enough to put a strain on even a decent relationship."

"It must be an interesting job, though." That was a

bit inane, but Bryce had the excuse he'd never had to make small talk with someone investigating him before.

"It can be." Her mouth quirked at the corner. "You're a pretty good example of that. I like intelligent men."

He'd been thinking about another roll, but her comment jerked his attention up. The words had a soft edge of innuendo, but he doubted it was really intended the way he wanted to take it.

"But I don't like smart killers," she went on, as if discussing murder over the dinner table was perfectly normal. For her, maybe it was. "Tell me, Dr. Grantham, with the degree from MIT, if you were me, how would you go about solving this case?"

He had no idea what to say for a moment. "You want advice from *me*?"

Ellie wasn't into games, but if she were, why not play catch-the-killer? "There's no law that says I have to take it, but yes. Sure. Why not? I'm going to guess you've been thinking about this almost as much as Rick and me, if not maybe even more the past few days."

"That could be true," he acquiesced with a wry smile. "Can I add I wish it wasn't?"

"I can imagine." She sipped wine and looked at him expectantly.

"One other favor. Please just call me Bryce. The Dr. Grantham thing makes me think of Dr. Grantham, the suspect."

"All right." She inclined her head. "Over dinner . . . sure."

"I think you've got a risk taker on your hands." He said it slowly. "From what I read in the paper, whoever is abducting these women actually stopped two of them somehow on roads that might not be busy but still see cars. I can't imagine how he could force them alive into his car, but I can't see him killing them on the side of the road either. However it happens, he is taking an awful risk someone will drive by and see him."

The arrival of their dinners kept her from commenting.

She dipped a french fry into her tartar sauce instead of using ketchup. "That's true. He started with a campground abduction, and even when Melissa Simmons was taken from her house there was no forced entry we could find. So how does he do it?"

"Hypothetically speaking, of course?" It was impossible to not notice the ironic edge to his tone.

"Of course."

He ate another bite of fish. The people at the table next to them were laughing at something one of them said, the sound loud even in the din of the Friday night crowd. It was absurdly normal. He finally played along and expounded, "I'm going to guess he has their trust in some way. Who do you open your door for, Detective? The UPS man? What about a police officer? I'd roll down my window to listen to him."

She used the malt vinegar on her fish liberally, her arm energetic. "Not a bad start, but we've thought of that too. Unfortunately, there isn't a link we can see. There *has* to be a link."

"It could be random."

"Maybe. But usually even random has a pattern. If these are impulse killings, he still has to find the victims a certain way."

"The women are young and alone, aren't they?"

"Go on."

"I don't really have any other ideas."

"Keep thinking. If you come up with something, I'd be interested."

"Maybe," he said with deliberate emphasis, "I'm not as smart as you think I am."

Unfazed, Ellie gazed at him and responded with quiet conviction, "You see, I think you are."

The lights and noise and mostly the food, at a guess, had done him good. The man sitting across from her didn't look nearly so hollow and his plate was already almost empty.

Ellie had kept him talking through the entire meal, prodding with small questions, and she had the feeling he knew exactly what she was doing. When he excused himself to go to the restroom, she thoughtfully watched him walk away. He had a nice build, so it wasn't exactly a chore.

If her instincts were worth anything, he had nothing to do with the disappearances or the strangulation of Margaret Wilson.

But, she reminded herself as philosophically as possible, until they had the killer, she couldn't be sure of anything.

He came back, slid into the opposite seat, and put two creams in his coffee, no sugar. Slowly he stirred it. "If I stay here in Merrill tonight, when should I go back to the cabin? I don't even have a razor with me."

"We'll be out there as soon as it's light." Ellie drank her coffee black though she usually used milk. It was sharp and hot. "The sheriff will want your statement of course. You know the drill. He's sent out officers to block the drive, tape the area off, and keep anyone out until it's processed."

"I'll feel like an idiot if it turns out to be someone's idea of a joke and those are deer bones, or something like that." Bryce lifted his cup and took a cautious sip.

"Deer don't have hands," she reminded him.

"I know." The strained look crossed his face again.

"I expect we will want to interview you tomorrow." Ellie kept her voice level. "And maybe DCI. We just didn't have anything to offer them before these past few days. With the bodies surfacing, I'd guess they're going to get more involved."

"Great." Bryce cradled his coffee cup and looked bleak. "Something to look forward to, I'm sure," he muttered. "I need to call my parents and warn them this is all happening."

"Might be a good idea. The sheriff has been pretty careful about your name so far in his dealings with the press," she pointed out, trying to stay neutral, "but it's obviously leaked out somehow. It's easy enough to find out from your last name where you live. Deeds are a matter of public record."

He regarded her with a singular intensity. "Believe me, that has occurred to me. It also strikes me whoever is doing all this has kept track of his victims. He knew just where those bones were if he went and retrieved them. I think that means something. These woods are sort of homogenous when you think about it. Lots of trees, no real landmarks except lakes and streams. Your quarry has a handle on the out-of-the-way spots where people don't go often or someone besides me would have found something."

"He's local." Ellie nodded. "I think so too. He had to know your elderly friend, Mr. Paris, no longer used that piece of property. The only problem is we have a lot of outdoorsmen around here. You practically *have* to be an outdoor type to live here year-round."

"Aside from a bit of fishing, I'm not."

She took in the flat declaration with a mental lift of an eyebrow. He was probably telling the truth again. The fashionable expensive leather jacket sat on the vinyl seat of the booth next to him, her memories of the chic loft swimming back into her mind. If she tried to picture him sitting at a desk, frowning in concentration at a computer screen, she bought it. An image of Bryce Grantham perched in a deer stand wearing camo gear wasn't quite as convincing. "No," she agreed with a small smile. "You do seem more the academic type, though they aren't mutually exclusive."

"I don't know how emasculating it is to admit this to a law enforcement officer, but I've never even fired a gun." His return smile was a ghost of the real thing.

"The person we're looking for strangles his victims. At least he did according to the ME on the Margaret Wilson case."

His cup rattled as he put it back in the saucer. "I haven't done that either."

He had nice hands. Long graceful fingers like a surgeon or a musician. The arrival of the waitress with their bill kept her from commenting. He offered to pay it, but Ellie stood firm.

"I invited *you*," she said setting her credit card down on the slip of paper. "My idea all the way, so I pay."

He looked at her across the table, his mouth lifted at one corner. "You can be very stubborn, Detective MacIntosh, and in the current situation, I don't think I have much leverage. All right. My turn next time?"

"That can be negotiated." She did her best to look bland. "I tell you what, when we catch him, you take me out to celebrate. I warn you, I can be an expensive date."

He gave her an undecipherable look. "I'll start saving up. If it happens soon, I'll throw in dessert."

She couldn't help it, she laughed.

It sounded ridiculous under the circumstances, but she had enjoyed having dinner with him.

Outside it was clear and cold, the night sky a blanket studded with a smattering of brilliant stars. He walked her to her car, hands in his pockets, his shoulders hunched against the freezing temperature. "Why don't you call me in the morning and let me know when I can get in. You have my cell number."

She pressed a button and her car started. "That sounds like a good idea." After a brief hesitation, she said quietly, "I have no idea if the sheriff plans on getting a warrant or not. Friday night is a tough time to reach a judge. You might want to give us permission."

The parking lot had spotlights perched on poles and the illumination washed his face to bones and angles. "A warrant for what?"

"To search the cabin."

"The bones are in the woodpile."

"I know, but . . ." She shrugged.

For a moment, he didn't seem to know what to say. Then he let out a resigned sigh, his breath a frosty puff. "I can't think of any reason to object except a general feeling of violation over the premise. It should take them all of two minutes. Other than my tackle box and fishing pole, the only thing that's really mine in the place is what I brought in my suitcase to wear during my stay, my laptop, and a briefcase with business papers and notes."

She refrained from pointing out what they'd be looking for was something *not* of his. Some serial killers took trophies. According to her husband, Margaret

Wilson might have been wearing pearl earrings the day she was abducted. He didn't remember if she'd specifically been wearing them the day she disappeared, but they weren't in her jewelry box and she hadn't had them on when she was found. She murmured, "Like I said, I am not sure if the sheriff is even going to go that direction, but it would helpful if you'd just let us."

"Fine." He looked away, all at once remote, the warmth gone. "I'll even give you the key if you want. Help yourselves."

When he pulled the ring from his pocket and extracted a key from the bunch, Ellie accepted it with mixed feelings. His demeanor said they weren't going to find anything.

She hoped they wouldn't. It was contrary to the best interests they had in the case, because if there was any scrap of evidence then they would finally nail the killer right to the wall and it would all be over.

She just didn't *want* it to be him.

It was ironic, but maybe the interview with his ex-wife had been a turning point for her. As much as Suzanne Colgan-Grantham had wanted to defame her husband, she hadn't been quite able to do it. It supported the underlying feeling Ellie had that he wasn't who they were looking for.

"Thanks." Ellie put the key in her pocket. She tilted her head to look up at him. "Get a good night's sleep. I'll call you tomorrow."

Chapter 16

It was an art form. The selection was the grand finale, the conclusion of the love affair. Since he'd given one up, he could choose a new one, but it didn't feel right, like that place still belonged to someone else. He'd lain awake last night, dreaming of this, fitful in turns and then ecstatic, aroused when he thought about the bones, so carefully layered between those logs, a puzzle for the police to put together, and yet with a missing piece he couldn't give up.

The Hunter rearranged the tarp, got into his vehicle, and flicked on the heater. Cold morning . . . November now. He should be looking forward to deer season more, but truthfully, he didn't care about it as much as usual, and he'd been afraid of that all along.

The game sucked you in, took hold with an inexorable grip, and once you were a player, he suspected it was impossible to walk away.

Dammit, he'd tried to distance himself. But he needed it, like air. As he accelerated along the country road, he reminded himself that he had as much a right to survival as anyone else. If this was what he had to have, that was nature speaking. Just as much as a pack of wolves relaying a deer, he hunted. Not for food, but food for the soul.

Yes, that was it.

Without the killing, he might go crazy . . .

A long time ago, back in the thirties, there had been a farmhouse out by Otter Lake. There was nothing left but a few mossy rocks from the foundation, tumbled like broken teeth, this morning covered in a thin film of frost. He parked by an untidy spruce in what had once been the front yard and got out to go around and remove the top of the old cistern.

As a choice for a hiding place, it was nothing less than perfection.

It wasn't the finest way to spend Saturday day morning. Rick stamped his feet and blew on his hands, standing on the periphery of the yellow crime scene tape. One of the other deputies had brought coffee in a stainless steel thermos, but it was already gone. The drop in temperature had caused a thin mist under the trees, the drift of the fog ghostly and thick in spots. Frost touched everything with spidery white fingers.

Pearson, his gaze perpetually scanning the scene, stood next to him. "This feels like we're being led."

Rick wished he'd put on his thermal socks before he left the house. He'd just been in too much of a damned hurry to get to the scene, but standing around like this his feet were cold despite his heavy boots. "I agree," he said grimly.

"We've recovered a body and have evidence of another possible homicide. Blood, the shoes . . . So the bastard gives us a third one, but just pieces. Like this is a goddamned game."

"Do we know that it's human remains yet?" Rick watched the crime scene unit move logs, each removal followed by a painstaking sweep for possible evidence. Everyone had his collar up and a red nose. Two technicians, one of them Tom Jessup, who didn't look too happy to be sacrificing part of his hunting weekend, had bags and tweezers, their gloved hands sifting through piles of leaves around the woodshed.

"The whole skeleton isn't here." Pearson rubbed his jaw, which showed an early morning grazing of stubble. "God, it sounds gruesome put this way, but the skull seems to be missing."

"*If* this is one of our victims."

"Do you think for a minute it isn't?" Ellie asked the question, a Styrofoam cup in her hand. Rick hadn't noticed her walk up and he turned. Her hat was small and powder blue, sprinkled with embroidered snowflakes and instead of her long dark wool coat, she wore a lightweight parka in a matching color of her hat. The ensemble made her look about eighteen. She added, "Come on, Rick, if it's human, it has to be Julia Becraft or Patricia Wells, and the coroner says those are human bones."

"It's likely," he agreed, wiggling his toes to maintain circulation. "The real question is, how much do we believe Grantham at this point?"

"He's cooperating." Ellie watched as another log was removed, her expression neutral.

"Or playing us. This could be a seriously brilliant move on his part."

"How so? To direct more suspicion on himself? Because no one with half a brain who was under consideration in a murder case would plant a body on their own property and then call the police." She shook her head, blond wisps of hair sticking out from under her cap brushing her shoulders. "It's too much of a stretch for me to believe it."

Rick wasn't as sure. "I think Grantham is a complicated guy and we know he went to see a shrink. Let's not forget his recent divorce. This could be a trick, a way to get his rocks off by giving us another body and make it look like he's being victimized."

"He went to see a therapist, but so do a lot of people, that's why there *are* therapists," Ellie pointed out briskly. "And as for the divorce, it happens. It happened to you, didn't it? That means nothing."

She didn't think the guy was guilty. He'd already gotten that impression. Not from anything she'd said really, but just a feeling. He wasn't half as sure. Or a third as sure. Maybe even a quarter . . .

"Except for the timing," he said.

She looked as if she going to argue, but the sheriff interrupted.

"I hate this damn case," Pearson said heavily, fiddling with the zipper on his jacket, his face drawn into a frown. "My first reaction is to think the bones were put here by whoever is abducting these women as gesture to implicate Grantham. That I'll admit. Now that bodies are popping up, the perpetrator wants control again. I think that's probably what's happening." His restless gaze skittered over to where Bryce Grantham stood leaning against his SUV, looking none too happy in the morning cold. "But, let's face it. One guy has now uncovered two bodies and he's tied to another disappearance. It's too unlikely to just be chance."

"He didn't hesitate to let us search the cabin." Ellie sounded subdued.

"Maybe he assumed we would and was ready for

it." Rick had to admit he didn't like what he sensed might be a personal interest in Grantham from his partner. Ellie was usually very professional, but she almost sounded defensive. "If he was going to plant the bones and let us know about it, he'd make sure the cabin was clean. I know *I* would. It's logical. Come on."

"How in the hell do you figure out the logical thought processes of someone who kills people?" Sheriff Pearson skimmed his gaze across the scene again and answered the question himself. "I can't. I don't even want to put myself in those shoes. There's an FBI profiler to help us out now that we have this latest development. I'll set up a phone interview. I'm also thinking we should try to get a subpoena for Dr. Grantham's psychotherapy records. At the very least, you need to go talk to his doctor. See if he'll cooperate to the extent of maybe not violating confidentiality issues, but just give us an overall evaluation on the stability of his patient."

"Duty to warn," Ellie argued, gesturing with her cup, sending a gentle curl of steam into the air. "If his therapist thought he was going to do harm to anyone, the doctor would have had to report it already."

Pearson shifted from foot to foot, restless as usual. "I don't need to know if he thinks his patient is psychotic, Detective. All I need to get is an idea if he thinks Grantham is stable."

"His ex-wife hasn't called us yet with the name. She seemed pretty uninterested."

"Then get her interested," Pearson said shortly. "This is a murder investigation."

"If Bryce Grantham had nothing to do with all this, we're concentrating a lot of energy in the wrong place, sir." Ellie looked at the subject of their conversation, her mouth just a little tight.

"If you have other leads, Ellie, I'd love to hear about them." The sheriff wasn't precisely sarcastic, but his frustration came through anyway. "Besides Grantham, we're empty-handed."

"Rick had a pretty solid idea. I think we should request credit card statements from all of the families for the day our victims disappeared. If we can link even two of them to the same place, such as a gas station, it would be a place to start."

Rick interjected, "Margaret Wilson was going by the store for a few things. The second victim, Patricia Wells, ran into town to pick up beer according to her parents. It isn't much of a pattern, but it is something."

"Follow whatever you have but keep DCI in the loop. Do what they want, when they want it. Show me, and them, there's nothing you overlooked." Pearson added with a mutter, "I need more coffee. I could use a cigarette too, but I promised my wife I wouldn't."

When he stalked away, Rick looked at Ellie. "This is getting to him."

"It's getting to all of us," she answered, sipping coffee. "They're finding little bones scattered all over the place. The guy dumped the body like so much garbage on the ground behind the woodpile and then proceeded to move the logs and layer the bigger bones in. There are fragments everywhere."

"Yeah, that's what Jessup said."

She leaned against the cruiser with one hip. "I'll call Ms. Colgan-Grantham and tell her we need that therapist's name right away, not on her time schedule."

"I'll get someone to start requesting credit and debit card statements."

"If they paid with cash, we're out of luck."

He knew it was true. "It's just a long shot but what else are we supposed to do?" Rick rubbed his cold fingers together.

"It isn't Grantham," Ellie said, her voice firm. She looked distracted but confident. "He doesn't feel like the one."

It was more likely she didn't want him to *be* the one. When she'd shown up with the key to the cabin, it seemed logical to ask how she'd gotten it and she'd admitted to meeting with the guy. Not that there was anything inherently wrong with that because he wasn't an official suspect, but Rick wasn't exactly blind.

The phone clipped to his belt vibrated. He checked it and answered shortly. "Jones."

"What do you want for dinner? I'm cooking tonight. I'm in the mood."

He knew what it meant when Jane had that domestic tone. She cooked, they had sex afterward. He'd never gotten the connection, but he always got the message. A home-cooked meal meant a pretty nice evening. Had the circumstances been different he would have smiled, but instead he said shortly, "I'm at a scene."

"Oh, God, Rick. Not another murder."

"I can't talk right now." With effort, he softened his voice, aware of Ellie's frown over his abruptness. "Whatever you want for dinner would be great. Hopefully I won't be late."

"Okay." She sounded subdued, the enthusiasm wiped from her voice, which made him wince. Maybe he should have left Jane a note, he thought as he pressed a button. When Pearson had called with the news he'd done little more than pull on some clothes and leave the house.

"Jane?" Ellie's tone held a hint of criticism.

"Yeah."

"You could have talked to her longer, Rick. We're just standing here for now."

"She wanted to know what I wanted for dinner. Sorry that I'm not in mood to pick out a menu. Those are human remains they are hauling out of Grantham's woodpile." He said with as little inflection as possible, "I'd rather it was one of Walters brothers myself. Grantham is at least a productive part of society instead of being an obvious dirtbag. I'll give you that. But, keep in mind, staying objective is important."

Ellie straightened. "What the hell does that mean?"

"Just a comment."

Her eyes narrowed. "Are you implying I'm *not* objective?"

He came up with a few responses, none of which seemed a good idea. He wasn't out to piss off his partner by pointing out he thought she might be leaning toward being sympathetic to Grantham, where he wasn't nearly as convinced.

Way less than a quarter by now.

Rick had heard that tone in a woman's voice before and he wasn't too fond of it. Vivian was a master at combining outrage with contempt. "Come on. There's nothing more we can do here until we get the report. It's the weekend. I bet we can start making a few calls and maybe even reach someone."

He'd had better starts to a day.

Since he didn't understand the situation himself, Bryce could hardly blame his father for the utter silence on the end of the phone. He added, "They haven't precisely said so, but I think I'm stuck up here for a little while."

"We've heard about it." The delayed response was measured. "It's been in the paper. I read about it in the *Sentinel*. I just didn't know it was you."

"Yes, well I think you can probably expect a little more on it by tomorrow. Just a word of warning. I hope not, but my name may pop up." Bryce looked out the window by the kitchen sink. There were still several vehicles in the drive and people walking the perimeter of the property. "My bad luck isn't exactly making whoever is doing all this happy."

"Good heavens, this is unreal, Bryce."

"Oh, you have no idea." His smile was wry.

"Maybe your mother and I should come up."

"To what purpose?" Bryce rubbed his temple. "No. Don't. As soon as I can, I'm going home. I'll call you."

When they signed off he stood there for a moment and then automatically began to straighten the cabin. Things had been moved around and rifled, and while it wasn't a mess, it wasn't neat like his mother had left it after her last visit. Had they found anything they considered suspicious, Bryce was sure he'd be under arrest, so at least that part of it was promising.

If the killer could plant bones around the cabin, what else might he do? He wasn't exactly being clued in by law enforcement, but he gathered they were still looking for more of the victim's skeleton.

A knock on the door made him look up from trying to arrange a stack of magazines back in some semblance of chronological order.

It was Deputy Jones, large and exuding what might not be precisely ill will, but wasn't the warmth of friendship either. A comical hat with flaps kept his ears warm, but the rest of him looked cold as hell. Bryce could relate, because he'd frozen half to death waiting as well. The deputy held out a hand that was chapped and reddened, the key to the cabin in the palm. "Thanks for the cooperation."

"They took my laptop," Bryce said, not really in the enthusiastic spirit of joyous communion with the local authorities in the aftermath reality of the search. "What, do you think I'd plot my diabolical intentions in some file labeled 'My victims and how I did it'?"

Jones elevated his brows at the outrage in his tone but kept his response even. "Now you see, sir, sarcastic remarks like that don't help."

"I can't work without my computer," Bryce said flatly, not bothering to conceal his annoyance and sense of intrusion.

"Thought you were up here for a little R and R." Jones smiled but it was brittle and hardly heartfelt. "Sorry for the inconvenience but it should be back to you soon."

"I'm up here to work on my book. So far it has been a bust. Can you even take it without charging me or a warrant?"

"You gave us permission to look for evidence."

The open door was letting in the cold but Bryce wasn't in the mood to invite the man inside so they could continue the acrimonious conversation. "*Is* it evidence? Because, quite frankly, I don't see how."

"We'll know that as soon as forensics checks it out. Be happy you still have your cell phone."

Fuck.

Bryce closed the door as Jones turned away, his hands shaking. Not that there was anything on his computer to raise any forensic red flags, but it made him feel helpless to have something taken from him that was pretty personal. E-mails were like reading a diary in his opinion, and he sure as hell didn't want anyone seeing the unedited, unfinished first draft of his novel.

It was a little depressing to know he didn't have any secrets that would raise any eyebrows, he thought sardonically. Was that why he was so pissed off? That some technician somewhere would discover he was actually a pretty lackluster individual?

Maybe that would be the headline: "*Possible Serial Killer Exonerated! Police Certain Grantham Too Boring to Have Committed the Crimes.*"

It would be nice if he could laugh about it, but he was beyond laughing and well into the frozen tundra emotional stage. It was also pretty much of an energy drain to deal with the combined suspicious hostility and confused sympathy of the law enforcement community he was coming to know pretty well. If he was a victim of circumstance that had been brought to the attention of a vicious killer, they were all sorry for him.

If he was the killer, trying to pull a sleight-of-hand fast one and make them all look like incompetent fools, they wanted his blood in a figurative sense . . . or maybe a real one.

The situation was untenable at best.

Bryce glanced at the moose clock. The hands were at rump and left antler. Three o'clock.

As he pulled out his cell phone he wondered how much Alan Silver charged for calls on the weekends. Maybe he needed to go ahead and get a lawyer.

Chapter 17

There were police everywhere, but while he took chances, he only took calculated ones.

It was tantalizing, like a childhood dare, but they all didn't draw him like Ellie MacIntosh. He saw the crime scene tape across the drive, smiling inwardly as he spotted her four-wheel-drive . . .

She was there, and they were wondering about those bones, about how they got there, about Dr. Bryce Grantham.

Good, that was exactly what he wanted.

Fall was turning, getting nasty, winter flexing its claws as it prowled on the sidelines.

Restless, like him.

Perfect hunting weather.

"I wish we had the goddamned head."

Ellie raised her brows and flicked off her brights. It was going to snow tonight, she could feel it. "Now that's not something you hear every day."

Rick shifted in his seat, running his hand through

his hair in a rough gesture. "Sorry, that came out all wrong."

"Maybe just a little," she agreed, braking carefully because there were thin veins of frost already all over the road and icy surfaces were more treacherous than deep snow. "But I agree wholeheartedly that a skull would have been valuable, so yeah, I also wish we had it."

"The bastard did it on purpose." Rick's voice held the same frustration she felt. "He deliberately kept it from us so we don't know who she is. I get this feeling that before he was getting off on kidnapping women and killing them, but now he's playing with *us*. New game and game is *on*."

"Seems to me Grantham is his new playground buddy."

"*If* Grantham isn't our boy." His tone held a hint of belligerence. They didn't like each other. Ellie had already gotten that loud and clear, but it didn't mean Bryce Grantham was a killer.

"If," she agreed, but more and more she just didn't think so. Ellie pulled into Rick's driveway. His house was a prefab one level, but it was nice enough, with pines all around and a circle of asphalt in the front with a small garden at this time of year filled with dead zinnias and withered marigolds. "I can't pretend I know what makes our perp think murder is a game, but I promise you, as careful as he's been, he knows it isn't a legal sport. From everything I've ever heard, these individuals enjoy getting away with it as part of the power trip."

She parked the car by a Jeep that had seen better days, rust holes starting to eat along the sides like acid through the metal. The house was well lit and another vehicle, a tan sedan, sat next to Rick's cruiser. Obviously Jane wasn't working this evening.

Ellie didn't often regret her single state because she liked both solitude and autonomy, but tonight she wished the lights would be on in *her* house when she got home.

As if he could sense the vague melancholy, he said, "Why don't you come on in and have dinner with us."

"I doubt Jane would appreciate the spontaneous invitation."

"She picked up Chinese food. I talked to her about an hour ago. There's always more than enough and she bitches at me for not eating the leftovers. The argument I'm not home much doesn't seem to get through."

"I thought she was going to cook and wanted a menu."

"She changed her mind, anticipating my not-so-festive mood. Come on."

He got out, his breath a small plume of steam in the cold, and slammed the door. It did beat sitting around brooding over this bizarre case, Ellie decided philosophically, and followed. Besides, she'd liked Jane the few times she'd met her, though they didn't know each other all that well. Pine needles were slick under her boots and she shoved her hands deep into her pockets as he unlocked the front door.

Residual fatigue from the morning—from the past damn week—made her passively accept Jane's offer of a beer though she wasn't really in the mood for it. Rick gave Jane a perfunctory kiss. "We had a quite a day. Tell me you got garlic chicken."

"Like I wouldn't. You're predictable, Jones, in case you didn't know it. Beef and broccoli and shrimp lo mein too. Pork eggrolls. We have all the common proteins going." She motioned at the counter as she moved to take out another place mat from a drawer.

Silverware rattled. "There's plenty. I'm glad to not be eating by myself, if you want the truth. Your call wasn't exactly brimming over with information."

Ellie had heard that tone of voice before. It was called I-Date-a-Police-Officer irritation. She'd dealt with it herself a time or two. Amused for the first time all day, she took a sip of her beer and watched Rick handle it.

He predictably didn't catch it, or if he did, he was immune to it. With a noncommittal male grunt—she'd heard that before too—he sat down and reached for one of the white containers on the table.

"And that," she said to Jane with as much equanimity as possible, "is why I'm not married."

"Be careful, MacIntosh," her partner said with a sour smile as he set his elbows deliberately on the floral tablecloth, "or I'll eat all the garlic chicken."

"He does anyway," Jane said with a quirky smile. "So that's not much of a threat."

They ate, talking about small things—not the case, not in front of Jane—and an hour later Ellie thanked them and got up to leave. Rick walked her out, both of them donning their coats, the night holding a thin northern wind that made the trees groan and rustle.

"Snow." The word was succinct but said it all.

"I know." The icy breath of Mother Nature wafting across her unprotected face made it impossible to ignore. The most inconvenient part of winter was all the extra clothing and gear.

He walked beside her as they went the short distance to her car. "Just three inches maybe they said on the radio. That'll probably melt off, but we're on a time frame."

"I'm uneasy leaving Bryce Grantham alone out there." She felt the sting of the breeze wheeze past.

"Pearson thought about a detail but decided against it for several reasons." Rick watched her take out her keys, his features shadowed. "The first is obvious. But Grantham isn't in danger if he's our killer, Ellie. I'm thinking more and more he's just messing with us."

She did her best to keep her tone even. "And if he isn't? That means our killer visited his property recently. Very recently. I don't know about you, but that would make me uneasy as hell. He already looks like he hasn't slept in about a month."

"If that's what's happened, whoever put those bones there isn't likely to do it again so soon."

"And we know this because we understand this guy so well we nabbed him right away, correct?"

Rick shook his head over the sarcastic tone of her voice. "Grantham isn't typical of the victims either. First point of fact, he's not female. Our guy doesn't want him dead if he really is trying to frame him. He wants him healthy and ready to be charged with murder. Grantham might be the safest person in northern Wisconsin tonight."

"Did you pay *any* attention to my last observation?" She unlocked the door and got in her car, shaking her head. "We don't know what our killer is thinking, Rick. If we did, we might have managed to arrest the asshole before now."

There was a reason, Bryce decided, why people didn't stay at lake cabins all winter. It wasn't complicated and he probably should have remembered that the inhospitable seasons were why the government gave you a tax break for adding insulation or new windows, because the cottage had neither.

The snow fell as silently as the temperature. He tossed another piece of wood into the stove and shut the door, hearing the welcome crackle as the flames caught the seasoned pine.

The musical tones of his cell phone startled him and he realized part of it was the complete and utter quiet. He hadn't even bothered to turn on the radio or put a movie in the DVD player to watch on the twelve-inch television. Instead he'd sat by the window and watched the reflection of his own face in the black glass and wondered what someone—some*thing*—out there was thinking.

Until now, with police cars swarming all over the property, he'd felt more like an observer. A detached force who'd inadvertently stumbled into horror but wasn't actually attached to it in any way.

The visceral vision of those naked bones among the stack of firewood was going to haunt him forever, as was finding Margaret Wilson. He flipped open his phone, considered not answering, and then expelled a breath and took the call. "Ellie."

There was a moment when she didn't speak and he wondered himself why he'd used her first name, but maybe it was the night, the cold, the pressure, but it had just come out that way.

When she spoke her voice sounded ordinary enough. "Hi. I was wondering how you were doing. Everything quiet?"

Now that was something new. Suzanne knew of this mess—Alan had told him so—and she certainly hadn't bothered to call, though in her defense, he wouldn't have talked to her anyway. "It's snowing, Detective."

"This is nothing up here. This is nothing down in Milwaukee. I repeat my question, all quiet?"

"Worried about me?"

It was really wrong to get sarcastic with someone who had been decent to him so far, but his conversation with Alan Silver hadn't been all that reassuring.

Don't cooperate with the police unless they threaten to charge you and if they do that, call me before you utter the first word.

Last Bryce knew, this was America and the police were supposed to be the good guys.

All true, unless they thought *you* were one of the bad guys. That was when you hired someone at an exorbitant rate to keep them at bay.

One body, a partial skeleton, and a missing woman's blood-stained shoe later, he wasn't even sure he could blame the law enforcement powers that be for whatever conclusions they had reached. Worse, he wasn't sure Alan, who'd known him for years, was positive he was innocent even though Bryce had said so repeatedly. On the other end of the line was a strictly no-comment vibe to those assertions. Alan had evidently been lied to by clients often enough he kept an open mind, for he'd brushed off the small matter of innocence or guilt and just gave ambivalent advice that would apply to both scenarios.

They have to have probable cause to arrest you, though they can hold you for twenty-four hours for questioning. If either happens, shut up and call me.

Ellie MacIntosh said, "Yes, I am worried about your safety." It actually sounded like she meant it. "If I were you, I'd be crawling up the walls."

It stopped Bryce in his self-centered, poor-me tracks.

The strange thing was—and he couldn't quite explain it—he really wasn't worried about the killer coming after him, or if so, not consciously. He just wondered what this psychopath was going to do next to screw with his life, or even worse, to end someone else's.

"I am a little bit crawling up the walls," he said carefully. "And I am not actually supposed to talk to you anymore unless you plan to arrest me."

"That's a lawyer speaking right there. I wondered when you'd take that course." She didn't blink a figurative eye that he could tell. He could picture her with that smooth honey gold hair and formidably serious composure.

"Are you at home?" he asked without thinking it out. "Doors locked, lights blazing?"

"Worried about me?" she shot back, but under the flippant tone, he thought he caught something else. "Are you at home?" Detective MacIntosh countered, "Lights blazing?"

"Blazing might be an exaggeration. Kitchen light and one small lamp."

She laughed on a small breathy exhale. "Don't go macho on me now. I was just starting to like you."

He liked her too. In the vast desert of sexual loneliness of the past year—longer than that if he counted the insidious slide his marriage had made toward first ambivalence and then acrimony—he hadn't pursued any kind of a relationship. This seemed like an awkward as hell time to start.

"Macho? Me? I don't think so. Trust me, I'm probably more scared over what might happen next than anyone else around here, but maybe not for the same reason."

"I can only imagine." She paused. "You should have gone back to the motel. I think a good night's sleep would really help you out."

A polite way of saying he looked like hell. Okay, he conceded he probably did register on a scale somewhere between haggard and half dead, but the sterility of the motel room hadn't really done much for him the night before. He was tempted to explain he planned on going back to Milwaukee, but suspected that fell into the "don't tell" category Alan had cautioned him about. "I appreciate the concern, Detective."

Another brief hesitation, and she said, "Good night then."

"Good night." He flipped the phone shut and rose wearily to his feet. His footsteps sounded unnaturally loud as he walked into the kitchen. If it hadn't been so late when the last technician and police officer left the property, he might even have driven home this evening. However, at least he had the sense to know fatigue, darkness, snow, and a four-hour drive were a bad combination. Besides, the cabin had to be closed up properly, which included draining the pipes and pump, not terribly time consuming but difficult in the dark.

One more night. He could endure one more night.

Tomorrow they could either arrest him, or he was going home.

Chapter 18

Dawn. Quiet as death, cold, snowy, with an icy kiss in the air.

It was time to up the ante. The Hunter moved with methodical care because the ground was slick, the blanket of white snow from the night before pristine and unmarred.

A small sound made him glance up in time to see a startled doe lope off in a graceful bound, her shadowed form fading into the gloom. The drive was long, wooded, and went up a hill. Except for the conifers, the trees were mostly bare, so there wasn't much cover, but he approached obliquely, knowing his tracks would be there for a while anyway, but they wouldn't tell anyone much, and if the wind picked up like the forecasters predicted, they'd be gone soon enough.

The weather was getting worse. He'd have to get in and get out fast.

He had a gift to deliver . . . rather like Santa Claus, stealing in under the cover of the now waning darkness.

The comparison made him laugh.

* * *

Ice clicked against the window, the crisp sound ominous. Ellie didn't mind snow so much. Everyone in northern Wisconsin knew how to handle snow. Ice storms took down power lines and rendered roads impossible to navigate.

The file slapped down on the desk dangerously close to her cup of coffee. She looked up, startled. Pearson was usually calm despite his restless habits, but his unruffled Midwest composure was seriously *ruffled.* He eased half his skinny ass down on the edge of her desk and said, "Read that. I'll sit right here."

She flipped open the folder, scanned the forensic report, almost missed what had him not devouring a cholesterol-bonanza egg and cheese bagel at his desk as usual this time of day and instead propping himself on hers, and then scanned over the line again. A flicker of excitement went through her. "There was other blood on her clothes. Margaret Wilson had someone else's blood on her clothes? Seriously?"

"Would I lie? After talking to the ME on the phone to get his initial report I thought we were done." Pearson heaved himself back to his feet, his face as gray as the still snowy sky outside. "All I heard was there were no defensive wounds on the victim, nothing under her fingernails, no sign of struggle other than the bruising around her neck and the bump on her knee. But there was that strange cut on her face so I assumed it would be hers. Apparently forensics found out otherwise. I should have just brought the file right over to you. I finally had a minute to read the report but it has been on my desk since yesterday morning."

In the next heartbeat of a moment Ellie reminded herself that elation was premature, but this was another piece of physical evidence. Pearson hadn't ever supervised a case like this one—with this much urgency, and neither had she worked one like it. She took in a breath. "I take it there is no DNA match."

"Nope. Too soon. There were a lot of hair samples from her car, and though we can check it against the Simmons case, the others have to go through their families to narrow down the probability genetically, which isn't an instant process. The blood's human though, and like it says right there, not hers. Rick wouldn't have known it at the time of autopsy, because during the actual procedure, the lab results weren't in, of course. They rushed it through as it is."

"Okay. All right." Ellie blew out a short frustrated breath. "One step forward and two steps back. We're all up in the air over this case anyway. So the delay probably means nothing without more information. How long before we hear from DCI on how they are going to handle this?"

It was a bit of a tough question to ask because she'd been on this investigation since the first disappearance.

"I recommended they keep you and Jones on their task force, and they agreed."

Ellie felt a surge of relief. She had an emotional investment in this case, and she knew Rick did too. Even if someone else was handling it, she'd still be on it. "Thank you, sir."

"You know I have never thought all that much about this profiling business, but we've got a phone conference set up this afternoon to talk to one of the FBI's best." The sheriff frowned, his tanned face drawn into linear planes and vertical lines. "I hope it helps us," he added bluntly. "We've got a bit of egg on our face right now with one dead, three missing, and nothing solid."

"Yes, sir. I take it you want me to deal with the phone consultation."

"It's like you read my mind."

"God forbid, sir."

That at least wrung a bark of a laugh. "I'm just saying you've at least come close to this before so talk to the profiler, keep the notes we'll need, and let Jones do the legwork, okay?"

Ellie tapped the report with a forefinger, thinking hard. *The other blood? What did that mean?*

"Rick has a theory. He thinks he keeps them somewhere alive, but I disagree. I think he just keeps their bodies." She sat back and stared out at the bleak parking lot with the beginning of snow ruts that would persist the entire winter. "He stores them in the same place."

Suddenly nothing seemed more distant and cold than the steely sky outside.

"Keeps them?" Pearson looked more gray than ever.

"Human blood on her clothes. Think about it. If the blood isn't hers, it might be *his,* but as you pointed out, there were no defensive wounds. Other missing women and human blood. He has a storage place. That's why when they initially disappear, we can't find them with cadaver dogs and search teams. Then, when the case goes cold, he maybe dumps them."

"Makes sense to me, though I wish like hell it didn't. Jesus. I hate this investigation." The sheriff walked away across the cracked linoleum floor to where the coffeemaker and a stack of Styrofoam cups sat on a steel cart by the fax machine. He poured himself a cup and went back into his office, shutting the door.

The phone call came about an hour later, transferred to her desk. The man on the end of the line identified himself as special agent Montoya, said he'd read the reports faxed to him, and waited politely for her to interject something.

Ellie flipped a pencil around with her fingers. "As for reading the file, that must have taken all of about fifteen minutes. We don't have much, I know. "

"Maybe more than you think."

"That's music to my ears. Keep talking." She had paper ready for notes and turned the pencil to a more businesslike position. "We have only one suspect right now, but not a very viable one. Not one shred of physical evidence against him and the only reason he's on our radar is he was the person to last see Melissa Simmons, he's the one who found Margaret Wilson, and skeletal remains were discovered—also by him—on his property."

"I've been reading about it. The press picked it up even here in Virginia and now on the national news. It's interesting, Detective."

CNN. Great.

"Tell me *how* interesting." Her tone was reasonable and she hoped objective, but she couldn't help but remember how Bryce Grantham looked, pallid and shaken, his hands in his pockets, as the crime scene crew tore apart his parents' property.

"We'll get to the latest disappearance later. Let's talk about what evidence we do have. The first remains were found in a remote property off a county road, correct?"

"Yes. The medical examiner concluded strangulation, but the decomposition was out of sync with the disappearance in the professional opinion cited in the autopsy."

"I see the notes. Another possible victim was placed on our suspect's property?"

"That's accurate, sir, with the emphasis on *placed*. Stacked between rows of logs in the woodpile."

"Were you at the scene?"

"Of course. This is a fairly small county in terms of manpower."

"Tell me about the case from your perspective. What are your impressions of what is happening, Detective MacIntosh?"

She didn't usually deal in impressions, she wanted to point out, as police were not supposed to draw conclusions but just support facts. On the other hand, he was in Virginia and she was dealing with this case.

"The skeletal remains were planted and we know Margaret Wilson was manually strangled. We also believe our man is very familiar with the area. He's comfortable with the environment and athletic. Not everyone would walk through the woods in the cold with a skeleton, much less could carry a body to a deserted lake and store it in the boathouse. That, so far, to me, is our common denominator. He's young, I'd guess, no more than forty probably."

"I'd agree. Pretty classic profile otherwise, but the knowledge of the area seems undisputed, including the outdoorsman persona. You are looking for someone who is using his tools as a predator to utilize the country up there."

"Great." Ellie resumed twirling the pencil, her jaw set. "It doesn't narrow the field. Have you ever gone deer hunting up here in November? Some of these idiots get up at four in the morning to freeze their asses off in deer stands with their .30-06 Springfield rifle because they think it's fun in subzero wind chills. So far, you aren't helping a great deal."

He had the gall to sound amused. "Give me a few more minutes."

"A few? I'm not sure we have it. Anyone sitting in the stone-cold ignorance of a blind investigation and facing a winter that will bury any possible evidence would count every second, Special Agent Montoya. It's your turn."

She thought there was a tinge more respect in his tone when he cleared his throat and said, "He's methodical. Good at what he does, and that's why no one has caught him at it yet. He's a hunter, not an impulse killer. He plans. Don't make the mistake of thinking it's spur of the moment. No one does four murders in eighteen months without a bit of trace evidence if he isn't careful. It speaks of some sort of training. Medical, military, the business world, something like that. If the blood found on Margaret Wilson's clothes belongs to another one of the victims, he has set up shop, Detective MacIntosh, and unfortunately, it is in your neck of the woods."

He'd deliberately given that last phrase an irritating southern accent, but she chose to ignore it. "What can we expect next? Any ideas?"

"I wish we had more than one certain manner of death. I don't think—because of the blood in the Melissa Simmons' case and maybe on the other victim's clothes—he limits himself to strangulation. He's careful, but a sportsman. A real dangerous combination. The best serial killers are opportunists, but they also know when not to strike. I'm guessing you have potential victims out there who escaped because the timing wasn't right."

"Lovely," she muttered.

"In a way, he is. Picture a lion hunting a zebra. Waiting, tail twitching, in the long grass. Not necessarily a bigger animal, just a much more deadly one. On the hunt, nothing personal in it, but the game is the kill. That's it in a nutshell. The thrill of the hunt is getting him off. I doubt he knows the victims, or if he does, it's in passing only. According to the report, you can't link them together. There's a reason. Except for a relative age similarity and that they are female, there just *is* no link."

"Margaret Wilson wasn't sexually assaulted."

"It can still be a sexually based crime." His tone was pragmatic and clinical. "Not all murderers are rapists and not all rapists are murderers. He might hate women, or he might choose them because they are generally smaller and easier to kill. Often the arousal is in the danger, the control, and when he kills them is the culmination."

"I'm not getting real reassured here, Agent Montoya."

"So you shouldn't be. You need to keep in mind all the talented ones break rules."

Talented ones? If she could have broken the pencil in one crisp snap, she would have. Ellie pushed her blotter two inches to the left. "Outline the rules to me like I've never investigated a serial before, would you?"

"You never *have* investigated a serial before, have you?"

"Nope."

"A virgin, then."

She had to laugh, but then sobered when he went on in a cool, even voice. "If you've never handled someone like your guy, you haven't a damn clue, Detective. I've profiled for five years now. Trust me on this one. He's bad news. This one sends a chill up my spine that has nothing to do with your shitty weather up there. He's *methodical*."

That was exactly what she was afraid of hearing. Ellie squared her shoulders as she propped her elbows on the desk. With a heavy tone, she said, "I'm taking notes here. Give me all of it. What do you think he'll do next?"

His next words chilled *her* and she'd have thought she was beyond it.

"He's showing off, Detective."

"I've already figured that out," she said curtly. "He's enjoying rubbing our noses in it."

Montoya said quietly, "I don't think it's just for us. I need to know more about Grantham."

It wasn't until he got halfway up the steps from the cabin to the hill that Bryce realized he had a flat tire. Passenger rear from the telltale tilt of the vehicle.

Can't anything go right?

The thought of changing a tire in this mess held about as much appeal as a root canal without anesthetic. The snow had turned to icy rain an hour ago and already coated the trees and his car in a thick glistening blanket.

It was going to be one hell of a drive home, he thought as he tried to open the driver's-side door and found the handle frozen in place. Finally he managed to wrench it free, but fifteen more minutes of this crap and he'd have been locked out. He slid in and started the engine, setting the defrost on high and cursing steadily under his breath.

At first he hadn't been able to fall asleep, and the result was when it finally happened, he slept later than he intended. After a hasty cup of coffee he'd set out to close up the cabin properly: bed stripped, power unhooked, water lines drained, refrigerator propped open and emptied, shutters closed and locked in place, floor swept, woodstove cleaned out of all ashes. He'd methodically completed each chore and checked the dire predictions of the fickle weather forecast on his phone with a growing knot in his stomach.

Now this.

Bryce got out of the car and tried to ignore the sting of icy rain on his face even with the hood of his parka up. He'd almost not brought a heavier coat and only tossed it in his duffel bag with his fishing gear at the last minute in case it did get really cold. Not that it was all that cold right now. That was part of the problem with temps just hovering around freezing. He'd even thought he'd heard a boom of thunder earlier. Ice storms didn't happen all that often this far north. He hoped it would turn into snow for the drive back to Milwaukee. Snow he could handle, but this mix was treacherous.

He'd popped the trunk from inside but the back hatch was still frozen firmly in place and the keyhole coated over with ice. His gloved hands just skidded across the metal as he tried to heave it open. *Shit.*

A small gleam of something was next to the depressingly flat tire, glittering like the ice so at first he thought the glimpse of it was an illusion. Pelted with freezing rain, he bent over, and saw it was metal, encased in ice like a fly in amber.

A pair of earrings. Not small studs, but the dangling kind some women liked, silver, with small hoops, maybe two inches long.

With a chill that had nothing to do with the weather, he realized they were carefully laid out on *top* of the snow that had fallen the night before.

Crouched there, he stared at the bizarre find, resisting the urge to try to dig it out, and then his head whipped up and he stood, looking around, scanning the empty woods, the ping of ice on ice warring with the sudden roar in his ears. Nothing moved. Even the birds were silent, huddled against the storm.

Flat tire. It happened, he reminded himself, and tried to work some saliva into his dry mouth. A slow leak from a nail he picked up somewhere might render the tire dead flat with showing any signs of going low first . . . it was possible.

The earrings, however, he couldn't explain. A crime scene unit had spent hours going over the area around the cabin just yesterday. They *would* have found it.

This time he didn't wait. He took out his phone, realized he was standing in the inhospitable elements for no reason, and went around to wrangle the door open again. Nothing like having a police officer programmed into your phone, he thought ironically, turning down the full blast of the heater so he could hear. The defroster hadn't made a dent in the ice and snow and it felt like a white cave.

Ellie's voice mail was on, which just about followed the current pattern of luck he was having lately, but he left a message saying it was urgent and could she call him back. Before he even could slip his phone back into the pocket of jeans, it rang.

"Bryce? What is it?"

His breath went out in an emotional expulsion. "I think I had a visitor again."

"Is that so?" Her voice went from businesslike to terse. "More bones?"

"No." He explained about the tire and the earrings.

"Are they pearl earrings? Margaret Wilson was wearing pearl earrings when she disappeared. She wasn't when we found her."

"No. These are silver."

Silence.

The wind hissed around his car and he felt vulnerable sitting there, unable to see out. He started to say, "Maybe it's nothing, but—"

"It isn't nothing until we determine it isn't important. Look, don't touch it. Don't move your car either."

Moving his car was becoming less and less of an option by the moment. If he waited to change the tire, he was screwed. As it stood, he wasn't sure he could open the back to get out the jack and the spare. "I've closed up the cabin. I'm heading back to Milwaukee. The power went out about two hours ago anyway. Forgive me if I don't want to freeze my ass off in the dark in the middle of nowhere during a storm when a serial killer seems to be dropping by like an annoying neighbor."

"I didn't really think you should stay out there by yourself last night either, but I got outvoted. If we'd had an officer there, maybe he'd have seen something. We don't have a ton of manpower."

He was less concerned with his sleepless night and more worried about getting home. "Fine. No hard feelings on suspecting me of murder, no problem with ransacking my parents' cabin; I'm not even as pissed about my laptop in light of this new development. I just want to get the hell out here. Can you blame me?"

"I'm on 17 right now. The roads are really getting bad. I can be there in about fifteen minutes, I think. Maybe twenty."

Considering his vehicle at the moment was like claustrophobic ice-covered closet, that time frame sounded like an eternity. For all he knew, whoever had left him the two macabre presents stood right outside the driver's side door wielding an ax. He wouldn't be able to see him.

Now that was a cheery thought. "Fine," he said grimly. "I suppose another fifteen minutes won't hurt."

Chapter 19

It was dark and cold and his footsteps scraped across the cement floor. Outside the wind was hushed, and in this place, he was safe.

And so was she.

Tucked into her bower, her sanctuary, safe from the elements that would eventually tear her apart, bit by bit until she was naked, ivory white, vulnerable to obscurity. The Hunter didn't want that to happen to one of his girls. There was something mystic about being chosen and he refused to let that go easily, to trade the immortality of it.

Most people were born quietly and died the same way, but some were special.

He lifted the lid of the freezer and stared inside. She looked like she was sleeping except for the ice crystals around her nostrils and eyelids. Her dark hair was frosted with white.

"It's cold outside too," he whispered and gently closed the lid again.

* * *

The enormous tree—she thought it was an elm—had not just fallen across the drive, but it had taken down two other trees in its dramatic descent, leaving a thick jumble of broken trunks, skeleton branches, and other assorted debris right across the small lane that led to the Grantham cabin. Considering thick woods hemmed the drive on either side, no one was getting in or out anytime soon, especially not in this malevolent weather.

Ellie stopped the car on the small road and even with pumping her brakes it slid about fifteen feet father than she intended. She called Bryce on his cell. He picked up immediately. "Yes?"

"You've got a tree down. I can't get in."

She was pretty sure he said *fuck* with a forgivable level of vehemence.

"Right. It also means you can't get out." She paused. "I'm not for leaving you there another night." She might have added she'd debated asking if he wanted her to come out and sleep on his couch the night before. At least she was armed and by his own admission, he wasn't. In the end, after flipping her phone open several times and then closing it without calling, she decided it wasn't the best idea from a professional standpoint.

Instead she told him, "I'm waiting on the road outside the drive. Hurry. They've just declared this county under a weather emergency. No one is supposed to be on the roads."

"I'm not for staying here another night either."

He cut off the call, and though it seemed longer by the clock on the dash it was only a few minutes before she saw him climbing over—there wasn't much choice—the uprooted tree, a vague figure in the precipitation that seemed to vary from rain to snow at intervals. He skidded on the icy pavement and saved himself with a hand on the hood of her car before opening the passenger door and climbing in, dropping a small duffel bag at his feet. "I'm soaking wet. Sorry."

"How could you not be wet as hell? This sucks." She eased the car into drive again, the windshield wipers on high and not helping much. It was three o'clock in the afternoon and it was dark as dusk. "I can deal with snow—we get lots of snow up here, but the ice . . . ugh. There are power outages everywhere."

It was true, and the big elm was not the only casualty. The weight of the ice had broken branches strewn all over the roadsides. Bryce shoved back his hood and stripped off his gloves, showing reddened hands as he held them out to the heating vent on his side of the car. "Thanks for picking me up."

"Thanks for calling in," she said neutrally. "You could have just changed your tire and gone on your merry way."

"Wrong. I could have changed the tire . . . or *maybe* I could have. The hatch was frozen shut, and I'm pretty sure what I thought was thunder earlier was that tree going down. I didn't know it before you told me, so you'll just have to take my word for it."

The wind whipped a veil of moisture with force against the windshield, making her slow to a crawl on the treacherous road. "I think your new friend left you a token of his regard with those earrings."

"A trophy?"

She dared a quick inquiring look. In profile his face was reminiscent of what she imagined in a Brontë hero, an almost melancholy sort of handsome. There was a dark curl plastered against his lean cheek. He smiled, but it had nothing to do with humor. He said, "I had some time to think about it, waiting for you. I'm not a psychologist, believe me, but I'm connected to two victims. At first I thought the bones were planted to incriminate me, but now I'm wondering. Maybe he's . . . sharing, or something really insane like that. I mean, he must know you'd searched the property pretty thoroughly."

"You're assuming no one thinks you flattened the tire and planted the earrings to lead us off."

That silenced him. He stared at the slick ribbon of dark road as if he didn't even see it, which could be true because she was having a hard time seeing it herself.

After a harrowing moment in which they passed a snowplow hogging most of the road, he said quietly, "I can't win, can I? If I didn't call you; if I'd just changed the tire, put the earrings in my pocket, and drove off, what if I was stopped for whatever reason and they were found on me, and the evidence linked back to one of the missing women? What if I tried to dispose of them and someone saw me do it, or about any scenario in between?"

"It would look bad," Ellie agreed.

"Even more important, what if telling you about it can help you catch him?"

"Noble of you, I suppose."

He caught the slight sardonic inflection. "Not so noble. I'm tired of being Public Enemy Number One. When you catch him, at least I'm exonerated. And I'd just as soon not see any more of his . . ."

"Work." she supplied when he trailed off. "An interesting way to put it, but I spent part of my morning talking to a profiler." Ellie squinted at the road. With so many branches coming down she was being careful anyway, but she really didn't want to encounter a live power line.

"Great." His voice was heavy with irony. "With the way my luck is running, let me guess what he said. Your killer is from Milwaukee, designs computer software, and most likely has dark hair."

She let out a muffled laugh. "He wasn't quite that precise. He did mention serial killers often feel possessive of their victims and can usually pinpoint burial spots even years later. Some return to 'visit' the bodies, according to the agent I talked to."

"What a lovely image."

"None of this is lovely."

"I agree." He sounded tired. "Years later? Our man hasn't been at it all that long, has he?"

"Eighteen months around here. That doesn't mean he isn't imported. VICAP . . . , sorry, the Violent Criminal Apprehension Program, is trying to analyze any similarities to other murders in different parts of the country."

"Any luck?" He unzipped his sodden jacket a little.

"I can't discuss specific evidence with you, I'm sorry."

"That's understandable, I suppose," he said dryly. "I was kind of hoping you'd found something. Other than college, I've always lived in Wisconsin."

"I know."

"That's right. How could I forget? You've even met my ex-wife and visited the house I no longer own because I lost it in the divorce. I was surprised you hadn't yet contacted my parents."

"We haven't had time. You keep unearthing bodies for us." She spoke with equanimity and guided them into a dicey turn back onto the county highway in which she gained the opposite lane more than the one she wanted. Righting the car, she made the decision she'd been toying with anyway, hoping she wasn't the biggest fool in the history of Wisconsin law enforcement. As casually as possible, since they were about to slide right off the road and she was with the prime suspect in a murder investigation, she said, "I'm not driving into Merrill, not in this, and I'm going to guess the motels are full from traffic from the freeway, besides probably out of power. I hope you don't mind staying at my place tonight."

It was difficult to get a clear impression of Ellie's house since the dark afternoon rendered visibility null and void and the ice had whimsically changed back to snow that swirled up in banshee sheets around them. Now, as if to solidify the ice, Mother Nature had decided to plunge the temperature and cause real problems.

They discovered her power was out when she attempted to switch on the lights. Two clicks—why did everyone try it twice when normally the lights came on at once—and the hallway was still dark and already chilly.

"I have a generator," she said in her usual pragmatic tone, slender and so small she barely came up to his shoulder, but seemingly at ease with someone her department suspected of killing four women. "I'll go out and get it started."

"I can do it, if you'll tell me where it is," he offered, not positive he could deliver. His last experience with a generator had been at his grandparents' farm about two decades ago.

"No need," Ellie told him, her eyes only a glimmer

in the shrouded hallway. "It's a matter of throwing the switch and a push of a button. I'll be right back."

He dropped his duffel bag near the door, stamped off the snow from his boots, and tried to ignore that his jeans were wet and stiffly cold. In a few moments he could hear an engine come to life and the furnace kicked on with an audible whirl. She emerged from the door off the kitchen and pulled off her gloves. "At least we won't freeze to death."

"Which I might have if I hadn't called you." Bryce took off his damp coat and hung it on a coat tree near the front door. "Listen to that wind."

"Impossible not to." Ellie also slipped out of her parka and flicked on a table top lamp with a deep blue shade. "I hate these early winter storms."

"The generator is a good idea."

"My father insisted. He gave it to me as a housewarming present when I bought this place. It doesn't run everything, but takes care of the essentials. Furnace, well pump, hot water heater, refrigerator, and the kitchen outlets."

He looked around at soothing taupe walls, the various levels of steps and rooms an interesting architectural touch, and the fireplace a real beauty with river stone that rose two stories in the great room. "This is very nice, Detective."

"I was in the half-million-dollar loft you owned in Milwaukee so I doubt you're impressed, but thank you." She headed off toward the galley-style kitchen, as businesslike as ever.

Three quarters of a million, he thought ironically, but didn't argue it. The housing market was pretty much in flux right now, so she could be right, but that was Suzanne's problem. It must have killed her to write that check when the divorce was settled because she'd insisted on buying out his half. He followed, still cold but at least not shivering. What would he have done if he'd never found those earrings but still had a gigantic fallen tree between him and Milwaukee?

Spent a cold, comfortless night in the cabin at a guess, with no water and no electricity, and from the way the weather was cooperating, maybe his stay would have been more extended than that.

The killer had done him a bizarre favor.

"Obviously the power has been off for a couple of hours at least, but it should warm up soon." She hung up her coat on a peg by the back door, set her gloves on the radiator vent, and ran slender fingers through her blond hair. "I think we should probably start a fire."

"That I can do," Bryce offered.

"Thanks. I'm going to scrounge up some candles."

There was kindling in a basket on the hearth and a few logs stacked nearby, though it wouldn't last them long. Bryce knelt and went to work, pondering the hysterical humor of fate in general. Was he really going to spend the night at the house of a pretty cop investigating him in a serial murder case?

The flame caught, licked upward through the kindling, and he carefully added a log, aware of Ellie moving around, lighting candles, and the howl of the wind outside. The panes in the windows actually rattled at times.

"Wine?"

Straightening from his crouch, he turned.

She was at the counter now, the flickering light playing over her face, a corkscrew in hand. "I know you like wine," she said as if she felt the need to fill in the quiet with conversation. "It's only late afternoon, but it sure feels later."

"That sounds great."

"We might as well. No television." She gestured at a blank screen perched on a small stand in the corner. "A fire and wine is going to be about the best we can do, though the generator will at least allow us to have something to eat later. You might be stuck with canned soup and a sandwich. Just fair warning."

"Wine and a fire? Considering what my evening might have been like, that's pure luxury." He did his best to keep his tone light, though he was trying to imagine what she was thinking. Trapped in a cabin in an ice storm with a suspected murderer? "I'm going to have one hell of a time getting that tree cleared out."

"The county might help out." Ellie handed him a glass, and then sat in a somewhat worn chair close to the fire. "We need to get technicians in there to look at the earrings and your flat tire."

"Maybe I should just make up another set and give them keys to the cabin." He was only half joking.

Her gaze was assessing in an unsettling way. If she was afraid at all, it didn't show. "Maybe you should, the way this is going. You didn't hear anything at all? Notice anything unusual?"

"I couldn't sleep." He took a sip of wine. It was a white, probably a Riesling and a little sweet for him, but the cabin was warming up and the fire beginning to go and he had no complaints. Still sitting on the hearth, Bryce shook his head. "I finally nodded off close to dawn. From the way the earrings were on top of the snow, he had to have let the air out of my tire sometime this morning, pre-ice."

She digested that, her glass suspended in her fingers,

her face drawn into a small contemplative frown. "The profiler agreed with what you told me in the restaurant the other night. The killer is a risk taker, but a careful one. An opportunist, but also a plotter. Somehow he stopped Margaret Wilson on the road, abducted his first victim from a campsite in broad daylight, and even went to the house of Melissa Simmons when she didn't have her car or cell phone and convinced her to open the door. How the hell did he manage it?"

All of that had been in the papers, so it wasn't as if she was revealing anything new. He murmured, "He couldn't know I wouldn't come outside and see him last night. He had to have used a flashlight."

"Or night-vision goggles. Lots of hunters have them."

How pleasant was that thought? Bryce drank more sweet wine and tried to ignore how damp his jeans were from the knee down. "What else did the profiler say, or is that privileged information also?"

After a short pause, she shrugged. "I can't see that there's an advantage one way or the other to keeping his comments secret. What it comes down to is this: It's educated guesswork, but still guesswork. Evidence is a different matter."

"I would agree that when working with the human psyche, that is always true. There are no certainties."

Ellie set her wineglass on a small table and leaned forward to unlace her wet boots and pull them off. "Our killer is probably a white male, between twenty and forty, athletic, an outdoorsman, intelligent, and he most likely isn't a drifter."

"Not stellar psychological deductions there, if you ask me." He propped an elbow on his bent knee. "I could have told you that."

"How so?" She lifted a brow and curled up in her chair, legs tucked under.

"Not because I know personally," he said with a humorless smile. "It's just common sense. He carried Margaret Wilson's body to a remote place where it was unlikely to be found, so he must be athletic, and he must know the area. I'm guessing he counted on no one going there for months, maybe the entire winter . . . longer even. If I'd decided to take a week or two up here in the spring instead of now, I would never have looked in the boathouse. It was the smell. By then, there wouldn't be."

That distinct odor he would never forget. The wine might be a little sweet, but he took a quick gulp anyway.

"Chance tripped him up then." She didn't pose it as a question, and he chose to not treat it as one either.

Yes.

"Weird as *hell* chance." Rather like finding himself in Ellie MacIntosh's house, drinking wine with her around the fire, he thought. "And do me a favor and skip quoting the astronomical odds of finding two bodies so close together, all right?"

"One was chance, the other was design, and Melissa Simmons is still missing," she said, looking unfazed by his acerbic tone. "We aren't dealing with chance any longer. There's someone out there, and he's watching. According to my profiler, he's excited by all this. You walked into his life, and you turned his work into an exhibition."

"Lucky me," Bryce muttered.

"So he now relates to you."

"I'm feeling better by the second."

"Law enforcement is grateful for the break, if that does make you feel better."

"It doesn't. I'd rather be almost anything else than a divining rod for dead bodies."

For the first time, she looked amused. "That sounds heartfelt and I, for one, believe you."

Chapter 20

The exhilaration of the bad weather was exactly what he'd needed. It was as if the spirits understood, felt that raw need and supplied the backdrop. It was frigid, the roads impassable, and the odds against him.

And still he hunted.

He liked nothing more. Nothing more and here it was, just the beginning of November. This winter offered such possibilities for a true sportsman.

Her car was just ahead. He'd followed close, waited until the right moment, and then accelerated to pass on a curve, skidding a little too close, forcing the sedan to the side.

It wasn't hard. Not in this weather. She swerved, caught the edge with no traction, and he'd seen in the rearview mirror the nose of the hood at a crazy angle against the backdrop of ice-covered trees as she went off to the side, the lights pointing upward.

All his fault.

Tsk tsk tsk, no one should be out driving in this mess. The Hunter stopped, backed up his truck, and got out, going around the side of the car in the ditch, half sliding on the icy pavement, and knocked on the driver's window.

He smiled, friendly, unthreatening, apologetic. "I'm so sorry. I was going way too fast. In a hurry to get home, I guess. Need some help?"

It was really getting damn cold outside.

Temperatures falling through the floor. Ice. Blackness. All the amenities.

But inside, no. Inside it was warm with candlelight, with the fire burning brightly, with the smell of chicken noodle soup and grilled cheese, and the scent of red wine.

Second bottle of wine. Was that a wise idea?

Curiously, Ellie was unafraid. Or maybe it wasn't so curious, she thought, sipping from her glass. Instincts were worth something in police work. If she had to gauge it, she'd say she was 95 percent sure Bryce Grantham was nothing but what he seemed. A successful, sensitive, good-looking man who was having the most macabre vacation imaginable. As for the other 5 percent, well . . . the only person she knew for certain wasn't the murderer was herself. It could be anyone capable of carrying Margaret Wilson to the boathouse. Gravelly, the surly bartender where Melissa Simmons had encountered car trouble. Some other patron there that night. A friend they didn't even know she had . . . one of the definitely sleazy and unsavory Walters brothers . . .

Bryce came in, shaking snow out of his dark hair, carrying more wood. He'd insisted on being the one to go out for it, and truthfully, she wasn't interested in the biting cold wind or trying to carry in logs with a glazing of ice on them, so she'd only argued for about two seconds before acquiescing and dropping the hostess routine. By the fire it was nice and cozy, and she sat with her legs curled under her, watching him stack the wood in the carrier and tug off his gloves.

Nice hands, as she'd noticed before. He had long graceful fingers, right now held out to the fire as he crouched by the hearth. A droplet of moisture ran along the clean line of his jaw. "Pretty nasty out there."

"I'll bet." The shriek of the wind under the eaves bore out his assertion.

"Just snowing now, though."

That was something, but with all the ice already on the trees, the wind was more of the problem now. "I shut the weather radio off," she said with a grimace. "I can't take the alert going off every few minutes."

"Sort of ruins the ambience," he agreed, and smiled as he rose to settle back down near the fireplace.

Ellie was pretty sure she'd never seen him genuinely smile before, though that was hardly a wonder. Crime scenes had been their main interaction except for that one dinner in Merrill the other night, and even then the case was the reason they were together and the main topic of discussion.

"Tell me about the chair."

"What?"

He gestured with his wineglass toward where she sat. "I'm not exactly an interior decorator but it doesn't fit with the rest of your taste. Why do you keep it?"

There wasn't a reason not to tell him. "It belonged to my father."

"I see."

"He died a year ago. Heart attack. We didn't expect it. My mother moved to Florida, which is what she's always wanted to do anyway. She likes the sun. But, no thanks. Too many people."

"Even on a night like tonight?"

"You have a point." She glanced at the window. "It really is ugly out there."

"Brothers? Sisters?"

"One sister, no brothers."

"Are you close?"

The interest seemed sincere. "Actually, we are, but she's the respectable married one with three little girls, and I'm the police officer." She shrugged. "We're different, but maybe that is why we get along. She lives close by so we get together fairly often, especially now since my mother moved. It's nice that she's busy, and I'm busy, but we do make time for each other. I have friends, but truthfully, most of them move away to warmer climates and better job opportunities, so I suppose she's my best friend."

Maybe she should tell Jody that someday. It hadn't occurred to her she'd never said it. Her choice of career wasn't conducive to warm, fuzzy emotions.

"My family is pretty tight-knit too. Sounds like we are both lucky. Not everyone has that in their life."

"I didn't feel lucky at all when my father died . . . but you're right. It seemed like we were all so autonomous until we needed each other."

"I think it works that way. That until you lose something, you don't appreciate what you have." His smile was wry. "I can't say I've felt very lucky this past week, but at least I have you."

He seemed at once to realize how that sounded, for he added quickly, "What I mean is that my impression is you are determined to find the truth. My confidence in that has made this all bearable. Or at least partially bearable."

"That's my job."

"I doubt everyone is quite so dedicated." He smiled again.

A part of her wished he hadn't.

Ellie pondered the dark red liquid in her glass and wondered if she had made some kind of inner decision when she'd taken the turnoff instead of driving into the nearest town with a motel. Not that her reasons weren't valid because they were logical. According to the reports the freeway was a mess, power out everywhere, and dumping him off at some motel probably not actually an option. Maybe the sheriff would give her points for baby-sitting their only tie to the killer.

Rationalization? Could be. It was her habit to be honest with herself but at the moment, soothed with alcohol, food, and warmth against the ferocious temper of the north woods, she wasn't in the mood for rational.

How long had it been since she'd had a romantic relationship? Two years, at least, since she and Brian had parted ways and he'd transferred to the Twin Cities.

And what the hell did that have to do with anything?

Crime scenes were not a good way to meet men, she reminded herself wryly. *Maybe you should lay off the wine and just go to bed. By yourself.*

"This isn't the most hospitable time of the year to visit the area." She shifted a little in her chair. Just a very little, but she saw him notice. Just a glimmer in his dark eyes and something about his posture.

They were very aware of each other, but they had been almost since that first moment when they met outside the cabin where Melissa Simmons had been abducted.

And now they were alone.

Very alone in an icebound county with impassable roads and no power. The attraction was a problem. He wasn't a suspect really, but he was *involved*. Not directly. By accident, but still . . .

"I have to agree. Inhospitable neatly sums up my visit this time." Bryce had been nursing his wine but he finally finished it. Candlelight did nice things to the planes of his face. "I love it here in the summer but don't usually come up in the late fall like this. I was just looking for a little solitude."

"Not exactly how it worked out." Ellie realized her pulse had started to quicken and she tried to quell the response with a casual laugh. "You're stuck here with me."

"Stuck is definitely *not* how I'd put it." His response was rueful. "More like you are stuck with me."

"That's not how I'd put it either."

She shouldn't have said that. It wasn't the words so much as it was the soft tone of her voice. He caught it too, and it made her get hastily to her feet. "I should probably wash the dishes by hand. It doesn't look like we're going to get power tonight."

"I'll wash, you dry." He stood also, in an easy movement. "You know where the dishes go."

Considering the extent of the mess was one saucepan, a nonstick skillet, two plates, two bowls and two spoons, cleanup was not a matter of more than a few minutes. They stood next to each other at the sink, and when their fingers brushed as he handed her a wet bowl, Ellie felt it all the way to the tips of her toes like some oversexed adolescent.

Damn. Time to get the hell away from him and into bed. She was having some pretty impure thoughts about their main link to a murder investigation. Unprofessional, to say the least.

"You've been the only good thing about any of this," he said quietly after he switched the water off. "This is kind of a tired line, but I wish we'd met under different circumstances."

"Pretty tired," she agreed in an even voice. He was tall enough she had to tilt her head back to look him in the eye.

But even though they stood close still, she didn't step back.

It was charming—in a time when few men were charming any longer—to watch him convince himself to misunderstand her body language. "Speaking of tired, I'm going to guess we both are," he said after a telling moment, his arms hanging at his sides, his hands still wet. "Like I said, I didn't sleep much last night."

Unassuming. He wasn't smooth, didn't immediately make a move. She liked that. Working with cops provided enough testosterone blasts to last a lifetime. But she really wasn't thinking about sleep at this moment.

You shouldn't do this.

And though the case still hung there in her mind, 5 percent doubt had shrunk to 2 percent during the course of the evening.

"This way." She walked through the living room to the hallway, and went into her bedroom. It was dark without the power on, but earlier she had lit one candle on the dresser and it flickered, sending shadows along the wall.

For a moment the doorway was empty and she wasn't sure he was going to follow her, but then his silhouette appeared, tall in the wavering light. He'd taken off his boots after getting the wood and moved into the room silently.

It took a minute, but he seemed to get it was her bedroom, and though a brief look of surprise crossed his face, it was just as quickly replaced with something else.

Neither of them spoke, which was fine with her. They'd been talking for hours already, about anything and everything. He'd been born in Sun Prairie and moved to Milwaukee with his parents and one sister when he was five. He wasn't a football fan, but had run track instead in high school and walked onto the team as a freshman in college. He liked classical music but didn't care for jazz . . .

He knew how to kiss, she discovered a moment later. Not too fast and furious, not too slow or sloppy, but with enough pressure of lips and tongue she could feel his sexual hunger, and his damp hands spanned her waist, drawing her in close. He smelled good, like wood smoke mingled with a little designer cologne, and when she slid her arms around his neck, his thick hair softly brushed her fingers.

They undressed each other, her fingers busy on the buttons of his denim shirt, then dropping to his fly, slipping the button free. He kissed the side of her neck as she pressed her palm against the hard length of his arousal through the material of his briefs, and he gave a low, telling exhale.

"You sure?" He touched her cheek with the backs of his fingers.

"It's a little cold in here. Feel free to wait for me in the bed," she murmured against his mouth as they kissed again, her blouse now on the floor. "I'll be right back."

She'd also lit a candle in the bathroom off her bedroom, and she squinted as she opened the bottom drawer of the vanity and took out a box. Did condoms expire? She guessed they might, but surely they lasted longer than two years and Brian had helpfully left a new box. Their sex life had been the first thing to go as the relationship started to splinter apart. Ellie extracted a couple of foil pouches, brushed her teeth, and undressed completely in the muted light. Outside, the wind moaned and caressed the house in unsubtle blasts of snow. It wasn't late, but it was dark and cold and bed sounded like the perfect place to be.

Naked and prepared, she went back into the bedroom.

The next hour passed in a blur of half whispers, exploring fingers, and sensual pleasure. Bryce made love with same restraint as he kissed, unhurried with no adolescent rush, no urgency, his mouth warm and experienced as he tasted and touched. His body was lean and well muscled, hard under the questing investigation of her hands,

She liked, especially in that blinding moment of pleasure, that he wasn't a selfish lover but knew how to give as well take.

Then . . . quiet breathing in the dark. His damp skin against hers, their bodies nestled together in the aftermath, his fingers carefully smoothing her tangled hair away from her face. Bryce said in a thick voice, "I think someone with a doctorate in literature should be more eloquent, but holy shit."

"Yeah," Ellie confirmed, liking the solid feel of him, the cocoon of warmth.

She could swear it wasn't five seconds before he slid

into sleep. Not a normal sleep either, but the dead sleep of the truly exhausted, his body still, his face peaceful in repose. One lax hand cradled her bare breast and she left it there, tired and replete herself, listening to the assault of the storm.

No living soul would be out in it was her last coherent thought before she drifted off.

The woods were *impassable with deep drifts, the snow cold and sticky, his eyes stinging. The trail was lost, the lake now just a flat snowy surface. He stumbled, trying to keep his balance as he ran, and the icy air dragged at his lungs, drowning him.*

The first spots of blood were there, crimson shocking against the pristine white, then spots became splotches, and finally there was crimson everywhere, in huge piles of soaked snow and the wind keening above it all, like some shrill phantom voice . . .

Bryce came awake with a start from the dream, sweating, heart pounding, disoriented in the dark. It took a moment but he registered the softness of the bed, the scent of sex that lingered, and of course, most telling, the curve of a naked female body next to him. Soft blond hair spilled across the pillow.

Detective MacIntosh.

No. Ellie. The woman he'd held in his arms and touched and felt respond to him wasn't the cool blonde with a notepad and a calculating gaze. She'd been unself-consciously passionate and right now was curled against him in deep slumber.

Just a damned dream, he told himself as his heart rate began to slow, and no wonder, with everything that had been going on. Even now the sweat on his body made him cold as he sank into the reality of the present.

Ellie slept, her breathing easy, slender body relaxed. If he cast back over the evidence, he didn't blame the police for their conclusions, so the trust involved in the current situation was a pivotal point in their relationship.

He eased away, relinquishing the warmth of her body with reluctance, and went into the bathroom. The candle she had in there was practically gutted, the flame more of just a glow. Bryce flushed the toilet, washed his hands, and gratefully found a freshly wrapped toothbrush in one of the drawers. He brushed his teeth, still trying to shake off the dream, and then padded back to climb into the bed again. She mumbled something as his cold hands brought her back against him.

"Hmm."

"I'm sorry I woke you."

She said drowsily, "That's okay. What time is it?"

"Power is still out. I have no idea." He lifted her hair and kissed the nape of her neck.

"The wind is supposed to die out by dawn."

"Then it isn't dawn. Listen."

"I hear it." She rolled over, into him, and touched his face with her fingertips. "Are you a dream?"

"Let's not talk about dreams." His lips brushed her eyebrows, her cheekbones, and then the dip of her mouth.

"That's nice." She kissed his bare shoulder and leaned into him, her eyes half closed.

"Go back to sleep." He knew she was still tired—they both were, and as ironic as it might be, the storm was like a gift, a buffer against the real world.

An illusion, but a welcome one. He was warm, drifting, safe.

But tomorrow, he had a feeling it would be damned cold again.

Chapter 21

Hibernation was for animals, and he was up a level on the food chain.

The Hunter loved this kind of weather, but tonight he was tired, pleasantly so, and there was no need to leave, to brave the howl of the wind. It vaguely reminded him of wolves he'd once heard on a camping trip with his dad.

Lonely, but he doubted the animals were. They lived in dens together, but in other ways they were very alike.

Hungry.

Always hungry.

Maybe he was an animal after all, but for the moment, he was satisfied.

The front had rolled over the northern counties like a bulldozer, and so at first, he hadn't worried too much about it. Jane wasn't home. He'd expected her to be late.

Not *this* late.

Rick sat straight up on the couch, realized he'd fallen

asleep a little after midnight, and rubbed his gritty eyes. He'd worked a sixteen-hour shift and was due to go back on duty in four hours.

Jane had stayed at the hospital, he told himself. The early shifts couldn't get home, the later shift couldn't get in, and the hospital still needed staff no matter what the weather was like. It had happened before.

The roads were impassable, the county on lockdown, and he just needed to go back to sleep. As it was, he'd barely made it back to his house due to the icy conditions and blocked roads. If it wasn't for the woodstove and thermal underwear, he'd be freezing.

But try as he might, he only managed to roll around in the bed and curse the howl of the wind until he dropped off into a restive doze.

Coffee boiled on the stove, like her grandmother used to make, wasn't really all that great. Ellie sipped from her cup and nodded, reluctant to criticize anything she didn't have to exert herself to make. "It's not bad."

"It's hot and resembles a dark liquid consumed at breakfast." Bryce moved efficiently between the stove and the counter where two plates were laid out. "The coffeemaker isn't working. At least we can have something to eat. How many eggs?"

She planted her elbows on the table and admired how he looked in just jeans and a T-shirt. That just-up tousled look worked well on him, and so did the shadow of a dark beard. "Two. Can you cook?"

"Eggs? Yes."

"Anything else?" She was admittedly curious, especially now. The night—and this morning—had been . . . different for her.

Yes, that was the right word, different. She didn't

pick up guys, bring them home, and invite them into her bed.

However, if that scenario always worked out like what had happened between her and Bryce Grantham, she might decide to make it a habit. It could have been the most memorable sex of her life.

"Bacon." He bent over and peered into her refrigerator, retrieving a clear package. "Of which you have three slices."

"Of questionable shelf life probably." It was hard to not admire the view. He had a nice ass.

"It smells okay."

"Go for it." She grinned and drank more overboiled coffee. "Cook the hell out of it and it can't hurt us, right? Besides, I like my bacon really crisp."

"Crisp it is."

"Over easy on the eggs."

"A woman after my own heart."

The day had dawned cold and gray and dismal, not bright and sunny like so often after a storm. Mother Nature wasn't done quite yet. Tree branches, still laden with ice, drooped unnaturally outside the big picture window, the sill crusted with crystalline snow like small prisms. At least the wind had died down, but according to the weather radio, it was supposed to pick up again later.

Bryce put a pat of butter in a frying pan, cracked two eggs as if he knew what he was doing, and peered at the bacon, which had started to sizzle. In the thin light coming in the big window, he looked less strained, she thought. The taut lines near his mouth had eased.

"Getting a little sleep did you some good," she remarked, sitting on one of the two stools at the small bar that separated her kitchen from the great room.

"It wasn't just the sleep." He glanced over at her with a brief smile.

Swathed in her favorite robe, wearing thick socks, and with her hair uncombed, Ellie didn't feel too sexy at the moment, but his smile did some interesting things to the pit of her stomach.

Nothing like getting laid, is there?

It was funny, though, she didn't think he would ever put it that way. She worked with too many men; that was the problem. Not all of them were crude, but some certainly were, and she had never gotten that impression from Bryce.

Her cell phone was on the counter and she opened it for the third time since she'd gotten up. "Still no signal. I'm wondering if the storm took out the closest tower."

"I'd guess you're right. I'm surprised I still have it after the search the other day, but you can try my phone if you want." He flipped the bacon over with impressive expertise and reached into his pocket to slip out his cell phone and set it within reach.

"We can check the records of your calls through your server just as easy, so there was no need to take it," she said wryly. "Don't worry, if you talk to your mother four times a day, we'll know it."

"I don't," he said after a short pause and a shrug. "I suppose it shouldn't bother me, but it still does. Invasion of privacy, I guess. My nondescript life bared for all to see."

"Not all," she corrected, sympathetic but also thinking about the case. About those lonely bones strewn in that woodpile. About Margaret Wilson's decomposing body. "Just the detectives and officers involved need to know everything. We want to nail this guy. I'm sure you understand we can't leave a single possibility loose on this."

He deftly slid out the two eggs onto one of the plates she taken from the cupboard and nodded. "I've cooperated."

"We appreciate it."

He glanced up, a lock of dark hair falling over his brow. "Don't go all detective on me now, Ellie."

"Sorry. It's part of the package."

The part that intimidated most men, or turned them off, or whatever it was that prevented her from having anything but mediocre dates since Brian that led strictly nowhere. For that matter, Brian had led nowhere too.

"Well, that's fair warning. Thanks." He took the bacon out of the skillet, drained it briefly on a paper towel, and added two strips to the eggs before bringing it over to put the plate in front of her. "Go ahead and eat while it's hot. Mine will be done in a minute."

He did join her a minute or two later, perching on the next stool, his long fingers wrapped around a thick mug that said, ironically, *Cops Make Better Lovers,* given to her as a joke by a colleague her rookie year. "I think you might be able to get footprints by my Land Rover."

"I hate to break it to you, but we had some nasty weather last night."

"I noticed, but it might be in our favor."

That seemed unlikely but Ellie dipped a piece of bacon in her egg yoke and took a bite, lifting her brows in unspoken inquiry. She was all ears. Anything to help solve this damned case.

He took a sip of coffee, his face thoughtful. "I looked around a little, but by then the ice was coming down pretty good. However, it snowed first, and he definitely put the earrings on top of the snow before the ice started. I couldn't even tell what was there at first. Even with all the wind and fresh snow on top of it, the ice probably preserved his trail, so to speak. The wind didn't really start until the line of the front shifted."

That was all probably true, but she was doubtful any evidence survived the storm.

Bryce went on doggedly. "Whoever flattened my tire must have parked somewhere nearby and walked through the woods. Maybe you could get tire imprints. This is a big area as far as the countryside goes, but it has a small population with few stores. Most people I know shop for tires pretty close to home."

"True enough, but it isn't nearly as easy as it looks on television to match evidence like that and tire casting in ice and snow might be impossible, not to mention getting investigators to the scene right now."

"If it can be determined where he parked, that alone will tell you something. I'm going to guess whoever was there headed home. Any outdoorsman would know the roads were going to get bad. Whatever direction he drove off in gives you at least a starting point."

"I wouldn't get my hopes up too much. The evidence will start to deteriorate the minute the weather improves."

Bryce snapped a piece of bacon in half and took a bite, then laid the uneaten part back on his plate. His dark eyes were somber. "You'll get more chances."

It was very quiet except for the outside drone of the generator and the crack as resin snapped in a log in the fireplace. "If you have a theory, don't stop now," Ellie prompted, one elbow propped on the counter, her gaze on his face. "Go on. Maybe you aren't law enforcement but you have a stake in this, I'll acknowledge that."

"The game has changed, I think," he said in measured tones. "At first he killed these women and hid them because it was his little special secret. I don't know how much media the disappearances got, but I do know that the discovery of the bodies has gotten a lot of press all over the state."

"Oh, you're right." And he was. It was one of the points of this case that irked the hell out of her. She told him, "He's a celebrity now. One of two things is going to happen. He's going to stop and lay low until it all calms down, or he is going to up the stakes."

"How? You're the homicide detective. A bit of a warning would be nice. I must admit I'm damn sick of his surprises."

"I'm going to guess," she said slowly, "he is really going to want to impress you. After all, you are getting credit for his work."

"Jesus, Ellie." Bryce set aside his coffee as if he couldn't stomach another sip.

She was just too damn afraid she was right. "He's already giving us evidence," she said with a small nod. *Bastard,* she thought. "But *through* you now. I listened to the profiler from the FBI and I don't doubt what he said was accurate to the extent of the information we gave him, but I'm living these cases and have been for a year and a half. He's punishing you for finding Margaret Wilson, but he's also enjoying the partnership."

"We aren't partners."

"Aren't you? Four women dead. You've been in contact one way or the other with three of them. It gets him off. He likes the danger. Most killers do."

"He's gotten away with it four times," Bryce agreed. In profile, his clean-cut features were remote. "I'm going to guess it's like freestyle mountain climbing.

Daunting as hell at first, exhilarating when you make it to the top, and then as you get better and better at it, the fear goes away and you think you'll never fall."

"An interesting analogy."

"Uh-oh. I recognize that look now." He almost visibly shook off the conversation and cut into one of his eggs. It was perfect, not too runny, not too firm, the edges of the white just a little bit crispy. "Let me forestall the question. No, I've never been freestyle rock climbing. I picked that because I've always wondered why the hell anyone would ever take the risk."

"Like murdering someone and hiding the body."

He looked at her steadily. "I've never done that either."

They were at 99 percent now. Almost one hundred. Ellie said calmly, "If I thought you had, do you think you'd really be here? Would last night have happened?"

"We just confirmed there are risk takers out there. Are you one, Detective?"

She wasn't sure how she would have answered that question, but all of a sudden someone pounded on her door, making her jump. It wasn't that early—after eight o'clock now, and she wasn't due on duty until ten—but with the insulation of the aftermath of the storm, she didn't expect it. Ellie slid off the stool with a mutter, and was only halfway to the door when the person pounded again.

"Coming," she called, padding across the floor in stocking feet, taking a moment to peek out the glass panel next to the front door. Snow, more snow, and one very large police officer, square jaw, thick shoulders . . .

She undid the dead bolt and opened the door. "Rick?"

"You aren't answering your cell." He stamped in past her, bringing a swirl of cold air and not a small amount of snow, which wasn't in character. Yes, he was impatient, but he wasn't rude normally.

Or agitated, she realized a second later, when she registered his reddened cheeks weren't totally due to the freezing temps. "I don't have signal at the moment because of the weather. What is it?"

"Get dressed. We've got a double homicide."

The raspy statement registered as he swung around. "What?" she repeated incredulously.

"Reginald Walters and someone we can't identify. No sign of Keith. So much for the happy family unit." He ripped off a glove. "Do I smell coffee? I hope you don't mind if I grab some while you put some clothes on."

"I'll get it."

At the sound of Bryce's voice, Rick's head whipped around. "What the fuck?"

Bryce wasn't surprised over Deputy Jones' reaction, but he wasn't exactly flattered either. However his partner felt about the case, it was clear Jones wasn't nearly as assured Bryce wasn't still running in first place as the guilty candidate in Wisconsin's race for the current most notorious murderer.

"I called in his report," Ellie said briskly, walking past toward the bedroom. It wasn't as if she was wearing a blinking sign that said SLEPT WITH SUSPECT, but Bryce could tell she was at least a little uncomfortable. "Tree fell across the drive to the cabin and he couldn't get out, but it sounds like our killer might have left another present for us on the Grantham property. I'm hoping we can get *something* when a crime scene team can get in there. Give me about two minutes."

She disappeared into the bedroom and Bryce went ahead and took a cup from the cupboard and poured some coffee into it from the pot on the stove, and wordlessly went to hand it over.

"Thanks," Jones said sarcastically, his eyes assessing as he took the cup, his jaw stuck at a dangerous angle.

"No problem." He was taller and Bryce knew maybe it was useless male pride, but he didn't sit back down. Despite Bryce's superior height, Ellie's partner probably outweighed him by forty pounds and he didn't trust the man's impartiality at the moment.

"She brought you *here*?"

The answer was obvious enough that Bryce didn't say anything, just lifted his brows a little.

"You've got to be kidding." Rick took a gulp of coffee that might have drained half the cup and shook his head, his mouth tight.

"And oddly enough, she's still alive." Bryce didn't keep the edge out of his voice. "Do I get points for good behavior?"

"No comment, though, trust me, I'd love to." Jones brushed at some snow on his parka, heedless of the floor. "I'd *really* love to."

"I get that impression."

"If you think, Dr. Grantham, that I don't want to slam my fist into someone right now, think again. This is supposed to be a quiet place and people are dying all over the county." He adjusted the flap on his hat and his pale blue eyes held a hint of unmistakable anger. "I wouldn't push it."

"They aren't dying because of me." Bryce had his

own sense of anger, his own violation to deal with, not least of which was invasion of his privacy by the police. "Someone flattened my tire yesterday and left evidence by my car on top of everything else. I expected to be home by now, away from all this."

"That so? Remind me to tell the sheriff you were going to leave the county."

"Remind me to tell my lawyer you want to detain me without probable cause." Bryce leaned against the counter and folded his arms across his chest.

"Probable cause? I'll give you probable cause. How about all those human remains showing up wherever you are?" Rick finished his coffee and slapped the cup down on the counter.

It was a hard point to argue. Luckily, he didn't have to. Ellie emerged in record time, her hair caught carelessly back in a no-nonsense ponytail, no cosmetics but her face scrubbed clean, a bulky sweater and jeans punctuated by midcalf-high boots.

She looked fantastic even swathed head to foot in warmth-generating material. Unfortunately, she barely glanced at him, Bryce noted. "Do you know how to turn off the generator if the electricity comes back on?"

"Walk me through it quickly," he said, her change in demeanor not surprising but still disconcerting.

"I'll be in the car." Jones stomped out, his face grim.

For whatever reason, Bryce wanted to apologize, but he wasn't sure for what. Instead he followed her into the garage and out the side door, to where the generator sat in a small side structure with an outlet that sent a plume of exhaust into the frigid air. He listened to her instructions on how to flip the switch and shut off the machine, and nodded.

"I've got to go." She didn't look at him.

"I get that."

"It'll be hours."

"Double homicide and the storm. I get that too."

Finally, she glanced up. "Sorry."

"For what?" He needed to know the answer. The garage was cold and his breath was visible. He shoved his hands into his pockets. "Last night?"

"No." The look she gave him was unfathomable, detached, as if she'd checked out of being that woman who had slept against him in the dark.

"Ellie," he said impulsively, because he didn't want to be shut out, because the past week had been hell.

"Like I said, this will take awhile," she said in a calm voice. "Make yourself at home."

And then she walked away.

Chapter 22

She was still alive . . . he did that sometimes. It was like a double-dipped cone, twice the treat. The basement was cold, but it was cool even in the middle of summer, which was part of the charm. If cement walls, a single bulb hanging from the ceiling, and a freezer full of body parts could be charming.

She was bound, and not yet conscious, though he could see she'd moved a little on the blanket.

The entire county was rebounding from the storm. It would probably be hours before she was really considered missing.

November was always the best time to hunt . . .

Even with the cold keeping it contained, the place smelled rank; a musty combination of cigarette smoke, old carpet, and unwashed bodies mingled with the unforgettable odor of death. Rick decided he could go the rest of his life without smelling that again. He pulled off his heavy gloves, slipped on latex examining substitutes, and knelt on the grimy floor near the closest body. "This is Reginald all right. Shotgun blast to the chest. Close range from the blood splatter. Took him right out. Lots of attractive Reggie debris everywhere."

"Kind of hard to define that in this place." Ellie professionally skittered the beam from her flashlight over plies of newspapers, a sagging couch, the cold rusted woodstove on bricks in the corner, and a coffee table laden with overflowing ashtrays and the crumpled remnants of fast-food bags. "I'm glad all possible insect life is dead. If it was summer, this place would be crawling. It's filthy."

"I do think their housekeeper could be on vacation." Rick said. "I don't make this guy." The second body was a stranger, young, clean shaven, his cheeks bearing some nasty acne scars, his hair shaved almost to his scalp. He wore an army fatigue jacket, dirty jeans, and socks. His wound was different. If Rick had to guess—but crime scene forensics was not his area of expertise—a nine-millimeter bullet through the left temple. The dead man's glassy eyes stared at the ceiling. "We've got two shooters or two weapons," he commented tersely.

"I see that." Ellie sounded curt, but subdued. "Quite the party. Left a mess."

"I don't think cleaning was high on Reginald's list of priorities," Rick agreed and rose. He looked at the state trooper standing by the door. The guy was shaken, but trying to look confident, as if he stumbled across two dead bodies every day of his life. "Where's the electric company guy who found them?"

"Gone." The patrolman looked sheepish, and his Adam's apple bobbed as he swallowed hard. "I hope that's okay. I got his cell number and the company number, but there are lines down everywhere and they need every man they can get. I took his statement and told him we might want to talk to him again later."

"Let's hear it." Ellie was brusque but not unfriendly, as always.

Except Rick was fairly sure she'd been more than friendly with Grantham. It had been one hell of a shock to find her in her robe and their lead suspect—*only* suspect—having breakfast in her house after having spent the night. Maybe Grantham slept on the couch, but there had been a vibe between them since the beginning, and somehow, he doubted the evening had passed in a platonic way. He wasn't a damn prude . . . hell, far from it, and if Ellie wanted to sleep with someone, he didn't care, but Grantham was just plain and simple a stupid choice and she wasn't at all a stupid woman.

"Lines down across the county road there." The officer pointed east. Through a cracked window, a stand of timber held a ghostly pall of snow. "Maybe a hundred yards or so from this place. The technician stopped by the house to tell the occupants they couldn't drive out that way until a team came to clear the mess . . . some of the lines might be hot even though the power is out to the house itself. The door was open when he came up on the porch. It clued him in something was wrong, since there are two vehicles in the driveway and it's twenty degrees. He peeked in. He saw the bodies and called his dispatch, who called it in to us."

"Not 911?"

"Lines are clogged with calls. This weather suc— Er . . ."—he shot a sidelong look at Ellie and straightened it out—"stinks."

That was probably true about the call delays. Rick

asked, "Any time estimate on the arrival of the coroner?"

"With the roads, sir, hard to say." The young man fidgeted with his notebook.

"Nice." He turned to Ellie. "We have to get word out about Keith. All points on that son of a bitch. It's a cinch call he did this, if you ask me."

She peered out the door, her cheeks pink from the cold. "That must have been his truck here last week. I don't see it. Any idea at least who the friend is?"

"None," Rick admitted grimly, gazing down at the sprawled body. "Like I said, I can't make him. He's a new attractive addition to Lincoln County. He'll look good in the cemetery. Should we start processing the scene? This is going to take hours."

"Maybe we could begin here." Ellie picked up a pair of hemostats with gloved fingers from a rickety gray TV tray that served as an end table. "I'm guessing they haven't been performing a lot of surgery in here."

"Some fishermen use them." Rick glanced into the kitchen and saw nothing but filthy linoleum, dishes in the sink, and an old-fashioned refrigerator with a broken handle. "You can remove fishhooks easier."

"Where are their poles and tackle and why is there a roach in the ashtray next to it?"

"Good point." He gingerly moved around the perimeter of the room. With a double like this, there was going to be a CS team. It was disturbing how he'd never handled a murder before all this started and now he wasn't getting used to it exactly, but he didn't have the frozen-in-the-headlights look of the young trooper either.

"Do you think this has a link back to the serial murders?" Ellie put the hemostats into a plastic bag.

Her face was averted. "You brought up Keith Walters in the first place. Apparently a good call."

"This isn't linked and you know it." Rick had thought so at one time, but not any longer. Neither did she, he could tell. With a fingertip he ruffled a stack of unopened mail sitting on what might have been a dining room table for the occupants before the Walters brothers.

He wasn't all that diplomatic, he never had been, but he made an effort to smooth over the awkward moment. "While I think Keith Walters could be capable of the brutality necessary for the abductions, and certainly for killing these two lowlifes, I doubt he'd ever have the subtlety to put those bones in Grantham's woodpile or save a pair of earrings, much less sneak in and drop them by the tire of the Land Rover."

"I agree." Her voice was quiet, concentrated, as she examined carefully the area around one of the bodies. "So all this means is we have another two unconnected murders to solve."

"Maybe." He'd make bank on it. This one could be drug related, but the missing women didn't have that connection.

"It was too much to hope it would be this easy," Ellie muttered, even her slim form bulky in her parka, a stray strand of blond hair falling forward as she peered under the sofa and grimaced. "They had mice. Didn't they mind?"

"When you're high, you overlook a lot of things," Rick answered, finding a small dusting of something that looked like powdered sugar in the debris on the table. He was pretty sure neither Keith, Reginald, nor the other dead guy used it on their doughnuts. "Look at this. Coke, I'd guess."

She turned, the young state kid's eyes widened, and Rick said matter-of-factly, "If they had a stash, I'm guessing Keith took it with him when he ran for it. The question is, were they running drugs through the county? I never pictured Reginald as the outdoor type and it would explain that shiny new truck Keith drove here from Stevens Point. The last time we were here I wondered how the hell a scumbag like him could afford it. We should have run the VIN. That shitty Ford out there must belong to Reginald, and the car to his friend here. Maybe we can make him from the tags."

"If we find more evidence than a trace of cocaine and something to suggest they might do more than some recreational weed, we can call the DEA. In the meantime, it's going to take forever to get the team here," she responded, as cool as ever, professional and collected. "Let's start processing the scene."

Bryce put down the book he'd picked up, too edgy to read any longer, even if it was *For Whom the Bell Tolls*. Apparently Ellie was a Hemingway fan, for she had every volume the man had written.

Cabin fever, he wondered. Maybe this was what it felt like. In someone else's house, no vehicle, no electricity except for the basics provided by the generator, his phone still useless, and no way of knowing exactly what was going on out there in the real world except for the local radio station that only wanted to cover the weather.

That he knew about. The house had nice windows with a panoramic view of the woods. As the day wore on, the temperature rose, and the ice-covered trees had begun to drip as did the eaves, in a soft, soporific sound. The clouds had thinned too, so the sky was a hazy steel color and the forecaster kept promising there might even be a peek of sun later in the day, but it was already four o'clock so that seemed doubtful.

At least he'd thought to take a minute and stuff his shaving kit and a change of clothes into his duffel bag when Ellie had told him about the tree. He'd expected to be sequestered yet again in a sterile motel room. It had passed the time to shower, put on clean jeans and a pullover sweater, make the bed, clean up their half-eaten breakfast, put more wood on the fire . . . but not enough time. The night before had left him exhilarated—and restless.

No scenario could be a worse way to start a relationship. If that was even the way to define what had happened between him and Ellie MacIntosh. Maybe it was just one night of consensual sex, shared between two people who were attracted to each other . . .

The sudden ring of his cell phone made him start. He'd left it on the counter and he jumped up to answer it, as if he hadn't spoken to a real person in days, instead of just hours.

He glanced at the number and a now familiar trepidation settled over him. "Alan."

"Good, I've got you," his friend said in his no-nonsense attorney voice. "I was beginning to worry you were in jail and because of the storm, you couldn't call me. I've been trying most of the day."

That didn't sound promising. Bryce sat down on one of the stools abruptly. "Service has been out but, no, I'm not in jail, and what's so urgent?"

"I wanted to let you know the story broke this morning here. Quite frankly, I'm surprised it hasn't before this."

Great. Bryce rubbed his forehead, glad he'd taken the time to call his parents and warn them. "Maybe you'd better tell me exactly what's going on."

"Let me read you the headline from this morning's paper."

"Okay."

"'*Psychic or Psycho? Local Man Leads Police to the Bodies of Three Murdered Women in a Bizarre Twist to the Recent Lincoln County Disappearances.*'"

Maybe not worse than what he'd imagined, but the implication was pretty bad, just the same. "You might have said brace yourself," Bryce muttered.

"Look, you've turned up two bodies and are implicated in another disappearance. What did you expect? Actually, something just like this is my guess, or you wouldn't have called me. The gist of the article is a rundown of your background, your connection with the area, a few oblique references to the police taking a close look at you as a possible suspect that we can't sue them over, and then a lot of bleeding heart references to the families of the victims."

Vaguely sick, Bryce closed his eyes, took a deep breath and exhaled. There went his career, his *life*.

"It's on the front page." Alan's voice sounded polished, urbane, and detached in a typical lawyerly manner Bryce recognized all too well from those years with Suzanne. "If the national news networks don't pick this up, I will be surprised, so I thought I should warn you."

"Thanks," he said ironically.

"I thought you were coming back here."

"A serial killer and a fallen tree got in the way."

Alan was silent for a moment. "Care to explain?"

He outlined briefly the afternoon before, leaving out how he'd spent the night in Ellie's bed. As far as he was concerned, that was no one's business but theirs.

"That sounds like a complication."

Complication? That was a simplistic way to put it. "Tell me about it."

"Where are you now?"

"Staying with a friend."

"I'm going to have to think about this." Alan sounded thoughtful, his words measured. "The killer has obviously taken an interest in you. Maybe you can help the police. Talk to them. Be cooperative."

Testily, Bryce said, "I've been so cooperative they've searched my parents' property, confiscated my laptop, and now someone is vandalizing my car and planting evidence. It doesn't seem to be getting me anywhere. If I remember correctly, you told me not to talk to them."

"I've changed my mind. Besides, they have nothing at all. Proof positive is that you aren't in jail."

"That's because I haven't done anything wrong," Bryce told him, his knuckles whitening as he clutched his cell too tight.

"If you think that's how it works, my friend, think again," Alan said succinctly. "If it did, I'd be out of a job. Keep me informed."

Chapter 23

The first time he'd kept her forever.

Well, perhaps that was an exaggeration, but he'd carefully kept her hidden, just for him. He'd thought about her every morning when he woke, when he was making a sandwich at lunch, when he brushed his teeth . . .

And then he started to forget. It scared him frankly, because the Hunter was so tuned to death, he knew it very well.

So he'd replaced her with a new memory. It had worked too, for months, and he'd visited the new shrine until he'd grown restive and knew she wasn't enough.

It wasn't as if he didn't realize each time made it more dangerous. He did. But he couldn't help it, or maybe didn't want to help it—the semantics didn't matter so much as to why, but they did as to effect.

There was a leak in the roof. He could hear the steady drip on the floor and he took out a cigarette and lit it, sitting back sprawled in an old rocker and listening to the soothing sound.

Inhaled deeply. Blew the smoke out slowly.

He had patience. All good predators did.

Then finally, two more nonfilters later, he heard something else besides the rhythm of melting snow and the creak of his chair. What he'd been waiting for: that beautiful, beautiful sound.

The first terrified whimper.

"The scene was too deteriorated by the melt off." Pearson toyed with his glasses, taking them on and off twice. Since he'd quit smoking he was so fidgety that they had all considered telling him to just go back to it. "They were able to follow some indentations that were tracks to the road through the woods, but then again, anyone could have walked out there. It could have been Grantham himself."

Sitting at her desk, Ellie rubbed her temples to try and ward off the onset of a throbbing headache. It all came back to Bryce each time, as it had from the beginning. Of all the times for the unpredictable weather to do a fickle upturn, this had to be it. "Any sign of a vehicle parked along the road where the tracks came out of the woods?"

"All kinds of signs." The sheriff put his glasses on again and pushed them up his nose with a forefinger. "Several of the deputies pulled off in that location. How could they know? We had no perimeter designation on this, Detective. A plow had been by anyway, so the point is moot. We wouldn't have found anything."

He was probably right and it was a miracle he'd found personnel to go out there at all. "The earrings?" she asked.

"They were there all right, by the back rear tire, which was flat, just like Grantham said."

"And for all we know he did it himself." Rick had kept his mouth shut fairly well so far about finding Bryce in her house, but the silence between them to and from the Walters crime scene had been tense. "Have you told her yet about the call we got this afternoon?"

Her head swiveled as she glanced from one of them to the other. Pearson said heavily, "Apparently Grantham was in the tavern, asking about the patrons the night Melissa Simmons disappeared. Wanting to know who might have seen them together. The owner recognized him from the picture in the paper. Said he was acting a little weird."

"Weird how?" This wasn't exactly welcome news and Ellie had no idea what to make of it. "Are we talking about Gravelly, who has a record? Who might very well smoke the same brand cigarette as our killer?"

"Grantham asked if all the other people in the bar were locals."

"How is that weird?"

"I'm just quoting Tom Gravelly."

Phones were still ringing all around them, making it difficult to hold a conversation. The aftermath of the storm held on, like a bad cold. Ellie said moderately, "If someone followed him when he took Melissa Simmons home, it makes sense they might have been in the bar. It isn't a bad line of questioning. We've been in there ourselves. Dr. Grantham"—she deliberately kept it as professional as possible—"isn't stupid. I'm sure once he figured out he was our number-one suspect, he thought it might be a good idea to look around a little himself."

Pearson glanced at his watch. "There's a meeting in an hour in my office. Lieutenant McConnell from DCI is now officially in charge of the task force and these cases."

Ellie had worked with McConnell before on a homicide case involving a child abduction by the guilty spouse and he was not just professional but intuitive. She had no problem at all with him running the task force as long as she was still on it.

"He taking care of the Walters case too, sir?" she asked.

Pearson's face was haggard with lack of sleep. "Depends if the two are connected. The Walters case looks drug related from the report I read. Any word on Keith Walters?"

"Everybody's looking for him," Rick said, drinking what was probably stale coffee, his short, fair hair sticking up because he'd taken off his hat. "He didn't register his truck, and he didn't buy it under his own name. We don't have a plate number or a VIN. Just the description."

"If he even bought it," Pearson said in disgust. "For all we know it's stolen."

"We should have checked it when we were out there the first time," Ellie admitted. "But we were investigating a possible murder, not car theft. We were trying to get a feel for Walters and his alibi for Margaret Wilson's disappearance."

We fucked up. She and Rick exchanged a glance. It didn't have plates. They should have insisted on the registration.

"The problem is, we're not used to this," Pearson said heavily. "There's homicide, and then there's something out of control like our killer. For one thing, we don't have the manpower. As it is, Ellie is spending all her hours on this damn case, so I'm short a detective, and we have other problems. Investigating the disappearances is a lot different than investigating four serial homicides, but I've pushed to keep you both in on this because of the time you've put in until now. We have this nut job now bringing us evidence. Let's make sure we use it. Thanks to Grantham, one way or the other, we have those earrings and they mean something. Find out what it is."

One way or the other. Ellie kept her mouth shut but it took some effort.

The sheriff went on. "This county has only one decent-size town and pretty much everything else is unincorporated villages and rural housing. Lots of trees, lots of lakes, and our killer is moving around out there. We need to catch him fast and you two know the terrain."

"Sir—" Rick started to say, his face set.

Pearson held up a hand impatiently. "The jewelry is in evidence right now. I'd say take pictures of it and contact the families of the women who are still missing. Let me know what you find out. In the meantime, let's stick a deputy on Grantham. No matter how you swing it, he's in the thick of this. Either he's dangerous, or he's in danger."

Stick a deputy on . . . Ellie felt her face heat.

"I think you can find a volunteer for that duty," Rick muttered, not quite under his breath.

"Hey, Rick." One of the deputies came into the room, his face showing the same strain they probably all felt. "I thought you might need to see this. We're getting a list of the stranded vehicles as they are reported. Just routine, but . . . well, here." He extended a piece of paper. "I recognized the name. They found it out on county road B."

Rick took the report, scanned down it, and lifted his head, lines suddenly by his mouth. "Jane's car? She's at the hospital."

"Call her," Ellie said immediately, because she *felt* it. The surge of unwelcome unease, the sickening twist in her stomach. "Call the hospital. If she went off the road, no doubt someone gave her a ride. There's a whole list of stranded cars."

"She was at work when this started," Rick said. "It doesn't make sense—"

"Then she's at home," Pearson interjected, but his fingers, which had been endlessly toying with the button on his shirt, began to work overtime. "*Call* her."

Rick's hand was visibly unsteady as he whipped out his cell and began punching buttons.

No answer. All four of them waited, taut, worried. The deputy was young, and looked vaguely guilty, as if he was responsible because he'd brought the news.

"Call the house."

"Motherfucker—"

"Call the house." Pearson said it in staccato tones.

Rick did, his knuckles white as he clenched his phone.

Ellie picked up the phone on her desk, and punched in the number to the hospital. Calmly as possible, she asked for the surgical floor, and when the nurse's station picked up, for Jane.

Jane Cummins, she was informed, had left the day before, around one o'clock when it was starting to get really bad. Their patient load was light, said the unconcerned staff nurse, and since she was scheduled to be off the next day, the shift supervisor had let her duck out a couple of hours early because of the storm so she wouldn't be stuck there.

In the fluorescent lighting, Rick had gone from ruddy to a dull gray. "She wasn't at home last night. She wasn't at home. *Goddammit,* she never came home."

The repetitive monologue didn't make anyone feel better. Ellie swallowed a lump that had suddenly risen in her throat and said evenly, "Parents? Friends? If she slid off the road, she would have called someone."

"Me. She would have called *me.*" Rick's voice sounded harsh and abrasive.

"Cell towers were down," Ellie argued, her mind rejecting the possibility something was actually wrong beyond the ice and snow dumped all over northern Wisconsin. "I had no signal at my house."

It was as if she hadn't spoken. "I went home, I *slept,*" he said, as if it was a crime. The office had gone quiet, and Ellie could hear him breathing in raspy bursts.

"We don't know she's missing," she insisted.

But she had a dismal feeling that was untrue, and from the sheriff's expression, he agreed.

Bryce found a package of ground chuck in the freezer, thawed it in the microwave since the power had come on around four o'clock, and tossed it into a pot with a little olive oil. He chopped an onion and some garlic while he browned the meat, stirred it all together with some tomato sauce he'd come across in the pantry, and liberally added spices. Ellie didn't have any spaghetti noodles but he did find some penne and Parmesan cheese—the real stuff, not the shaker—and she had romaine, so he could improvise a salad.

Simple, but then again he wasn't a superstar cook, just adequate, yet after a long day, maybe she'd appreciate something hot to eat.

If she came home at all.

By seven, he was starting to think maybe it wouldn't happen and his level of disappointment told him a great deal about how he felt about the night before. When he met Suzanne he'd been at first attracted, then infatuated, and then embarked on a journey he'd told himself in retrospect he knew was a lapse in judgment fueled by a lot of factors, not the least of which was the timing. It sounded inane, but he'd been almost thirty, and his friends had been getting married, having children, and it seemed like the timing was right. He should have asked himself one crucial question; opposites may attract, but how often do they solidify into the cement of a true relationship?

Older now. Wiser, right? Maybe not. Here he was, stirring spaghetti sauce on the stove of a woman he knew only because of a murder investigation . . .

His emotional reflexes did not appear to be any more honed now that he was supposedly older and wiser, he thought wryly.

The hands on the clock crawled to eight. Ellie didn't call, didn't return.

He was tempted to try her cell phone, but didn't. It wasn't as if he had any right to ask her when she'd be home, and the excuse of all time for being late had to be investigating a double homicide. Any homicide investigation was not in the realm of his experience.

And thank God for that, he thought as he drained the pasta and set about making two plates finally, hoping she'd walk through the door at any moment. Penne, sauce, grated cheese, a little salad with vinaigrette on the side. He sat at the kitchen bar, since her dining room table was covered with papers, and ate his dinner methodically.

Walters. He didn't recognize the name, but obviously Ellie had.

None of the four women missing had that last name, he knew that much from the papers.

The sound of a car door was his first clue she might be home after—a glance at his watch told him—eleven hours. It was pitch dark now and had been for some time, but maybe that long of a day for her was normal. He had to admit he didn't know the ins and outs of a detective's schedule.

Unfortunately, he was starting to be more clued in all the time.

Ellie's face was drawn into lines and angles; creases in the forehead, along the jaw, her mouth tight. She came in the door, but didn't discard her scarf or gloves, just gave a cursory scrape of her boots on the mat, and then lifted her head. "I don't know what to say to you."

Whatever he expected, it wasn't that curt statement. Bryce hesitated, silent, not sure what it was he saw in her eyes. A hollowness, a grim resignation that cut through him like a razor.

Another car had pulled in, the swinging arc of the lights visible against the kitchen curtains.

What the hell *now*?

"While we wait for a judge to grant us—and he will—a search warrant for your car and the cabin, we'd like you to come in for questioning."

"You already searched the cabin." He made a helpless gesture with his hand. "Jesus, Ellie."

Too evenly, she said, "That was two days ago. We need to go over it again."

"Why?" he asked flatly, arms at his sides.

"You can ride with me, or with the two deputies outside. Your choice."

Bryce just stared at her. There were dark circles under her eyes and her shoulders drooped. He well remembered how her slender body had fitted to his, how they'd intimately moved together in perfect communion, how her lips parted and her eyes squeezed shut when she climaxed and breathed his name in his ear . . .

More important, how she'd slept trustingly against him, warm and vulnerable in the night.

"What's happened?" His voice was hoarse.

"I'm sorry." Her voice dropped. "This isn't my call."

"You won't tell me?"

"No."

"Because I'm a suspect?

"Yes."

"How nice to be upgraded from . . . what was it, person of interest? I'd love to know what I was supposed to have done sitting here stranded in your house all day, most of it without electricity."

"Trust me, you still had a better day than I did." She briefly closed her eyes as if the memory of the past hours could be erased that way.

Bryce had a healthy aversion to the idea of a police station and that had steadily grown since the moment he'd decided a week or two of north woods solitude might clear his mind. The solidification of the nightmare was an unwelcome development, and call him a coward, but the idea of a jail cell made him turn clammy from head to toe. "Am I under arrest?"

"Not yet." She turned away, remote, her voice tired. There was a glassy look to her eyes that might have been tears. "It's pretty cold outside. Get your coat."

He took it from the rack by the glass panel framing the front door, apprehension and anger bubbling through his nerve endings like fizz from soda water. There was no way he could resist saying, "I made you dinner. It's covered and in the refrigerator."

The look she gave him said that was a cheap shot, and it had been, but then again, she wasn't the one being hauled off to the police station either. Her response was low, so quiet he almost couldn't hear it. "I've already told you this isn't how I'd play it, but I'm not in charge, the sheriff is, at least for now. This is getting worse, Bryce. It's so . . . awful."

The way her voice cracked and from the look on her face, he decided grimly, it was, but he'd also figured out she wasn't going to tell him just how awful. He zipped up his coat. "I have no idea what on earth I can tell you I haven't already, but let's get this over with."

Chapter 24

They'd have evidence for the first time.

From a nosebleed. Fuck.

Simple enough, but it had never happened before and it had been too late to back out, to decide the kill wasn't worth the risk.

Sometimes things go wrong, he reminded himself. Like the time he was crossing Deer Creek and somehow his foot went through the ice, which should have been thick as his forearm. His boot had taken on icy water and he'd had to sit down in the snow and remove it, wring out his sock, which was already turning stiff in the below-zero temps, and then put it all back and head for his truck as fast as possible, his foot feeling prickles like needles stabbing in his flesh the whole way. If he had broken his ankle, or the water had been deeper, he could have been in real trouble.

A small mishap a resourceful man could deal with, if he could stay calm.

November . . . When he'd started to drag her from the car she'd hit him and blood was splashed in crimson splotches in the snow and on the driver seat . . .

Bitch.

They'd find the blood, and the car, and she'd be missing, and they'd look for her.

For him.

Not that it frightened him. They were always looking for him, searching but not finding as he quietly laughed and went about his life.

Still, he thought as he turned off the light and went up the stairs, he wished they didn't have the blood.

The cold, filtered light from a dismal sky didn't do anyone favors and Ellie had the feeling she looked as washed out as a bleached bit of driftwood. She hadn't slept now for twenty-two hours and her eyelids were gritty each time she blinked.

If Jane wasn't the one missing, they might or might not have been up most of the night, but as it was, going home to sleep was out of the question.

"No matter if he's telling the truth or not, it would have been a really tight time frame." McConnell, the DCI lieutenant, drove like he did everything else, competently. He was in his forties probably, but looked older, with a lean face and heavy-lidded eyes.

Ellie nodded, her muscles jerking because of fatigue. She'd stopped by her house to shower and change, but she could swear despite the cold she felt sticky. "Grantham called me at two forty-seven. That means if Jane left her shift at one, it would still take her nearly half an hour to get to where her car was found, and with the weather we were having, maybe longer. That would give him an extremely short amount of time to pull it off."

"Tight." McConnell braked for a light.

"He would have had to walk back to the cabin.

That's four miles from where her car was found. " It was the most damning part. The car was so close and Jane didn't usually take that route. It was out of her way, but then again, roads had been closing all over the place.

"In that shit we had coming down? That might take two hours alone right there."

She agreed, but she had to be honest. "It's still possible though. Maybe she wasn't abducted where we found her car. If he waited for her right outside the hospital that changes everything."

"I suppose our man might have driven it there deliberately into the ditch."

Just close enough to walk. Smart move.

Dammit.

"Maybe. But it would have to be a matter of precision timing." McConnell pulled into the hospital parking lot. "Suppose he *was* waiting, stopped her, abducted her, and drove her car to where we found it?"

It would mean taking a serious chance, but their killer had proved he wasn't above doing just that. "How the hell did he get to the hospital? How did he know when she'd get off work early with the storm?"

"He could have gotten a ride there and waited. People tend to be helpful when the weather is going south."

"That doesn't answer my last question."

"Detective, you are assuming he was targeting one specific victim. I'm going more with the assumption he was just waiting for the opportunity. Hospitals have lots of nurses and most are female."

"What I don't buy is that someone who has kept us guessing for long would leave so much to chance."

"Just because we haven't caught him yet, doesn't mean he isn't capable of mistakes."

"Rick thinks this is a deliberate strike back at him. But I don't agree. How would Grantham even know he had a girlfriend, or who she was, where she works?" She didn't buy it, but was trying to stay as unbiased as possible. If word got out she and Bryce had a personal relationship of any kind, she'd get booted right off the case. And she was much too invested to allow that to happen. Professionally and on an emotional level too. She was good at her job . . . good enough to catch whoever was doing this. Maybe someday she might think about federal law enforcement again. It had occurred to her. She liked the chase, the challenge, and she especially liked it when she won.

However, at this moment, she wasn't happy with any aspect of this case. They weren't winning, they were losing. Big time.

McConnell took a moment. "No one has had our suspect under constant surveillance. It's difficult to draw conclusions over what he might or might not know."

Ellie took a moment and drew a measured breath. "The tree was down a good hour before Grantham called me. I saw it. Must have been. It was covered in ice an inch thick on the horizontal surface of the trunk and there had to be enough weight to bring it down in the first place. The crime scene techs also say they don't think his car was moved after it started to snow the night before despite the melt they encountered when they finally got there. He didn't drive back. If we are postulating with him as the suspect, he would have had to be on foot. Then what did he do with the body? Jane isn't a small woman." McConnell berthed the car in an empty spot a good distance from the front doors of the hospital. The plows had been at work and piles of snow defined the space, but it was supposed to get in the forties later and there was already opaque slush at the edges and watery puddles.

"I have no idea. We have the blood to go on anyway and let's just hope it isn't hers." He opened his door and slid out. In the gray morning light, his leathery skin looked drawn. "Let's find out what's going on."

The lobby was moderately busy, and the minute Ellie said who they were, the reception desk directed them upstairs, the older woman in charge nodding after a sharp-edged glance at their identification.

In small towns and a small county, news traveled fast. They took the elevator, not speaking, and followed the signs to the surgical floor. There were two nurses behind the high desk, both tapping away on computers, and they glanced up as Ellie and her companion fished out their badges again and explained why they were there.

One of them checked the log, and nodded. "I'll get Lori and Stephanie. They were both working Jane's shift." Subdued, she got up, the other nurse no longer typing but bowing her head and brushing the back of her hand furtively across one cheek.

Ellie didn't blame her. She felt a little like sitting down and crying herself. Pearson had driven Rick home, ignoring the protest Rick could be on the job; that he *needed* to be on the job, and this morning at first light, search parties had started to fan out from the location of Jane's abandoned car.

There was more too. Forensics was working on those damned bloodstains on the cloth seat. They'd swabbed Bryce for his DNA, but that wasn't a fast test, and Ellie didn't want to think about his state of humiliation over having to allow it.

Stephanie came around the desk, her blond hair drawn into a ponytail, and if she wore makeup it had long ago worn off. After all the extra hours the smudges under her eyes were distinct, and she sat heavily in a chair and looked defeated and tired, her pink scrubs rumpled. "Jane said she wasn't interested in the overtime. We had next shift nurses coming in who knew in a few hours they wouldn't be able to get here, so she volunteered to leave early."

Ellie sat in a chair across the low desk and nodded. "What else did she say?"

Stephanie fiddled with the file in front of her, bending the edges. "I don't really remember. We were all running around."

McConnell leaned a hip on the desk and imitated a sympathetic cop, but he only came off as a top brass DCI in his suit and tie and polished shoes. "She was going right home then?"

"As far as I know."

Lori finally arrived, pushing a cart, her expression also strained and her shoulders slumped. She was older, also visibly tired, and had wispy hair pushed back by a white band. "She told me they were out of milk. It's ridiculous. A little weather moves in and everyone raids the grocery stores, acting like we're going to be snowed in for weeks. Jane mentioned to me she was going to stop for milk and a few other things."

Ellie exchanged a look with McConnell. Margaret Wilson was also out running errands when she disappeared. If she wasn't so sick at heart, she might be elated at that small connection. "Did she say where she was going?"

"No. She just said on the way home."

McConnell asked a few more questions that yielded nothing and they left.

There was something positive in living in this remote part of the country. That limited the choices. "The grocery in Merrill, or else Hathaway's," Ellie said as they exited the building. "Those were on her way home. Unless she stopped at a gas station."

"At least it won't take forever to do the interviews." McConnell unlocked the doors, his face set in grim lines. "We've only got a handful of possibilities. From what I understand everything shut down early as the ice came in. As far as investigation goes, this should be easy."

"There were no groceries in her car." Ellie got in and slammed the door. There was a two-foot pile of snow tinged with dirt in front of the car from the plows. "Just her purse. It was clean. No prints but hers and Rick's."

She pictured Jane laughing and spooning out Chinese food not even a week ago. "Except for the blood," she said out loud in a bleak voice.

The house was cold, quiet, desolate. Rick sat at the table, in his underwear, deliberately torturing himself. Normally he would wear sweats at least, and switch on the television, maybe eat something he shouldn't. Jane would complain about it too. Point out that if a hot dog had 170 calories in it, 140 of them were from fat and it was an unhealthy ratio.

Not one bit as bad as running into the wrong person who might, who had . . .

Oh shit.

He wanted to cry. No, he wanted to weep. Put his

head down and sob, because he knew . . . he knew, she couldn't be missing for this long without calling him. Her purse and cell phone had been in the car, and there was blood.

As a police officer, he was worried. As a man, he was . . . terrified.

He'd been relieved of duty and sent home. Not that Pearson was wrong, because quite frankly, Rick knew his mind had started to come to a grinding stop the minute he'd heard about her stranded car.

It was useless, superfluous, but now he wondered why he hadn't ever asked Jane to marry him. Scared, he'd guess. His first marriage had ended up such a disaster. He ignored the chill eddy as the furnace kicked on, the first blast of air never all that warm.

What he needed was to be reflective about this, to be analytical and calm, to view all the evidence with dispassionate dissection.

What he wanted was something else altogether.

Putting his fist into someone's face was one of the most tempting options, satisfying a primal urge, if nothing else. Blood, broken teeth . . . they all held a particular primitive appeal that wouldn't help Jane.

Because he had the awful singular preknowledge that sometimes happened when investigating a crime that told him unequivocally that though the crime might someday be solved, as desperately as the loved ones of the victim might want to think it was not the ugly, unacceptable truth, justice might be the only benefit of the investigation.

His cell phone migrated across the table as it vibrated. He eyed it with disinterest. It wasn't Jane's ring but he recognized it. Finally he flipped it open with weary resignation. "Jones."

"Rick." It wasn't as possible to sound as tired as he felt, but Ellie came close. "You holding up?"

"No." The truth might be unwelcome, but he was beyond the point to conjure up any kind of a lie, much less a good one.

"She left the hospital around one. After the snow, but before the ice. Were you out of milk?"

How the fuck would he know? Jane drank it, but he didn't. "I'm . . . I'm not sure."

Gently, Ellie urged, "Go look, okay?"

That meant hauling himself from his chair and three steps across the room. The energy required was too damned much.

"It won't do you any good to just sit there," she said in a very soft tone. "Look in the refrigerator. If there is no milk, the answer is yes."

"Why is it important?" He couldn't process like he should—he knew it. Shock, most probably, but oddly enough, it left him numb enough the panic was gone. It worked. He didn't want to think about it, about her, about the quiet house and her bathrobe hanging on the hook of the bathroom door . . .

"It might be important, it might not, Rick. Look, will you?"

"Where the hell is Grantham?"

"Don't worry about that right now. Just tell me if you think Jane might have stopped off somewhere to buy some groceries."

Swearing, he got up and padded, half naked and barefoot, to the refrigerator. They were out of eggs and milk, he saw, standing there, shivering. "Yes."

"Thanks." A pause. "I'll be by in a few hours. Give you an update. Get some sleep, will you?"

He just hung up. Maybe someday he could care about food, or sleep, or even being moderately polite, but for right now, he just . . . didn't.

Didn't care about anything.

It was the weirdest feeling.

The room smelled faintly sterile, like disinfectant and something unidentifiable that should be bottled and labeled "Motel" but then again, no one would want to buy it.

The questioning hadn't really been the bad part, Bryce thought, lying on the bed and staring at the television, the picture just a blur of color. Long and tiring, yes, but he'd answered the interrogation, stuck by his story, and then they had let him go.

So to speak. He'd ended up at one of the local motels because there was still that huge tree down across the lane to the cabin, and as far as he knew, the Land Rover still had a flat tire. Just because the local sheriff's department didn't have enough to hold him meant very little in the middle of the night when it was impossible to rent a car. One of the deputies had obligingly driven him to the motel at his request, where he'd lain sleepless for most of the night—*that* was beginning to become an unwanted habit. The couple of hours of drifting in and out of consciousness left him lethargic and disoriented.

The cell phone lay on the mattress next to him. He was tempted to call Ellie . . . God, *more* than tempted, but wasn't sure what to say. There was someone else missing, he'd figured that out easily enough from the questions they'd asked him, and he was probably the last person on earth she'd give the details to.

Mozart's Night Music belted out suddenly, making him jump. Bryce flipped the phone open and debated whether or not to answer the call.

What did Suzanne want anyway?

He blew out a breath. Did he need this now? But she never did anything without a reason, and he sure didn't have anything else to do, so why not answer it?

"Hello."

"Hi, honey."

Honey? He hadn't been honey for about two years, one year of which he had still been married to her. "What do you want, Suzanne?"

"It's all over the news."

"I know. Alan called me."

"He told me you'd retained him. Are you really in trouble or is what we're seeing journalistic sensationalism?"

He sighed and rubbed a jaw liberally graced with stubble. What the hell was he watching? A cartoon mouse and cat bounced across the screen. He was tempted to turn the volume up rather than talk to his ex-wife. "I don't think I'm so much a suspect as just an unwilling participant, but you'd have to ask the police if you want to know what they're thinking. They sure aren't telling me."

Her voice was dry. "I'm not your counsel. I doubt they'd tell me either."

"Then what exactly is the point of this conversation? Your last foray into wifely concern was slapping me with a restraining order." He adjusted his position on the bed, restive, wishing he hadn't answered, wishing he didn't react to the sound of her voice. Once, he'd loved her, but that was dead, gone, blown to dust, but there were enough memories left he really didn't need this. Not *now*.

"Did you really find four bodies?"

Four?

"No," he was able to say honestly, wondering where the fourth one had come from. One body, one incomplete set of bones, a shoe, and the earrings. It was bad enough. "That's an exaggeration."

"What's true and what isn't?"

"What are you, a reporter?"

That got her. He knew it would. "Don't be an ass," Suzanne said heatedly. "I'm worried about you, that's all."

"You didn't worry about me when we were married, why start now?" He gently pushed the end button.

The ceiling looked exactly as it had a few minutes before. He clasped his hands behind his head and stared at it.

What he really wanted was to talk to Ellie.

Chapter 25

He went about his business, because he always did. Unobtrusive and smiling.

But he thought about her. The entire time.

He'd tied her hands. And then her feet. He didn't want to necessarily, but there were no chances that could be taken and he was methodical by nature. He'd explained, but she hadn't listened . . . none of them did. She had struggled and didn't seem to understand it was . . . over.

The hunt was complete and she belonged to him.

The grocery turned up nothing except two overworked clerks, wet floors as the tracked in snow started to melt, and one freezer that had disobediently not come back on with the power. The manager was harried and covered in melted ice cream and had given them permission to question anyone they wanted.

Ellie had refrained from pointing out they would have done that regardless. No one remembered Jane coming in that day.

Two convenience gas stations were about as helpful, but the local store in Carney was a little more productive.

"Bad storm." Russell Hathaway, gray-haired and efficient, moved behind the counter, nodding at a passing customer. "Hello, Bobby."

"Hey, Russell." The man wandered down an aisle. The place smelled like an old-fashioned store; aged wood with a hint of freezer burn.

Ellie produced the picture of Jane she'd rummaged around for and found in Rick's house. He'd been no use whatsoever, just sank into a chair and held his head in his hands.

Her worst fear . . .

Jane had wanted a gun. He'd told her no, just get some pepper spray.

And the sight of his gray face had made Ellie wince inwardly because she'd never interviewed a victim's family that didn't ask that question. *What could I have done differently to prevent this?*

She pushed the photo across the counter. "Was this woman by chance here day before yesterday when the bad weather came in?"

Hathaway peered at the photograph, put on the glasses hanging around his neck by a chain, and looked at it again. "I've seen her."

"Day before yesterday?"

He shook his head. "No, but I can tell you she shops here now and then. Neil ran the store that day. We closed early. Good thing, since the power went out. Besides, we ran out of the staples everyone rushes out to buy."

"Can we talk to Neil?" McConnell asked, bland in his suit, which was decidedly out of place.

"He's at the back."

"Thanks." Ellie followed the nod of the older man's head and walked down an aisle lined with boxes of cereal on one side and assorted cans of juice, coffee, and teas. Neil proved to be young, bulky, and energetic, at the moment reloading the deli case with bratwurst and hamburger. He wore a navy blue shirt, an apron, and faded blue jeans, his fair hair cut short, and his eyes were a light ice blue that contrasted with his bronzed skin.

"Neil?"

"Yeah?" He straightened with a good-natured smile.

"I'm Detective MacIntosh and this is Lieutenant McConnell. Can we talk to you for a moment?"

The smile vanished. "Sure," he said uneasily, which was a pretty typical reaction. When she held out the picture, he stripped off a latex glove and took it, frowning. She said, "Was she in here day before yesterday?"

"Day before yesterday?" he repeated.

Ellie nodded. "Right before the storm closed everything down."

The young man looked up, his broad face creasing in dismay. "Is she the one missing?"

"We have reason to believe she might have stopped here. Did she?" Ellie asked, deliberately not answering though she knew the rumors about another disappearance had spread all over the place, like lit gasoline on a dry pile of brush.

He licked his lips, and his hand trembled just a fraction as he handed back the picture. "Yeah. I remember pretty well. She was the last customer. The power had just gone out. I was getting ready to lock up. We have generators though, for the meat freezers, and I had to get that going. She came rushing in. Wanted a few things."

This is probably the last person to see Jane before she disappeared.

Well, second to last. A chilling realization. The murderer would be the last one . . .

"She alone?" McConnell had taken a pad out and was jotting down notes.

"Yes." Neil dragged his hand across his face. "No . . . I don't know. There was a man in here too. He followed her in, but didn't buy anything. I didn't see him leave. I checked her out and was going to lock up because I didn't want to get trapped here either by the ice, and I looked around for him, but he'd obviously left. They might have been together, but I don't think so. They spoke, but I didn't hear it. It might have just been a hello or something."

At last, not just a lead, but maybe a *sighting* of the killer. Ellie said tersely, "Can you describe him?"

Neil leaned on the meat case, his eyes wide. "Is it important? Christ, do you think—"

"What did he look like, sir?" McConnell interrupted, polite but firm.

"I . . . I don't know," the young man stammered.

"Do your best," Ellie urged, a flare of excitement igniting in the pit of her stomach. *An eyewitness . . . if they had an eyewitness*

"Just relax, think back. Was he wearing a cap? What color was his coat? Could you determine his race?"

"Let me think." His face creased in concentration. "Definitely Caucasian. No hat. I remember I thought that was crazy because it was sleeting pretty good by then. Dark hair, tall, dressed nice . . . expensive leather jacket, which was also crazy in that weather. I don't mean this to sound queer or anything, but he was a good-looking guy, you know?"

The excitement turned into a stab of nausea as Ellie's stomach seemed to flip upside down and muscles turned to knots. A clammy flush prickled across her skin.

No, God, no. She'd trusted her instincts. All good cops did.

This time, had she been wrong? And not just a little wrong, when she thought about the other night. Was it possible she'd *slept* with a murderer? Her hands were shaking and she shoved them deep into her pockets.

McConnell, who hadn't met Bryce, just noted the description. "Anything else we could use to ID the man who was in here but disappeared? A distinguishing mark? Color of his eyes?"

"Hey, I didn't look that close." Neil rattled the tray cart of bratwurst toward the case. "I was anxious to get out of here. When I left it was just a few minutes later and the parking lot was empty."

"Thanks for your help," Ellie managed to say and she woodenly followed McConnell out to the car, but her knees felt weak.

He didn't notice until they slid into their seats, then his eyes narrowed. "You okay? You've gone dead pale."

Deep breath. Steady. Whatever happened next, she needed to do her job. "I think we may have him, Eric. He wasn't wearing a leather jacket when I picked him up, but I know he has one."

Tall. Dark-haired. Leather jacket. Another missing woman.

It just . . . fit.

"Who has one?"

In a tired voice, she went on. "The description fits Bryce Grantham right down to the leather jacket. There was blood in her car. If the search of his cabin and car turns up the jacket and there's a trace of her blood on it, he's done. It's pretty difficult to move someone who is bleeding and not get some of it on you."

"If it *doesn't* turn up the jacket, that also gives us some solid circumstantial evidence," McConnell pointed out, swinging the car back onto the slushy county road. "From what I understand, he's no idiot; far from it. If he walked back from where we found her car, he wouldn't have any time to dispose of anything except to dump it. If he did, we'll find it."

The fatigue was shutting her down. Ellie could feel it thrumming through her veins with each sluggish beat of her heart. She rested her head on the back of the seat and watched the road wind in front of them. "I agree. He might have tossed it in the woods somewhere."

No. She didn't believe it.

No.

"It's an easier search with a defined area and we have teams out there now, looking for Cummins. We have a starting point and an ending. Son of a bitch," McConnell said with a smile, "I think you're right. I think you've got him. He must have shit when he got back to the cabin, changed clothes, and went to leave and found he couldn't. Fast thinking on his part. Then he realized that he needed to alibi himself as fast as possible, so he flattens the tire, produces the earrings, and calls you."

"Maybe." She was too exhausted to think straight anymore, her body slumped in the seat. "Why did

Jane stop? If it was Grantham, how would he manage it? The story has been all over this part of Wisconsin. She lives with Rick, for God's sake, and she was scared enough, according to him, she talked about getting a gun."

With chilling logic, McConnell said, "What better time to get someone to stop than right before a major weather event? Especially a well-dressed, nice-looking guy who might have had car trouble, or gone into the ditch, trudging through the snow on the side of a country road."

"She saw him in the store, McConnell."

"Our friend Neil said he *thought* they spoke to each other."

The words made sense. Horrible sense in a case that made little sense to begin with. Dully, she murmured, "I never sensed it was him. From the beginning, I liked him. Even now, I don't *believe* it. I would stake my life he's a *nice* man."

And she had. She'd spent the night alone with him in a raging storm with closed roads, no power, no available help.

McConnell's profile was defined against the glass, and he didn't smile, his voice somber. "Didn't your mama warn you all men are assholes, Detective MacIntosh?"

"It isn't true," she argued, weariness giving her voice an uncharacteristic throatiness. "I adored my father. Rick Jones is a good guy under his somewhat blustery exterior, and I even like *you*, so don't try to sell me that. If I didn't trust my instincts, I wouldn't be a good police officer, Lieutenant. If you want my take on this, we are putting an innocent man through hell and somewhere out there a killer is laughing at us."

Her companion glanced over. "You sound sure, Detective. How sure are you?"

In the face of Jane's disappearance, she said finally, "I thought it was one hundred percent."

Alan arrived in a suit that had Armani written all over it, his leather briefcase shining, his bland face sporting the usual bonhomie that was belied by the razor-sharp look in his eyes. He set down the briefcase on the plain table and asked pleasantly, "Are you charging my client?"

"Not yet." Pearson, the sheriff Bryce was getting to know despite the fact he wished just the opposite was true, folded and refolded a piece of paper in a methodic rectangle. "We're waiting on several reports back."

"In other words, you have nothing."

"I didn't say that."

"He's finished talking to you until there's a formal charge." Alan turned to Bryce. "Let's go."

"I won't hold him if he doesn't leave the county." Pearson stopped fiddling for a moment and his gaze was steely. "We might have more to talk about, Dr. Grantham."

Bryce stood, waiting for the sheriff to say something more, but there was no objection. Wearing the clothes from the day before made him feel grimy—especially next to Alan's sophisticated elegance—though he hadn't done anything at all except sit around and had taken a long, hot shower at the hotel. He silently followed Alan out of the interrogation room, and down an institutional hallway. They walked past the main desk, and he could feel the stares of the assorted county employees sitting there, the faint ring of a phone the only sound.

At least it was in the forties and sunny, he thought

ironically as they stepped outside in a puddle of melted snow. They'd taken his coat, adding it to a long list of possessions now held by Lincoln County. Car, laptop, clothes . . .

"You know the area," Alan said briskly. "Where can we go and get something decent to eat and talk? It's not a short drive up from Milwaukee and I could use a bite."

Decent by Alan's standards wasn't exactly available. Bryce said, "There's a place with some pretty good food on the edge of town."

Alan drove a sleek dark green Jaguar that he unlocked with a push of a button. "As far as I can tell, the entire town is on the edge of town. That works in your favor. Be happy you aren't dealing with big-city cops who sometimes bend the rules a little, because when you're overworked and underpaid, you tend to cut corners."

"I'll be sure to thank my lucky stars," Bryce muttered darkly when he slid into the leather seat.

His lawyer looked amused. "We'll talk when we get there."

The Antler Inn was a little less romantic in the late afternoon sunshine, or maybe it was that this time Ellie was not his companion. Alan looked askance at the red imitation leather seats, requested a far booth in a corner, and when they were seated, asked the thin blond waitress for two Beck's Darks and menus. She pointed at his place mat and walked away. Bemused, he finally realized what her gesture meant and scanned the offerings. "The half-pound Antler burger with chili fries," he mused, his mouth twitching. "My doctor is going to double my cholesterol medication, isn't he?"

"Probably," Bryce agreed. "Try the walleye."

"Everyone in Wisconsin says that."

"Cheese and great walleye. Not bad things for a state to be known for."

"There's also a plethora of serial killers here for some damn reason. Maybe it's the weather."

Not that Bryce was all that hungry to begin with, but Alan really knew how to do a number on someone's appetite. "I'm not one of them," he said evenly.

The other man's gaze was steady. "If you are, you should tell your lawyer."

Their beers arrived, halting the conversation. The background music was country, and at this hour, not even five o'clock yet, the place had only a few patrons.

"I can give you a better defense with the truth," Alan said after the waitress took their orders, resuming their conversation seamlessly, his fingers smoothing the label of his bottle of beer.

"You'd defend a serial killer? Excuse me if I think that's just plain wrong." The beer was ice cold and good, and Bryce took a second swallow, wondering at the dark side of the justice system.

"Everyone is entitled to due process and a fair trial."

"I'll take your word for it, if you'll take mine that the worst thing I've done in all of this is buy a young woman a drink and then give her a ride home. When I found her cell phone, I compounded my crime by trying to return it. I'm obviously a menace to society."

Alan, incongruous in his expensive suit against the worn wood of the booth, just looked at him for a moment. Then he nodded. "All right. Let's start with Melissa Simmons. Tell me about it as best you can remember. The cardinal rule of successful defense law is to never allow the prosecution to spring an unpleasant surprise on you because your client failed to mention a detail that will potentially convict him in the eyes of a jury." He leaned forward, his expression intent. "Keep in mind you may not recognize that detail, Bryce, but I will. It's why you retained me. So, tell me everything. Start at the beginning."

Everything? He wondered if that included sleeping with Ellie MacIntosh. Probably, but he doubted he was going to offer that up. It couldn't possibly pertain to the case and might just get her in trouble, and though at the moment he felt a bit betrayed, she also had a job to do. Bryce hesitated and then rubbed his eyes. "I'll need another beer."

"That's fine." Alan sat back and smiled. "You're paying, so what the hell?"

Chapter 26

It could be he'd just made his first mistake.

The Hunter didn't count the blood he'd left behind at the scene . . . that wasn't how it worked. There were incidents and there were errors. The blood was an incident, inevitable, out of his control.

The leather jacket was different.

That was definitely an error.

"The forensic evidence is inconclusive."

Ellie had slept three hours. It wasn't enough, but it helped, and she was sipping coffee even now at ten at night, sitting at the bar in her kitchen when the sheriff called. "How inconclusive?"

"The blood in the car isn't hers. Wrong blood type."

She took a minute and processed that. It changed . . . *everything*. "Then all we need is a solid suspect and we have him. Once Bryce is cleared . . ."

Her voice trailed off. She was tired or she never would have said that. Not used his first name. Three hours of sleep was *definitely* not enough.

"Detective, I'm aware of your opinion on Grantham's

possible guilt, but let's make sure we still have an objective approach to the case. If it is his, this is all over."

"Yes, sir."

Pearson went on inexorably. "It doesn't match the blood on Margaret Wilson's clothes either. A third party, and what do you know, we weren't invited to the festivities."

"Maybe not, but this is real progress. Did you find the leather jacket?"

"Yes. It was in Grantham's suitcase."

She stopped in the act of taking a drink, the cup halfway to her mouth. "And?"

"No blood." Pearson sounded defeated. Worn out. "We checked his clothes, his car, the cabin . . . nothing. Even took the heavier parka he was wearing when you picked him up but there doesn't appear to be anything on it."

Thank God. Relief poured over her, strong enough to make her blink and take a solid swallow of coffee. She wanted to catch the killer. There was nothing she wanted more, but . . .

But *this* was good news. Her job was to catch the man terrorizing this part of the state, not to clear Bryce, but if both ends could be achieved at the same timc . . .

"What condition was it in?"

"The jacket? All I asked was for them to call me if it tested positive for blood. There wasn't any. We'll have the written report by tomorrow, though they are complaining about Lincoln County overworking them."

"The jacket should still be wet. If he was out on the icy rain in a leather jacket, it would show it. He didn't have time for it to dry before he called me if he had really followed Jane into that store. Just walking down the driveway the parka he wore was soaked. If he packed his leather one away, it would be at least damp."

"They didn't mention it being wet, but you have a point. Feel free to call and ask for yourself and use my name. I don't have time. I've got a possible fifth victim, my phone beeps every five seconds, and I'm up to my earlobes in media coverage."

"I've sent pictures of the earrings to all the families but we still don't have a definitive link back to any of our victims. I'll check with the forensic lab tomorrow, sir, about the jacket, but it sounds like we still have no physical way to connect Grantham." Statement— not question.

"All right, all right. How solid is the witness testimony?"

She did her best to consider it dispassionately. "He described the man who was seen in the store the same time as Jane fairly clearly, and certainly Grantham fits, but Neil Hathaway wasn't all that close when we asked him for specifics. Unfortunately, we need to keep in mind the newspapers ran a piece on the finding of the bodies. You know how it is. We could get sightings of him all over the place now that his name is out there. Tall and dark-haired doesn't narrow the field to just a few suspects. It would be easy enough to get a description of Grantham if someone tried."

"Neil is your witness?" His voice perceptibly altered.

She set down her cup. The house was very quiet, the windows blank dark oblongs against the night. It smelled like coffee and a hint of oregano from the pasta Bryce had left for her. She'd been too hungry to feel guilty about eating it. "You know him?"

"Not him all that well, but his dad and I went to

high school together. We're in Rotary . . . old friends, though not exactly buddies. When you said a store clerk, I didn't realize you meant Neil. I've looked through too many reports lately."

"Is there a problem?"

"He's gotten in some trouble. After he graduated from high school at the top of his class, he went to UWM for a while, but dropped or flunked out. I don't know what went wrong. He's a bright kid, but likes to be outdoors. For a while he was living in northern Minnesota working for a logging operation, but moved back here a year or two ago."

A year or two ago. That was damned interesting, she thought, interest stirring despite her fatigue. A more specific date was something she'd look into. An image of him pulling off the latex glove came to her mind. That would explain the lack of prints in Jane's car. Carefully, she asked, "What kind of trouble?"

"Russ didn't say, but you can't blame him for that. Not something you advertise."

For the very first time, she had a glimmer of something that wasn't frustration or fear in the case. "Maybe we need to look into Neil Hathaway. Sir, he is admittedly the last person we know of to see her . . . well, to *see* her."

She refused to say "alive." That would assume that Jane was dead, and while it was frightening to think that might be the case, it was never a certainty without the body.

Pearson waited a minute and when he did speak his voice was tight. "Dammit, Ellie. He's the son of a friend."

Her fingers had tightened around the handle of the

cup and she had to consciously relax them before she snapped off the ceramic piece, her mind starting to pick up the pace. "Our killer knows the area really well, sir."

Silence on the other end. Pearson finally said, "Neil's been caught several times by the DNR hunting out of season, trespassing here and there. Got fined each time. Russell keeps an eye on him."

"What does that mean? Keeps an eye on him?"

"I doubt it means anything." Pearson was testy, unhappy. "I just hope if this all goes to trial with Grantham, his high-powered lawyer doesn't tear Neil to shreds as a witness. We need more than what we have."

Ellie swiveled on her stool, propping her feet on the lowest rung. "Well, we don't have it, sir. Not one shred of physical evidence."

"Except Grantham at every single scene where we've discovered anything related to the crimes except the cars."

"Where *he's* discovered anything we have. I'll grant you it's suspicious."

"Do you *think*, Detective?"

She ignored the sarcasm. "But nothing conclusive. Like you said, we need something more. You could arrest him, but there's no way we'd get an indictment and since he doesn't have a record or look like a flight risk, I've no doubt his lawyer would have him out on bail immediately and then what have we accomplished?"

"May I repeat myself and say I hope, Detective MacIntosh, you are keeping an objective view of this case. I pulled Jones off of it because he can't function without prejudice any longer. I'm aware Grantham stayed at your house the night of the storm."

"There wasn't much of a choice." Luckily, over the

phone Pearson couldn't see her face flush. "The circumstances were unusual. I felt safe enough, and look, here I am, still breathing."

"This whole damn thing is unusual and Grantham is too smart to do anything to you."

She'd made that point to Bryce once before. She was also going to have to process what happened between them later—after the case was over. She glossed it over. "I've been trying to get ahold of Rick. He won't answer his cell."

"Maybe he's asleep. He needs it. We all do." Pearson audibly sighed. "Let me know tomorrow anything you dig up, will you? I've a meeting with McConnell first thing in the morning."

"I will."

"Good night, then. Get some sleep. I don't know about you, but I feel like an eighty-year-old man."

"Sir?"

"Yes?"

"Neil Hathaway said he checked Jane out as his last customer right after the power went out."

"And?"

"I can see why we didn't find a receipt in her purse. That old-fashioned cash register doesn't operate on electricity and they use an adding machine next to it instead to print the receipts. It's very possible he waited on her, just like he said. But I'd like to know why we didn't find the groceries in her car."

His response was emotionless. "Me too. When you figure it out, let me know."

The laugh she gave was hollow and she disconnected.

Tried Rick again.

Nothing.

* * *

The knock on his door roused him from a semidoze. The television was still on, but very low, and Bryce glanced at the illuminated numbers on the clock radio next to the bed. It was after eleven o'clock, Alan had left hours ago to drive back to Milwaukee, and Bryce really couldn't think of anyone else who might come calling at his generic motel room this time of night. He was naked, so he jerked on his twice-worn jeans and went to the door but didn't open it. "Yes?"

"Deputy Jones."

Bryce raked his hand through his hair and contemplated not opening the door. He was sick of the police. "Isn't it a little late? Besides, I won't talk to anyone without my lawyer present."

"I've got a warrant for your arrest."

Not the best news this late at night—or at any other time. It was strange, but having his worst fear realized was calming. "I need to get dressed."

"Grantham, you need to open this door immediately or we'll knock it down."

The only thing worse than being arrested was having an entire motel full of people witness the degrading event. Knocking the door down involved a lot of noise. At least he was wearing pants. He flipped the latch on the door and opened it.

The first blow was to the face and took him off guard. Bryce staggered backward into the room and swore, throwing up his arms, stumbling sideways enough that he tripped over the cord of the tall lamp by the table and went down in a graceless sprawl. His head thudded against the wall. Jones was on him right away, throwing another punch, this one low, and if Bryce hadn't managed to twist, it would have hit him solidly in the gut. The other man's arm came down across his throat, and his weight pinned him to the cheap carpet.

"Where is she?" Deputy Jones' breath hissed out, his face just inches away. "Tell me, you fucker, where is she?"

Had Bryce wanted to say something, it would have been impossible. He managed an incoherent gurgle. Two hundred–plus pounds of angry deputy had put a lot of force into that punch and he was little dazed, not to mention oxygen deprived, at the moment.

"Rick, are you crazy?" The female voice registered dimly, familiar but with a hysterical edge to it. "What the hell are you doing here? You've lost it. God, please, get off him before I arrest you for assault."

Yeah, Rick, please get the fuck off me. Black dots danced on the periphery of Bryce's vision.

A thick forearm pressed harder against Bryce's Adam's apple. Jones said harshly, "Fine. Arrest me."

"We've got something new. I swear to you, it's a solid lead. I came here to ask Bryce about it."

To his relief the pressure eased. The buzzing growing in his ears decreased. Jones struggled to his feet, breathing heavily. As Bryce managed to focus again, he saw the deputy wipe his eyes, his face wet. He was dressed in street clothes: jeans, a turtleneck sweater under a windbreaker. "Goddamn it, Ellie, you'd better not be lying to me."

"I'm not." Ellie stood there in her long dark wool coat just inside the door. She looked tired, but her eyes were alive. "I swear I'm not."

"Tell me." As if he hadn't just assaulted someone, Jones wandered over to the bed and sat down like a collapsing balloon.

Bryce fingered his jaw and sat up, the taste of blood metallic in his mouth. He was going to have one hell of a bruise but didn't think anything was broken and at least he hadn't lost a tooth. Cautiously he got to his feet but it was as if Jones didn't see him anymore.

Ellie shut the door and shot Bryce a quick glance. "You okay?"

"I'll live," he said grimly, leaning back against the wall, his face already throbbing. "If I ever stop seeing stars. Mind explaining to me what's going on here?"

"He's not himself." Her voice was strained.

"Well then my official position is I liked the old him better before, and I didn't like *that* persona all that much." He wiped his mouth and saw a smear of blood on his palm.

Jones sat strangely silent, as if he was numb, his gaze fastened on Ellie. His hands hung limply between his knees. He looked shell-shocked, or maybe intoxicated, and certainly his behavior didn't indicate rational thought. It also seemed to Bryce they'd arrived independently, and that was damned confusing.

"I need to ask you a few questions." She brushed past Bryce, close enough he caught the scent of her shampoo, clean and floral. The dark coat went on the floor, and Ellie sat on the edge of the chair by the laminated desk, clasping her hands in her lap. She wore faded jeans and a light green sweater, and her hair fell into its usual shining curtain to her shoulders. She looked incredible, except for the charcoal shadows under her eyes. "I've been thinking."

"No offense, but that isn't one of my favorite phrases from a woman," he said sardonically. "The voice of experience tells me that declaration isn't often followed by good news."

"This one might be." Her voice was quiet, closed. And her gaze *examined* him. "How often do you go into Hathaway's general store?"

Whatever he expected, that question wasn't it.

"I don't know. Why?"

The smile that curved her mouth was faint. "Haven't you learned by now, we ask the questions? Just answer it, Bryce. It's not ten miles from your cabin. Surely you go in there."

The use of his first name was the first glimmer of hope he'd had in a hellish day.

"Occasionally. I was in there the other day." He really couldn't see the harm in telling the truth, but he was starting to get wary when it came to the police. His lawyer's advice was sound for a reason. Still, this was *Ellie*. "They carry a decent grocery selection and you can buy minnows and other bait. My parents have shopped there for years. Decades, I guess."

"Have you ever worn your leather jacket in there?"

Where the hell is this going?

Bryce was bare chested and the room was a little cold, and he crossed his arms. It was late, he was more than tired, and Jones not a small guy and knew how to throw an effective punch. His jaw hurt like hell.

"In the summer obviously not . . . but since I've been up here for this charming visit, I don't know. Maybe . . ." After a second, he said slowly, "Actually, yes. I remember changing into my windbreaker in the car before I went fishing. I stopped in Hathaway's to get my license."

"Were you there the day of the storm?"

He stared, wondering what the hell she was getting at. "On the day of the storm I closed up the cabin and came out to find I had a flat tire. Maybe you remember my phone call?"

"I remember. Are you saying you weren't in Hathaway's that day at all?"

"Ellie," he said in exasperation. "I was with *you*, remember? Besides, there was a giant tree—still is—across the lane."

"I remember." The line of her mouth was vulnerable for a moment but then her lips firmed. "But not until midafternoon. And if the tree was brought down by the ice, that could have happened not long before you called me."

"Jane shops there." Jones sounded like a mechanical toy, wound up but not quite human, his voice jerking like links missing in a mechanism. "At Hathaway's. She shops there pretty often when we need just one or two things." He stopped and added almost inaudibly, "Like milk."

"No, I wasn't in Hathaway's that day and who the hell is Jane?" Bryce said stiffly, not following the conversation and not liking the implied accusation. But a logical voice in his mind pointed out, Ellie looked focused, just not on him.

Not on him. It hurt a little considering they'd spent a night he'd never forget together.

"We have an eyewitness that described you pretty convincingly as the only other person in the store at the same time as Jane Cummins, our latest missing woman." Ellie spoke softly.

That brought his uninvited guest back to life. Rick Jones's head came up and he stared at Bryce with bloodshot eyes, his hands clenching into fists.

"But, hold it," Ellie went on in an inexorable voice.

"I *am* starting to wonder about this witness. Pearson knows him. He's apparently an outdoorsman, been in trouble, but as of now we don't know what kind, and I think he lied to us. I've been trying to figure out why."

"Lied how?" Jones asked. The area around his nostrils was pinched and white and his breathing was heavy.

"He said the man in the store was wearing a leather jacket. Made quite a point of it. Tall, dark-haired, good-looking, wearing an expensive impractical coat in really bad weather."

"And you thought of me. I'm flattered," Bryce said sarcastically.

"Shut up, Grantham." Deputy Jones didn't move, sitting like a lump of clay on the side of the bed. "Who's the witness?"

"Neil Hathaway. He works at his father's store."

"Don't know him. What've we got?"

"I'm calling Minnesota tomorrow. Pearson heard from his father that Neil had a run-in there. I didn't get the impression he served time or anything, but maybe there's an arrest record." She added with slow emphasis, "He knows this area, Rick. He grew up here and he's a hunter. DNR has picked him up a couple of times for out-of-season violations."

"And at least one of the victims disappeared when running out for something at the store," Jones said slowly.

They'd both forgotten him. Bryce had that impression, their faces intent, eyes locked on each other.

"We've both thought all along he's local. Dammit, he fits."

"What about Keith Walters?" Jones had the unfocused eyes of an addict, or maybe someone who needed a couple of centuries of sleep. "We can't forget him. He left two bodies in a bloody mess in a fishing shack the day Jane disappeared, and one them was his brother."

"He didn't hide them." Ellie shook her head. "No finesse. A dirtbag, but not *our* dirtbag. You don't think so either, Rick."

"No," he agreed heavily, "I don't. Son of a bitch."

Then, to Bryce's consternation, the deputy started to cry.

Chapter 27

He couldn't sleep. It happened often enough . . . the midnight wakefulness, the cold sweats, the itch. If it didn't happen one night, it didn't matter because he knew sooner or later, it would come back.

The. itch. It was strong now, and the anticipation had him strung like a taut wire, but he wanted to bide his time. It was always over too fast.

Not that he minded danger, but he liked it clean, he liked it slick and remote, and he liked most of all making the kill.

He had to make sure they didn't take it away from him.

Exceptional circumstances required a change in plans.

There was no way he could keep this one. It was time to let her go.

There was every chance he'd lose his job. Rick didn't care, and it was surprising to realize it. He dealt with the harsh realities of life on a daily basis. Yes, up here, it wasn't so bad. Not the concentrated evil of crime in big cities where poverty, prejudice, and just plain too many life forms were crammed into too few square miles contributed to the problem, but bad things did happen.

Not like this, though.

Grantham drank his coffee black. He sat across the vinyl-covered table of the busy little café, his gaze wary, his jaw already darkened to what was destined to become a pretty spectacular bruise. Rick had put a lot of frustrated hate into that punch and if the circumstances were different—if he could feel anything at all—he might even be sorry.

He wasn't. Maybe he'd find it in himself later, when the icy clutch of despair loosened—if it ever did. Right now, that seemed optimistic. In the meantime, he couldn't take the inaction anymore, and if Grantham was innocent, then fine, he'd maybe apologize one day. If he wasn't innocent—

It wasn't out of the realm of possibility he would kill him with his bare hands. From the very first instant he'd realized Jane was truly missing, his greatest fear was that she was *gone*.

He didn't think he could bear it. He wasn't just afraid for her, he was afraid for *himself*.

"Since neither of us seems to be very hungry," Grantham began in a subdued tone, nestling his coffee cup in the thick white saucer, "mind telling me just what you have in mind?"

Rick had to acknowledge his hamburger and fries were just as untouched. He studied his companion. Ellie had taken Grantham to a Walmart that morning where he'd bought a clean shirt—that must have caused Mr. MIT a moment of pain, shopping at a discount store—because forensics still had all his clothes, and obviously also a razor because he'd shaved. He was still a pretty boy, but there was a haggard cast to his face that spelled either guilt—though Rick was coming around to the conclusion maybe Grantham wasn't the killer—or the kind of emotional distress that culminated in too little sleep and no appetite. Rick wasn't all that anxious to look in the mirror either. He hadn't shaved in three days.

"I want you to help me find her."

"I've already told you." Grantham's voice was ragged, hoarse, and too loud, and heads turned. He lowered the pitch. "I have no idea what happened to *any* of the missing women."

"No? All right, let's say I agree with that . . . but you do *find* them. Maybe Jane is dead." The words came out in a low, painful hiss. "The killer has a distinct pattern and it doesn't involve leaving his victims alive when all is said and done. Ellie thinks he maybe stores them somewhere until the search dies down, but he doesn't do it with them still alive. Margaret Wilson had no defensive wounds, nor had she any evidence of adhesive on her wrists or mouth. He'd killed—then *kept*—her."

Ellie's lover looked at him like he was crazy. Yeah, Rick knew they were lovers because once you'd slept with someone, there was something there that didn't go away. Even if you hated each other the way he detested Vivian now, the memory stayed between you. Ellie and Grantham had that connection.

He'd regret the rest of his life not marrying Jane. It might make no difference now to her, but he regretted his hesitation, and if he could have her back . . . *Goddammit, please let me have her back.*

He swallowed with difficulty and stared at his cup.

"Maybe she's dead," he repeated, trying to come to terms with it, but not succeeding. "But what if she isn't? What if I sit here, feeling sorry for myself, while he has her locked up somewhere? Laws are all about following rules, but you know, *he* isn't following rules. I don't want to either. Not anymore. Aren't you the slightest bit pissed to be dragged into his personal hell?"

Bryce Grantham made a sound that might have been a laugh but had nothing to do with mirth. "Are you kidding me? "

"All right then. Help me."

"I don't know *how*."

All around them people ate, talked, the smell of burnt coffee and pancake syrup heavy in the air. It was almost too warm, and the homey atmosphere cloying. Rick had shown up at the motel at noon, invited the other man to lunch, and maybe because he was bored being stuck there, maybe out of curiosity, maybe because this sucked for him too, Grantham had accepted.

"Think about it," Rick urged, waving off an approaching waitress with a coffee pot. "You've got that high-class education and hopefully that indicates a level of intelligence that can be useful."

"I can't help you." Grantham rubbed the bruise on his jaw with what looked an absent mannerism, and winced. "I wish I could, believe me. But everything that has happened up until now has been either chance or due to whoever is perpetrating the crimes. I'm not some sort of psychic, Deputy."

Desperation crawled along every quivering nerve ending. Rick rasped out, "But the asshole is communicating with you. The bones, the earrings . . . he feels a connection. You two have shared something special."

"Special? Good God." Grantham shook his head and looked sick.

Rick folded his hands on the table. "I'm off duty right now. Unofficial vacation. You can't leave the county. Maybe we can help each other pass the time. Ellie's going to be wrapped up in seeing if she has enough evidence to convince a judge for a search warrant of Hathaway's house and vehicle. She doesn't, by the way. All she has is your word that you didn't go into town. You haven't been charged because we don't have any real physical evidence and Ellie's been pressuring Pearson to drag his feet about going to the district attorney. With Neil's testimony they could build a circumstantial case against you that might stick at least enough to go to the grand jury."

"Are you supposed to tell me that?"

"No."

Fuck my career, Rick thought as he took a gulp of tepid coffee. Screw it. He was giving away information but he didn't care. He went on. "Your expensive lawyer will get you off, I'd guess, because we have nothing on you really, but a trial would not be pleasant. Trust me, none of them are."

Grantham looked away, his face taut. "I don't need to trust you. I've figured that out for myself, but thanks anyway. What is this all about?"

"It could be Hathaway, but we have even less on him. No judge is going to give the sheriff's office a search warrant based on Ellie's hunch the guy was lying. Maybe Judge Branscum if he's in a good mood, but I've worked here for years now. Take my word on it; it's going to be tough."

"Didn't have any problem getting a warrant with me."

"You were already morphing into our favorite suspect. You kept giving us evidence. Hathaway is only someone who's lying if *you're* telling the truth."

"What the hell ever happened to innocent until proven guilty?" Grantham muttered resentfully.

"That was a bill of goods sold to us from the beginning from the conception of the judicial branch of our government. Sue our founding fathers." Rick tapped the tabletop with an emphatic fingertip. "Want the modern practical view? It translates to if you're the most obvious suspicious person in a case like this the police are going to hunt you down like a rabid dog. At this point, you're all they've got and the public wants proof they are at least trying to do their job. Better be able to prove you weren't in the wrong place at the wrong time."

"Your cynical take is really reassuring, Deputy."

Sometime in the bleak wilderness of the past two days a blackness had settled into Rick's mind—he wasn't a poetic person—but maybe even his soul. He'd never wanted to be a player, but suddenly was one. "Let's go rattle his cage."

"Hathaway?" Grantham stared at him.

Rick looked down at his hands. They'd somehow managed to become wound together so tight he was surprised the knuckles didn't snap like twigs. "If he's the one, you walking through the door is going to be like a birthday party for him. You find his bodies. He brings you gifts. You want to know what I think? On a psychological level, he connects with you because in his freakish asshole way, he thinks you've shared something with him. I mean, the police come calling, asking about a missing woman. Who does he think of right away? In fact, he blatantly tries to deflect suspicion onto you. I want to see how he reacts if you and he come face to face."

"Doesn't sound like a good idea. What if we tip him off that there *is* some suspicion? Aren't we interfering with the case?"

Rick said with blunt, emphatic force, "You got a better way to spend the day? This could clear you." He added in a more controlled tone though his voice cracked, "And what if we can find Jane? Think about her for a minute. Please."

If he could have erased that pleading note, he would have, but apparently it was impossible.

This was important. So . . . *important*.

The other man looked away for a moment, his averted face set. Then his mouth thinned, and he said unexpectedly, "Wait a minute. There's a place on the Prairie River."

"What?" Rick couldn't mentally make the leap.

Bryce Grantham pushed his plate away as if he couldn't stand to look at it anymore. "It's privately owned and no one uses it. I think there's a cabin there. It's owned by someone named Jack, but he and Hathaway seemed to be good friends and it was made clear to me that it isn't used except for fishing." A muscle in Grantham's cheek tightened visibly. "Jack would remember offering to let me fish there . . . right in front of Neil Hathaway, who gave me directions. But I didn't go there, I went to Luke's place instead, where I found Margaret Wilson, so I'd guess he would remember it."

Rick wasn't completely dead, because the police officer inside him felt the familiar quickening of his pulse whenever a case started to turn. Sometimes it was just a hunch, but it seemed as if good officers had a sense for what was a long shot and what might end up in an arrest. "If he's the one, he sure as hell would."

"If I was trying to implicate someone, I might use a place I could prove the suspect knew about." Grantham didn't have the same flare of excitement; instead he looked sick, the bruise emphasizing the bloodless pallor of his skin. "If Ellie hadn't said anything about Hathaway, it wouldn't even have occurred to me."

"It's a possibility." Rick stood up and tossed some money on the table.

"Maybe we should go take a look."

Ellie put her head in her hands, took a deep breath, and tried to focus. The information swam in front of her. Four victims. Possible number five gone only a few days. Nothing definite from the search of Jane's car . . .

Jane. Oh, God.

These weren't just statistics, put on a piece of paper for analysis; these were cold, lethal hard facts and this last victim wasn't faceless either. She knew her and it was much too personal.

"Pearson's at the airport. More DCI due here soon." One of the younger deputies sauntered past her desk, his face irritatingly alight from the excitement. "McConnell is calling in reinforcements. The case is making every single major newspaper by the end of today."

Okay, it was usually a very quiet county, but this kind of attention they could all do without. "No one will be happier than me to have as many investigators on this case as possible," she said with biting emphasis. "But in the meantime, can we keep in mind Officer Jones has a very personal stake in the outcome of this? Can I have a cup of coffee, please? I'm waiting on a call."

The smug smile vanished. "Sure, Detective."

The phone rang and she snatched it up, still waiting to hear from Minnesota on the follow-up on Hathaway. It was Pearson instead. "Got anything else? We're stopping at a Perkins for lunch . . . oh hell, I guess dinner. I don't even know what time of day it is."

"They serve breakfast all day."

Pearson at least could still wring out a laugh. "Hey, it's on the county. Have you seen our budget? They're lucky. I could have picked a Burger King. What's going on?"

She tugged out the notepad, full of scribbles. "Neil Hathaway has no convictions, and no charges that stuck. He was arrested for battery. Girlfriend. She dropped."

"I see." He sounded subdued. "It could mean something and it could mean nothing, but we don't have much else but Walters and Grantham."

She wished she didn't have to agree. "I'm trying. I called back to find out about missing persons cases that occurred during the time Hathaway lived in Ely to see if any fit the profile of what's been happening here. I'm still waiting."

"Good idea." There was a heavy pause. "How's Rick?"

She didn't want to tell Pearson about Rick's out-of-line behavior the night before. Assaulting a suspect—or witness—whatever you wanted to call Bryce, was *so* out of line he might get suspended, but under the circumstances she couldn't bring herself to censure someone in that much pain.

Bryce had been surprisingly decent over the incident too, but when she thought about it, he was as touchy as Rick. "He's a little out there but who can blame him?"

"Not me," Pearson said heavily. "I can't blame him one bit, Ellie, that's why I took him off the case. Let me know what the Minnesota boys say, okay?"

"Of course."

She hung up, noting the deputy hadn't brought her cup of coffee. That was fine, she hadn't wanted it anyway. Taking a chance, she picked up the phone and dialed the number she'd gotten from the faxed report for the fifth time. The woman had probably moved, and how long it might take to find her, if she even *could* be found—

To her surprise, someone answered. "Hello?"

"Laura George?"

"Yes." Tentative admission, wary of telemarketers probably.

"This is Detective MacIntosh working with the Lincoln County Sheriff's Department. I've been trying to reach you."

"I saw the messages . . . I've been at work. Why do you want to talk to me?"

"Can I have a moment of your time to discuss Neil Hathaway?"

There was a perceptible pause. "Neil? I . . . I suppose."

"Can you tell me about the night you called 911 two years ago?"

"Why?" The woman didn't sound too happy. "I told it all to the police then. How do I even know you're a police officer?"

"His arrest is a matter of public record." Ellie pointed it out with practical reassurance. "And feel free to contact the sheriff's department to confirm my identity. I'll give you the number of my supervisor. Or," she paused, "if you don't want to go to that trouble, just give me the gist of what happened that night after asking yourself who besides a police officer would care. Young women get roughed up too many times to mention in this country. It's happening now to someone as we speak. I have a report that says at one o'clock on a November afternoon he pinned you to the floor and choked you until you lost consciousness. Do you have anything to add?"

"Like what?" The young woman sounded not hostile, but uncertain. "That says it all. We had an argument. It happens."

If she could take the time, Ellie wished she could do this face to face, but Jane had been missing for several days now.

Rick's theory the killer kept them alive had better be accurate.

Unfortunately, she didn't think it was.

"Yes, people argue, but not every man chooses to assault his fiancée. What did you fight about?"

"I don't even remember. It . . . just happened."

"Ms. George, this is pretty important."

"Why?"

"Until I can confirm you aren't still communicating with Neil Hathaway, I can't really tell you."

"I'm not," the young woman said faintly. And then she added in a stronger voice, "I'm *no*t. The bastard."

"Your help would be appreciated."

"Okay . . . fine. One minute we were just there, watching television, and then the next arguing over something. I got up to get a beer, and then he caught me from behind, and I was on the floor, and he had . . .

he had—" She stopped, and Ellie could hear her make a small sound of distress in the background. "He had a knife. Big one. The one he uses for hunting. He ran the tip of the blade down my face before he choked me. That asshole. I have a scar."

That rang a bell. Ellie shuffled papers on her desk, breaking out in a light sweat. *Wasn't there* . . . didn't she remember . . . hell yes, there it was. Her gaze focused on the page and she took in a breath.

Margaret Wilson had an unexplained cut on her face, not postmortem, and she'd been strangled.

This, Ellie thought, *I might be able to take to a judge.*

Wound to the face, the medical examiner's report said, but nothing specific about the knife.

She found her voice. "Why did you drop the charges?"

"Look, I just told you he attacked me. When I thought about it, I decided it was best to not piss him off even more. Neil seems like a friendly guy, but he has some real creepy issues. I packed up, moved down to Hastings with my mother, and tried to forget about the whole thing."

That was hardly a new story. It was exactly why more men weren't prosecuted for assaults on the women they supposedly loved.

Ellie said, "I'm going to need a deposition from you. I'll send an officer over. Tell him everything you just told me."

She called Pearson back. "Over your chef salads, tell McConnell this little story about Neil Hathaway. Maybe *he* can get us a warrant without any physical evidence."

Chapter 28

There was a time to stay very, very still, usually before the kill. It was that definitive deep breath between recognition that this was the moment, and the rise of excitement before it. Stealthy was better than the raging charge.

Animals knew it. Instinct was a powerful force.

He needed to be low, to be invisible.

It could be done. He'd walked past a doe once, dropping a fawn. She'd been resting against a log, not making a sound, the birth arrested by his presence, but in the end he'd spotted her and lifted his rifle.

Sometimes fate just wasn't in your corner.

Not much sport in a kill like that. He always needed more.

The drive was heavy with slush from the melted snow and ice, and barely discernible except as a break in the trees. The filmy light lent the scene odd depth and definition, like a blurry Ansel Adams photograph.

"There's a gate." Rick Jones braked the car and slid

to a stop by the paved road access. "We'll have to go in on foot."

Bryce was surprised at the deputy's resolution, because, quite frankly, they hadn't liked each other from the beginning, and here Jones was, willing to take his word on it. He opened the car door. "He said it was private. I don't know anything about this place. I haven't been here before."

"I don't need a disclaimer, Grantham."

The property was butted up against a county forest, the road a dead end, and as they got out of the vehicle, the isolation reached out to curl around him. In the summer, it would be wooded and lovely, but right now . . . now, it just seemed lonely.

Circumventing the gate was just a matter of climbing the fence on one side, and at the top of a good-size hill they found a stone and timber structure, about as old as the cabins on Loon Lake, weathered to a dull gray, lichen on the warped roof. The drive was tangled with weeds, the separate garage shuttered and locked. The branches whispered eerily over their heads as they approached the walk and scrunched through piles of wet leaves. Rick had his hands inside his jacket, and his eyes were still bloodshot, but more focused than earlier. "I'm still not sure what you think we'll find here, but with your track record, I'm willing to take your word for it. Any ideas?"

There wasn't much question the man was both edgy and strung out to a degree that Bryce registered as dangerous. "No."

Is this a huge mistake?

They were alone. In a remote place. The thin autumn wind brushed past, carrying the fecund scent of rotting leaves. The snow from the storm was melting, but not gone, and there were piles of ice next to the foundation of the decrepit building.

Jones had a gun. Bryce realized it, but it hadn't been a particular concern, just something he'd *known*. If the guy snapped again, he could easily shoot him and conceal his body, or maybe even invent a story that would make it all seem like self-defense.

Now he wished he'd called Ellie to fill her in on their destination. He hardly wanted to be gunned down and chucked into the river.

"This was *your* theory." Rick's face was strained.

It had been. Now he was second-guessing himself. If Jones really thought he'd done something to his girlfriend, they were alone and the man was edgy . . .

"Where do we look?" Jones insisted, his face drawn, his boots scraping the snow- crusted gravel.

"Inside the garage?" Bryce rubbed his hands together. It really wasn't that cold, but he was uncomfortable in this remote place. The river was a sheet of dark glass in the disappearing sunlight, and the forest thick around them, silent, watching. "I don't know. This is much more your area than mine."

"Yeah, well, if you're thinking understanding a psycho is part of my job, think again. We catch them. We don't ever try to understand them."

He squared his shoulders. "Look, it's remote and Hathaway said something about it to me. I think we need to break into the cabin."

Rick looked at him with that squared-jawed thrust he'd seen before. His breath frosted in the cold air. "You think we'll find Jane in there?"

The strong underlying feeling they both had she was dead wasn't necessarily a brotherhood he wanted to be a part of. Bryce said, "I think we might find . . . something."

With a mutter Bryce couldn't quite catch, Jones walked to the front door, picked up a rock from a clump of dying weeds next to the stoop, and smashed in the window at the top. The sound of breaking glass was loud in the shrouded silence.

The deputy reached in, unlocked the door, and said, "Here we go."

Not being able to get ahold of Rick or Bryce this late in the afternoon made her uneasy. If the victim had been anyone but Jane, Ellie would trust Rick implicitly, but he wasn't really stable right now and she didn't blame him, but she didn't trust him at the moment either.

She pressed the end button on her cell and sat in her car in the parking lot outside the sheriff's office, repressing the urge to toss her phone out the window.

If Neil Hathaway was really a suspect, and Rick knew it, what would he do? If Bryce was the number-one suspect, what *would* he do?

For the first time in her career, she had serious reservations about a fellow officer, and it wasn't that she doubted Rick, it was just logic. In his shoes . . . well . . .

Shit.

At least the weather was better, she decided, as she started her car and pulled out of the lot.

She tried Bryce again. No answer.

The five minutes from the station seemed to take forever. The motel sat in its asphalt lot, squat and generic, and the clerk at the desk inside confirmed that Dr. Grantham had not checked out, yet when Ellie went up to his room, he wasn't there. She went back downstairs, got the clerk to give her a key card, and checked out his room. The new razor sat by the sink, and one of the new shirts he'd bought was on the bed, still on the hanger. He'd left all right, and not without the intention of coming back. His duffel bag sat on the floor.

But where the hell was he?

If Rick had gone off the deep end, it could be bad.

The sense of panic she felt was unexpected and telling. And the conclusion was she was worried about both of them.

Maybe Bryce had gotten someone to take him out to the cabin so he could change his tire and arrange to have the tree moved. Or maybe Rick had showed up again.

It seemed logical to take Highway 17 south. Hathaway's parking lot was nearly deserted when she pulled in, only one car in the closest spot to the door, and Ellie got out and stared at the façade of the building. She probably should have called McConnell. He and Pearson could still be in their meeting, but this might warrant a heads-up.

On the other hand, if she did, Rick could get in trouble and she couldn't risk it. Rick was off the case.

Why weren't either of them answering their damn phone?

"Dumbasses," she muttered.

It was almost closing time. The sky was a deep, dark indigo and the woods had thickened with shadows to the point the opaque visibility would soon be an issue. She got out, checked her weapon, and walked up the steps to the door of the store. A small bell jingled as she went inside.

The lone customer was a young man buying ham salad and a six-pack of beer. He nodded at her and picked up his package, and Russell Hathaway thanked him by name. The older man recognized her as well, she could tell, and though he smiled affably enough, unless it was her imagination, his eyes took on a certain wariness.

"Evening, Detective."

She nodded. "I have a few more questions for Neil, Mr. Hathaway. Is he here?"

"No, ma'am. Sorry. He got off at four."

"Is he at home?"

"Couldn't say. He didn't tell me his plans."

Ellie considered the older man with a level look. "I understand he was arrested up near Ely for assaulting his girlfriend a couple of years ago."

Russell Hathaway's face visibly tightened. "Yes, he told me about it. They were drinking, got into an argument and it got out of hand. She dropped the charges."

"Out of hand? Did he mention he disfigured her with a knife and choked her until she was unconscious?"

Neil had obviously left out the details, from his father's reaction. After a moment, Russell shook his head, his expression strained as he braced his hands on the counter. "No. I admit I hadn't heard that."

"Do you believe he's capable of it?"

"Ma'am, I am not going to answer a question like that about my own son."

And that, she thought, *was answer enough.*

"I'll need his address." They could question him again tomorrow when McConnell was with her. No way she would go after him on her own. Not the way it was all shaking out.

"He lives with me. Here's the address." Russell reached under the counter and pulled out a small pad of paper, took a pen from a cup near the old cash register, and jotted something down. He handed it over, his hand not quite steady. "Though I doubt he's there right now. My son spends a lot of time out of doors."

She hesitated and then asked, "Has anyone else been by, looking for Neil?"

"No."

Where the hell is Rick? Where is Bryce?

"Thanks, Mr. Hathaway. Have a good evening."

No response. The older man stood there, unmoving, as she pushed open the door, the little bell ringing.

It was ten miles to the Grantham cabin, dusk glimmering down, low-hanging clouds that had thickened all afternoon lending a premature darkness under the trees. The big elm was still there, in a lifeless sprawl across the curve of the drive, splinters of wood and cracked branches everywhere. With the general damage from the storm, not even the county had been able to get a tree-removal service out there and the crime scene investigators had to hike for it when they searched the cabin and Bryce's car the second time.

Ellie parked to the side, the area rutted from other law enforcement vehicles, and got out, her breath frosty. She pulled on gloves and climbed a low bank, going around the barricade of the giant fallen tree on foot. Soil still clung to the roots, exposed like naked, dirty veins.

It was silent except for her passage as she trudged up the lane, only a whisper of a breeze stirring the branches overhead. The crunch of her footsteps was loud, and as she crested the hill, she saw the Land Rover still sitting in crooked isolation, the cabin silent and closed, the lake black ice in the background. She went down the steps and peered into the portion of the interior she could see through the crack in the curtains in the window by the front door.

Nothing moved.

Bryce was definitely not here.

Impatient, frustrated, she stopped and stood there, the quiet almost oppressive.

So quiet she jumped when her phone rang. She registered the number with relief, flipping the phone open. "Rick. Where the hell are you? I've been trying—"

"We have another body, Ellie."

His voice sounded dead, empty.

Another body.

"Jane?" The single word was barely audible. She didn't want to ask, didn't even want to know.

"No. It's Melissa Simmons." His voice shook. "Jesus, Ellie, we've found the dickwad. We've caught him."

"Can you clarify? Where are you?" Then, because she somehow had known it all long, she asked sharply, "Is Bryce with you?"

"He is . . . how the hell else do think I would have found another body? He identified her."

That couldn't have been easy. "Where . . . how . . . is he okay?"

"Let's just say this isn't his line of work." His caustic tone was loud and clear. But then he audibly relented a little. "I might have had the same reaction. He's understandably not the happiest person right now."

"You shouldn't be doing this, Rick. Off alone with a suspect when Pearson pulled you from the case—"

"Oh, you're one to preach at me."

Good point. She inhaled a cleansing breath. "I didn't think you believed he was innocent."

"Desperation makes for interesting partnerships.

The body is here near a cabin on the Prairie. We searched the entire property twice before we found fresh upturned earth over by what once used to be a shed. If the snow wasn't melting, we would never have seen it. The grave is shallow, but I'm wondering if that isn't on purpose."

"Get the hell out of there."

"Exactly. The place is owned by a friend of Hathaway's father. Can you call Pearson? He's going to be pissed enough at me. We don't have a search warrant and if this isn't handled just right, the court will refuse to let us admit it. We're going to leave before we do any more damage to the scene."

"Hell yes, I'm calling him, though I am going to have to dance all over the place about how I know what I know. Can I talk to Bryce, please? He isn't answering his cell."

There was a brief pause before Bryce's voice, slightly hoarse, said, "Ellie."

At least he was alive. She'd have to address how much she found she cared about that somewhere down the line.

"What's going on?" she asked more sharply than she should, but a tension between her shoulder blades that was almost a physical pain eased a fraction. "Why are you with Rick? Do you feel safe? Where did you—"

"I'll explain later, probably from prison," he interrupted with audible fatalistic cynicism and a ragged tone. "I was just trying to help. How in the hell do you *do* this?"

"Can I ask for at least the third time, where exactly are you? Prairie River is pretty vague. I'm at your cabin now, looking for you."

"I'll give you directions."

She listened, her brain on automatic pilot now, taking in the facts. At the very same moment she was about to end the call, she realized she wasn't alone. Ellie froze, her phone in hand. Then she slowly turned and stared at the man at the top of the steps.

Blond hair, cut short, wide shoulders, athletic build. He wore pack boots, jeans, and a dark lightweight coat. A rifle hung loosely in the crook of his arm and his good-natured smile surfaced easily. "Good evening, Detective. My father told me you were looking for me."

Chapter 29

It was odd, but when a man embarked on an epic journey, he knew it would be long and hard, and of course he realized it was a mystery how it would end. How the finale happened was a matter of personal choice, and the Hunter was not one to back away from a little glory.

He'd earned it, he thought, having fooled the police so easily for so long, and if there was a full-scale investigation complete with so much law enforcement and alerts to the surrounding states, he could do no less than live up to his reputation.

This was nice . . . the ultimate hunt. He got a thrill scenting the fear, seeing the dawning realization of fate in the eyes of his quarry—especially the pretty hazel eyes of Detective MacIntosh.

She was a hunter too. She was hunting him.

Time for a bit of role reversal.

Hathaway had called and warned his son.

Ellie hadn't expected it, and that was perhaps a fatal error.

There was an advantage to being a police officer, trained to handle dangerous situations, but first and foremost she was a normal human being and the jolt of adrenaline that shot through her held her paralyzed for a long, crucial heartbeat. Ellie stared at Neil and *knew* he was the one they were looking for.

Even worse, he knew she knew. They saw it in each other's eyes, and at a moment like this, trying to deny it seemed futile.

The way the cabin was built into the hillside, with the panorama of the water view from the back showcase of windows, gave Ellie no place to go. The steps down to the front stoop where she stood were landscaped stone and actually set into the slope of the hill, so she was virtually hemmed in at the moment, and at the top stood . . . death.

It was a melodramatic thought, but three murdered women and two missing made it less so.

Still she tried to stay calm, conscious she hadn't ended her call with Bryce. "You needn't have gone through so much trouble, Mr. Hathaway. We just have a few more questions. Lieutenant McConnell and I will drop by tomorrow."

"Close your phone."

She did so at the uncompromising order. There were some points you didn't argue. His weapon was at ready. Hers wasn't.

"If you move your hands," Hathaway said evenly, "even attempt to move for the gun I know you carry, keep this in mind: By the time you reach inside your coat, which is buttoned, and take the safety off your service revolver, I'll have lifted this"—he did a mock demonstration—"taken aim, and fired. I'm a damned good shot. It isn't my preferred method, but any decent outdoorsman occasionally runs across situations that test his ability to improvise. Seems like this is one of them."

"I just told my partner where I am," she said, surprised her voice was calm, a part of her in disbelief it was all happening. "How can you possibly think they won't apprehend you, whether or not you kill me? I feel obliged to mention the state of Wisconsin frowns on citizens who shoot their law-enforcement personnel."

"I don't want to shoot you, Detective, believe me."

"Really?" Ellie said coolly. If she took her chances and dove down, was there enough cover to wedge her body under the front step until she could pull out her Glock?

No. There wasn't.

"That's predicated on whether or not it gets really sticky from here, and whether they can catch me. You must admit you all haven't done so well so far." The infuriating note of satisfying conviction in Hathaway's voice spoke of the cold eighteen-month investigation that had given it to him. "Canada is just hours north and I have a valid passport. Lots of country. Plenty of great hunting there."

She knew he didn't mean game.

Bastard.

No death penalty in Canada. Wisconsin didn't execute its killers either. She'd been afraid all along their quarry was aware of that.

What she needed was a little time. Time to get her weapon free. She couldn't go forward, but she could go backward.

In a sense.

The window next to the door was just behind her

right shoulder. It was old glass, probably original to the cabin, and maybe four feet high and two feet wide.

Enough to get through?

It didn't matter if she miscalculated at this point, because standing in front of a serial killer armed with a hunting rifle limited her options to an extremely small number.

Hesitation was the enemy of salvation. As often as police officers have to make split-second decisions that might save or take a life, she knew this, so Ellie angled her body backward just a fraction so she could see the window out of the corner of her eye.

Then she turned and dived, literally, into the glass.

The window shattered as she propelled herself against it, her coat shielding much of her body, her arms flung up to protect her face. It didn't work as perfectly as she hoped, for her legs caught the sill, sending her sprawling inside in a cascade of shattered glass. The first shot thudded into the floor near her head and she scrambled up, slamming into the nearest door, which ended up being a bedroom. She managed to get her coat open and yank her weapon free.

Gun out, held in trembling hands—she did her best to get her bearings. The bedroom wasn't a good option because she was trapped. She peered out the doorway, saw Hathaway framed in the window, but he ducked back before she could take a shot.

No warning to freeze if she got a clear shot now. He was past that. She didn't owe him anything. He'd fired at a police officer. Screw procedure, and besides, it was just the two of them.

To get to her, he had to come in, and she could cover the entrances to the cabin. If she could only call for help . . .

But staying alive and talking on the phone seemed to be mutually exclusive at the moment as she edged along a pine paneled wall and ducked into the hallway, risking him taking a sniper shot from the hill through the broken window, but now seemed a better time to try before he could settle into place.

She couldn't get out, but she hoped he couldn't get in either, and she had her phone. He'd have to run for it before help arrived.

Except, she realized, holding her weapon in still shaking hands, she *didn't* have her phone. When she'd jumped through the window, she'd dropped it. It was lying there on the floor just inside the door in a pile of broken glass when she peeked around the corner from the kitchen.

Son of a bitch.

Reconsider. Calmly. *Think.*

Did he know she'd dropped it? Maybe, since he had the scope on his rifle, but then again, it was getting dark. Would it help him? Maybe, maybe not. Magnified darkness was just more darkness.

In the dark, this game would get more interesting, and Hathaway knew she'd told Bryce where she was. How long would it take for him and Rick to realize she'd never had a chance to call Pearson?

An hour? Two?

She might not last an hour. How long would they wait before they assumed something was wrong? Had they overheard anything of her exchange with Hathaway?

What a question.

Surely she could shimmy out of one of the bedroom windows. On her stomach, Ellie lay on the kitchen floor, the shrouded gloom disconcerting. Maybe if she knew the house better it wouldn't be so confusing, but discovering the floor plan with an armed killer outside didn't lend a lot of encouragement to calm, rational tactics. She'd been in there a couple of times, had a glass of wine in the living room, but the rest of the layout wasn't too clear.

The offensive came from the opposite direction.

A spray of gunfire shattered the windows, one by one, facing the lake. Glass rained everywhere, the noise was deafening, and she was close enough she could feel the flying debris in stinging cuts on her face. Cold air streamed inside. She slid to a more sheltered position by the refrigerator, her back to the wall, knees up.

That had been petty. He couldn't get into the cabin that way. The hillside was too steep. Scare tactics, that was all.

But he was out back now, not out front.

Just as she had the urge to jump and run for the front door, she told herself he'd probably counted on just that and stayed put, the cold linoleum beneath her body reflecting a grim inner chill. He was probably in a position where he could catch her long range if she reached the top of the steps.

Her phone began to ring out in the glass-strewn hallway.

She muttered a word her mother probably didn't know existed. Ellie's male associates would approve and agree the timing was just right for her to start using it.

Neil Hathaway shot another round, this time the bullets hitting the ceiling and one smashing into a rack of plates on a shelf in the kitchen. Debris went everywhere. *Still on the hillside. Really making a point of having me know it too.*

The front door was not an option.

She moved toward the hallway off the kitchen where she assumed there was another bedroom. The carpet was musty and the ghost of a hundred wood fires lingered in the air. The bed was a rough oblong from her position, but she did see curtains even from the floor.

Don't think about it too much. She heaved herself to her feet, crawled across the stripped bed, and peeked out the corner of the drape on the right side. It looked clear, but it was dark enough now outside she couldn't tell.

Her orphaned phone started ringing again as she detached the window screen.

The drop was about ten feet because of the slope of the hill. She gauged it, wondering how she'd hit the ground and still be able to fire if he was waiting for this move. The only luck on her side was that no one person could watch all four sides of the same structure at once.

While it might be instinct to go still and hide like an injured rabbit, she knew waiting was lethal. So was indecision. She cranked the window open and levered herself over the sill. The ground was soft and gave as she hit. She'd miscalculated in an ungraceful disaster of how she imagined her descent, going down on one hip in a jarring landing, the slick pine needles making her slide a good three feet. Hastily, she scrambled to regain her feet, jerking up her gun, the adrenaline of possible escape a rush that took her breath from her lungs. In the summer, the thick woods could provide a perfect cover of leaf and branch, thicket and fern, but now it was bleak and stripped naked and if she ran and he had a good bead . . .

She was dead.

But it was a lot harder to hit a moving target and

enough trees down here and there she might be able to find some sort of a hiding place.

These were big woods.

If there was another law he could break, Bryce wasn't positive he could think of what it might be. Trespassing . . . hell, he was doing that enough lately it wasn't even a concern. Breaking and entering. Failure to report knowledge of a crime . . . and now reckless driving. He'd forgotten the exact penalty, but he had a feeling it involved handcuffs and jail time.

Could be worse. If they hit a deer right now—and on these winding tree-lined roads at dusk it happened all the time—it would be quite an accident at this manic speed. A detached part of his brain computed the statistic. An average citizen of the great state of Wisconsin hit two deer in his lifetime. Crap. He didn't even have *one* under his belt yet. He was due.

He was also driving a police car, no less. There was probably another penalty for that, because while Jones had handed over the keys pretty easily, he might be off the payroll by now anyway and at a guess neither one of them should be driving it. Jones had the nothing-to-lose attitude of a man who thought it was all over. Case in point, breaking into someone's cabin without permission or warrants, or whatever else Bryce unfortunately knew too much about since he'd decided to take this vacation.

"She's still not answering." Rick shook his head.

"Keep trying." Bryce took a curve way too fast, barely kept the car on the road, and noted Jones didn't seem to care much about a possible accident. Good thing, because he had no intention of slowing down.

The headlights flashed against the white slender

trunks of hovering birch, the sturdier hemlock, and white pine, sprinkled with the occasional thick oak.

Almost there.

When Ellie's car flashed into view, he slammed on the brakes and stopped so abruptly his seat belt shoulder lock engaged. He missed her rear bumper by inches.

"She's still here." Jones had his weapon under his coat and checked it in a movement that was obviously automatic. "You're sure you heard him on the phone?"

"Why is her car here and she isn't answering?" Bryce didn't wait, but slid out, the cruiser askew in the middle of the road. He'd put it in park—or he thought he had, but didn't turn off the engine and ran toward the fallen tree. Let Jones worry about his squad car.

He went over the top of the fallen tree instead of around, tearing through the branches and sliding on the slippery bark, his boots thudding onto the lane, his heart pounding.

The rush of the woods as he went up the hill, the cold, the descending night . . . Bryce blundered into a pile of brush in the darkness and grunted at the impact.

A hard hand grasped his arm and a voice hissed in his ear. "I heard you coming like you were blasting a fog horn. You sound like a herd of rabid moose. Where's Rick? At least he's armed. Hathaway is out there."

Ellie. Still breathing, warm, supple, safe . . . and after seeing Melissa's corpse, still half frozen . . .

He wanted to collapse to the ground, with her in his arms, and either cry or laugh or both. "I—"

"Shh. Just listen. Don't move unless I tell you to, got it? This isn't a software seminar. Where?" she whispered tersely, not looking at him. Alert. Dangerous.

She held a handgun with expertise and crouched there in the thin, distorted light. There was blood on her face and mud smeared on her coat.

"He's right behind me," he said as low as possible, easing up enough he could at least let his eyes adjust to the darkness and cast a quick look around. "Look, we can do whatever is it is you do . . . call for backup—"

"He's not going to wait around for that." In the shadows he could see the hard set of her mouth. "This isn't your call. I'm nailing him. But I need to be close. Really close. My .45 isn't all that accurate otherwise."

Fine. He knew a lost argument when he heard one. She was right, this was her territory.

It was dark enough that he could barely make out her expression when she turned. The air was cold, the woods silent. "You already have a connection," she said, her gun extended as they crouched behind the log. "He has some sort of a vibe with you that even I don't understand, and *I* might be actually having a real love affair with you. Tell him about this new body."

"What?"

"Tell him."

"Maybe you'd better specify how you'd like me to do that."

"Call out, but don't stand up."

"You *want* him to shoot at us?" he asked incredulously.

"Yes, I do," she answered evenly. "And trust me, so does Rick. Hathaway is going to find us eventually anyway. Think about the noise you just made. He's going to know you're here. Just get him close enough for one of us to take him out. I need the sound of his voice."

"Academia doesn't prepare you for this," he muttered.

"That's why," she said calmly, as if a serial killer wasn't out there in the woods, her weapon gleaming in her hand, "the university doesn't issue you guns. Now, do it. Tell him you found another body."

Chapter 30

This was one of those moments. He'd always imagined it. Oh, hell yes, it was a rush to go after a good-size black bear with a bow, but . . . it wasn't this.

The minute the pretty detective had walked up and introduced herself, he'd known she was next.

Would Grantham appreciate the gesture?

He thought he would.

In the dark, the Hunter smiled.

This wasn't the time for cold calculation, but knowing she had backup made all the difference in the world to Ellie as she crouched down and sharply inhaled the cold air. There was a reason Rick had not come running wildly through the woods. No one who had a modicum of self-preservation would have done it.

Except Bryce.

If they lived through this, he would get a lecture on the futility of desperate heroics.

At the moment, it was a toss-up whether or not he would ever live to hear it or she would live to give it.

Despite the tension and gravity of the situation, she had to have a flicker of introspection. Who knew she favored sensitive men? Not her. Maybe that's why all her relationships had been a disaster so far.

The pile of three crisscrossed fallen logs was thick enough for cover, but rotten, and heavy with the scent of decay and probably wouldn't do much as a shield. She tried not to think about it. The cold truth was, as she'd said, she needed Hathaway pretty damned close. His rifle against her sidearm was not an even match. Should she draw him in with Bryce, who was unarmed and inexperienced? No. She wasn't supposed to endanger the life of a civilian, and on a personal level, especially not him. But on the other hand, she had Rick out there somewhere, and if she didn't play this right, it could go south pretty quick. Maybe they'd even shoot each other. That would be some nice irony.

She couldn't even be sure Rick had called in that they were out there and in trouble. Normally, yes, but that was before his girlfriend had been kidnapped by a serial killer and he'd decided to trespass, endanger the case by searching without a warrant, and otherwise lose his mind.

Fuck.

Wet cold leaves surrounded her knees. She couldn't see more than about twenty feet now, and the thin wind made enough sound that every crackle of the waving branches made her jump. "Tell him who you are and what you just found," she said softly. "That's enough. Then, *don't* move. If he says anything back, don't respond. Not a word."

She had her gun. Rick was presumably armed. The odds had improved considerably, but she didn't want to shoot Rick accidentally, and definitely didn't want him to shoot either her or Bryce. He needed to know where they were, and maybe it would draw a response from Hathaway. If Rick could get in close, it would be enough. Maybe Hathaway didn't even know Bryce hadn't come alone.

"If you're sure, here goes," Bryce muttered, crouched next to her behind the logs, and raised his voice to a shout. "Hathaway, this is Grantham. I just found the body you hid at Jack's cabin on the river."

One of two things would happen now, Ellie calculated. Either Hathaway would take off through the woods to escape, or he'd try to slip around behind them for the best shot.

Something moved off to their left. Just a snap of a twig, a subtle rustle, but she heard it, and so did Bryce, his head whipping around that direction.

For the first time in her life, she wished she'd gone in for deer stands in the frigid early mornings and learned to gauge if your quarry was thirty feet away, or thirty yards. It was too dark to make out much in such indistinct light, the pall of clouds from the day hanging on. It didn't help her heart pounded loudly in her ears, and she had to exert effort to control her breathing.

Leaves rustled. Wind? Or something else? She strained against the darkness, praying she and Rick were thinking along the same lines, because now Hathaway had a good sense of their direction, and so did Rick, but she couldn't afford to wait until she figured out which one to fire at if all hell broke loose. By then it might be too late.

Then she caught it, a hint of movement in the black shadows, something a little darker, creeping through the trees but then moving fast all at once, circling, close enough she could hear the whistle of his breath . . .

But, dammit, he didn't try and shoot, and until he did, she couldn't be sure it wasn't Rick. Bryce swiveled with the arc of the footsteps now openly cracking twigs and he made a small incoherent sound as they were now no longer protected by the barricade of rotted logs, but the mover was behind them, no longer caring if they heard him.

There was a flash of noise to her right and she pivoted on the balls of her feet, still crouched down, but nothing came close and there was still someone off to the left too.

Had she miscalculated, she wondered with a sense of panicked anger? If she and Bryce were caught in a crossfire exchange, that wasn't going to be good either.

A bullet from a different direction tore through the sleeve of her coat before she even heard the retort, but it was answered so quickly by return fire—not hers, she still couldn't tell which shooter might be where. By now Hathaway had to realize they weren't alone. "Down," she barked at Bryce, half rising, "You can't help. Rick, where are you?"

Searching, searching, where the hell are you?

"To your right," he shouted from the trees. "I can see you."

So could Hathaway. Another flash from the left. This one grazed her thigh, she could feel the sting and the bullet thudded into the logs with a spat and chips flew.

God, he's close, close . . . both she and Rick fired, the noise deafening.

Then . . . quiet.

Hathaway hadn't fired back.

Eerie, drifting quiet in the aftermath. There was

blood running down her leg, she realized, warmly seeping through her jeans. Her ears were ringing, her hands still tight around her extended weapon.

We didn't get him.

Rick confirmed it, coming out of the dark haze of trees, snapping another round into his weapon. His face resembled soapstone, gleaming with sweat in the cold, and white as a ghost. "He's running. Going toward the road. I'm not letting that motherfucker get away."

"You're bleeding." Bryce caught her arm as Rick ran into the darkness down the hill toward the road, yanking her back around. "Ellie, you're hurt."

She shook him off. "It's a graze. Look, we need backup. My cell is in the cabin, right inside the door. Call Pearson, will you? His number is programmed in there. He'll get things moving faster than 911. Tell him roadblocks on every possible access out of here. Do it!"

Then she plunged after her partner into the darkness.

There was glass everywhere, and next to the front door of the cabin gaped a black square hole since the glass from the window was gone. For expediency Bryce managed to get over the sill with only several minor cuts from the jagged edges in his hurry. It was actually a good thing it was broken. The only keys he had were on the ring he'd given to Ellie for the search of his car and the second dissection of the cabin.

Bryce swore, plucking a piece of glass from the palm of his hand. It was so dim inside he had to grope across the floor to try and find Ellie's cell phone, finally locating it as he accidentally swept it with his hand underneath a small table. That took another precious few seconds.

The screen illuminated as he scrolled down through her address book for Sheriff Pearson. He was still rattled from the impromptu volley of gunfire, and the sight of Ellie, her face cut, her leg bleeding. His hands shook.

"MacIntosh?" Pearson answered with impatient irritation almost immediately. "You were supposed to be here for a meeting at—"

"This is Bryce Grantham. Look, Sheriff, there have been shots fired here at my parents' cabin . . . Ellie is wounded and last I saw she and Jones were chasing Hathaway through the woods. She asked for backup and full roadblocks on any way out of the area."

"What the f— Hathaway? Are you sure?" Pearson's voice was raspy now, deeper. "And what is Jones doing there? Don't answer . . . we're coming—" he broke off on an explosive exhale and the call ended.

The cabin was dead cold. Bryce shivered, wondering how much of the chill was inside him, still kneeling in broken glass, Ellie's phone in his hand. It felt absurdly like he should call someone else, not just ineffectually sit there. He wanted to help, but unarmed, he was more of a liability and he knew it, but it chafed just the same to let Ellie run off in the darkness after a man who had killed five women.

I might be actually having a real love affair with you . . .

Heaving himself to his feet, Bryce put Ellie's phone into his jacket pocket. He'd put new batteries into the flashlight and he took it from the shelf, flicking it on. Like a spill of shattered ice, glass lay in glistening disarray. He walked toward the ruined windows facing the lake. Everywhere his booted feet crunched glass, the icy breeze scented with pine. He felt as if he'd attended a rock concert, his hearing hollow from the gunfire.

The beam hit the darkness, lighting the trees on the steep hill in a yellow arc. From the woods there was nothing. Nothing.

What a mess, he thought, his mind abstractly taking in the disaster. It was something to concentrate on other than whatever might be happening out there. Or the image of Melissa's body . . .

He'd have to hire someone to clean up the glass and board up the windows for the winter, someone else to remove the tree from the drive . . . his parents might never want him to use the cabin again, and who could blame them. He swung the light around unsteadily, noting with dismay his mother's favorite old dishes in pieces on the kitchen floor. There was a bullet hole in the wall near the stove, another in the ceiling in the living room above the fireplace, and when he flashed the light into the bedroom down the short hall, he saw the screen crooked and discarded on the floor, and the window open.

Methodically, he closed the window, replaced the screen, and sat down on the stripped bed. He felt useless, and it wasn't pleasant. He wasn't stupid enough to think he could charge out there and help, but then again, there wasn't much point in sitting in a freezing cabin either.

As he stood up, the beam of the flashlight hit the corner of the room. At least the bedroom was fine as he ran the light over the walls. No holes, no . . .

What the hell?

The attic stairway was cracked open.

That hadn't been that way when he'd closed up the

place. He knew for sure, because his father was fanatical about how squirrels got in that way and it was on the stringent list for how to close the cabin.

Bryce ran the flashlight beam over the square opening in the ceiling. No, definitely not shut like he'd left it, but then again, the windows were gone, the place shot up, so maybe it was part of what happened.

Normally there was a pole with a hook stored under the bed. It was used to catch the ring that would pull the folding ladder down, and the wooden apparatus dropped far enough someone could flip open the narrow stairs, but it was so rarely accessed he couldn't remember the last time he was up there.

So why was it open?

He groped under the bed for the pole, didn't find it, and then caught it in the beam of the flashlight leaning instead against the wall. Definitely not there when he'd left the place. He picked it up and tugged down the ladder.

Halfway up the stairs, he *knew*. It was just a small sound, not even enough to qualify as a moan, but he heard it and froze before he scrambled up the rest of the way.

The beam of his flashlight caught a tumble of red hair, a dark coat, and a pale oval face, the fine pure outline of her profile, turned toward him. He didn't even finish the climb but leaned his head against the closest rung, swallowed convulsively, and felt a flare of disbelief at the realization that the woman now lying bound and gagged in his parents' tiny attic was staring at him with wide eyes. Incongruously she was next to a stack of rubber tire tubes they used for swimming, and a set of pink flippers and a snorkel.

Alive.

What a wonderful word.

And paradoxically, he hoped, in that definitive moment, for another human being's death. At this point, as far as Bryce could tell, Neil Hathaway had forfeited any sort of humane sympathy. Bryce wanted him killed, shut down, eliminated.

"Jane?" he asked tentatively.

In the glare of the flashlight, she nodded, just barely. There was a long streak of dried blood on her cheek. Her clothes were soaked and he could see her trembling in the cold.

"It's okay," he said quietly, awkward in the moment, not certain what a savior was supposed to do, and just as certain that if she'd really endured several days of captivity, not to mention that assault on the cabin, what the hell could he say that would make her think any of this was going to get better. "I'm a friend of Rick's."

That was certainly stretching it.

She might have sobbed, but even as he moved to try to decide how to free her—the knives were in the kitchen—he heard the thud.

His head came up as someone shoved open the front door of the cabin, his heavy breathing loud, and footsteps crunching glass. It hadn't even occurred to Bryce it *was* unlocked. When he'd left the other day during the ice storm, he'd locked it himself. Earlier, he'd come in through the broken window because he was sure it was as he left it.

He almost did it. Almost called out: *In here. She's alive.*

* * *

She'd never been shot before.

Ellie could feel the blood pooling in her boot, the warm insidious slide soaking her jeans, the pain just a dull ache, but like any injury, she expected it would get worse.

Not a good time for this particular experience. Her foot was also slippery now and the ice didn't help and she lost her balance, skidding sideways.

Stupid of her to think she could chase Hathaway down in the frozen woods. Let her take inventory. Cold. Wet. Dark. Bleeding everywhere.

Those four elements did not make up a perfect evening she decided as she levered up, winced as her palm slid in the wet leaves, and realized Rick had gone on without her. The left side of her body was soaked, her sense of direction skewed, and she didn't know if it was the wound or the adrenaline that was making her dizzy.

Maybe both. She tried to wipe off the crusted snow and looked around.

Hathaway and Rick were both gone, and try as she might, she could not slow her breathing to the point where she could hear them. After all these months of hunting an elusive killer, because of Jane's disappearance, she knew Rick was going to kill the son of a bitch. She didn't disagree, but the idiot might go to jail for it if she didn't do something.

The cabin. Her phone was in the cabin. Bryce would have been in touch with Pearson by now.

She staggered to her feet. Crap, her sock was soaked. The warm squish between her toes as she moved to go forward gave her pause. *How bad is it?*

Ellie slipped, going down again, one elbow digging into the snow, her breath exhaled in a low grunt as she caught herself with the other hand. The leg might be worse than she first thought.

Pearson would bring reinforcements. *If* Bryce had gotten through.

She needed her phone.

The footsteps stopped but not before Bryce had already realized that whoever had come in knew the door was unlocked.

The simple calculation left him colder than ever. Someone had put Jane Cummins in the attic, and to do it he would have had to go through the front door, no question about it.

There was a certain quality to the silence that also spoke to him more than words. If it was a police officer he would identify himself.

Bryce was committed to the staircase already. It didn't take much to ease upward and slither backward on the attic floor. It was rough plywood and he might have made a sound, but Hathaway's breathing was labored and he had to be as deafened as Bryce by the recent gunfire, if not more so.

Thoughts went rapid fire through his brain as Bryce joined the latest kidnapping victim in macabre camaraderie in the small space, cognizant he still didn't have a weapon. A stealthy glance revealed only shadows, but he couldn't chance the flashlight . . . Shit, what *was* stored up here?

Think.

Old plastic floatation rafts, worthless but not discarded for whatever reason. Bait buckets, a few metal, but lightweight; a rolled-up musty hammock, no doubt so moth-eaten it would fall apart if unrolled; part of the old umbrella his father had once bought his mother for the dock, the top part now completely disintegrated. He groped along, blind now, the darkness like a suffocating blanket, but if he used the flashlight, Hathaway might catch a glimpse and shoot right up through the ceiling—the place was hand built and hardly square and no doubt there were cracks here and there. He tried, hoping for something, anything . . .

Jane didn't make a sound but her breathing was louder, the panic communicated effectively even without words. Bryce was sweating in the November cold, his hands skittering in his frantic quest for a weapon.

Hathaway headed toward the kitchen. Coming closer. Having a crushed-glass floor didn't make for silent progress, so Bryce could clearly make out the other man's movements.

Hell.

Crunch. Crunch.

"I understand you found another of my girls." Hathaway's voice was so normal it was morbid, and close enough he must be in the room now. "I think we're playing a game, Dr. Grantham. I hide, you seek. Only right now, you're hiding and I'm seeking. I doubled back, old hunter's trick. Only two of the three of you with a weapon out there, and I figured police officers wouldn't let you tag along in a pursuit like that, so you might come back here. Good call, wasn't it?"

Bryce should have been petrified. Maybe deep down he was, but the truth was, he only felt a lethal sort of calm calculation. The musty smell, the dusty floor, the utter dark. The lack of light would help a little because Hathaway would have to shoot blind, but the space was only about eight feet square. Eventually he'd find his target.

There was nowhere to go.

Surely there's something up here.

A creak on the first rung of the ladder. Hathaway continued his toneless monologue. "You see, at first it was interesting. I was intrigued. All that time and they belonged only to me, but then you met the one that was to be November. It rushed things. I don't like to be rushed. Two in the same month? I've never done that before."

One of Bryce's groping hands encountered the wooden base of the big umbrella. It was two inches around at least, and heavy, like a thin elongated baseball bat. The rotted top part was no longer attached. He hefted it in his palm. Jane was crying now. He couldn't hear it, but he saw the glistening trail on her cheeks because of the reflected illumination of the flashlight below.

There was a distant wail of sirens.

Hathaway didn't seem to care. The ladder squeaked again. "I couldn't believe it when you found October."

Bryce was still, crouched under the eaves, his legs aching, his mouth dust dry. This was *it*.

"As a gesture of appreciation, I gave you July." The tone of the eerie recital dropped, was even quieter. "And I was going to leave November here for you, right in your family's place. Be a nice little surprise next spring, wouldn't it? I liked the idea of that, of killing her here. How long would it take for someone to find her? And the circle would come around to you again. The police wouldn't know what to make of it, would they? But I think we're done with our game."

A head crested the opening, barely visible in the gloom. Hathaway had the rifle angled, the dim silhouette not exactly reassuring.

Bryce lunged and swung, catching only the tip of

the gun, but he put his full weight into that blow. Even with it deflected he heard the satisfying thud of wood on skull as Hathaway went backward down the stairs. Bryce also went sprawling forward with the momentum of the effort, half in the attic and half spilling onto the staircase, his tenuous grip keeping him from pitching downward eight feet to the floor on top of Hathaway.

Any hope he'd incapacitated the man was dashed as Neil sat up, but Bryce did notice with detached satisfaction a runnel of blood down the side of his face. The beam of the flashlight was skewed upward, a circle on the ceiling.

Hathaway reached for the rifle first, finding it with the unerring instincts of a true hunter, slowly getting to his feet.

"The police know it's you," Bryce said, and normally he would be embarrassed his voice was so unsteady. He cleared his throat. "You aren't going to get far."

"Farther than you." Neil Hathaway audibly released the safety on his weapon. "You'll be my easiest kill yet. It's over."

Trapped, Bryce wondered if this was how someone felt when he was drowning, knowing he couldn't hang on another second and then welcoming the first lungful of suffocating water.

Jane began to sob and it occurred to him abstractly he should say something to comfort her, but then again, he didn't have much comfort to offer.

The shot was as loud as he expected, maybe louder in the small space. He recoiled, the sound echoing, the world exploding . . .

No pain, no definitive moment, he realized as the echo went on, and when he opened his eyes, he saw that Hathaway was sprawled next to the wall, a dark stain spreading under his head, one arm outstretched . . .

Dimly he heard someone say in the aftermath, "Police officer. Don't move, you son of a bitch or I'll fire."

The flash of blue and red lights once again cast rainbow shadows against the trunks of the trees lining the narrow road, reminding Ellie of that moment when she'd stood outside Margaret Wilson's car. Having Bryce call Pearson personally had been a good idea, because reinforcements arrived in record time. Everywhere there were officers on their radios, some from DCI with cell phones to their ears. McConnell was there too, and he'd been the first one to interview her.

"We lost him almost right away." Ellie was lightheaded, from the precipitous flight through the wet, half-frozen woods, from the rush of it, and maybe from blood loss also. A paramedic had wrapped a bandage around her thigh and they were trying to insist she get into the ambulance. "Ask Rick. Hathaway had the advantage of the moonless night, of his superior weapon for the chase, of knowing the area like the back of his hand. We hadn't even located his vehicle yet."

"We've got this covered." Pearson leaned in the window of the cruiser. She would still be cold but the engine was running and the heater mercifully on. He said, "I've sent two officers in to collect Grantham and get his statement. Rick isn't officially on duty, so looking to him for backup on what happened is only going to tick me off, Detective.

"However, since he is still in the employ—temporarily,

probably—of the Lincoln County Sheriff's Department, why don't you let him run you into the hospital? You're pretty scraped up and that leg is still bleeding. He's heading over there anyway, I assume."

Jane had been taken away first, dehydrated and suffering from hypothermia, but at least alive.

"Hell, yes, I am," Rick said grimly.

"Go." Pearson straightened and walked away.

Not a request. She knew that tone.

As the car nosed away, the beams catching all the activity, McConnell, who had to be freezing in his dress coat and suit, flashed them a glance and gave a half wave of dismissal. Rick said, "You all right?"

"I keep telling everyone it's a graze, but truthfully, it hurts like hell."

"Not what I meant."

"If this is an inquiry as to my emotional state, why don't we just save it for later? I'll make you a promise to let you know if I ever regret what happened this evening, okay? I shot a serial killer, for God's sake. I just saved the state of Wisconsin a lot of money. I have serious doubts I'll lose sleep over it."

To her surprise, Rick, who could be tenacious, dropped it. "Jane was so weak when they brought her out she could hardly do more than whisper my name, but she's going to be okay. God, if we'd gone to that cabin just a little earlier—"

Her thigh throbbed in rhythm with her heart and Ellie leaned her head back, suddenly very tired. "Come on, Rick. All of life is like that. What if you'd stepped out in the street earlier in the path of the oncoming car, if your parents hadn't caught the same bus and met you wouldn't exist . . . please don't expect me to be philosophical right now."

She thought maybe he sent her a sidelong glance. Damn, she was exhausted.

"Yeah," he agreed softly. "And sometimes your parents do meet on that bus. Think of it that way, dammit."

Chapter 31

It was three in the afternoon, he noted, and he might be the only one who had gotten any sleep. Actually, when he'd been delivered back to the motel, he'd fallen onto the bed and slept like a baby.

Amazing, considering everything.

Bryce sat in the designated chair and surveyed the room of inquiring faces. Ellie looked pale, but somehow softer; not as taut. Pearson had told him her wound had been stitched and she'd insisted on being in on the conference.

It was nice to be downgraded from interrogation to conference.

"I have here your statement, Dr. Grantham." One of the many official-looking people in the room, immaculate in his white shirt and dark tie, tapped a piece of paper. "We do appreciate your cooperation. But can we ask about a few points?"

He folded his hands on the table and nodded. "Fine."

Pearson flipped his pen around in his fingers like a practiced baton twirler. "Most of this has been cleared up. Russell let us search the store. There's a freezer they don't use anymore—he'd all but forgotten about it—down in the basement. It still works. We found blood in there. That's why we could never find them. He kept them there until the search died down. We postulate that he might have kept the last victim's body until he had another one."

It made sense, or as much sense as any of it could make. Bryce sat back in his chair, the memory of that moment on the attic stairs still too fresh and dark.

"We *can* guess, and I'm sure you've gone there, too. Because of you, he kept Jane alive when we doubt that was his normal pattern. Killing her at your cabin upped the stakes, and he was thumbing his nose at us too, capitalizing on our suspicion of you and keeping you engaged in his life," Ellie said in a somber voice. There were a least a dozen tiny cuts from flying glass on one side of her face. "In the game."

He'd told them about Hathaway coming into the cabin, about how he'd found Jane, about what the other man had said . . . before Ellie had shot him.

It had occurred to him he should be more upset over having another person killed right in front of him, but then again, Hathaway wasn't all that human, he reminded himself.

"You are the only witness to the actual shooting besides Detective MacIntosh. Can you please go over it again?"

Ah, that was what this was about. To make sure Ellie wasn't in the hot seat. She just looked at him with no expression whatsoever.

He did so. Same words as before. "Hathaway had seen me come into the cabin. When I saw the loft was open, I went up and found Jane Cummins there, and he had us trapped. I did my best to disarm him but failed, and Detective MacIntosh arrived, not to be cliché about it, just in time. Had she not taken decisive action, he would have killed us. He'd told us both, and while Jane Cummins might not have seen the shooting, I'm sure she will corroborate that Detective MacIntosh ordered him to drop his weapon but had no choice but to fire."

Well, she'd ordered it afterward, but Bryce wasn't about to split hairs over it. Had she waited, he wasn't sure he'd still be alive.

Luckily, that seemed to satisfy everyone. Pearson even smiled slightly.

"What gave you the idea to look up at the cabin on the river?" The officer introduced as McConnell looked at him with a quizzical expression, as if he was an animal he couldn't quite place in the genus hierarchy.

"Something he said when I was in the store once." Bryce had prepared himself for this question. He explained slowly, "I'd bought some minnows and he told me about a place on Prairie that wasn't used anymore that was great fishing. As soon as I realized he might be the killer, it occurred to me. I'm not a trained psychologist, but if he was in the tavern the night I took Melissa Simmons home, it's obvious now he followed us and killed her, so maybe he couldn't resist mentioning it because he had every intention of putting her body there eventually. He kept calling it a game and I don't know how clever he was, as much as cunning. He liked taking chances. Instead of taking his advice, I went out to the Paris place and accidentally found Margaret Wilson instead. He must have been stunned over the irony of it. I know I am. If I had to call it, I would guess at that moment he considered me a part of it all."

"Better you than me," McConnell said dryly.

"We found two sets of tracks at the river cabin where you discovered the body. Did Rick Jones accompany you, Dr. Grantham?"

That's right, Ellie wasn't the only one who'd bent a rule here and there. "For my own protection," Bryce flat-out lied, but all in a good cause, looking the sheriff in the eye. "I told him I was going to go look, and he insisted on coming because I don't even own a weapon, and let's face it, gentlemen, he was right. Hathaway was a dangerous man. Officer Jones tried to talk me out of breaking the window, but truthfully, I was getting pretty desperate to prove that whoever was doing all this wasn't me."

Not a single person in the room believed he'd told the exact story of what happened, but Pearson nodded and stood, practically congenial, and said, "Thank you, Dr. Grantham."

A definite step up from his other interviews with the Lincoln County Sheriff's Department, and to his relief, this seemed to be the last one.

Bryce walked with Ellie to the door of the station house, opened it for her, and stepped out into temperatures bordering on freezing. "Give you a ride home?' he said jokingly, since he'd been duly picked up and delivered by a deputy as his car was still immersed in a crime scene, not to mention the tree and the flat tire.

She glanced at him, the collar of her coat flipped up against the cold. Her hair shimmered gold. "Yes." She fished her keys out of her pocket. "If you drive, I'll let you make me dinner, how's that? I have to admit my leg is really sore. I could use a glass of wine."

The flicker of hope he'd kept carefully banked, flared a little as he caught the toss. "That's a deal."

"You've looked there since I have. Anything edible in my freezer?"

Before he thought about it, he said, "We could stop and pick up something."

"I'd just as soon not." The wince she gave as she slid into the car wasn't feigned and he carefully closed the door for her and got into the driver's side. "It'll be awhile before I look at a friendly store clerk the same way. We're pretty sure that's how he targeted his victims. A young woman alone comes in, pays cash, and if there is no one else in the store, he might have just locked up and followed them. Hathaway's is a family-run business. They close up early now and then; just stick a sign on the door if something comes up. No one would think anything about it."

Bryce started the car. "Why would the women stop for him?"

"Maybe he flashed his lights, got them to at least pull over, and walks up all nice and friendly, pretending that something didn't get into their bag. We've all left a store and had a clerk come after us because we left something behind. You wouldn't think a thing about it. That's probably how he got Melissa Simmons to open her door also. He knocked, apologized real nice for not putting the animal crackers or whatever in her bag the day before, we'll never quite know. He did the friendly, easygoing Neil pretty well and she was up here alone, and she might easily have told him the location of her rental cabin one day when she stopped by the store. She might even have been abducted right before you pulled in because we know the rain didn't stop until the middle of the night. Maybe by then she'd realized her cell was missing and was grateful to have someone she knew who could possibly help her. When she unlocked the door, he had her."

"Rick said Jane was really wary. To the point of asking him about getting a gun. It didn't sound to me like she'd stop, even for a ruse like that."

As they pulled out of the parking lot, Ellie stared straight ahead, her expression tinged with anger, even if Hathaway was dead. "He ran her off the road in the storm. She didn't realize it wasn't an accident until she'd already rolled down her window. God, it was so simple. It shouldn't be that simple. It should never, *ever* be that simple."

There was nothing he could think of to say, so he just braked at the red light and sat silent.

Ellie cleared her throat and turned to finally look at him. "Thanks."

"For what?" His laugh was incredulous.

"There might have been an inquiry if you'd told them exactly what happened."

"I get that impression, but why? He'd fired his weapon already, he'd even shot you."

She shrugged. "I still should have given him a chance to surrender, but sometimes you have to go with your gut. However, the public doesn't like it when police officers kill suspects."

"Some of the public does. My hearing will never be the same. All I know is that he was going to shoot me, and you came to the rescue. It's a bit of a blow to my ego, but I'm already over it, Detective."

"Glad to hear it," she said dryly. She went on after a

moment. "Those earrings belonged to Julia Becraft, his first victim. I sent pictures to all the families and her younger sister recognized them. They tore apart the basement below the store and the cabin and still can't find a trace. Nothing."

Bryce stared at the road as a truck passed. There was slush in the gutters that hit the hood in a thick spray. "I'm not surprised."

"I'm not either. You go first and tell me why."

"Just a feeling. Nothing based on fact of any kind."

"Yeah, well, I'm starting have some respect for these *feelings*. Tell me."

"She was June, wasn't she?"

"What?"

"Something Hathaway said to me. He didn't call them by their names, but by the months when he killed them. He gave me July. The bones in the woodpile. Wasn't that the second one? She was the first one."

"I'm thinking the same thing. She'd be special. He'd be really careful then, maybe scared. If I had to guess, he hid her very well. She was abducted from her tent. I'm going to also guess it set the pattern. She'd been in the store, maybe chatted with Neil, and she told him where she was camping. He was a hunter. Maybe he watched them, saw her friends leave, and decided he had the opportunity."

They slid out of town into the countryside. He liked the quiet, he'd found, even with the bleak trees and utter absence of life. The road was wet, but clear, and the trunks and branches just black silhouettes.

"You don't think we'll ever find her."

"No." Ellie gazed at him from the passenger seat. "Just speculation, but I believe he must have been thinking about doing something like this—like murder—for a long time. None of the killings were an act of rage. Just like a favorite deer stand or fishing spot, he had a special place in mind to put her before he ever settled on his first victim. He didn't rush around, tossing the body in a ditch after the killing, or leaving messy clues. He killed each woman and planted them all around the county in strategic spots he knew first-hand were remote and unlikely to be discovered."

A thin rain had started and Bryce tried to figure out how to turn on the wipers in an unfamiliar car. Ellie frowned, reached over and did it for him, and settled back.

The pain medication made her sleepy, so she declined to take it, opting for a glass of zinfandel instead. Bryce had somehow managed to make a delicious soup out of what was left in the cabinets. Along with some bread toasted in the oven, it was not bad at all for a self-proclaimed average cook.

She liked him in the kitchen, Ellie thought, watching him settle into the club chair he seemed to have chosen for his own. Actually, she liked *him*. Period. No problems with his masculinity. No pretention or affectations. Didn't flaunt he had a good job and made some money, but didn't hide it either. He was good-looking and aware of it, but not arrogant.

Was he perfect? Hell no, but she was well aware perfect didn't exist. She had a feeling he thought too much about every detail before he acted, and that was the reason he was drawn to confident women like his ex-wife because they took the initiative in most cases. Despite that he'd essentially helped solve a serial murder case; the circumstances had been forced on him, not a choice. He preferred to avoid confrontation at all costs usually. He sought quiet, solitude, and a structured life.

She was a cop and her life was so rarely structured that every day when she got up in the morning, she had no idea what might happen out there. She liked the risk, fed off the challenges, and was passionate about her job. It was going too far to say being a police officer was her life, but it was definitely a lifestyle. She wasn't ever going to be easy to live with, and she was never going to apologize for that either. Law enforcement was still, in her opinion, very much a man's world, but she could hold her own. This case had taught her a lot, not just about investigation, but about herself.

Hathaway wasn't the only hunter.

She and Bryce were pretty opposite in a lot of ways.

Still, she mused as she watched the flicker of the firelight over his face, this might be . . . workable.

Yes, Dr. Bryce Grantham was definitely workable if she chose to pursue whatever might happen next.

She was almost positive she would go that direction.

"Think Russell Hathaway will sell the store?" Bryce asked, his long legs extended, a wineglass hanging loosely in his fingers. "It's been there for decades."

"What would you do?"

"Yeah, I get your point. I think I'd rather be the serial killer than the parent of one. God knows the world would look at you and wonder what the hell you did wrong."

She understandably hadn't been one of the officers who delivered Mr. Hathaway the news, but she knew he'd taken it hard. All of it, from the grim truth, to his son's death.

"People are stuck on trying to figure out why things happen a little too much. Take Keith Walters. They apparently picked him up yesterday in Missouri because he ran a red light. Still had the gun with him that killed his brother. Why'd he do it? And if he did it, why he'd keep the weapon? What an idiot."

Bryce just shook his head and drank some wine, his expression drawn in the flickering light. "It doesn't sound to me like Reginald Walters was much of a loss to this earth, but I do feel bad for Neil's father. It isn't just because none of this is his fault. I keep thinking about my parents. They love coming up here and with everything that has happened . . ." He made a helpless gesture with his free hand.

By tacit agreement they hadn't talked about the case during dinner, but both of them had been thinking about it, so maybe it was better to just discuss it. Ellie had changed into sweats and was fairly comfortable in her father's old recliner, a blanket over her lap. No wonder he'd loved the chair so much. The wound felt tight from being stitched, and hurt, but it wasn't bad. She tucked the blanket more around her and shook her head. "I don't know. Something like this is never easy for anyone."

"Neil Hathaway destroyed a lot of lives, and not just those of his victims."

"True." She eyed him over the rim of her glass. "But along came you."

He immediately shook his head, as she'd known he would. A lock of dark hair curled against his cheek. He really could use a haircut, but she kind of liked it a little too long. "I was simply an unwilling participant, believe me. I think it more appropriate to say along came *you*."

Ellie took a sip of wine, pondered what to say next, and finally, because she really didn't believe too much in subtlety, stated quietly, "You essentially rescued Jane. I think you're right, he kept her alive because he wanted to kill her where it would affect you the most personally."

"You sent me to the cabin for your phone." His face was shuttered and distant for a minute. "Ellie . . . God, what if I hadn't noticed that open attic access?"

"You have a lot to learn about police work."

"No thanks."

There was an urge to laugh at his emphatic declaration, but then again, she thought she understood too. "I know it feels wrong that chance is part of the process, but it is. Look at it this way. You *did* find her."

"You saved her, not me."

"Maybe so." She was going to go to sleep soon, the fatigue was creeping in. She whispered, "And the next time you wonder what might have happened if we hadn't been there, remind yourself that his December girl is safe."